Towing Jehovah

Towing Jehovah

JAMES MORROW

A HARVEST BOOK

HARCOURT BRACE & COMPANY

San Diego   New York   London

Requests for permission to make copies of any part of the work
should be mailed to: Permissions Department,
Harcourt Brace & Company, 6277 Sea Harbor Drive,
Orlando, Florida 32887-6777.

Library of Congress Cataloging-in-Publication Data
Morrow, James, 1947–
Towing Jehovah/James Morrow.—1st ed.
(A Harvest Book)
p.   cm.
ISBN 0-15-190919-9
ISBN 0-15-600210-8 (pbk.)
I. Title.
PS3563.0876T6   1994
813´.54—dc20   93-35022

A leatherbound, signed edition of this book has been
privately printed by The Easton Press.

Designed by Lisa Peters
Printed in the United States of America
First Harvest edition 1995

G H F

*To the memory
of my father-in-law,
Albert L. Pierce*

ACKNOWLEDGMENTS

I OWE A SINGULAR debt to my friend Able Seaman Gigi Marino, a splendid writer who taught me everything I wanted to know about oil tankers. The insights of my editor, John Radziewicz, were likewise invaluable, as was the support of my agent, Merrilee Heifetz. Throughout the composing process, I maintained close contact with many friends, colleagues, and relatives, probing them for their reactions to particular scenes as well as for their general views on theothanatology. Each of the following people will know the special reasons for which I am grateful to him or her: Joe Adamson, Linda Barnes, Deborah Beale, Lynn Crosson, Shira Daemon, Sean Develin, Travis DiNicola, Daniel Dubner, Margaret Duda, Gregory Feeley, Justin Fielding, Robert Hatten, Michael Kandel, Glenn Morrow, Jean Morrow, Elisabeth Rose, Joe Schall, Peter Schneeman, D. Alexander Smith, Kathryn Smith, James Stevens-Arce, and Judith Van Herik. And, finally, a hearty thanks to the Sycamore Hill Writers' Conference for improving the Eucharist.

WE HAVE LEFT the land and have embarked. We have burned our bridges behind us—indeed, we have gone farther and destroyed the land behind us. Now, little ship, look out! Beside you is the ocean: to be sure, it does not always roar, and at times it lies spread out like silk and gold and reveries of graciousness. But hours will come when you will realize that it is infinite and that there is nothing more awesome than infinity! Oh, the poor bird that felt free and now strikes the wall of this cage! Woe, when you feel homesick for the land as if it had offered more *freedom*—and there is no longer any "land."

—Friedrich Nietzsche,
"In the Horizon of the Infinite,"
The Gay Science

And the Lord said, "Behold . . . I will take away mine hand, and thou shalt see my back parts: but my face shall not be seen."

—*The Book of Exodus*

CONTENTS

Part one

Angel

THE IRREDUCIBLE STRANGENESS of the universe was first made manifest to Anthony Van Horne on his fiftieth birthday, when a despondent angel named Raphael, a being with luminous white wings and a halo that blinked on and off like a neon quoit, appeared and told him of the days to come.

That year, 1992, Anthony's Sundays were always the same. At four P.M. he would descend into the New York subway system, take the A-train north to 190th Street, hike across the rocky hills of Fort Tryon Park, and, after melding with the tourists, enter the simulated European monastery known as the Cloisters and slip behind the altar in the Fuentidueña Chapel. There he would wait, holding his breath and enduring his migraine, until the crowd went home.

The lead-off watchman, a rangy Jamaican with a limp, always made his rounds faithfully, but at midnight a new guard normally came on duty, an emaciated N.Y.U. student who made no rounds but instead entered the Unicorn Tapestries Room bearing an aquamarine nylon backpack jammed with textbooks. After seating himself on the cold stone floor, the student would switch on his flashlight and begin poring over his *Gray's Anatomy*, endlessly rehearsing the parts of the human body. "Gluteus medius, gluteus medius, gluteus medius," he would chant into the sacred precincts. "Rectus femoris, rectus femoris, rectus femoris."

That particular midnight, Anthony followed his usual custom. He stole out from behind the Fuentidueña altar, checked on the student (hard at work, drilling himself in the fissures and sulci of the left cerebral hemisphere), then proceeded along an arcade of Romanesque columns capped by snarling gargoyles and down a flagstone path to the gushing marble fountain that dominated the open-air Saint-Michel-de-Cuxa Cloister. Reaching into his freshly washed chinos, Anthony removed a translucent plastic box and set it on the ground. He climbed out of his pants, then pulled off his white cotton jersey, immaculate undershirt, spotless Jockey shorts, polished shoes, and clean socks. At last he stood naked in the hot night, his skin burnished by an orange moon drifting across the sky like a huge orbiting pumpkin.

"Sulcus frontalis superior, sulcus frontalis superior, sulcus frontalis superior," said the student.

Anthony picked up the plastic box, popped the lid, and removed the egg-shaped cake. Pressing the soap against his chest, he leaned into the Cuxa fountain. In the golden pool he saw himself—the broken nose, the weary eyes sinking into bogs of flesh, the high forehead eroded by sea spray and baked hard by equatorial sun, the tangled gray beard spreading across a lantern jaw. He lathered up, letting the cake slide down his arms and chest like a tiny toboggan, catching it before it hit the flagstones.

"Sulcus praecentralis, sulcus praecentralis, sulcus praecentralis . . ."

Ivory soap, mused Anthony as he rinsed, Procter and Gamble

at its purest. At that exact moment he felt clean—though the oil, he knew, would be back the next day. The oil always came back. For what soap on earth could scrub away the endless black gallons that had spilled from the fractured hull of the SS *Carpco Valparaíso*, what caliber of purity could erase that particular stain?

During the cold months, Anthony had kept a Turkish bath towel handy, but now it was mid-June—the first day of summer, in fact—and a simple jog through the museum would be sufficient to get him dry. And so he put on his Jockey shorts and ran, moving past the Pontaut Chapter House . . . the Nine Heroes Tapestries Room . . . Robert Campin Hall with its homey *Annunciation*: the angel Gabriel advising Mary of God's intentions as she sits in the bourgeois parlor of the artist's patrons, surrounded by tokens of her innocence—fresh lilies, white candle, gleaming copper kettle.

At the entry to the Langon Chapel, beneath a rounded arch set on lintels carved with blooming acanthus, a sixtyish man in a flowing white robe stood weeping.

"No," he moaned, his low, liquid sobs echoing off the limestone. "No . . ."

Except for the man's wings, Anthony might have assumed the intruder was a penitent like himself. But there they were, huge and phosphorescent, sprouting from his shoulder blades in all their feathered improbability.

"No . . ."

The glowing man looked up. A halo hovered above his snowy hair, flashing bright red: on-off, on-off, on-off. His eyes were rheumy and inflamed. Silver droplets rolled from his tear ducts like beads of liquid mercury.

"Good evening," said the intruder, convulsively catching his breath. He laid his hand on his cheek and, like a blotter pressed against some infinitely sad letter, his palm absorbed the tears. "Good evening and happy birthday, Captain Van Horne."

"You *know* me?"

"This is not a chance meeting." The intruder's voice was wavering and fragmented, as if he were speaking through the whirling blades of an electric fan. "Your schedule is well known among us angels—these secret visits to the fountain, these sly ablutions . . ."

"Angels?"

"Call me Raphael." The intruder cleared his throat. "Raphael Azarias." His skin, yellow aspiring to gold, shone in the moonlight like a brass sextant. He smelled of all the succulent wonders Anthony had ever sampled on his journeys, of papayas and mangoes, guanabanas and tamarinds, guavas and guineppes. "For I am indeed the celebrated archangel who vanquished the demon Asmodeus."

A winged man. Robed, haloed, delusions of divinity: another New York lunatic, Anthony surmised. And yet he did not resist when the angel reached out, wrapped five frigid fingers around his wrist, and led him back to the Cuxa fountain.

"You think I'm an impostor?" asked Raphael.

"Well . . ."

"Be honest."

"Of course I think you're an impostor."

"Watch."

The angel plucked a feather from his left wing and tossed it into the pool. To Anthony's astonishment, a familiar human face appeared beneath the waters, rendered in the sort of ersatz depth he associated with 3-D comic books.

"Your father is a great sailor," said the angel. "Were he not in retirement, we might have chosen him over you."

Anthony shuddered. Yes, it was truly he, Christopher Van Horne, the handsome, dashing master of the *Amoco Caracas*, the *Exxon Fairbanks*, and a dozen other classic ships—the soaring brow, lofty cheekbones, frothy mane of pearl gray hair. JOHN VAN HORNE, his birth certificate read, though on turning twenty-one he'd changed his name in homage to his spiritual mentor, Christopher Columbus.

"He's a great sailor," Anthony agreed. He chucked a pebble into the pool, transforming his father's face into a series of concentric circles. Was this a dream? A migraine aura? "Chosen him for what?"

"For the most important voyage in human history."

As the waters grew calm, a second face appeared: lean, tense, and hawklike, perched atop the stiff white collar of a Roman Catholic priest.

"Father Thomas Ockham," the angel explained. "He works over in the Bronx, Fordham University, teaching particle physics and avant-garde cosmology."

"What does he have to do with me?"

"Our mutual Creator has passed away," said Raphael with a sigh compounded of pain, exhaustion, and grief.

"What?"

"God died."

Anthony took an involuntary step backward. "That's crazy."

"Died and fell into the sea." Raphael clamped his cold fingers around the tattooed mermaid on Anthony's naked forearm and abruptly drew him closer. "Listen carefully, Captain Van Horne. You're going to get your ship back."

There was a ship, a supertanker four football fields long, pride of the fleet owned and operated by Caribbean Petroleum Company, Anthony Van Horne in command. It should have been a routine trip for the *Carpco Valparaíso*, a midnight milk run from Port Lavaca, spigot of the Trans-Texas Pipeline, across the Gulf and northward to the oil-thirsty cities of the coast. The tide was ripe, the sky was clear, and the harbor pilot, Rodrigo López, had just guided them through the Nueces Narrows without a scratch.

"You won't hit any icebergs tonight," López had joked, "but look out for the drug runners—they navigate worse than

Greeks." The pilot jabbed his index finger toward a vague smear on the twelve-mile radar scope. "That might be one now."

As López climbed into his launch and set out for Port Lavaca, a migraine flared in Anthony's skull. He'd experienced worse—attacks that had dropped him to his knees and shattered the world into flaming fragments of stained glass—but this was still a killer.

"You don't look well, sir." Buzzy Longchamps, the chronically jolly chief mate, strode onto the bridge to begin his watch. "Seasick?" he asked with a snorty laugh.

"Let's just get out of here." Anthony clamped his temples between his thumb and middle finger. "All ahead full. Eighty rpm's."

"All ahead full," echoed Longchamps. He moved the twin joysticks forward. "Speedy delivery," he said, lighting a Lucky Strike.

"Speedy delivery," Anthony agreed. "Ten degrees left rudder."

"Ten degrees left," echoed the able-bodied seaman at the wheel.

"Steady," said Anthony.

"Steady," said the AB.

Ambling up to the twelve-mile radar, the chief mate touched the amorphous target. "What's that?"

"Wooden hull, I suspect, probably out of Barranquilla," said Anthony. "I don't think she's carrying coffee beans."

Longchamps laughed, the Lucky Strike bobbing between his lips. "Stu and I can manage up here." The mate tapped repeatedly on the able seaman's shoulder, as if translating his own words into Morse code. "Right, Stu?"

"You bet," said the AB.

Anthony's brain was aflame. His eyes were ready to melt. *In the presence of any navigational or meteorological hazard, two officers must be on the bridge at all times*: so ran one of the few truly unambiguous sentences in the *Carpco Manual*.

"We're only two miles from open water," said the mate. "A twenty-degree turn, and we're outta harm's way."

Longchamps snapped up the walkie-talkie and told Kate Rucker, the AB standing lookout in the bow, to keep her eyes peeled for a rogue freighter.

"You sure you can handle this?" Anthony asked the mate.

"Chocolate cake."

And so Anthony Van Horne left the bridge—the last time he would do so as an employee of Caribbean Petroleum.

Nameless as a wild duck, the mahogany steamer came out of the night at thirty knots, loaded to her gunwales with raw cocaine. No running lights. Dark wheelhouse. By the time Able Seaman Rucker screamed her warning into the walkie-talkie, the steamer was barely a quarter mile away.

Up on the bridge, Buzzy Longchamps cried, "Hard right!" and the helmsman responded instantly, thereby setting the tanker on a direct course for Bolivar Reef.

Lying in his bunk, prostrate with pain, Anthony felt the *Valparaíso* tremble and lurch. Instantly he rolled to his feet, and before he was in the corridor the obscene odor of loose oil reached his nose. He rode the elevator to the weather deck, ran outside, and sprinted down the central catwalk, high above the writhing tangle of pipes and valves. Fumes swirled everywhere, sweeping past the kingposts in palpable clouds and spilling over the sides like absconding ghosts. Anthony's eyes watered, his throat burned, his sinuses grew raw and bloody.

From out of the darkness, a sailor shouted, "Holy shit!"

Descending the amidships stairway, Anthony dashed across the weather deck and leaned over the starboard rail. A searchlight swept the scene, the whole stinking hell of it—the black water, the ruptured hull, the thick, viscous oil gushing from the breach. Eventually Anthony would learn how close they'd come to foundering that night; he would learn how Bolivar Reef had lacerated the *Val* like a can opener cutting the lid off a cocker spaniel's dinner. But just then he knew only the fumes—and the stench—and the peculiar lucidity that attends a man's awareness that he is experiencing the worst moment of his life.

To Caribbean Petroleum, it hardly mattered whether the *Val* was lost or saved that night. An eighty-million-dollar supertanker was chopped liver compared with the four and a half billion Carpco was ultimately obliged to pay out in damage awards, lawyers' fees, lobbyists' salaries, bribes to Texas shrimpers, cleanup efforts that did more harm than good, and a vigorous campaign to restore the corporation's image. The brilliant series of televised messages that Carpco commissioned from Hollywood's rock-video mills, each new spot trivializing the death of Matagorda Bay more shamelessly than its predecessor, went ridiculously over budget, so eager was the company to get them on the air. "Unless you look long and hard, you probably won't notice her beauty mark is missing," the narrator of spot number twelve intoned over a retouched photograph of Marilyn Monroe. "Similarly, if you study a map of the Texas coast . . ."

Anthony Van Horne gripped the rail, stared at the pooling oil, and wept. Had he known what was coming, he might simply have stayed there, transfixed by the future: the five hundred miles of blackened beaches; the sixteen hundred acres of despoiled shrimp beds; the permanent blinding of three hundred and twenty-five manatees; the oily suffocation of over four thousand sea turtles and pilot whales; the lethal marination of sixty thousand blue herons, roseate spoonbills, glossy ibises, and snowy egrets. Instead he went up to the wheelhouse, where the first words out of Buzzy Longchamp's mouth were, "Sir, I think we're in a peck of trouble."

Ten months later, a grand jury exonerated Anthony of all the charges the state of Texas had leveled against him: negligence, incompetence, abandoning the bridge. An unfortunate verdict. For if the captain wasn't guilty, then somebody else had to be, somebody named Caribbean Petroleum—Carpco, with its understaffed ships, overworked crews, steadfast refusal to build double-hulled tankers, and gimcrack oil-spill contingency plan (a scheme Judge Lucius Percy quickly dubbed "the greatest work of maritime fiction since *Moby-Dick*"). Even as the legal system was vindicating Anthony, his bosses were arranging their revenge. They told him he would never command a supertanker again, a prophecy they proceeded to fulfill by persuading the Coast Guard to rescind his license. Within one year Anthony went from the six-figure salary of a ship's master to the paltry income of those human marginalia who haunt the New York docks taking whatever work they can get. He unloaded cargo until his hands became mottled with calluses. He tied up bulk carriers and Ro-Ros. He repaired rigging, spliced mooring lines, painted bollards, and cleaned out ballast tanks.

And he took showers. Hundreds of them. The morning after the spill, Anthony checked into Port Lavaca's only Holiday Inn and stood beneath the steaming water for nearly an hour. The oil wouldn't come off. After dinner he tried again. The oil remained. Before bed, another shower. Useless. Endless oil, eleven million gallons, a petroleum tumor spreading into the depths of his flesh. Before the year ended, Anthony Van Horne was showering four times a day, seven days a week. "You left the bridge," a voice would rasp in his ear as the water drummed against his chest.

Two officers must be on the bridge at all times . . .

"You left the bridge . . ."

"You left the bridge," said the angel Raphael, wiping his silver tears with the hem of his silken sleeve.

"I left the bridge," Anthony agreed.

"I don't weep because you left the bridge. Beaches and egrets mean nothing to me these days."

"You weep because"—he gulped—"God is dead." The words

felt impossibly odd on Anthony's tongue, as if he were suddenly speaking Senegalese. "How can God be dead? How can God have a body?"

"How can He not?"

"Isn't He . . . immaterial?"

"Bodies *are* immaterial, essentially. Any physicist will tell you as much."

Groaning softly, Raphael aimed his left wing toward the Late Gothic Hall and took off, flying in the halting, stumbling manner of a damaged moth. As Anthony followed, he noticed that the angel was disintegrating. Feathers drifted through the air like the residue of a pillow fight.

"Insubstantial stuff, matter," Raphael continued, hovering. "Quirky. Quarky. It's barely there. Ask Father Ockham."

Alighting amid the medieval treasures, the creature took Anthony's hand—those cold fingers again, like mooring lines dipped in the Weddell Sea—and led him to an anonymous Italian Renaissance altarpiece in the southeast corner.

"Religion's become too abstract of late. God as spirit, light, love—forget that neo-Platonic twaddle. God's a Person, Anthony. He made you in His own image, Genesis 1:26. He has a nose, Genesis 8:20. Buttocks, Exodus 33:23. He gets excrement on His feet, Deuteronomy 23:14."

"But aren't those just . . . ?"

"What?"

"You know. Metaphors."

"Everything's a metaphor. Meanwhile, His toenails are growing, an inevitable phenomenon with corpses." Raphael pointed to the altarpiece, which according to its caption depicted Christ and the Virgin Mary kneeling before God, interceding on behalf of a prominent Florentine family. "Your artists have always known what they were doing. Michelangelo Buonarroti goes to paint the Creation of Adam, and a year later there's God Himself on the Sistine Chapel—an old man with a beard, perfect. Or take William Blake, diligently illustrating Job, getting everything right—God the Father, ancient of days. Or consider the evidence before you . . ." And indeed, Anthony realized, here was God, peering out of the altarpiece: a bearded patriarch, at once serene and severe, loving and fierce.

But no. This was madness. Raphael Azarias was a fraud, a con man, a certifiable paranoid.

"You're molting."

"I'm dying," the angel corrected Anthony. Indeed. His halo, previously as red as the Texaco logo, now flickered an anemic pink. His once-bright feathers emitted a sallow, sickly aura, as if infested with aging fireflies. Tiny scarlet veins entwined his eyeballs. "The entire heavenly host is dying. Such is the depth of our sorrow."

"You spoke of my ship."

"The corpse must be salvaged. Salvaged, towed, and entombed. Of all vessels on earth, only the *Carpco Valparaíso* is equal to the task."

"The *Val*'s a cripple."

"They refloated her last week. She's in Connecticut at the moment, taking up most of the National Steel Shipyard, awaiting whatever new fittings you believe the job will require."

Anthony stared at his forearm, flexing and unflexing the muscle, making his tattooed mermaid do a series of bumps and grinds.

"God's body . . ."

"Precisely," said Raphael.

"I would imagine it's large."

"Two miles fore to aft."

"Face up?"

"Yes. He's smiling, oddly enough. Rigor mortis, we suspect, or perhaps He elected to assume the expression before passing away."

The captain fixed on the altarpiece, noting the life-giving

milk streaming from the Virgin's right breast. Two miles? *Two goddamn miles?* "Then I guess we'll be reading about it in tomorrow's *Times*, huh?"

"Unlikely. He's too dense to catch the attention of weather satellites, and He's giving off so much heat He registers on long-range radar as nothing but a queer-looking patch of fog." As the angel guided Anthony into the foyer, his tears started up again. "We can't let Him rot. We can't leave Him to the predators and worms."

"God doesn't have a *body*. God doesn't *die*."

"God has a body—and for reasons wholly obscure to us, that body has expired." Raphael's tears kept coming, as if connected to a source as fecund as the Trans-Texas Pipeline. "Bear Him north. Let the Arctic freeze Him. Bury His remains." From the counter he snatched up a brochure promoting the Metropolitan Museum of Art, its cover emblazoned with Piero della Francesca's *Discovery and Proving of the True Cross*. "A gigantic iceberg lies above Svalbard, permanently pinned against the upper shores of Kvitoya. Nobody goes there. We've hollowed it out: portal, passageways, crypt. You merely have to haul Him inside." The angel plucked a feather from his left wing, eased it toward his eye, and wet the nib with a silver tear. Flipping over the brochure, he began writing on the back in luminous salt water. "Latitude: eighty degrees, six minutes, north. Longitude: thirty-four degrees . . ."

"You're talking to the wrong man, Mr. Azarias. You want a tugboat skipper, not a tanker captain."

"We want a tanker captain. We want you." Raphael's feather continued moving, spewing out characters so bright and fiery they made Anthony squint. "Your new license is in the mail. It's from the Brazilian Coast Guard." As if posting a letter, the angel slid the brochure under the captain's left arm. "The minute the *Valparaíso*'s been fitted for a tow, Carpco will send her on a shakedown cruise to New York."

"Carpco? Oh, no, not those bastards again, not *them*."

"Of course not *them*. Your ship's been chartered by an outside agent."

"Honest captains don't sail unregistered vessels."

"Oh, you'll get a flag all right: a Vatican banner, God's own colors." A coughing fit possessed the angel, sending tears and feathers into the sultry air. "He hit the Atlantic at zero by zero degrees, where the equator meets the prime meridian. Begin your search there. Quite likely He's drifted—east, I'd guess, caught in the Guinea Current—so you might find Him near the island of São Tomé, but then again, with God, who knows?" Shedding feathers all the way, Raphael hobbled out of the foyer and toward the Cuxa Cloister, Anthony right behind. "You'll receive a generous salary. Father Ockham is well funded."

"Otto Merrick might be right for a job like this. I think he's still with Atlantic-Richfield."

"You'll be getting your ship back," the angel snapped, steadying himself on the fountain. He breathed raggedly, wheezingly, as if through shredded lungs. "Your ship—and something more . . ."

Halo sputtering, tears flowing, the angel tossed his quill pen into the pool. A tableau appeared, painted in saturated reds and muddy greens reminiscent of early color television: six immobile figures seated around a dining-room table.

"Recognize it?"

"Hmmm . . ."

Thanksgiving Day, 1990, four months after the spill. They'd all gathered at his father's apartment in Paterson. Christopher Van Horne presided at the far end of the table, overbearing and elegant, dressed in a white woolen suit. To his left: wife number three, a loud, skinny, self-pitying woman named Tiffany. To his right: the old man's best friend from the Sea Scouts, Frank Kolby, an unimaginative and sycophantic Bostonian. Anthony sat opposite his father, bracketed on one side by his hefty sister, Susan, a New Orleans catfish farmer, and on the other by his then-current girlfriend, Lucy McDade, a short, attractive steward from the *Exxon Bangor*. Every detail was right: the cheroot in Dad's mouth, the Ronson cigarette lighter in his hand, the blue ceramic gravy boat resting beside his plate of mashed potatoes and dark meat.

The figures twitched, breathed, began to eat. Peering into the Cuxa pool, Anthony realized, to his considerable horror, what was coming next.

"Hey, look," said the old man, dropping the Ronson lighter into the gravy, "it's the *Valparaíso*." The lighter oriented itself vertically—striker wheel down, butane well up—but stayed afloat.

"Froggy, take it easy," said Tiffany.

"Dad, don't do this," said Susan.

Anthony's father lifted the cigarette lighter from the boat. As the greasy brown gravy ran down his fingers, he took out his Swiss Army knife and cut through the lighter's plastic casing. Oily butane dripped onto the linen tablecloth. "Oh, dear, oh, dear, the *Val*'s sprung a leak!" He plopped the lighter back into the boat, laughing as the butane oozed into the gravy. "Somebody must've run her into a reef! Those poor seabirds!"

"Froggy, *please*," wailed Tiffany.

"Them pilot whales ain't got a chance," said Frank Kolby, releasing a boorish guffaw.

"Do you suppose the captain could've left the bridge?" asked Dad with mock puzzlement.

"I think you've made your point," said Susan.

The old man leaned toward Lucy McDade as if about to deal her a playing card. "This sailor lad of yours left the bridge. I'll bet he got one of those headaches of his and, *pfft*, he took off, and now all the egrets and herons are dying. You know what your boyfriend's problem is, pretty Lucy? He thinks the oily bird catches the worm!"

Tiffany burst into giggles.

Lucy turned red.

Kolby sniggered.

Susan got up to leave.

"Bastard," said Anthony's alter ego.

"Bastard," echoed the observer Anthony.

"Gravy, anyone?" said Christopher Van Horne, lifting the boat from its saucer. "What's the matter, folks—are you afraid?"

"I'm not afraid." Kolby seized the boat, pouring polluted gravy onto his mashed potatoes.

"I'll never forgive you for this," seethed Susan, stalking out of the room.

Kolby shoveled a glop of potato into his mouth. "Tastes like—"

The scene froze.

The figures dissolved.

Only the waterborne feather remained.

"That was the worst part of Matagorda Bay, wasn't it?" said Raphael. "Worse than the hate mail from the environmentalists and the death threats from the shrimpers—the worst part was what your father did to you that night."

"The humiliation . . ."

"No," said the angel pointedly. "Not the humiliation. The brute candor of it all."

"I don't understand."

"Four months after the wreck of the *Val*, somebody was finally telling you a truth the state of Texas had denied."

"What truth?"

"You're guilty, Anthony Van Horne."

"I've never claimed otherwise."

"Guilty," Raphael repeated, slamming his fist into his palm like a judge wielding a gavel. "But beyond guilt lies redemption, or so the story goes." The angel slipped his fingers beneath the feathers of his left wing and relieved himself of an itch. "After completing the mission, you will seek out your father."

"Dad?"

The angel nodded. "Your aloof, capricious, unhappy father. You will tell him you got the job done. And then—this I promise—then you will receive the absolution you deserve."

"I don't want *his* absolution."

"*His* absolution," said Raphael, "is the only one that counts. Blood is thicker than oil, Captain. The man's hooks are in you."

"I can absolve myself," Anthony insisted.

"You've tried that. Showers don't do it. The Cuxa fountain doesn't do it. You'll never be free of Matagorda Bay, the oil will never leave you, until Christopher Van Horne looks you in the eye and says, 'Son, I'm proud of you. You bore Him to His tomb.'"

A sudden coldness swept through the Cuxa Cloister. Goose bumps grew on Anthony's naked skin like barnacles colonizing a tanker's hull. Crouching over the pool, he fished out the drifting feather. What did he know of God? Maybe God *did* have blood, bile, and the rest of it; maybe He *could* die. Anthony's Sunday school teachers, promoters of a faith so vague and generic it was impossible to imagine anyone rebelling against it (there are no lapsed Wilmington Presbyterians), had never even raised such possibilities. Who could say whether God had a body?

"Dad and I haven't spoken since Christmas." Anthony drew the soft, wet feather across his lips. "Last I heard, he and Tiffany were in Spain."

"Then that's where you'll find him."

Raphael staggered forward, extended his chilly palms, and collapsed into the captain's arms. The angel was surprisingly heavy, oddly meaty. How strange was the universe. Stranger than Anthony had ever imagined.

"Bury Him . . ."

The captain studied the spangled sky. He thought of his favorite sextant, the one his sister had given him upon his graduation from New York Maritime College, a flawless facsimile of the wondrous instrument with which, nearly two centuries earlier,

Nathaniel Bowditch had corrected and emended all the world's maps. And the thing worked, too, picking out Polaris in an instant, filtering the brilliance of Venus, sifting banded Jupiter from the clouds. Anthony never sailed without it.

"I own a precise and beautiful sextant," Anthony told Raphael. "You never know when your computer'll break down," the captain added. "You never know when you'll have to steer by the stars," said the master of the *Valparaíso*, whereupon the angel smiled softly and drew his last breath.

The moon assumed an uncanny whiteness, riding the sky like God's own skull, as, shortly before dawn, Anthony hauled Raphael Azarias's stiffening body west across Fort Tryon Park, lowered it over the embankment, and flung it facedown into the cool, polluted waters of the Hudson River.

Príest

THOMAS WICKLIFF OCKHAM, a good man, a man who loved God, ideas, vintage movies, and his brothers in the Society of Jesus, wove through the crowded Seventh Avenue local, carefully maneuvering his attaché case amid the congestion of pelvises and rumps. On the far wall a map beckoned, an intricate network of multicolored lines, like the veined and bleeding palm of some cubistic Christ. Reaching it, he began to plot his course. He would get off at Forty-second Street. Take the N-train south to Union Square. Walk east on Fourteenth. Find Captain Anthony Van Horne of the Brazilian Merchant Marine, sail away on the SS *Carpco Valparaíso*, and lay an impossible corpse to rest.

He sat down between a wrinkled Korean man holding a potted cactus on his lap and an attractive black woman in a ballooning maternity dress. To Thomas Ockham, S.J., the New York subway system offered a foretaste of the Kingdom: Asians rubbing shoulders with Africans, Hispanics with Arabs, Gentiles with Jews, all boundaries gone, all demarcations erased, all men appended to the Universal and Invisible Church, the Mystical Body of Christ—though if the half-dozen glossy photographs in Thomas's attaché case told the truth, of course, there was no Kingdom, no Mystical Body, God and His various dimensions being dead.

Italy had been different. In Italy everyone had looked the same. They had all looked Italian . . .

The Church faces a grave crisis: thus began the Holy See's cryptic plea, an official Vatican missive sliding from the fax machine in the mailroom of Fordham University's physics department. But what sort of crisis? Spiritual? Political? Financial? The missive didn't say. Severe, obviously—severe enough for the See to insist that Thomas cancel his classes for the week and catch the midnight flight to Rome.

Hiring a cab at the *aeroporto*, he'd told the driver to take him straight to the Gesu. To be a Jesuit in Rome and not receive communion at the Society's mother church was like being a physicist in Bern and not visiting the patent office. And, indeed, during his last trip to Geneva's Conseil Européen pour la Recherche Nucléaire, Thomas had taken a day off and made the appropriate pilgrimage north, eventually kneeling before the very rosewood desk at which Albert Einstein had penned the great paper of 1903, *The Electrodynamics of Moving Bodies*, that divinely inspired wedding of light to matter, matter to space, space to time.

So Thomas drank the blood, consumed the flesh, and set off for the Hotel Ritz-Reggia. A half-hour later, he stood in the sumptuous lobby shaking hands with Tullio Cardinal Di Luca, the Vatican's Secretary of Extraordinary Ecclesiastical Affairs.

Monsignor Di Luca was not forthcoming. Phlegmatic as the moon, and no less pocked and dreary, he invited Thomas to dinner in the Ritz-Reggia's elegant *ristorante*, where their conversation never went beyond Thomas's writings, most especially *The Mechanics of Grace*, his revolutionary reconciliation of post-Newtonian physics with the Eucharist. When Thomas looked Di Luca directly in the eye and asked him about the "grave crisis," the *cardinale* replied that their audience with the Holy Father would occur at nine A.M. sharp.

Twelve hours later, the bewildered priest strolled out of his hotel, crossed the courtyard of San Damasco, and presented himself to a plumed *maestro di camera* in the sun-washed antechamber of the Vatican Palace. Di Luca appeared instantly, as dour in the morning light as under the Ritz-Reggia's chandeliers, accompanied by the spry, elfin, red-capped Eugenio Cardinal Orselli, the Vatican's renowned Secretary of State. Side by side, the clerics marched through the double door to the papal study, Thomas pausing briefly to admire the Swiss Guard with their glistening steel pikes. Rome had it right, he decided. The Holy See was indeed at war, forever taking the field against all those who would reduce human beings to mere ambitious apes, to lucky chunks of protoplasm, to singularly clever and complex machines.

Armed with a crozier, draped in an ermine cape, Pope Innocent XIV shuffled forward, one gloved and bejeweled hand extended, the other steadying a beehive-shaped tiara that rested on his head like an electric dryer cooking a suburban matron's hairdo. The old man's love of ostentation, Thomas knew, had occasioned debate both within the Vatican and without, but it was generally agreed that, as the first North American ever to assume the Chair of Peter, he had a right to all the trimmings.

"We shall be honest," said Innocent XIV, born Jean-Jacques LeClerc. His face was fat, round, and extraordinarily beautiful, like a jack-o'-lantern carved by Donatello. "You weren't anyone's first choice."

A Canadian pope, mused Thomas as, steadying his bifocals, he kissed the Fisherman's Ring. And before that, the Supreme Pontiff had been Portuguese. Before that, Polish. The Northern

Hemisphere was getting to be the place where any boy could grow up to be Vicar of Christ.

"The archangels regard you as rather too intellectual," said Monsignor Di Luca. "But when the Bishop of Prague turned us down, I convinced them you were the man for the job."

"The archangels?" said Thomas, surprised that a papal secretary should harbor such a medieval turn of mind. Was Di Luca a biblical literalist? A fool? How many pinheads can dance on the floor of the Vatican?

"Raphael, Michael, Chamuel, Adabiel, Haniel, Zaphiel, and Gabriel," the beautiful Pope elaborated.

"Or has Fordham University done away with those particular entities?" A sneer flitted across Monsignor Di Luca's face.

"Those of us who labor in the subatomic netherworld," said Thomas, "soon learn that angels are no less plausible than electrons." Tremors of chagrin passed through him. Not two days in Rome, and already he was telling them what they wanted to hear.

The Holy Father smiled broadly, dimpling his plump cheeks. "Very good, Professor Ockham. It was in fact your scientific speculations that inspired us to send for you. We have read not only *The Mechanics of Grace* but also *Superstrings and Salvation*."

"You possess a tough mind," said Cardinal Orselli. "You have proven you can hold your own against Modernism."

"Let us ascend," said the Pope.

They rode the elevator five floors to the Vatican Screening Room, a sepulchral facility complete with digital sound, velvet seats, and hardware capable of projecting everything from laserdiscs to magic-lantern slides but most commonly used, Orselli explained, for Cecil B. DeMille retrospectives and midnight revivals of *The Bells of St. Mary's*. As the clerics sank into the lush upholstery, a short and tormented-looking young man entered, a stethoscope swaying from his neck, the surname CARMINATI stitched in red to his white vestment. Accompanying the physician was a sickly, shivering, gray-haired creature who, beyond his other unsettling accouterments (halo, harp, phosphorescent robe), sported a magnificent pair of feathered wings growing from his shoulder blades. Something nontrivial was in the air, Thomas sensed. Something that couldn't be further from Cecil B. DeMille and Bing Crosby.

"Every time he makes his presentation"—Cardinal Orselli gestured toward the haloed man and released an elaborate sigh—"we become more convinced."

"Glad you're here, Ockham," said the creature in the sort of thin, scratchy voice Thomas associated with early-thirties gangster movies. His skin was astonishingly white, beyond Caucasian genes, beyond albinism even; he seemed molded from snow. "I'm told you are at once devout"—he stood on his toes—"and smart." Whereupon, to Thomas's utter amazement, the haloed man flapped his wings, rose six feet in the air, and stayed there. "Time is of the essence," he said, circling the screening room with an awkwardness reminiscent of Orville Wright puddle-jumping across Kitty Hawk.

"Good Lord," said Thomas.

The haloed man landed before the red proscenium curtains. Steadying himself on the young physician, he set his harp on the lectern and twiddled a pair of console knobs. The curtains parted; the room darkened; a cone of bright light spread outward from the projection booth, striking the beaded screen.

"The Corpus Dei," said the creature matter-of-factly as a 35mm color slide flashed before the priest's eyes. "God's dead body."

Thomas squinted, but the image—a large, humanoid object adrift on a bile-dark sea—remained blurry. "What did you say?"

The next slide clicked into place: same subject, a closer but equally fuzzy view. "God's dead body," the haloed man insisted.

"Can you focus it any better?"

"No." The man ran through three more unsatisfactory shots of the enigmatic mass. "I took them myself, with a Leica."

"He has corroborating evidence," said Cardinal Orselli.

"An electrocardiogram as flat as a flounder," the creature explained.

As the last slide vanished, the projector lamp again flooded the screen with its pristine radiance.

"Is this some sort of a joke?" Thomas asked. What else could it be? In a civilization where tabloid art directors routinely forged photos of Bigfoot and UFO pilots, it would take more than a few slides of a foggy something-or-other to transform Thomas's interior image of God along such radically anthropomorphic lines.

Except that his knees were rattling.

Sweat was collecting in his palms.

He stared at the rug, contemplating its thick, sound-absorbent fibers, and when he looked up the angel's eyes riveted him: golden eyes, sparkling and electric, like miniature Van de Graaff generators spewing out slivers of lightning.

"Dead?" Thomas rasped.

"Dead."

"Cause?"

"Total mystery. We haven't a clue."

"Are you . . . Raphael?"

"Raphael's in New York City, tracking down Anthony Van Horne—yes, *Captain* Anthony Van Horne, the man who turned Matagorda Bay to licorice."

As the angel brought up the house lights, Thomas saw that he was coming unglued. Silvery hairs floated down from his scalp. His wings exfoliated like a Mexican roof shedding tiles. "And the others?"

"Adabiel and Haniel passed away yesterday," said the angel, retrieving his harp from the lectern. "Terminal empathy. Michael's fading fast, Chamuel's not long for this world, Zaphiel's on his deathbed . . ."

"That leaves Gabriel."

The angel plucked his harp.

"In short, Father Ockham," said Monsignor Di Luca, as if

he'd just finished explaining a great deal, when in fact he'd explained nothing, "we want you on the ship. We want you on the *Carpco Valparaíso.*"

"The only Ultra Large Crude Carrier ever chartered by the Vatican," the Holy Father elaborated. "A sullied vessel, to be sure, but none other is equal to the task—or so Gabriel tells us."

"What task?" asked Thomas.

"Salvaging the Corpus Dei." Bright tears spilled down Gabriel's fissured cheeks. Luminous mucus leaked from his nostrils. "Protecting Him from those"—the angel cast a quick glance toward Di Luca—"who would exploit His condition for their own ends. Giving Him a decent burial."

"Once the body's in Arctic waters," Orselli explained, "the putrefaction will stop."

"We have prepared a place," said Gabriel, listlessly picking out the *Dies Irae* on his instrument. "An iceberg tomb adjoining Kvitoya."

"And all the while, *you'll* be on the navigation bridge," said Di Luca, laying a red-gloved hand on Thomas's shoulder. "Our sole liaison, keeping Van Horne on his appointed path. The man's no Catholic, you see. He's barely a Christian."

"The ship's manifest will list you as a PAC—a Person in Addition to Crew," said Orselli. "In reality you'll be the most important man on the voyage."

"Let me be explicit." Gabriel fixed his electric eyes directly on Innocent XIV. "We want an honorable interment, nothing more. No stunts, Holiness. None of your billion-dollar funerals, no priceless sculpture on the tomb, no carving Him up for relics."

"We understand," said the Pope.

"I'm not sure you do. You run a tenacious organization, gentlemen. We're afraid you don't know when to quit."

"You can trust us," said Di Luca.

Curling his left wing into a semicircle, Gabriel brushed Thomas's cheek with the tip. "I envy you, Professor. Unlike me, you'll have time to figure out why this awful event happened. I'm convinced that, if you apply the full measure of your Jesuit intellect to the problem, pondering it night and day as the *Valparaíso* plies the North Atlantic, you're bound to hit upon the solution."

"Through reason alone?" said Thomas.

"Through reason alone. I can practically guarantee it. Give yourself till journey's end, and the answer to the riddle will suddenly—"

A harsh, guttural groan. Dr. Carminati rushed over and, opening the angel's robe, pressed the stethoscope against his milk-white bosom. Whimpering softly, Innocent XIV brought his right hand to his lips and sucked the velvet fingertips.

Gabriel sank into the nearest seat, his halo darkening until it came to resemble a lei of dead flowers.

"Pardon, Holiness"—the physician popped the stethoscope out of his ears—"but we should return him to the infirmary now."

"Go with God," said the Pope, raising his moistened hand, rotating it sideways, and etching an invisible cross in the air.

"Remember," said the angel, "no stunts."

The young doctor looped his arm around Gabriel's shoulder and, like a dutiful son guiding his dying father down the hallway of a cancer ward, escorted him out of the room.

Thomas studied the barren screen. God's dead body? God had a body? What were the cosmological implications of this astonishing claim? Was He truly gone, or had His spirit merely vacated some gratuitous husk? (Gabriel's grief suggested there was no putting a happy face on the situation.) Did heaven still exist? (Since the afterlife consisted essentially in God's eternal presence, then the answer was logically no, but surely the question merited further study.) What of the Son and the Ghost? (Assuming Catholic theology counted for anything, then these Persons were inert now too, the Trinity being ipso facto indivisible, but, again, the issue manifestly deserved the attentions of a synod or perhaps even a Vatican Council.)

He turned to the other clerics. "There are problems here."

"A secret consistory has been in session since Tuesday," said the Pope, nodding. "The entire College of Cardinals, burning the midnight oil. We're tackling the full spectrum: the possible causes of death, the chances of resuscitation, the future of the Church . . ."

"We'd like your answer now, Father Ockham," said Di Luca. "The *Valparaíso* weighs anchor in just five days."

Thomas took a deep breath, enjoying the rich, savory hypocrisy of the moment. Historically, Rome had tended to regard her Jesuits as expendable, something between a nuisance and a threat. Ah, but now that the chips were down, to whom did the Vatican turn? To the faithful, unflappable warriors of Ignatius Loyola, that's who.

"May I keep this?" Thomas lifted a stray feather from the floor.

"Very well," said Innocent XIV.

Thomas's gaze wandered back and forth between the Pope and the feather. "One item on your agenda confuses me."

"Do you accept?" demanded Di Luca.

"What item?" asked the Pope.

The feather exuded a feeble glow, like a burning candle fashioned from the tallow of some lost, forsaken lamb.

"Resuscitation."

Resuscitation: the word wove tauntingly through Thomas's head as he emerged from the fetid dampness of Union Square Station and started down Fourteenth Street. It was all highly speculative, of course; the desiccation rate Di Luca had selected for a Supreme Being's central nervous system (ten thousand neurons a minute) bordered on the arbitrary. But assuming the *cardinale* knew whereof he spoke, an encouraging conclusion followed. According to the Vatican's OMNIVAC-5000, He would not be brain-dead before the eighteenth of August—a sufficient interval in which to ferry Him above the Arctic Circle—though it had to be allowed that the computer had made the prediction under protest, crying INSUFFICIENT DATA all the way.

The June air fell heavily on Thomas's flesh, an oppressive cloak of raw Manhattan heat. His face grew slick with perspiration, making his bifocals slide down his nose. On both sides of the street, peddlers labored in the sultry dusk, gathering up their shrinkwrapped audiocassettes, phony Cartier watches, and spastic mechanical bears and piling them into their station wagons. To Thomas's eye, Union Square combined the exoticism of *The Arabian Nights* with the bedrock banality of American commerce, as if a medieval Persian bazaar had been transplanted to the twentieth century and taken over by Wal-Mart. Each vendor wore a wholly impassive face, the shell-shocked, world-weary stare of the urban foot soldier. Thomas envied them their ignorance. Whatever their present pains, whatever defeats and disasters they were sustaining, at least they could imagine that a living God presided over their planet.

He turned right onto Second Avenue, walked south two blocks, and, pulling Gabriel's feather from his breast pocket, climbed the steps of a mottled brownstone. Crescents of sweat marred the armpits of his black shirt, pasting the cotton to his skin. He scanned the names (Goldstein, Smith, Delgado, Spinelli, Chen: more New York pluralism, another intimation of the Kingdom), then pressed the button labeled VAN HORNE— 3 REAR.

A metallic buzz jangled the lock. Thomas opened the door, ascended three flights of mildew-scented stairs, and found himself face to face with a tall, bearded, obliquely handsome man wearing nothing but a spotless white bath towel wrapped around his waist.

He was dripping wet. A tattooed mermaid resembling Rita Hayworth decorated his left forearm.

"The first thing you must tell me," said Anthony Van Horne, "is that I haven't gone crazy."

"If you have," said the priest, "then I have too, and so has the Holy See."

Van Horne disappeared into his apartment and returned gripping an object that disturbed Thomas as much for its chilling familiarity as for its eschatological resonances. Like members of some secret society engaged in an induction ritual, the two men held up their feathers, moving them in languid circles. For a brief moment, a deep and silent understanding flowed between Anthony Van Horne and Thomas Ockham, the only nonpsychotic individuals in New York City who'd ever conversed with angels.

"Come in, Father Ockham."

"Call me Thomas."

"Wanna beer?"

"Sure."

It was not what Thomas expected. A captain's abode, he felt, should have a sense of the sea about it. Where were the giant conches from Bora Bora, the ceramic elephants from Sri Lanka, the tribal masks from New Guinea? With a half-dozen Sunkist orange crates serving as chairs and an AT&T cable spool in lieu of a coffee table, the place seemed more suited to an unemployed actor or a starving artist than to a sailor of fortune like Van Horne.

"Old Milwaukee okay?" The captain sidled into his cramped kitchenette. "It's all I can afford."

"Fine." Thomas lowered himself onto a Sunkist crate. "You Dutchmen have always been merchant mariners, haven't you—you and your *fluytschips*. This life is in your blood."

"I don't believe in blood," said Van Horne, pulling two dewy brown bottles from his refrigerator.

"But your father—he was also a sailor, right?"

The captain laughed. "He was never anything else. He certainly wasn't a father, not much of a husband either, though I believe he thought he was both." Ambling back into the living room, he pressed an Old Milwaukee into Thomas's hand. "Dad's idea of a vacation was to desert his family and go slogging 'round the South Pacific in a tramp freighter, hoping to find an uncharted island. He never quite figured out the world's been mapped already, no *terrae incognitae* left."

"And your mother—was she a dreamer too?"

"Mom climbed mountains. I think she needed to get as far above sea level as possible. A dangerous business—much more dangerous than the Merchant Marine. When I was fifteen, she fell off Annapurna." The captain unhitched the bath towel and scratched his lean, drumtight abdomen. "Have we got a crew yet?"

"Lord, I'm sorry." Even as the sympathy swelled up in Thomas, a sympathy as profound as any he'd ever known, he felt an odd sense of relief. Evidently they were living in a non-contingent universe, one requiring no ongoing input from the Divine. The Creator was gone, yet all His vital inventions—gravity, grace, love, pity—endured.

"Tell me about the crew."

Thomas twisted the lid off his beer, sealed his lips around the rim, and drank. "This morning I signed up that steward you wanted. Sam somebody."

"Follingsbee. I'll never get over the irony—the sea cook who hates seafood. Doesn't matter. The man knows exactly what today's sailor wants. He can mimic it all: Taco Bell, Pizza Hut, Kentucky Fried Chicken . . ."

"Buzzy Longchamps turned down the first mate's position."

"Because he'd be working for me again?"

"Because he'd be working on the *Valparaíso* again. Superstitious." Thomas set his briefcase on the AT&T spool, popped the clasps, and removed his *Jerusalem Bible*. "Your second choice said yes."

"Rafferty? Never sailed with him, but they say he knows more about salvage than anybody this side of . . ."

The captain's voice trailed off. A faraway look settled into his eyes. Taking a large gulp of humid air, he ran the nail of his index finger along the belly of his tattooed mermaid, as if performing a caesarean section.

"The oil won't go," he said tonelessly.

"What?"

"Matagorda Bay. When I'm asleep, a heron flies into my bedroom, black oil dripping from its wings. It circles above me like a vulture over a carcass, screeching curses. Sometimes it's an egret, sometimes an ibis or a roseate spoonbill. Did you know that when the sludge hit their faces, the manatees rubbed their eyes with their flippers until they went blind?"

"I'm . . . sorry," said Thomas.

"Stone blind." Van Horne made his right hand into tongs, squeezing his forehead between thumb and ring finger. With his left hand he lifted his Old Milwaukee and chugged down half the bottle. "What about a second mate?"

"You mustn't hate yourself, Anthony."

"An engineer?"

"Hate what you did, but don't hate yourself."

"A bos'n?"

Opening his Bible, Thomas slipped out the set of 8 × 10 glossies that *L'Osservatore romano*'s photography editor had printed from Gabriel's 35mm slides. "It all happens tomorrow—an officer's call down at the mates' union, a seaman's call over in Jersey City . . ."

The captain disappeared into his bedroom, returning two minutes later in red Bermuda shorts and a white T-shirt emblazoned with the Exxon tiger. "Big sucker, eh?" he said, staring at the photos. "Two miles long, Raphael told me. About the size of downtown Wilkes-Barre." He dragged the edge of his hand along the blurry corpse. "Small for a city, large for a person. You figured His displacement?"

Thomas treated himself to a hearty swallow of Old Milwaukee. "Hard to say. Close to seven million tons, I'd guess." The enjoyment of cold beer was probably the closest he ever came to sinning—beer, and the pride he took in seeing himself footnoted in *The Journal of Experimental Physics*—beer, footnotes, and the viscous oblations that followed his occasional purchase of a *Playboy*. "Captain, how do you see this voyage of ours?"

"Huh?"

"What's our purpose?"

Van Horne flopped into his ruptured couch. "We're giving Him a decent burial."

"Your angel say anything about resuscitation?"

"Nope."

Thomas closed his eyes, as if he were about to offer his undergraduates some particularly difficult and disconcerting idea, like strange attractors or the many-worlds hypothesis. "The Catholic Church is not an institution that readily abandons hope. Her position is this: while the divine heart has evidently stopped beating, the divine nervous system may still boast a few healthy cells. In short, the Holy Father proposes we apply the science of cryonics to this crisis. Do you know what I'm talking about?"

"We should get God on ice before His brain dies?"

"Precisely. Personally, I believe the Pope's being far too optimistic."

An uncanny but entirely reasonable gleam overcame Van Horne, the inevitable luminescence of a man who's been given the opportunity to save the universe. "But if he's *not* being too optimistic," said the captain, a mild tremor in his voice, "how much time . . . ?"

"The Vatican computer wants us to cross the Arctic Circle no later than the eighteenth of August."

Van Horne chugged down the rest of his beer. "Damn, I wish we had the *Val* now. I'd leave with the morning tide, crew or no."

"Your ship arrived in New York Harbor last night."

The captain slammed the empty bottle onto the AT&T spool. "She's here? Why didn't you tell me?"

"Don't know why. Sorry." Thomas collected the photos and slipped them back into his Bible. He knew perfectly well why. It was a matter of power and control, a matter of convincing this strange, oil-haunted man that Holy Mother Church, not Anthony Van Horne, was running the show. "Pier Eighty-eight . . ."

In a flurry of movement the captain pulled on a pair of mirrorshades and a John Deere fits-all visor cap. "Excuse me, Padre. I gotta go visit my ship."

"It's awfully late."

"You don't have to come."

"Yes, I do."

"Oh? Why?"

"Because the SS *Carpco Valparaíso* is currently under Vatican jurisdiction"—Thomas offered the scowling captain a long, meandering smile—"and no one, not even you, can board her without my permission."

In his life and travels Anthony Van Horne had seen the Taj Mahal, the Parthenon, and his ex-fiancée Janet Yost without her clothes on, but he'd never beheld a sight so beautiful as the rehabilitated *Carpco Valparaíso* riding high and empty in the moonlit waters off Pier 88. He gasped. Until that exact and magical moment, he'd not fully believed this mission was real. But there she was, all right, the canny old *Val* herself, tied to the wharf by a half-dozen Dacron lines, dominating New York Harbor with all the stark disproportionality of a rowboat sitting in a bathtub.

In certain rare moments, Anthony thought he understood the general antipathy toward Ultra Large Crude Carriers. Such a ship had no sheer, no gentle ascending slope to her contours. She had no rake, none of the subtle angling of mast and funnel by which traditional cargo vessels paid homage to the Age of Sail. With her crushing tonnage and broad beam, a ULCC didn't ride the waves; she ground them down. Gross ships, monstrous ships—but that was precisely the point, he felt: their fearsome majesty, their ponderous glamour, the way they plied the planet like yachts designed to provide vacation cruises for rhinoceroses. To command a ULCC—to walk its decks and feel it vibrating beneath you, amplifying your flesh and blood—was a grand and defiant gesture, like pissing on a king, or having your own international terrorist organization, or keeping a thermonuclear warhead in your garage.

They went out to her in a launch named the *Juan Fernández*, piloted by a member of the Vatican Secret Service, a bearish sergeant with frazzled white hair and a Colt .45 snugged against his armpit. Lights blazed on every floor of the aft superstructure, its seven levels culminating in a congestion of antennas, smokestacks, masts, and flags. Anthony wasn't sure which of the present banners troubled him more—the keys-and-tiara symbol of the Vatican or the famous stegosaurus logo of Caribbean Petroleum. He resolved to have Marbles Rafferty strike the Carpco colors first thing.

As the launch glided past the *Valparaíso*'s stern, Anthony grabbed the Jacob's ladder and began his ascent to the weather deck, Father Ockham right behind. He had to say one thing for this control-freak priest: the man had nerve. Ockham climbed up the ship's side with perfect aplomb, one hand on his attaché case, the other on the rungs, as if he'd been scaling rope ladders all his life.

The retrofitted towing rig rose sharply against the Jersey City skyline: two mighty windlasses bolted to the afterdeck like a pair of gigantic player-piano rolls, wound not with ordinary mooring lines but with heavy-duty chains, their links as large as inner tubes. At the end of each chain lay a massive kedge anchor, twenty tons of iron, an anchor to hook a whale, tether a continent, moor the moon.

"You're looking at some fancy footwork." Ockham opened his attaché case and drew out a gridded pink checklist clamped to a Masonite clipboard. "Anchors brought down by rail from Canada, motors flown over from Germany, capstans imported from Belgium. The Japanese gave us a great deal on the chains—underbid USX by ten percent."

"You put this stuff out on *bid*?"

"The Church is not a profit-making institution, Anthony, but she knows the value of a dollar."

Boarding the elevator, they rose three stories to the steward's deck. The main galley was aswarm. Eager, robust, competent-looking women in blue jeans and khaki work shirts bustled through the great stainless-steel kitchen, filling the freezers and refrigerators with provisions: tubs of ice cream, wheels of cheese, planks of ham, sides of beef, sacks of Cheerios, barrels of milk, pools of salad oil sealed in 55-gallon drums like so much Texas crude. A propane-fueled Toyota forklift truck chugged past, its orange body peppered with rust, its prongs supporting a paddock piled high with crates of fresh eggs.

"Who the hell are these people?" asked Anthony.

"Vatican longshoremen," Ockham explained.

"They look like women to me."

"They're Carmelites."

"Who?"

"Carmelite nuns."

In the center of the kitchen stood portly Sam Follingsbee, dressed in a white apron and supervising the chaos like a cop directing traffic. Catching sight of his visitors, the steward waddled over and tipped his big, floppy cream puff of a hat.

"Thanks for the recommendation, sir." Follingsbee clasped his captain's hand. "I *needed* this ship, I really did." Swinging his formidable belly toward the priest, he asked, "Father Ockham, right?" Ockham nodded. "Father, I'm puzzled—how come a crummy Carpco voyage rates the services of all these lovely sisters, not to mention yourself?"

"This isn't a Carpco voyage," said Ockham.

"So what's the deal?"

"Once we're at sea, things will become clearer." The priest drummed his bony fingers on the checklist. "Now *I'll* ask a question. On Friday I put in a requisition for one thousand communion wafers. They look a bit like poker chips . . ."

Follingsbee chuckled. "I *know* what they look like, Father— you're talkin' to an ex-altar boy. Not to worry. We got all them hosts in freezer number six—couldn't be safer. Will you be celebratin' Mass every day?"

"Naturally."

"I'll be there," said Follingsbee, starting back into the heart of the hubbub. "Well, maybe not *every* day." His eye caught a Carmelite maneuvering a wheel of cheddar across the floor like a child playing with a hoop. "Hey, Sister, carry that thing—don't fuckin' *roll* it!"

The forklift truck pulled up, and a plump, ruddy nun climbed down from behind the wheel, a string of smoked sausages hanging about her neck like a yoke. Her step struck Anthony as remarkably lively, a sashay, really, if nuns sashayed. Evidently she moved to the beat of whatever private concert was pouring from the Sony Walkman strapped to her waist.

"Tom!" The nun ripped off her headphones. "Tom Ockham!"

"Miriam, darling! How wonderful! I didn't know they'd

recruited *you*!" The priest threw his arms around the nun and planted a sprightly kiss on her cheek. "Get my letter?"

"I did, Tom. Oddest words I ever read. And yet, somehow, I sensed they were true."

"*All* true," said the priest. "Rome, Gabriel, the slides, the EKG . . ."

"A bad business."

"The worst."

"There's no hope?"

"You know me, the eternal pessimist."

Anthony massaged his beard. The banter between Ockham and Sister Miriam bewildered him. It seemed a conversation less between a priest and a nun than between two passé movie actors encountering each other on a Hollywood set twenty years after their amicable divorce.

"Darling, meet Anthony Van Horne—the planet's greatest living sailor, or so the angels believed," said Ockham. "Miriam and I go back a long way," he told the captain. "At Loyola they're still using a textbook we wrote in the early seventies, *Introduction to Theodicy.*"

"What's theodicy?" asked Anthony.

"Hard to explain."

"Sounds like *idiocy*."

"Much of it is."

"Theodicy means reconciling God's goodness with the world's evils." Sister Miriam snapped off a smoked sausage and took a bite. "Dinner," she explained, chewing slowly. "Captain, I want to come along."

"Along where?"

"On the voyage."

"Bad idea."

"It's a splendid idea," said the priest. He gestured toward the sausages. "Would you mind? I haven't eaten all day."

"One PAC is enough," said Anthony.

Miriam snapped off a second sausage and handed it to Ockham.

"Let me put it this way." The priest nudged Anthony with his clipboard. "The Holy Father was never entirely sold on you. It's not too late for him to hire another captain."

The first insidious stirrings of a migraine crept through Anthony's brain. He rubbed his temples. "All right, Padre. Fine. But she won't like the work. All you do is chip rust and paint what's underneath."

"Sounds dreadful," said the nun. "I'll take it."

"See you in church tomorrow?" said Ockham, squeezing Miriam's hand. "Saint Patrick's Cathedral—0800 hours, as we say in the Merchant Marine."

"Sure thing."

Sister Miriam put on her headphones and returned to her forklift.

"Okay, so our galley's in good shape," said Anthony as he and Ockham approached the elevator, "but what about the rest? The antipredator matériel?"

"We loaded six crates of Dupont shark repellent this morning," said Ockham, devouring his sausage, "along with fifteen T-62 bazookas"—he glanced at his checklist—"and twenty WP-17 Toshiba exploding-harpoon guns."

"Backup turbine?"

"Arrives tomorrow."

They went up to level seven, the bridge. The place seemed untouched, frozen, as if some historical society were preserving the *Carpco Valparaíso* for tourism, the newest exhibit in the Museum of Environmental Disasters. Even the Bushnell binoculars occupied their customary spot in the canvas bin beside the twelve-mile radar.

"Bulkhead reinforcement beams?"

"In the fo'c'sle hold," Ockham replied.

"Emergency prop?"

"Look down—you'll see it lashed to the weather deck."

"I didn't like that crap you pulled back there, threatening me . . ."

"I didn't like it either. Let's try to be friends, okay?"

Saying nothing, Anthony grasped the helm, curling his palms around the cold steel disc. He smiled. In his past lay a dead mother, a mercurial father, a broken engagement, and eleven million gallons of spilled oil. His future promised little beyond old age, chronic migraines, futile showers, and a voyage that smacked of madness.

But at that precise moment, standing on the bridge of his ship and contemplating his emergency screw propeller, Anthony Van Horne was a happy man.

In the soggy, sweltering center of Jersey City, a twenty-six-year-old orphan named Neil Weisinger shouldered his seabag, climbed eight flights to the top of the Nimrod Building, and entered the New York Hall of the National Maritime Union. Over three dozen ABs and ordinaries jammed the dusty room, sitting nervously on folding chairs, gear wedged between their legs, half of them puffing on cigarettes, each sailor hoping for a berth on the only ship scheduled to dock that month, the SS *Argo Lykes*. Neil groaned. So much competition. The instant he'd finished his last voyage (a dry-cargo jaunt on the *Stella Lykes*, through the Canal to Auckland and back), he'd done as every able-bodied seaman does on disembarking—run straight down to the nearest union hall to get his shipping card stamped with the exact date and time. Nine months and fourteen days later, the card had acquired considerable seniority, but it still wasn't a killer.

Neil pulled the card from his wallet—he liked his ID photo immensely, the way the harsh glare of the strobe had made his black eyes sparkle and his cherubic face look angular and austere—and tossed the laminated rectangle into a shoe box duct-taped to the wall below a poster reading SHIP AMERICAN: IT COSTS NO MORE. Reaching into the box, he flipped through his rivals. Bad news. A Rastafarian with nineteen more days on shore than Neil. A fellow Jew named Daniel Rosenberg with eleven. A Chinese woman, An-mei Jong, with six. Damn.

He sat down beneath an open window, a thick layer of Jersey grime spread across its panes like peanut butter on a saltine. You never knew, of course. Miracles happened. A tramp tanker might arrive from the Persian Gulf. The dispatcher might post an in-port relief job, or one of those short trips up the Hudson nobody wanted unless he was as broke as Neil. A crew of methane-breathing Neptunians might land in Journal Square, their helms-man dead from an oxygen overdose, and sign him up on the spot.

"Ever had any close calls?" A tense voice, slightly laryngitic. Neil turned. Outside the window, a sailor lounged on the fire escape—a muscular, freckled, auburn-haired young man in a red polo shirt and tattered black beret, his seabag serving as a pillow. "I mean, really *close*?"

"Not me, no. Once, in Philly, I saw an AB come in with this card three hundred and sixty-four days old."

"Sweating?"

"Like a stoker. When the sheet went up, the guy actually pissed his pants."

"He get a berth?"

Neil nodded. "Twelve and a half minutes before his card would've rolled over."

"The Lord was lookin' out for him." The freckled sailor slipped a tiny gold chain from beneath his polo shirt, glancing at the attached cross like the White Rabbit consulting his pocket watch.

Neil winced. This wasn't the first time he'd encountered a Jesus aficionado. As a rule, he didn't mind them. Once at sea, they were usually diligent as hell, cleaning toilets and chipping rust without a whimper, but their agenda made him nervous. Often as not, the conversation got around to the precarious position of Neil's immortal soul. On the *Stella*, for example, a Seventh Day Adventist had somberly advised Neil that he could spare himself "the trouble of Armageddon" by accepting Jesus then and there.

"What're you doin' on the fire escape?"

"It's cooler out here," said the freckled sailor, unwrapping a package of Bazooka bubblegum. He scanned the comic strip and chortled, then popped the pink lozenge into his mouth.

"I'm Neil Weisinger."

"Leo Zook."

Drawing his plastic Bugs Bunny lunch box from his seabag, Neil climbed through the window. He'd always been a great admirer of Bugs. The rabbit was a loner, and liked it. No friends. No family. Smart, resourceful, rejected by the outside world. There was something rather Jewish about Bugs Bunny.

"Hey, Leo, I saw three killer cards in the box, and none of 'em belongs to you." The fire escape seemed no cooler than the hall, but the view was spectacular, a clear vista stretching all the way from midtown to the Statue of Liberty. "Why don't you leave?"

"The Lord told me I'd be getting a ship today." From the zippered compartment of his seabag, Zook retrieved a tattered booklet titled *Close Encounters with Jesus Christ*, the author being one Hyman Levkowitz. "You might find this interesting," he said, pressing the tract into Neil's palm. "It's by a cantor who found salvation."

Neil opened his lunch box, removed a green apple, and began to munch. He beat back a sneer. God was a perfectly fine idea. Indeed, before realizing he belonged on ships, Neil had spent two years across the river at Yeshiva University, studying Jewish history and toying with the idea of becoming a rabbi. But Neil's God was not the patient, accessible, direct-dial deity on whom

Leo Zook evidently predicated his life. Neil's was the God he'd found by going to sea, the radiant *En Sof* who lay somewhere below the deepest mid-Atlantic trench and beyond the highest navigational star, the God of the four A.M. watch.

"Do yourself a favor—read it through," said Zook. "I can't recommend eternal life highly enough."

At that moment, Neil would have preferred almost anyone else's company. An encyclopedia salesman's. An Arab's. Whatever their other foibles, his Arab mates never tried to convert him. Usually they just ignored him, though sometimes they actually became his friends—particularly when, during prayers, he helped them stay pointed toward Mecca while the ship made a turn. Neil always brought a magnetically-corrected compass to sea for expressly this purpose.

A pear-shaped woman with the demeanor of a fishwife waddled out of the office and headed for the board.

"Soup's on!" the dispatcher cried as Neil and Zook scrambled back into the hall. She jerked two thumbtacks from her mouth as if they were loose teeth and pinned a job sheet to the cork.

• OFFSHORE SHIPPING JOBS •

COMPANY:	*Lykes Brothers*
SHIP:	*SS* Argo Lykes
LOCATED:	*Pier 86*
SAILS:	*1500 Friday*
RUN:	*West Coast South America*
JOBS:	*Able Seaman: 2*
TIME:	*120-day rotary*
RELIEVING:	*J. Pierce, F. Pellegrino*
REASON:	*Time up*

"All right," said the dispatcher, "who's got 'em?"

"Nobody here be beatin' ten month plus fifteen day, eh?" said the Rastafarian.

"The other one's mine," said Daniel Rosenberg.

The dispatcher checked her watch. "Assuming no killer card shows up in the next six seconds"—she winked at the winners—"they're all yours. Step into the office, fellas."

Gradually the mob dispersed, forty disappointed men and women ambling morosely back to their seats. Eight sailors collected their cards and, conceding defeat, left. The dreamers and the desperate sat down to wait.

"The Lord will come through," said Zook.

Neil slumped onto the nearest folding chair. Why didn't he just admit it—he had no career, he was a failure. Somehow his grandfather had wrought an honorable and glamorous life from the sea. But that era was gone. The system was dying. Advising a young man to join the United States Merchant Marine was like advising him to go into vaudeville.

As a boy, Neil had never tired of hearing Grandfather Moshe recount his maritime adventures, wondrous tales of battling pirates on Ecuadorian rivers, transporting hippopotami to French zoos, playing cat-and-mouse with Nazi submarines in the North Atlantic, and, most impressive of all, helping to smuggle fifteen hundred displaced Jews past the British blockade and into Palestine on the *Hatikvah*, one of the dozen rogue freighters secretly leased by the Aliyah Bet. Four decades later, Chief Mate Moshe Weisinger had opened his mail to find a token of appreciation from the Israeli government: a bronze medal bearing the face of David Ben-Gurion in bas-relief. When Grandfather Moshe died, Neil inherited the medal. He always kept it in his right pants pocket, something to clutch in moments of stress.

The door to the hall swung open, and a wrinkled, lanky man wearing a black shirt and Roman collar entered, slapping a job sheet into the dispatcher's palm.

"Call this right away."

The dispatcher tacked up the priest's sheet directly over the *Argo Lykes* notice. "Okay, you packet rats," she said, turning to the hopeful sailors, "we've got this tramp tanker over at Pier Eighty-eight, and it looks like they're startin' from scratch."

• OFFSHORE SHIPPING JOBS •

COMPANY:	*Carpco Shipping*
SHIP:	SS *Carpco Valparaíso*
LOCATED:	*Pier 88*
SAILS:	*1700 Thursday*
RUN:	*Svalbard, Arctic Ocean*
JOBS:	*Able Seaman: 18*
	Ordinary Seaman: 12
	Food Handler: 2
TIME:	*90-day rotary*
RELIEVING:	*Not applicable*
REASON:	*Not applicable*

Grunts of dismay resounded through the union hall. Rumors swarmed like sea gulls feasting on a landfill. The *Valparaíso*, the infamous *Valparaíso*, the tainted, broken, bedeviled *Valparaíso*. Hadn't she been sold to the Japanese and converted into a toxic-waste carrier? Sunk in a Tomahawk missile test?

"Does this mean we're all hired?" asked a blobby man with bad teeth and five o'clock shadow.

"Every one of you," said the priest. "Not only that but you can figure on more overtime than you've ever pulled down in your lives. My name is Thomas Ockham, Society of Jesus, and we'll be spending the next three months together."

And then, as if he thought the U.S. Merchant Marine were a branch of the military, the priest saluted, made an abrupt about-face, and marched out of the room.

"I told you the Lord would come through," said Zook, licking a mustache of perspiration from his upper lip.

An eerie silence descended, settling into the dust, clinging to the cigarette smoke. The Lord had come through, mused Neil. Either the Lord or Caribbean Petroleum. Neil wouldn't be ferrying any Jews to Haifa or hippos to Le Havre this trip, he wouldn't be dodging any Nazi subs, but at least he had a job.

"Jesus hasn't let me down yet," the Evangelical went on.

A job—and yet . . .

"Christ never lets anybody down."

A ship like the *Valparaíso* should not be resurrected, Neil believed, and if she *were* resurrected, a smart AB would look elsewhere for work.

"You know, mates, this seems kinda creepy to me," said a buxom Puerto Rican woman in a tight Menudo T-shirt. "Why're we shippin' out with a *priest*?"

"Yeah, and why on the fucking *Titanic*?" asked a leathery old sailor with I LOVE BRENDA tattooed on the back of his hand.

"I'll tell you something else," said the blobby man. "I been to Svalbard on a bulk carrier once, and I can say for an absolute fact you won't find one solitary drop of crude up there. What're we takin' on, walrus piss?"

"Well, it's great to have a ship," said willowy An-mei Jong with forced enthusiasm.

"Oh, for sure," said Brenda's lover with artificial cheer.

Reaching into his right pants pocket, Neil squeezed his grandfather's Ben-Gurion medal. "Let's go sign up," he said, when in fact his impulse was to bolt from the room, find some unemployed sailor roaming the Eleventh Avenue docks, and give the poor bastard his berth.

Storm

FOR THE AVERAGE sea captain, handing one's ship over to a harbor pilot was a wrenching experience, an ordeal of displacement not unlike that endured by a husband finding an alien brand of condom in his wife's purse. But Anthony Van Horne was not the average sea captain. Harbor pilots didn't make the rules, he reasoned; the National Transportation Safety Board did. And so when a battered New York Port Authority launch tied up alongside the *Carpco Valparaíso* at 1735 hours on the evening of her scheduled departure, Anthony was quite prepared to be civil.

Then he recognized the pilot.

Frank Kolby. Unctuous old Frank Kolby, the idiot who'd laughed so uproariously on seeing Anthony's father reenact the wreck of the *Val* in a gravy boat.

"Hello, Frank."

"Hiya, Anthony." The pilot stepped into the wheelhouse and pulled off his black waterproof leggings. "I heard it was you on the bridge." He wore a blue three-piece suit, well tailored and neatly pressed, as if trying to pass himself off as other than what he was, a glorified parking-lot attendant. "They spliced the *Val* together real good, didn't they?"

"I expect she'll last another voyage," said Anthony, slipping on his mirrorshades.

The tugboats tooted their readiness. Kolby dropped his leggings next to the compass binnacle, then reached toward the control console and snatched up the walkie-talkie. "Raise anchors!"

Groaning, gushing steam, the fo'c'sle windlasses rotated, slowly drawing two algae-coated chains from the river. On the forward TV monitor Anthony watched globs of dark silt slide from the starboard anchor like Jell-O from a fork and plop into the Hudson. For an instant he imagined he saw Raphael Azarias's corpse wrapped around the flukes, but then he realized it was only an angel-shaped hunk of mud.

"Cast off!"

Snugging his John Deere visor cap down to his eyebrows, Anthony opened the starboard door and strode across the bridge wing. All along Pier 88, stevedores in torn plimsolls and ratty T-shirts scurried about, untying Dacron lines from bollards, setting the tanker free. Sea gulls wheeled across the setting sun, squawking their endless disapproval of the world. A half-dozen tugs converged from all directions, whistles shrieking madly as their crews tossed thick, shaggy ropes to the ABs stationed on the *Val*'s weather deck.

Anthony inhaled a generous helping of harbor air—his last chance, before shoving off, to savor this unique mix of bunker oil, bilge water, raw sewage, dead fish, and gull guano—and stepped back inside.

"Slow ahead," said Kolby. "Twenty rpm's."

"Slow ahead." Chief Mate Marbles Rafferty—a mournful black sailor in his early forties, lean and tightly wound, a kind of human sheepshank—eased the dual joysticks forward.

Gently, cautiously, like a team of seeing-eye tuna guiding a blind whale home, the tugs began the simultaneously gross and balletic business of hauling the *Valparaíso* down the river and pointing her into Upper New York Bay.

"Right ten degrees," said Kolby.

"Right ten," echoed the AB at the helm, Karl Jaworski, a paunchy sailor who carried the designation *able-bodied seaman* into the deepest reaches of euphemism. Eyes locked on the rudder indicator, Jaworski gave the wheel a lethargic twist.

"Half ahead," said Kolby.

"Half ahead," said Rafferty, advancing the throttles.

The *Valparaíso* coasted smoothly over three hundred westbound commuters stuck in the Holland Tunnel's regular six P.M. traffic jam.

"Is it true Dad and his wife are in Spain?" Anthony asked the pilot.

"Yep," said Kolby. "Town called Valladolid."

"Never heard of it."

"Christopher Columbus died there."

Anthony suppressed a smirk. But of course. Where else would the old man drag himself at the end of his life but to the site of his idol's passing?

"Know how I can reach him?"

As the pilot pulled a computerized Sanyo Life Organizer from his vest, Anthony flashed on the previous Thanksgiving: Kolby eating a helping of mashed potatoes saturated with giblet gravy and lighter fluid.

"I got his fax number."

Anthony grabbed a Chevron ballpoint and an *American Practical Navigator* from atop the Marisat computer. "Shoot," he said, opening the book.

Why did his father identify so fiercely with Columbus? Reincarnation? If so, then the spirit that occupied Christopher Van Horne was surely not the visionary, inspired Columbus who'd discovered the New World. It was the demented, arthritic Columbus of the subsequent voyages—the Columbus who'd kept a gibbet permanently installed on the taffrail of his ship so he could hang mutineers, deserters, grumblers, and all those who publicly doubted they'd reached the Indies.

"Dial 011-34-28 . . ."

Anthony transcribed the number across a diagram of the Little Dipper, filling the bowl with digits.

"Away with the tugs!" bellowed Kolby.

As the World Trade Center loomed up, its promontories rising into the dusk like bollards meant to moor some unimaginably humongous ship, a disquieting thought possessed Anthony. This seventy-year-old Sea Scout, this asshole friend of his icebox father, was within two hundred yards of hanging them up on the shoals.

"Come right ten degrees!" cried Anthony.

"I was about to say that," Kolby snapped.

"Right ten," echoed Jaworski.

"Dead slow!" said Anthony.

"And that," said Kolby.

"Dead slow," echoed Rafferty.

"Stern tugs gone," came the bos'n's report, rasping out of the walkie-talkie.

"You gotta be a little sharper, Frank." Anthony gave the pilot a condescending wink. "When the *Val*'s riding this light, she takes her sweet time turning."

"Forward tugs gone," said the bos'n.

"Steady," said Anthony.

"Steady," said Jaworski.

The tugs spun north, let out a high, raunchy series of farewell toots, and steamed back up the Hudson like an ensemble of seagoing calliopes.

"Wake up the pump room," said Kolby, plucking the intercom mike from the console and handing it to the chief mate. "Time we took on some ballast."

"Don't do it, Marbles," said Anthony.

"I need ballast to steer," Kolby protested.

"Look at the fathometer, for Christ's sake. Our barnacles can stick their peckers in the bottom."

"This is *my* harbor, Anthony. I know how deep it is."

"No ballast, Frank."

The pilot reddened and fumed. "It appears I'm no longer needed up here, am I?"

"Appears that way."

"Who's your tailor, Frank?" asked Rafferty, deadpan. "I'd like to be buried in a suit like that."

"Fuck you," said the pilot. "Fuck the lot of you."

Anthony tore the walkie-talkie from Kolby's hand. "Lower starboard accommodation ladder," he instructed the bos'n. "We're dropping our pilot in ten minutes."

"Once the Coast Guard hears about this," said Kolby, quivering with rage as he climbed back into his leggings, "it won't be a *week* before you lose your master's license all over again."

"Put your complaint in Portuguese," said the captain. The Statue of Liberty glided past, tirelessly lifting her lamp. "My license comes from Brazil."

"Brazil?"

"It's in South America, Frank," said Anthony, hustling the pilot out of the wheelhouse. "*You'll* never get there."

By 1835 Kolby was in the harbor launch, speeding back toward Pier 88.

At 1845 the *Valparaíso* began drinking Upper New York Bay, sucking its tides into her ballast tanks.

At 1910 Anthony's radio officer came onto the bridge: Lianne Bliss—"Sparks," as per hallowed maritime tradition—the bony little hippie vegetarian Ockham had dug up on Wednesday at the International Organization of Masters, Mates, and Pilots. "Jay

Island's on the phone." For someone so petite, Sparks had an astonishingly resonant voice, as if she were speaking from the bottom of an empty cargo bay. "They wanna know what we're up to."

Anthony ducked into the radio shack, thumbing the transceiver mike to ON. "Calling Jay Island Coast Guard Station . . ."

"Go ahead. Over."

"*Carpco Valparaíso* here, bound in ballast for Lagos, Nigeria, to take on two hundred thousand barrels of crude oil. Over."

"Roger, *Valparaíso*. Be advised of Tropical Depression Number Six—Hurricane Beatrice—currently blowing west from Cape Verde."

"Gotcha, Jay Island. Out."

At 1934 the *Valparaíso* slid across the ethereal line separating Lower New York Bay from the North Atlantic Ocean. Twenty minutes later, Second Mate Spicer—Big Joe Spicer, the only sailor on board who seemed scaled to the tanker herself—entered the wheelhouse to relieve Rafferty.

"Lay me a course for São Tomé," Anthony ordered Spicer. Grabbing the Exxon coffee Thermos and his ceramic Carpco mug, the captain poured himself the first of what he expected would be about five hundred cups of thick black jamoke. "I want us there in two weeks."

"I overheard the Coast Guard mention a hurricane," said Rafferty.

"Forget the damn hurricane. This is the *Carpco Valparaíso*, not some proctologist's sailboat. If it starts to rain, we'll turn on the windshield wipers."

"Can O'Connor give us a steady eighteen knots?" asked Spicer.

"I expect so."

"Then we'll be in the Gulf of Guinea by the tenth." The second mate advanced the joysticks, notch by notch. "All ahead full?"

The captain looked south, scanning the ranks of gray, glassy swells, the eternally shifting terrain of the sea. And so it begins, he thought, the great race, Anthony Van Horne versus brain death, decay, and the Devil's own sharks.

"All ahead full!"

July 2.

Latitude: 37°7′N. Longitude: 58°10′W. Course: 094. Speed: 18 knots. Distance made good since New York: 810 nautical miles. A gentle breeze, no. 3 on the Beaufort scale, wafts across our weather deck.

I wanted a real diary, but there wasn't time to visit a stationery store, so instead I ran down to Thrift Drug and got you. According to your cover, you're an "Official Popeye the Sailor Spiral-Bound Notebook, copyright © 1959 King Features Syndicate." When I look into your wizened face, Popeye, I know you're a man I can trust.

On this day in 1816, the French frigate *Medusa* went aground off the west coast of Africa—so says my *Mariner's Pocket Companion*. "Of the 147 who escaped on a raft, most were murdered by their mates and either thrown overboard or eaten. Only 15 survived."

I think we can do better than that. For a company cobbled together at the last minute, they seem like a pretty smart bunch. Big Joe Spicer brought his own sextant aboard, always a good sign in a navigator. Dolores Haycox, the *zaftig* third mate, passed the surprise quiz I gave her without a hiccup. (I had her calculate her distance from a hypothetical bold shore based on the interval between a ship's foghorn blast and the echo.) Marbles Rafferty, the gloomy first officer, is a particularly poetic choice for this mission—his great-grandfather was owned by a family of Florida Keys salvage masters, those vainglorious 19th-century sailors who were, Ockham informs me, "immortalized by John Wayne and Raymond Massey in *Reap the Wild Wind*."

I already knew Sam Follingsbee was a brilliant cook, but tonight's fried chicken was indistinguishable from Colonel Sanders's secret recipes, both Original and Extra Crispy. An odd talent, this genius for mediocrity. Crock O'Connor, the chief engineer, is the sort of affable Alabama yarn spinner who claims he invented the twist-off bottle cap but receives no royalties thanks to the knavery of an unscrupulous patent attorney. He's been giving us our 18 knots, so who am I to call him a liar? Lou Chickering, the blond and handsome first assistant engineer—our very own Billy Budd—is a stage actor from Philly who once tried to make it on Broadway and now spends his off-hours organizing talent shows in the deckies' recreation room. His specialty is Shakespeare, and even our illiterates were beguiled by his performance last night of Ariel's song from *The Tempest*. ("Full fathom five thy father lies . . .") Bud Ramsey, the second engineer, is a pornography collector, beer connoisseur, and seven-card-stud fanatic. It's refreshing, I think, when a man wears his vices on his sleeve. And backing us up: 38 gratefully employed sailors—23 men and 15 women—scattered among our decks, galleys, engine rooms, and cargo-control stations. I enjoy browsing through their resumes. We've got a minor-league center fielder on board (Albany Bullets), a former clown (Hunt Brothers Circus), an ex-con (armed robbery), a spot-welder, an auto assembly-line worker, a Revlon saleslady, an Army corporal, a dog trainer, a Chinese math teacher (junior high), a taxi driver, three Desert Storm vets, and a full-blooded Lakota Sioux named James Echohawk.

A great mass of spilled oil—one of those "floating particulate petroleum residues"—has coagulated off Cameroon: that's the story I've been feeding anybody who asks. When Carpco realized the Vatican had gotten wind of the disaster, they offered the Pope a deal: keep Greenpeace and the U.N. off our backs, and we'll remove the asphalt posthaste. And we won't just sink it, either.

We'll tow it to shore, chop it up, and refine the fragments into free oil for burgeoning African industries. Great, said Rome, but we're sending Father Ockham to supervise.

So: a secret operation, get it, men? Hush-hush, understand? That's why we don't signal passing ships, turn on our running lights, or let anybody phone home.

"Okay, but why so damn *fast*?" Crock O'Connor wants to know. "We're practicing to be the first supertanker ever to win the America's Cup?"

"The asphalt's a menace to navigation," I explain. "The sooner we get there, the better."

"Last night I left my empty orange-juice glass on the table," the man persists, "and the damn thing scooted right up to the edge and fell, singing all the way. We're vibrating, Captain. We're gonna crack the fucking hull."

He's right, actually. Run your ULCC in a straight line at 18 knots with empty cargo bays, and before long you'll start flapping apart like a '57 Chevy.

There are ways to soothe a shivering ship without losing too much time. I'm using every trick in the book: changing speed briefly, altering course slightly, shutting down entirely for a minute or two and coasting—anything to break the rhythm of the waves hitting our stem. So far it's working. So far we're still in one piece.

At dawn the sea turtles came.

Hundreds of them, Popeye, swimming through my dreams, their shells glistening with Texas crude. Then the snowy egrets arrived, black as crows, then the roseate spoonbills, the blue herons . . .

I awoke in a sweat. I took a shower, dried off, read Act I of *The Tempest*—Prospero raising the storm and drawing the royal ship to his enchanted island, Miranda falling hopelessly in love with the castaway prince Ferdinand—and drank a glass of warm milk. At 0800 I finally got back to sleep.

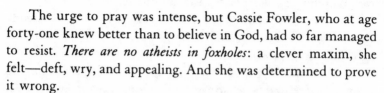

The urge to pray was intense, but Cassie Fowler, who at age forty-one knew better than to believe in God, had so far managed to resist. *There are no atheists in foxholes*: a clever maxim, she felt—deft, wry, and appealing. And she was determined to prove it wrong.

For over fifteen hot, wretched, thirsty hours Cassie had endured her aquatic foxhole, a rubber dinghy adrift in the North Atlantic, and in all that time she'd been true to herself, never asking God for assistance. Cassie was a woman of integrity—a woman who'd spent the first decade of her adulthood writing antireligious, money-losing off-Broadway plays (the sorts of satires the critics termed "biting" when authored by a male and "strident" if by a female)—a woman who, having devoted most of her thirties to acquiring a Ph.D. in biology, had elected to teach at dull, hidebound Tarrytown Community College, a place where the students were unlikely to form positive opinions about either feminism or evolution without her intervention, and where she was free to conduct oddball little experiments (her initial finding being that, given the opportunity, the male Norway rat exhibits instincts toward its young every bit as nurturing as the female) without pressure to pull down a grant or publish her results.

Were Cassie's situation any less desperate, it would have been comic, in a Samuel Beckett sort of way. Maneuvering the dinghy with a Ping-Pong paddle. Bailing it out with an Elvis Presley memorial drinking cup. Sheltering her bikini-clad body with a Betty Boop beach towel. "Help," she gasped into the transceiver mike, furiously working the generator crank. "Please, somebody . . . heading east . . . last known latitude, two degrees north . . . last known longitude, thirty-seven west . . . help me." No answer. Not one word. She might as well be praying.

To the east, she knew, lay Saint Paul's Rocks, a tiny volcanic archipelago strung along the equator. The Rocks promised little—a chance to gather her strength, a reprieve from the endless bailing—but at this point a meaningless destination was better than none at all.

An authentic reenactment of Charles Darwin's historic voyage undertaken on an exact replica of his ship: what a marvelous concept for a cruise, she'd thought on reading the brochure, a kind of Club Med vacation for rationalists. All during the flight to England, Cassie had imagined herself reporting back to her friends in the Central Park West Enlightenment League, proudly projecting her 35mm color slides of the Galápagos Islands' native finches and lizards (she was planning to shoot over fifty rolls of film), descendants of the very beasts from whose anatomies Darwin had inferred that Creation traced not to the hand of God Almighty but to something far more interesting—and she'd continued to indulge in such cheerful fantasies when, on June 12, the *Beagle II* left the Cornish port of Charlestown, her twenty-four berths jammed with an unlikely assortment of biology professors, armchair naturalists, and spoiled college dropouts being deported by their exasperated parents. The itinerary devised by Maritime Adventures, Incorporated, had the *Beagle II* following Darwin's precise route, with the exception of an about-face at Joas Pessoa so they might avail themselves of the Panama Canal and save seven months. Once they'd explored the Galápagos, a jetliner out of Guayaquil would take them back to England.

They never got past the equator. Hurricane Beatrice did not merely sink the *Beagle II*, it tore her apart like one of Cassie's sophomores dissecting a dogfish. As the ship went down, Cassie found herself alone on a frigid sea, clinging to a spar and clutching her Betty Boop towel, bitterly absorbing the fact that among the stratagems by which Maritime Adventures kept its Galápagos package under a thousand dollars per person was the elimination of life rafts, life jackets, and backup batteries for the shortwave radio. Only through a miracle of chance did she manage to fish a hand-cranked transceiver from the flotsam and haul herself aboard the *Beagle*'s errant dinghy.

"Heading east . . . last known latitude, two north . . . last known longitude, thirty-seven west . . . help, somebody."

Inexorably, maliciously, the sun came up: her one-eyed enemy, a predator as dangerous as any shark. The Betty Boop towel protected her from the rays, but her thirst soon became intolerable. The temptation to dip her Elvis cup into the ocean and drink was nearly overwhelming, though as a biologist she knew that would be fatal. Consume a pint of seawater, and along with those ten cubic inches of pure H_2O she would also ingest a quantity of salt far beyond what her body required. Take a second helping, and her kidneys would now have enough H_2O to process the salt in pint number one, but not enough to process the salt in pint number two. Drink a third pint—and so on, and so on, never getting ahead of the game. Inevitably her kidneys would turn imperialistic, stealing water from her other tissues. She would dry up, become febrile, die.

"Help me," Cassie moaned, painfully rotating the transceiver crank. "Last known latitude, two north . . . longitude, thirty-seven west . . . water . . . water . . ." I shall not cry out to God, she vowed. I shall not pray for deliverance.

And suddenly they appeared, Saint Paul's Rocks, six granite spires rising from the equator like aquatic stalactites, their peaks frosted with heaping mounds of seabird droppings. Briefly she savored the peculiar poetry of the moment. On February 12, 1832, the original *Beagle* had anchored here. At least I'll go out in Darwin's shadow, she mused. At least I've followed him to the end.

By dusk Cassie had made a landfall, maneuvering the dinghy against the lee side of the islet. Transceiver in hand, Betty Boop towel flung over her shoulder, she dragged herself up the highest spire, the jagged pumice tearing her palms and scouring her knees. An ice-cold can of Diet Coke hovered just out of reach;

a frosty pitcher of lemonade beckoned from a neighboring crag; a frigid geyser of Hawaiian Punch spewed heavenward from a tide pool. Reaching the summit, she stood up, the towel spilling down her back like a monarch's cape. It was all hers, the whole dreadful little archipelego. Her Royal Highness Cassie Fowler, Empress of Guano.

The wayfarers swooped down, squadron after squadron, brazen cormorants perching on her shoulders, bold gannets pecking at her hair. For all her terror and misery, she found herself wishing her students could see these birds; she was prepared to lecture about the *Sulidae* family in general and the blue-footed booby in particular. The blue-foot was a bird with a vision. While its red-shod cousin laid its eggs in a conventional nest built near the top of a tree, the blue-foot employed a *picture* of a nest, an elegant abstraction it created by squirting a ring of guano on the ground. Cassie loved the blue-footed booby, not only for its politics (the males did their fair share of sitting on the eggs and caring for the chicks) but also because here was a creature for whom the distinctions between life, art, and shit were less obvious than commonly supposed.

On all sides, the grim Darwinian rhythms played out: crabs eating plankton, gannets devouring crabs, big fish preying on little fish, an eternal orgy of killing, feasting, digesting, eliminating. Never before had Cassie felt so connected to brute evolutionary truth. Here was Nature, real Nature, red in claw, white in ca-ca, stripped of all Rousseauistic sentiment, rhapsodic as a cold sore, romantic as a yeast infection.

With the last of her strength she shooed the birds away, then squatted, Joblike, amid the guano. Ironically, Cassie's personal favorite among her plays, *Bible Stories for Adults, No. 46: The Soap Opera*, was a freewheeling sequel to Job. Two thousand years after being tortured, browbeaten, and bought off by God, the hero returns to the dung heap for a rematch.

Her tongue was a stone. She was too dry to weep. I shall not succumb to faith, she swore, staring across the vast, faceless sea.

There are no atheists in foxholes. "Help," Cassie rasped, cranking the transceiver. "Please. Help. The *Beagle* is a stupid name for a ship," she groaned. "Beagles are *dogs*, not ships. Help. Please, God, it's me," muttered the lapsed Darwinist. "It's Cassie Fowler. Saint Paul's Rocks. Beagles are dogs. Please, God, help me."

July 4.

Our fair republic's birthday. Latitude: 20°9′N. Longitude: 37°15′W. Course: 170. Speed: 18 knots. Distance made good since New York: 1106 nautical miles.

If I didn't know better, I'd say Jehovah himself had sent that hurricane. Not only did we survive, we got carried 184 miles at 40 knots, and now we're almost a day ahead of schedule.

A loaded tanker probably could've smashed those rollers apart, but we actually had to *ride* them—full speed ahead in the troughs, dead slow along the crests. There was so much foam, the waves turned pure white, as if the sea herself had died.

We had a good man at the helm, a moon-faced Jersey kid named Neil Weisinger, and somehow we bullied our way through, but only after a Marisat dome cracked in two and a starboard kingpost got torn out by the roots. Not to mention 4 lifeboats blown overboard, 15 shattered windows in the deck-house, 2 broken arms, 1 sprained ankle.

On a normal voyage, whenever the crew gets drunk and rowdy, I can usually scare them into sobriety by waving a flare pistol around. But on this trip, if things go as I expect, we'll eventually be arming the deckies with those damn antipredator weapons. I'm nervous, Popeye. A potted sailor and a T-62 bazooka are a bad combination.

It doesn't matter that alcoholic beverages are forbidden in

the U.S. Merchant Marine. We're not a dry ship—this I know. Judging from past experience, I'd guess we left port with about 30 cases of contraband beer and 65 bottles of hidden liquor. Rum is especially popular, I've noticed over the years. Pirate fantasies, I think. I myself keep 4 bottles of mescal in the chart room, secluded under Madagascar.

To date we've had only one minor setback. The Vatican was supposed to send us the cream of its film collection, but either the reels never arrived or those Carmelites forgot to load them, and the only picture that actually made it on board is a 16mm pan-and-scan print of *The Ten Commandments*. So we've got this fancy theater and just one movie to run in it. It's a pretty awful flick, and I suspect we'll be chucking tomatoes at the screen long about the tenth showing.

There are 4 or 5 VCRs kicking around, and dozens of cassettes with titles like *Babs Boffs Boston*. We've even got the notorious *Caligula*. But such fare tends to leave about a third of the men and nearly all the women cold.

Whenever I slip Raphael's feather from my sea chest and stare at it, the same questions run through my mind. Did my angel speak the truth? Is Dad really the one who can wash away the oil? Or was Raphael just making absolutely sure I'd accept the mission?

In any event, I'm figuring to return from the Arctic by way of Spain. I'll dock in Cadiz, give the crew shore leave, and hop on the first bus to Valladolid.

"I did it," I'll tell him. "I got the job done."

Although zero by zero degrees still lay half an ocean away, Thomas Ockham nevertheless found himself grappling night and day with the eschatological implications of a Corpus Dei. Beyond the information Rome explicitly requested—course, speed, position, estimated date of rendezvous—his daily faxes contained as much speculative theology as he thought the cardinals could stand.

"At first blush, Eminence," he wrote to Di Luca on the Fourth of July, "the death of God is a scandalous and enervating notion. But do you remember the riches certain thinkers mined from this vein in the late fifties and early sixties? I'm thinking in particular of Roger Milton's *Post Mortem Dei*, Gabriel Vahanian's *Culture of the Post-Christian Era*, and Martin Buber's *Eclipse of God*. True, these men had no actual body on their hands (nor do we, as of yet). I sense, however, that if we look beyond our immediate *angst*, we may find some surprises. In an odd way, this whole business is a ringing vindication of Judeo-Christianity (if I may use that mongrel and oxymoronic term), proof that we've been on to something all these centuries. From a robust theothanatology, I daresay, some surprising spiritual insights may emerge."

Truth to tell, Thomas did not believe these brave words. Truth to tell, the idea of a robust theothanatology depressed him to the point of paralysis. A dark and violent country lay beyond the Corpus Dei, the old priest felt in his heart—a landfall toward which Ultra Large Crude Carriers sailed only at their peril.

"Dear Professor Ockham," Di Luca wrote back on July 5, "at the moment we are not interested in Martin Buber or any other atheist egghead. We are interested in Anthony Van Horne. Did the angels pick the right man? Does the crew respect him? Was his decision to dive into Hurricane Beatrice wise or was it rash?"

In drafting his answer, Thomas addressed Di Luca's concerns as forthrightly as he could. "Our captain knows his ropes, but I sometimes fear his zeal will jeopardize the mission. He's obsessed with the OMNIVAC's deadline. Yesterday we entered a new time zone, and it was only with the greatest reluctance that he ordered the clocks set forward . . ."

Thomas typed the reply on his portable Smith-Corona—the same antique on which he'd written *The Mechanics of Grace*. He signed his name with an angel feather dipped in India ink, then carried the letter up to the wheelhouse.

It was 1700, an hour into the second mate's watch. From the very first, Big Joe Spicer had struck Thomas as the smartest officer aboard the *Valparaíso*, excluding Van Horne himself. Certainly he was the only officer who brought books to the bridge—real books, not collections of cat cartoons or paperback novels about telekinetic children.

"Good afternoon, Joe."

"Hi there, Father." Rotating ninety degrees in his swivel chair, the hulking navigator flashed a copy of Stephen Hawking's *A Brief History of Time*. "Ever read this?"

"I assign it in Cosmology 412," said Thomas, glancing nervously at the AB on duty, Leo Zook. The day before, he and the Evangelical had engaged in a brief, unsatisfactory argument about Charles Darwin, Zook being against evolution, Thomas pointing out its fundamental plausibility.

"If I understand this stuff," said Spicer, drumming his knuckles on *A Brief History of Time*, "God's out of a job."

"Perhaps," said Thomas.

"Don't be ridiculous," said Zook.

"In the Stephen Hawking universe," said Spicer, pivoting toward the Evangelical, "there's nothing for God to do."

"Then Stephen Hawking is wrong," said Zook.

"What would *you* know about it? You ever even *heard* of the Big Bang?"

"In the beginning was the Word."

Thomas couldn't decide whether Zook truly wished to discuss *A Brief History of Time* or whether he was irritating Spicer merely to relieve his boredom, the ship being on autopilot just then.

Declining the bait, the navigator turned back to Thomas. "Celebrating Mass today?"

"Fifteen hundred hours."

"I'll be there."

Good, the priest thought—you, Follingsbee, Sister Miriam, Karl Jaworski, and nobody else. The sparsest parish this side of the prime meridian.

As Thomas started toward the radio shack, wondering which profited the world more—the rhapsodic atheism of a Hawking or the unshakable faith of a Zook—he nearly collided with Lianne Bliss. Eyes darting, she dashed up to the navigator, swiveling him like a barber aiming a customer at a mirror.

"Joe, call the boss!"

"Why?"

"Call him! SOS!"

Six minutes later Van Horne was on the bridge, hearing how a Hurricane Beatrice survivor named Cassie Fowler had evidently landed a rubber dinghy on Saint Paul's Rocks.

"Could be a trap," said the captain to Bliss. Fresh water dripped from his hair and beard, residue of an interrupted shower. "You didn't break radio silence, did you?"

"No. Not that I didn't want to. What do you mean, a trap?"

Saying nothing, Van Horne marched to the twelve-mile radar and stared intently at the target: a flock of migrating boobies, Thomas suspected. "Get on the horn, Sparks," ordered the captain. "Tell the world we're the *Arco Fairbanks*, due south of the Canaries. Whoever reports in, give 'em Fowler's coordinates."

"Is it necessary to lie?" asked Thomas.

"Every order I give is necessary. Otherwise I wouldn't give it."

"May I call the woman?" asked Bliss, starting back into the shack.

Van Horne ran his index finger around the radar screen, encircling the birds. "Tell her help is on the way. Period."

At sundown Bliss returned to the bridge and offered her report. The *Valparaíso* was evidently the only ship within three hundred miles of Saint Paul's Rocks. She'd contacted a dozen ports from Trinidad to Rio, and among those few Coast Guard officers and International Red Cross workers who understood her frantic mix of English, Spanish, and Portuguese, not one commanded a plane or chopper with enough fuel capacity to get halfway across the Atlantic and back.

"What did Fowler say when you called her?" asked Thomas.

"She wanted to know if I was an angel."

"What did you tell her?"

Bliss shot an angry scowl toward Van Horne. "I told her I wasn't authorized to answer."

Setting *A Brief History of Time* atop the Marisat terminal, Spicer strode to the helm and snapped off the autopilot. "Course two-seven-three, right?"

"No," said Van Horne. "We're holding."

"Holding?" said Zook, grabbing the wheel.

"You're joking," said Spicer.

"I can't throw twenty-four hours away, Joe. That's everything we gained from Beatrice. Put us back on iron mike."

Thomas bit down, his molars clamping the soft flesh of his inner cheeks. Never before had he faced such a dilemma. Did the Christian course lie west, along the equator, or southeast, toward God? How many divine brain cells equaled a single human castaway? A million? A thousand? Ten? Two? His skepticism regarding the OMNIVAC's prediction did little to relieve his anxiety. Even *one* salvaged neuron might eventually prove so scientifically and spiritually valuable it would start to seem worth a dozen castaways—two dozen castaways—three dozen—four —the lives of all the castaways since Jonah.

Except that Jonah had been delivered, hadn't he?

The whale had vomited him out.

"Captain, you must bring us about," said Thomas.

Snatching up the bridge binoculars, Van Horne issued an angry snort. "What?"

"I'm telling you to bring us about. Turn the *Val* around and point her toward Saint Paul's Rocks."

"You seem to have forgotten who's commanding this operation."

"And you seem to have forgotten who's paying for it. Don't imagine you can't be replaced, sir. If the cardinals hear you neglected an obvious Christian duty, they won't hesitate to airlift in a new skipper."

"I think we should talk in my cabin."

"I think we should bring the ship about."

Van Horne raised the binoculars and, inverting them, looked at Thomas through the wrong ends, as if by diminishing the priest's size he could also diminish his authority.

"Joe."

"Sir?"

"I want you to plot us a new course."

"Destination?"

Mouth hardening, eyes narrowing, Van Horne slid the binoculars into their canvas bin. "That guano farm in the middle of the Atlantic."

"Good," said Thomas. "Very good," he added, wondering how, exactly, he would justify this detour to Di Luca, Orselli, and Pope Innocent XIV. "Believe me, Anthony, acts of compassion are the only epitaph He wants."

Dírge

WHEN CASSIE FOWLER awoke, she was less shocked to discover that an afterlife existed than to find that she, of all people, had been admitted to it. Her entire adulthood, it seemed, year after year of spiting the Almighty and saluting the Enlightenment, had come to nothing. She'd been saved, raptured, immortalized. Shit. The situation spoke badly of her and worse of eternity. What heaven worthy of the name would accept so ardent an unbeliever as she?

It was, of course, a pious place. A small ceramic Christ with blue eyes and cherry red lips hung bleeding on the far wall. A gaunt, rawboned priest hovered by her pillow. At the foot of her bed a large man loomed, his gray beard and broken nose evoking every Old Testament prophet she'd ever taught herself to mistrust.

"You're looking much better." The priest rested his palm against her blistered cheek. "I'm afraid there's no physician on board, but our chief mate believes you're suffering from nothing worse than exhaustion combined with dehydration and a bad sunburn. We've been buttering you with Noxzema."

Gradually, like cotton candy dissolving in a child's mouth, the fog evaporated from Cassie's mind. *On board*, he'd said. *Chief mate*, he'd said.

"I'm on a ship?"

The priest gestured toward the prophet. "The SS *Valparaíso*, under the command of Captain Anthony Van Horne. Call me Father Thomas."

Memories came. Maritime Adventures . . . *Beagle II* . . . Hurricane Beatrice . . . Saint Paul's Rocks. "The famous *Valparaíso*? The oil-spill *Valparaíso*?"

"The *Carpco Valparaíso*," said the captain frostily.

As Cassie sat up, the medicinal stench of camphor filled her nostrils. Pain shot through her shoulders and thighs: the terrible bite of the equatorial sun, her red skin screaming beneath its coating of Noxzema. Good God, she was alive, a winner, a golden girl, a beater of the odds. "How come I'm not thirsty?"

"When you weren't babbling your brains out," said the priest, "you consumed nearly a gallon of fresh water."

The captain stepped into the light, holding out a tangerine. He was better looking than she'd initially supposed, with a Byronesque forehead and the sort of sorrowful, vulnerable virility commonly found in male soap-opera stars on their way down.

"Hungry?"

"Famished." Receiving the tangerine, Cassie worked her thumb into its north pole, then began peeling it. "Did I really babble?"

"Quite a bit," said Van Horne.

"About what?"

"Norway rats. Your father died of emphysema. In your youth you wrote plays. Oliver—your boyfriend, we presume—fancies himself a painter."

Cassie grunted, half from astonishment, half from annoyance. "Fancies himself a painter," she corroborated.

"You're not sure you want to marry him."

"Well, who's ever *sure?*"

The captain shrugged.

She broke off a quadrisphere of tangerine and chewed. The pulp tasted sweet, wet, crisp—alive. She savored the word, the holy vocable. Alive, alive.

"Alive," she said aloud, and even before the second syllable passed her lips, she felt her exhilaration slipping away. "Thirty-three passengers," she muttered, her voice at once mournful and bitter. "Ten sailors . . ."

Father Thomas nodded empathically. His eyebrows, she noticed, extended onto the bridge of his nose, meshing like two gray caterpillars in the act of kissing. "It's tragic," he said.

"God killed them with His hurricane," she said.

"God had nothing to do with it."

"Actually I agree with you, though for reasons quite different from yours."

"Don't be so sure of that," said the priest cryptically.

Cassie finished her tangerine. In her irreverent sequel to Job, the hero's mistress kept repeating a line from the original, over and over. *And I only am escaped alone to tell thee.*

"This your cabin?" she asked, pointing to the ceramic Christ.

"Was. I've moved."

"You forgot your crucifix."

"I left it here on purpose," said Father Thomas without elaboration.

"Excuse my ignorance," said Cassie, "but do oil tankers normally carry clergy?"

"This isn't a normal voyage, Dr. Fowler." The priest's eyes grew wide and wild, darting every which way like bees who'd lost track of their hive. "Abnormal, in fact."

"Once our mission's accomplished," said the captain, "we'll ferry you back to the States."

"What're you talking about?"

"For the next nine weeks," said Van Horne, "you'll be our guest."

Cassie scowled, her broiled body hardening with confusion and anger. "Nine weeks? *Nine weeks?* No, folks, I start teaching at the end of August."

"Sorry."

"Send for a helicopter, okay?" Slowly, like some heroic, evolution-minded fish hauling itself onto dry land, she rose from the berth, and only after her feet touched the green shag carpet did she bother to wonder whether she was clothed. "Do you understand?" Looking down, she saw that someone had swapped her bikini for a kimono printed with zodiac signs. Glued by Noxzema, the silk stuck to her skin in large amorphous patches. "I want you to charter me an International Red Cross helicopter, the sooner the better."

"I'm not authorized to report our position to the International Red Cross," said Van Horne.

"Please—my mother, she'll go nuts," Cassie protested, not knowing whether to sound desperate or furious. "Oliver, too. Please . . ."

"We'll allow you one brief message home."

An old scenario, and Cassie hated it, the patriarchy wielding its power. *Yeah, lady, I think we might eventually get around to fixing your reduction gear, as if you knew what the hell a reduction gear is.* "Where's the phone?"

Blue veins bulged from Van Horne's brow. "We're not offering you a *phone*, Dr. Fowler. The *Valparaíso* isn't some farmhouse you stumbled into after getting a flat tire."

"So what *are* you offering me?"

"All communication goes through our radio shack up on the bridge."

A spasm of sunburn pain tore through Cassie's neck and back as she followed Father Thomas down a gleaming mahogany corridor and into the sudden claustrophobia of an elevator car. She closed her eyes and grimaced.

"Who's Runkleberg?" the priest asked as they ascended.

"I babbled about Runkleberg? I haven't thought of him in years."

"Another boyfriend?"

"A character in one of my plays. Runkleberg's my twentieth-century Abraham. One fine morning he's out watering his roses, and he hears God's voice telling him to sacrifice his son."

"Does he obey?"

"His wife intervenes."

"How?"

"She castrates him with his hedge clippers, and he bleeds to death."

The priest gulped audibly. The elevator halted on the seventh floor.

"Biology and theater"—he guided them down another glossy corridor—"the two disciplines aren't normally pursued by the same person."

"Father, I simply *can't* stay on this boat."

"But the more I think about it, the more I realize that the biologist and the dramatist have much in common."

"Not for nine weeks. I have to clean up my office, prepare my lectures . . ."

"Explorers, right? The biologist seeks to discover Nature's laws, the dramatist her truths."

"Nine weeks is out of the question. I'll die of boredom."

The *Valparaíso*'s radio shack was a congestion of transceivers, keyboards, fax machines, and telex terminals threaded together by coaxial cables. In the middle of the mess lounged a slender young woman with carrot-colored hair and skin the complexion of provolone. Cassie smiled, grateful for the two metal buttons pinned to the radio officer's red camisole: a clenched fist sprouting from the medical symbol for Woman, and the motto MEN HAVE UTERUS ENVY. Only the officer's pendant, a quartz crystal housed in silver, gave Cassie pause, but she had long ago accepted the fact that, when it came to the affectations with which radical feminists liked to impoverish their minds—crystal therapy, neo-paganism, Wicca—her skepticism placed her emphatically in a minority.

"I like your buttons."

"You look good in my kimono," said the radio officer in a voice so deep it might have come from someone twice her size.

"She gets one telegram, Sparks," said Father Thomas, backing out of the shack. "Twenty-five words to her mother—period. Nothing about a ship called the *Valparaíso*."

"Roger." The woman stretched out her bare arm, its biceps decorated with a tattoo of a svelte sea goddess riding the waves like a surfboard passenger. "Lianne Bliss, Sagittarius. I'm the one who picked up your SOS."

The biologist shook Lianne Bliss's hand, slick with equatorial sweat. "I'm Cassie Fowler."

"I know. You've had quite an adventure, Cassie Fowler. You drew the Death card, then Fate reversed it."

"Huh?"

"Tarot talk."

" 'Fraid I don't believe in that stuff."

"You don't believe in Oliver either."

"Jesus."

"There are no private lives on a supertanker, Cassie. The sooner you learn that, the better. Okay, so the boy's got a bankroll, but I still think you should drop him. He sounds like a popinjay."

"Oliver sends back the wine," Cassie admitted, frowning.

"I gather he plans to be the next Van Gogh."

"Much too sane. A Sunday painter at best . . . I'm alive, aren't I, Lianne? Incredible."

"You're alive, sweetie."

And I only am escaped alone to tell thee.

Extending her index finger, Cassie fiddled with a disembodied telegraph key, absently tapping out gibberish. "Now that all *my* secrets have been revealed, what about yours? Do you hate your job?"

"I *love* my job. I get to eavesdrop on the whole damn planet. On a clear night I might tune in a Tokyo businessman and his mistress having cellular-phone sex, a couple of ham-radio drug dealers planning an opium drop in Hong Kong, some neo-Nazis ranting to each other on their CBs in Berlin. I can pipe everything through to the deckies' quarters, and you know what they *really* want? Baseball from the States! What a waste. If I ever hear another Yankees game, I'll puke." She lifted a blue Carpco pencil to her mouth and licked the point. "So—what do we tell Mom?"

The radio shack, Cassie decided, would make a great set for a play. She imagined a one-act satire laid entirely in heaven's central communications complex, God working the dials, bypassing the screams of pain and the cries for help as He attempts to pick up Yankee Stadium.

Closing her eyes, she brought her mother into focus: Rebecca Fowler of Hollis, New Hampshire, a cheerful and energetic Unitarian minister whose iconoclasm ran so deep it shocked even her own congregation. BEAGLE II SUNK BY HURRICANE . . . I'M SOLE SURVIVOR . . . PLEASE TELL OLIVER . . .

Her thoughts drifted. *Mission*, Anthony Van Horne had said, a ship with a mission—and from the peculiar countenance Father Thomas had assumed back in his cabin, it was the most portentous mission since Saul of Tarsus had suffered an epileptic seizure and called it Christianity.

"I gather this isn't a regular voyage."

Lianne tugged on her UTERUS ENVY button. "It's a goddamn

cover-up, Cassie. Evidently Holy Mother Church has detected some huge tarball coagulating off Africa, but she's promised to keep the matter quiet if Carpco ropes the sucker in and gives it to charity. Personally, I think the whole arrangement stinks."

"I'm a charter member of the Central Park West Enlightenment League," said Cassie with a knowing nod, as if it went without saying that any charter member of the Central Park West Enlightenment League needn't be instructed in the defects of Holy Mother Church. "A vital organization, I believe, a real bulwark"—she pointed to Lianne's pendant—"though you wouldn't like our opinion of those things."

"Small tits?"

"Magic crystals."

"It got rid of my herpes."

"I doubt that."

"You have a better explanation?"

"The placebo effect."

"Know what, Cassie Fowler? You should spend more time on ships. Standing lookout in the bow, with the ocean roaring all around you and the entire universe spread over your head—well, you just *know* there's some sort of eternal presence out there."

"An old man with a beard?" said Cassie, suppressing a sneer.

"Sweetie, if I've learned anything during my ten years at sea, it's this. Never confuse your captain with God."

July 12.

Two days ago we reached our destination, 0°0′N, 0°0′E, 600 miles off the coast of Gabon. Both scopes remained clear, and I should've expected as much—Raphael told me the body's been drifting.

I guess I was hoping we'd find something.

Our search pattern is an ever-expanding spiral, south to north, west to east, north to south, east to west, south to north, a course that should bring us within sight of São Tomé by Tuesday. We're weaving a net in the sea, Popeye. Big gaps. But then again: big fish.

Crock O'Connor's still giving me my 18 knots, which means we'll hit the equator twice more before midnight.

That Cassie Fowler hates me, I can tell. No doubt she's one of *those*. Tree huggers, bug lovers, squid kissers—I can spot them a mile away, people for whom a polluter like Anthony Van Horne deserves to be eaten alive by ferrets. But I must say this: she's an appealing lady, voluptuous as old Lorelei here on my arm, with frizzy black hair and one of those long, horsy faces that look comical one minute, beautiful the next. I've decided to put her to work—scraping rust, maybe scrubbing a john or two. On the *Carpco Valparaíso* there are no free riders.

At dinner I issued a standing order. "Call me the minute anything odd shows on either scope, night or day." To which Joe Spicer replied, suspiciously, "All this fuss over a lousy hunk of asphalt."

We're not a happy ship, Popeye. The crew's fed up. They're sick of steaming in circles and seeing *The Ten Commandments* and wondering what I'm hiding from them.

Every time we cross 0° north, Spicer drops a penny on the equator.

"For luck," he says.

"We'll need it," I tell him.

"Captain, this is strange . . ."

Anthony recognized his navigator's voice, crackling out of the intercom speaker: his navigator's voice, and more—the same mix of incredulity and fear with which First Mate Buzzy Long-champs had delivered his verdict, *Sir, I think we're in a peck of trouble*, the night the *Val* slammed into Bolivar Reef.

He lurched toward the wall-mounted intercom, tearing at the sheets, clawing his way through his insomniac's daze. "Strange?" he mumbled, pressing the switch. "What's strange?"

"Sorry to wake you," said Big Joe Spicer, "but we've got ourselves a target."

Climbing out of his bunk, Anthony picked a tiny grain of sand from his eye and rolled it between thumb and forefinger, then glanced around for his shoes. He was otherwise fully dressed, right down to his ratty pea jacket and canvas Mets cap. Ever since reaching zero-by-zero, he'd stripped his life of irrelevancies, eating sporadically, sleeping in his clothes, letting his beard grow wild. For seventy-two hours, his mind had known only the hunt.

He grabbed his Carpco mug, shoved his knobby feet into his tennis shoes, and, without bothering to lace them, sprinted to the elevator.

A soft glow lit the bridge: radar scopes, collision-avoidance system, Marisat terminal, clock. It was 0247. Spicer stood hunched over the twelve-mile radar, fiddling with the rain-snow clutter control. "Captain, I've seen my brother-in-law's laserdisc of *Deep Throat* and just about every episode of *Green Acres*, and I swear to you"—he pointed to the target—"that's gotta be the weirdest thing ever to show on a cathode-ray tube."

"Fog bank?"

"That's what it looked like on the fifty-mile scope, but no more. This sucker's got bulk."

"São Tomé?"

"I checked our position three times. São Tomé's fifteen miles in the opposite direction."

"The asphalt?"

"Much too big."

Anthony made a fist. His chest tightened. The mermaid on

his forearm grew tense. "Steady," he told the AB at the helm, the brawny Lakota Sioux, James Echohawk.

"Steady," said Echohawk.

Anthony locked his bleary eyes on the scope. The screen displayed a long jagged blob, momentous as a shadow on a lung X-ray. Fuzzy, shapeless—and yet he knew exactly Whose electronically graven image he was beholding.

"So what is it?" asked Spicer.

"If I told you, you wouldn't believe me." Anthony grasped the throttles, dropping both screws to sixty-five rpm's. He hadn't pushed his ship past the recommended speeds and driven her through Hurricane Beatrice just so they could smash into their cargo and sink. "I'll stand the rest of your watch for you, Joe. Go grab some sleep."

The second mate looked into his captain's eyes. Silent signals traveled between the men. The last time an officer had left the bridge of the *Valparaíso*, eleven million gallons of oil had poured into the Gulf of Mexico.

"Thanks, Captain," said Spicer, joining Anthony at the console, "but I think I'll stick around."

"How's Follingsbee's coffee tonight?" Anthony asked the helmsman. "Strong enough?"

"You could prime a kingpost with it, sir," said Echohawk.

"Let's drop her another notch, Joe. Sixty rpm's."

"Aye. Sixty."

Anthony seized the Exxon thermos, splashing jamoke into the stained interior of his Carpco mug. "Come left ten degrees," he said, eyes locked on the radar. "Steady up on zero-seven-five."

"Zero-seven-five," Echohawk replied.

"Glass falling," said Spicer, fixing on the barometer. "Down to nine-nine-six."

Lifting the bridge binoculars from their bin, Anthony gazed through the grimy, rain-beaded windshield toward the horizon. Glass falling: quite so. Lightning flashed, dropping from heaven like a crooked gangway, illuminating a hundred thousand white-caps. Fat gray clouds hung in the northern sky like acromegalic sheep.

"Fifty-five rpm's."

"Fifty-five."

Anthony gulped his coffee. Hot, marvelously hot, but not enough to thaw his bowels. "Joe, I want you to place a call to Father Ockham's quarters," he ordered, pulling back the door to the starboard wing. The storm rushed in, spattering his face, twisting the fringes of his beard. "Tell him to transport his ass up here on the double."

"It's three A.M., sir."

"He wouldn't miss this for the world," said Anthony, starting out of the wheelhouse.

"Glass still falling!" the second mate shouted after him. "Nine-eight-seven!"

The instant Anthony stepped into the turbulent night, the odor hit him, roiling across the bridge wing. Sharp and gravid, oddly sweet, not so much the stink of death as the fragrance of transformation: leaves festering in damp gutters, jack-o'-lanterns wrinkling on suburban doorsteps, bananas softening inside their leathery black peels. "Fifty rpm's, Joe!" he screamed through the open door.

"Fifty, sir!"

Then came the sound, thick and layered, a kind of choral moan hovering above the drone of the engines and the roar of the Atlantic. Anthony raised the binoculars. A long, brilliant trident of electricity speared the sea. Another ten minutes, he figured, certainly no more than fifteen, and they'd have visual contact . . .

"That sound," said Father Ockham, pulling on his Panama hat and buttoning his black vinyl raincoat as he hurried onto the wing.

"Odd, isn't it?"

"Sad."

"What do you suppose . . . ?"

"A dirge."

"Huh?"

Even as Ockham repeated the word, a lightning bolt revealed the truth of it. *Dirge*, oh, yes. In the sudden brightness Anthony saw the mourners, flopping and rolling over the boiling sea, swarming across the churning sky. Pods of bereaved narwhals to starboard, herds of bereft rorquals to port, flocks of orphaned cormorants above. Flash, and more species still, herring gulls, great skuas, fulmars, shearwaters, petrels, prions, puffins, leopard seals, ringed seals, harbor seals, belugas, manatees—multitudes upon multitudes, most of them hundreds of miles from habitat and home, their voices rising in preternatural grief, a blend of every seaborne lung and aquatic larynx God had ever placed on earth.

"Come right ten degrees!"

"Right ten!"

"Forty-five rpm's!"

"Forty-five!"

Miraculously, each tongue kept its identity even as it joined the general lament. Closing his eyes, Anthony grasped the rail and listened, awed by the bottlenose dolphins' whistled elegies, the sea lions' throaty orations, and the low coarse keening of a thousand frigate birds.

"The smell," said the priest. "It's rather . . ."

"Fruity?"

"Exactly. He hasn't started to turn."

Anthony opened his eyes. "Joe, forty rpm's!"

"Forty, sir!"

Flash, a massive something, bearing zero-one-five.

Flash, a series of tall rounded forms, all aspiring to heaven.

Flash, the forms again, like mountains spread along a seacoast, each higher than the next.

"You saw that?"

"I saw," said the priest.

"And . . . ?"

Ockham, shivering, slipped a Sony Handicam from his rain-coat pocket. "I think it's the toes."

"The what?"

"Toes. I just lost a small wager. Sister Miriam believed He'd be supine"—Ockham choked up—"whereas I assumed . . ."

"Supine," Anthony echoed. "He's smiling, Raphael told me. You in trouble, Thomas?"

The priest tried sighting through the Handicam's viewfind-er, but he was trembling too badly to connect eye with eyecup. Rain and tears spilled down his face in equal measure. "I'll get over it."

"You aren't gonna faint, are you?"

"I said I'll get over it." On his second attempt, Ockham managed to elevate the Handicam and fire off a quick burst of tape. "It's rather poetic, seeing the toes first. The word has special meaning in my field. *T-O-E*: Theory of Everything."

"Everything?"

"We're looking for one, we cosmologists." The priest panned across the phalanxes of mourners. "At the moment, we've got TOE equations that work on the submicroscopic level, but noth-ing that"—his voice splintered—"handles gravity too. It's so hor-rible."

"Not having a TOE?"

"Not having a heavenly Father."

Another celestial explosion. Yes, Anthony decided, no ques-tion: ten pale and craggy toes, stiff with rigor mortis, arching into the gloomy sky like onion domes crowning a Byzantine city.

"Dead slow!"

"Dead slow!"

"Wish I could help you," said Anthony.

"Just try to understand." The priest returned the Handicam

to his raincoat pocket and pulled off his bifocals. "Try to understand," he said again, wiping the lenses with his sleeve. "Try," groaned Father Thomas Ockham, calling above the storm, the sea, and the mad, ragged music of the wake.

In the old days, Neil Weisinger mused, merchant ships had galley slaves: thieves and murderers who died chained to their oars. Today they had able-bodied seamen: fools and dupes who keeled over gripping their pneumatic Black and Decker needle guns. Chip and paint, chip and paint, all you did was chip and paint. Even on so extraordinary a voyage as this—a voyage on which a huge pulpy island lay off your starboard quarter, tirelessly attended by moaning whales and squawking birds—you got no relief from chipping, no respite from painting.

Neil was on the fo'c'sle deck, chipping rust off a samson post, when a voice screeched out of the PA system, overpowering the noise of his needle gun and penetrating the rubber plugs in his ears. "Ship's-com-pan-y!" cried Marbles Rafferty, the gun's racket fracturing his words into syllables. "Now-hear-this! All-hands-re-port-to-off-i-cers'-ward-room-at-six-teen-fif-teen-hours!"

Neil killed the gun, popped the earplugs.

"Repeat: all hands report . . ."

Ever since Neil's Aunt Sarah had come to him at Yeshiva and insisted that he stop wallowing in grief—it had been over five years, she pointed out, since his parents' deaths—the AB had labored to avoid self-pity. Life is intrinsically tragic, his aunt had lectured him. It's time you got used to it.

". . . sixteen-fifteen hours."

But there were moments, such as now, when self-pity seemed the only appropriate emotion. 1615 hours: right after he got off duty. He'd been planning to spend the break in his cabin, reading a *Star Trek* novel and nursing a contraband Budweiser.

Dipping his wire brush into the HCL bottle, Neil lifted the acid-soaked bristles free and began basting the corroded post. Dialogue drifted through his mind, verbal gems from *The Ten Commandments*. "Beauty is but a curse to our women. . . ." "So let it be written, so let it be done. . . ." "The people have been plagued by thirst! They've been plagued by frogs, by lice, by flies, by sickness, by boils! They can endure no more!" The *Val* had left New York with only one movie in her hold, but at least it was a good one.

It took him over twenty minutes to wash up. Despite his earplugs, goggles, mask, cap, and jumpsuit, the rust had gotten through, clinging to his hair like red dandruff, covering his chest like metallic eczema, and so he was the last sailor to arrive.

He'd never been on level five before. Twentieth-century ABs got invited to their officers' wardrooms about as often as fourteenth-century Jews got invited to the Alhambra. Billiard table, crystal chandeliers, teakwood paneling, Oriental rug, silver coffee urn, mahogany bar . . . so this was his bosses' tawdry little secret: spend your watches mixing with the mob, pretending you're just another packet rat, then slip away to the Waldorf-Astoria for a cocktail. As far as Neil could tell, everyone on board was there (officers, deckies, priest, even that castaway, Cassie Fowler, red and peeling but on the whole looking far healthier than when they'd pulled her off Saint Paul's Rocks), with the exceptions of Lou Chickering, probably down in the engine flat, and Big Joe Spicer, doubtless on the bridge making sure they didn't collide with the island.

Van Horne stood atop the mahogany bar, outfitted in his dress blues, the sobriety of the dark serge intermittently relieved by brass buttons and gold piping. "Well, sailors, we've all seen it, we've all smelled it," he told the assembled company. "Believe me, there's never been such a corpse before, none so large, none so important."

Third Mate Dolores Haycox shifted her weight from one

tree-stump leg to the other. "A corpse, sir? You say it's a *corpse?*"

A corpse? thought Neil.

"A corpse," said Van Horne. "Now—any guesses?"

"A whale?" ventured gnomish little Charlie Horrocks, the pumpman.

"No whale could be that huge, could it?"

"I suppose not," said Horrocks.

"A dinosaur?" offered Isabel Bostwick, an Amazonian wiper with buck teeth and a buzz cut.

"You're not thinking on the right scale."

"An outer-space alien?" said the alcoholic bos'n, Eddie Wheatstone, his face so ravaged by acne it looked like a used archery target.

"No. Not an outer-space alien—not exactly. Our friend Father Thomas has a theory for you."

Slowly, with great dignity, the priest walked in a wide loop, circling the company, corralling them with his stride. "How many of you believe in God?"

Rumblings of surprise filled the wardroom, echoing off the teakwood. Leo Zook's hand shot up. Cassie Fowler burst into giggles.

"Depends on what you mean by God," said Lianne Bliss.

"Don't analyze, just answer."

One by one, the sailors reached skyward, fingers wiggling, arms swaying, until the wardroom came to resemble a garden of anemones. Neil joined the consensus. Why not? Didn't he have his enigmatic something-or-other, his *En Sof,* his God of the four A.M. watch? He counted a mere half-dozen atheists: Fowler, Wheatstone, Bostwick, a corpulent demac named Stubby Barnes, a spidery black pastry chef named Willie Pindar, and Ralph Mungo, the decrepit guy from the union hall with the I LOVE BRENDA tattoo—and of these six only Fowler seemed confident, going so far as to thrust both hands into the pockets of her khaki shorts.

"I believe in God, the Father Almighty," said Leo Zook, "maker of heaven and earth, and in His only Son, Jesus Christ our Lord . . ."

The priest cleared his throat, his Adam's apple bumping against his Roman collar. "Keep your hand up if you think that God is essentially a spirit—an invisible, formless spirit."

Not one hand dropped.

"Okay. Now. Keep your hand up if you think that, when all is said and done, our Creator is quite a bit like a person— a powerful, stupendous, gigantic person, complete with bones, muscles . . ."

The vast majority of arms descended, Neil's among them. Spirit and flesh: God couldn't be both. He wondered about the three sailors whose arms remained aloft.

"Now you're talking about Jesus Christ," said Zook, his hand fluttering about like a drunken hummingbird.

"No," said the priest. "I'm not talking about Jesus Christ."

A falling sensation overcame Neil. Reaching into his jeans, he squeezed the bronze medal his grandfather had received for smuggling refugees to the nascent nation of Israel. "Wait a minute, Father, sir. Are you saying . . . ?" Gulping, he repeated himself. "Are you saying . . . ?"

"Yes. I am."

Whereupon Father Thomas lifted a gleaming white ball from the billiard table, tossed it straight up, caught it, and proceeded to relate the most grotesque and disorienting story Neil had heard since learning that the Datsun containing his parents had fallen between the spans of an open drawbridge in Woods Hole, Cape Cod, and vanished beneath the mud. Among its assorted absurdities, the priest's tale included not only a dead deity and a prescient computer, but also weeping angels, confused cardinals, mourning narwhals, and a hollowed-out iceberg jammed against the island of Kvitoya.

As soon as he was finished, Dolores Haycox jabbed her thick

index finger toward Van Horne. "You told us it was asphalt," she whined. "Asphalt, you said."

"I lied," the captain admitted.

From the middle of the crowd, the squat and wan chief engineer, Crock O'Connor, piped up. "I'd like to say something," he drawled, wiping his oily hands on his Harley-Davidson T-shirt. Steam burns dappled his cheeks and arms. "I'd like to say that, in all my thirty years at sea, I never heard such a pile of pasteurized, homogenized, cold-filtered horseshit."

The priest's voice remained measured and calm. "You may be correct, Mr. O'Connor. But then how are we to interpret the evidence currently floating off our starboard quarter?"

"A snare set by Satan," Zook replied instantly. "He's testing our faith."

"A UFO made of flesh," said Chief Steward Sam Follingsbee.

"The Loch Ness Monster," said Karl Jaworski.

"One of them government biology experiments," said Ralph Mungo, "gotten way outta hand."

"I'll bet it's just rubber," said James Echohawk.

"Yeah," said Willie Pindar. "Rubber and fiberglass and such . . ."

"Okay, maybe a deity," said Bud Ramsey, the chicken-necked, weasel-faced second assistant engineer, "but certainly not God Himself."

Silence settled over the wardroom, heavy as a kedge anchor, thick as North Sea fog.

The sailors of the *Valparaíso* looked at each other, slowly, with pained eyes.

God's dead body.

Oh, yes.

"But is He really *gone?*" asked Horrocks in a high, gelded voice. "Totally and completely *gone?*"

"The OMNIVAC predicted a few surviving neurons," said

Father Thomas, "but I believe it's working with faulty data. Still, each of us has the right to entertain his own private hopes."

"Why doesn't the sky turn black?" demanded Jaworski. "Why doesn't the sea dry up and the sun blink out? Why aren't the mountains crumbling, forests toppling over, stars falling from heaven?"

"Evidently we're living in a noncontingent, Newtonian sort of universe," Father Thomas replied. "The clock continues ticking even after the Clockmaker departs."

"Okay, okay, but what's the *reason* for His death?" asked O'Connor. "There's gotta be a reason."

"At the moment, the mystery of our Creator's passing is as dense as the mystery of His advent. Gabriel urged me to keep thinking about the problem. He believed that, by journey's end, the answer would become clear."

What followed was a theological free-for-all, the only time, Neil surmised, that a supertanker's entire crew had engaged in a marathon discussion of something other than professional sports. Dinnertime came and went. The new moon rose. The sailors grew schizoid, a company of Jekyll-and-Hydes, their bouts of *Weltschmerz* alternating with fresh denials (a CIA plot, a sea serpent, an inflatable dummy, a movie prop), then back to *Weltschmerz*, then more denials still (communism's last gasp, the Colossus of Rhodes emerging from the seabed, a distraction concocted by the Trilateral Commission, a facade concealing something *truly* bizarre). Neil's own reaction bewildered him. He was not sad—how could he be sad? Losing this particular Supreme Being was like losing some relative you barely knew, the shadowy Uncle Ezra who gave you a fifty-dollar bill at your bar mitzvah and forthwith disappeared. What Neil experienced just then was freedom. He'd never believed in the stern, bearded God of Abraham, yet in some paradoxical way he'd always felt accountable to that nonexistent deity's laws. But now YHWH wasn't watching. Now the rules no longer applied.

"Guess what, sailors?" Van Horne jumped from the mahogany bar to the Oriental rug. "I'm canceling all duties for the next twenty-four hours. No chipping, no painting—and you won't lose one red cent in pay." Never before in nautical history, Neil speculated, had such an announcement failed to provoke a single cheer. "From this moment until 2200," said the captain, "Father Thomas and Sister Miriam will be available in their cabins for private consultations. And tomorrow—well, tomorrow we start doing what's expected of us, right? How about it? Are we merchant mariners? Are we ready to move the goods? Can you give me an *aye* on that?"

About a third of the deckies, Neil among them, sang out with a choked and hesitant "Aye."

"Are we ready to lay our Creator in a faraway Arctic tomb?" asked Van Horne. "Let me hear you. Aye!"

This time over half the room joined in. "Aye!"

A high, watery howl arose, shooting from Zook's mouth like vomitus. The Evangelical dropped to his knees, clasping his hands in fear and supplication, shivering violently. To Neil he looked like a man enduring the monstrously conscious moment that follows hara-kiri: a man beholding his own steaming bowels.

Father Thomas sprinted over, helped the distraught AB to his feet, and guided him out of the wardroom. The priest's compassion impressed Neil, and yet he sensed that such gestures alone would not save the *Valparaíso* from the terrible freedom to which she was about to hitch herself. Inevitably the climax of *The Ten Commandments* flashed through his brain: Moses hurling the Tablets of the Law to the ground and thus depriving the Israelites of their moral compass, leaving them uncertain where God stood on adultery, theft, and murder.

"Ship's company—dismissed!"

Then said Jesus unto His disciples, "If any man will come after me, let him deny himself and take up his cross, and follow me."

Amen, thought Thomas Ockham as, wrapped in the tight rubbery privacy of his wetsuit, he made his way beneath the Gulf of Guinea. Except that the Cross in this instance was a huge kedge anchor, the Via Dolorosa an unmarked channel between the *Valparaíso*'s keel and the Corpus Dei. Although a PADI-certified diver, Thomas hadn't been underwater in over fifteen years—not since joining Jacques Cousteau on his celebrated descent into the submarine crater of the volcano that destroyed the ancient Greek civilization of Thera—and he didn't feel entirely sure of himself. But, then, who *could* feel entirely sure of himself while seeking to affix a thirty-foot, twenty-ton anchor to his Creator?

The dozen divers who constituted Team A had distributed themselves evenly along the kedge: Marbles Rafferty at the crown, Charlie Horrocks on the left fluke, Thomas on the right, James Echohawk and Eddie Wheatstone handling the shank, the others holding up the stock, the ring, and the first five links of the chain. Sixty yards to the south, Joe Spicer's Team B was presumably keeping pace, bearing their own kedge, but a curtain of bubbles and murk prevented Thomas from knowing for sure.

Arms raised, palms turned upward, the twelve men worked their flippers, carrying the anchor over their heads like Iroquois portaging a gargantuan war canoe. Within twenty minutes the divine pate, slightly balding, appeared. Thomas lifted his wrist, checked his depth gauge. Fifty-four feet, just right: their buoyancy compensators were inflated sufficiently to counterweight the anchor but were not so full as to float the divers above their target. Local inhabitants drifted by—a giant grouper, a pea-green sawfish, a school of croakers—either grieving in silence or keening below the threshold of Thomas's hearing, for the only sounds he perceived were his own bubbly breaths and the occasional clang of an oxygen tank hitting the kedge.

Wriggling to the left, the divers swam past a great swaying carpet of hair and aligned themselves with His ear. At Rafferty's signal, each man reached down and switched on the searchlight strapped to his utility belt. The beams played across the ear's numerous folds and crannies, painting deep curved shadows along the feature known as Darwin's tubercle. Thomas shuddered. In the case of *Homo sapiens sapiens*, at least, Darwin's tubercle was considered a prime argument for evolutionary theory: the manifest vestige of a prick-eared ancestor. What in the world did it mean for God Himself to be sporting these cartilaginous mounds?

They finned their way through the concha and into the external auditory meatus. Queasiness spread through the priest. Should they really be doing this? Did they truly have the right? Stalactites of calcified wax hung from the roof of the ear canal. Life clung to its walls: clusters of sargasso, a bumper crop of sea cucumbers. Thomas's left flipper brushed an echinoderm, a five-pointed *Asterias rubens* floating through the cavern like some forsaken Star of Bethlehem.

It had taken the priest all morning to convince Crock O'Connor and the rest of the engine-flat crew that opening God's tympanic membranes would not be sacrilegious—heaven wanted this tow, Thomas had insisted, displaying Gabriel's feather—and now the fruits of their efforts loomed before him. Fashioned with pickaxes, ice choppers, and waterproof chain saws, the ragged slit ran vertically for fifty feet, like the entrance to a circus tent straight from the grandest dreams of P. T. Barnum.

As the dozen men bore their burden through the violated drum, Thomas's awe became complete. God's own ear, the very organ through which He'd heard Himself say, "Let there be light," the exact apparatus through which the Big Bang's aftershock had reached His brain. Again Rafferty signaled, and the divers thrashed their flippers vigorously, stirring up tornadoes of bubbles and maelstroms of sloughed cells. Inch by inch, the anchor ascended, rising past the undulating cilia that lined the membrane's inner surface, finally coming to rest against the huge and delicate bones of the middle ear. Malleus, incus, stapes, Thomas recited to himself as the searchlights struck the massive triad. Hammer, anvil, stirrup.

Another sign from Rafferty. Team A moved with a single mind, guiding the anchor's right fluke over the long, firm process of the anvil, binding the *Valparaíso* to God.

Now: the moment of truth. Rafferty pushed off, gliding free of the kedge and gesturing for the others to do likewise. Thomas—everyone—dropped away. The anchor swung back and forth on the anvil, its great steel ring oscillating like the pendulum of some stupendous Newtonian clock, but the ligaments held, and the bone did not break. The twelve men applauded themselves, slapping their neoprene gloves together in a soundless, slow-motion ovation.

Rafferty saluted the priest. Thomas reciprocated. Flush with success, he hugged the chain and, like Theseus reeling in his thread, began following this sure and certain path back to the ship.

Christ was smirking. Cassie was certain of it. Now that she looked carefully, she saw that the face on Father Thomas's crucifix wore an expression of utter self-satisfaction. And why not? Jesus had been right all along, hadn't He? The world had indeed been fashioned by an anthropomorphic Father.

Father, not Mother: that was the rub. Somehow, against all odds, the patriarchs who'd penned the Bible had intuited the truth of things. Theirs was the gender the universe fully endorsed. Womankind was a mere shadow of the prototype.

Around and around Cassie paced the cabin, wearing a ragged path in the green shag carpet.

Naturally she wanted to explain the body away. Naturally she'd be delighted if any of the crew's paranoid fantasies—CIA plot, Trilateralist conspiracy, whatever—could be proven correct.

But she couldn't deny her instincts: as soon as the priest had named the thing, she'd experienced eerie intimations of its authenticity. And even if it *were* a hoax, she reasoned, the world's innumerable boobs and know-nothings, should they learn of its existence, would accept and exploit it anyway, just as they'd accepted and exploited the Shroud of Turin, the hallucinations of Saint Bernadette, and a thousand such idiocies in the face of thorough refutation. So, whether reality or fabrication, truth or illusion, Anthony Van Horne's cargo threatened to usher in the New Dark Ages as surely as the Manhattan Project had ushered in the Epoch of the Bomb.

Cassie wrung her hands, callus grinding against callus, by-products of the hours she'd spent chipping rust off the athwart-ships catwalk.

Okay, it was dead, a step in the right direction. But that fact alone, she believed, while of undoubted relevance to people like Father Thomas and Able Seaman Zook, did not remove the danger. A corpse was far too easy a thing to rationalize. Christianity had been doing it for two thousand years. The Lord's intangible essence, the phallocrats and misogynists would say, His infinite mind and eternal spirit, were as viable as ever.

Inevitably, she thought of her favorite moment from her irascible retelling of Abraham's near-sacrifice of Isaac: the scene in which Runkleberg's wife, Melva, smears her hands with her own menstrual flow. "I shall guard my son's blood with my own," Melva vows. "Somehow, some way—no matter what it takes— I shall keep this monstrous thing from happening."

Slowly, methodically, Cassie removed the crucifix from the bulkhead and, taking hold of the brad, worked it free.

Gritting her teeth, she pushed the tiny spike into her thumb. "Ow . . ."

As she withdrew the nail, a large red pearl appeared. She entered the bathroom, stood before the mirror, and began to paint, left cheek, left jaw, chin, right jaw, right cheek, pausing periodically to squeeze out more blood. By the time clotting occurred, a thick, smeary line ran around Cassie's face, as if she were wearing a mask of herself.

Somehow, some way—no matter what it took—she would send the God of Western Patriarchy to the bottom of the sea.

Now, only now, standing on the starboard wing with the wind howling, the sea roaring, and the great corpse bobbing behind him—only now did it occur to Anthony that the tow might not work. Their cargo was big, bigger than he'd ever imagined. Assuming the anchors held, the chains remained whole, the boilers stayed in one piece, and the windlasses didn't rip loose and fly into the ocean—assuming all these things, the sheer drag might still prove too much for the *Val* to handle.

Lifting the walkie-talkie to his lips, he tweaked the channel selector and tuned in the engine flat.

"Van Horne here. We got steam on deck?"

"Enough to make a pig sweat," said Crock O'Connor.

"We're gonna try for eighty rpm's, Crock. Can we do it without busting a gut?"

"Only one way to find out, sir."

Anthony turned toward the wheelhouse, waving to the quartermaster and giving Marbles Rafferty a thumbs-up. So far the first mate had acquitted himself brilliantly at the console, keeping the carcass directly astern and two thousand yards away, perfectly pacing the *Val* with her cargo's three-knot drift. (Too bad Operation Jehovah was a secret, for this was exactly the sort of venture that might earn Rafferty the coveted paper declaring him "Master of United States Steam or Motor Vessels of Any Gross Tons upon Oceans.") The kid at the helm knew his stuff, too: Neil Weisinger, the same AB who'd performed so splendidly during Hurricane Beatrice. But even with Sinbad the Sailor manning the throttles and Horatio J. Hornblower holding the wheel, winching in this particular load would still be, Anthony knew, the trickiest maneuver of his career.

Pivoting to stern, the captain surveyed the windlasses: two gargantuan cylinders twenty feet in diameter, like bass drums built to pace the music of the spheres. A mile beyond rose God's balding cranium, His white mane glinting in the morning sun, each hair as thick as a transatlantic cable.

The mourners had all left. Perhaps they'd completed their duties—"swimming *shivah*," as Weisinger liked to put it—but more probably it was the ship that had driven them away. At some level, Anthony believed, they knew the whole story: the Matagorda Bay tragedy and what it had done to their brothers and sisters. They couldn't stand to be in the same ocean with the *Carpco Valparaíso*.

He lifted the Bushnells and focused. The water was astonishingly clear—he could even see His submerged ears, the anchor chains spilling from their interiors like silver pus. Twenty-four hours earlier, Rafferty had taken an exploration party over in the *Juan Fernández*. After sailing into the placid cove bounded by the lee biceps and the corresponding bosom, they'd managed to lash an inflatable wharf in place, using armpit hairs as bollards, then rappel up the great cliff of flesh. Hiking across the chest, walking around on the sternum, the chief mate and his team had heard nothing they could honestly call heartbeats. Anthony hadn't expected they would. And yet he remained cautiously optimistic: cardiovascular stasis wasn't the same thing as brain death. Who could deny that a neuron or two might be perking away under that fifteen-foot-thick skull?

The captain changed channels, broadcasting to the men by the windlasses. "Ready on the afterdeck?"

The assistant engineers plucked the walkie-talkies from their belts. "Port windlass ready," said Lou Chickering in his actor's baritone.

"Starboard windlass ready," said Bud Ramsey.

"Release devil's claws," said Anthony.

Both engineers sprang into action.

"Port claw released."

"Starboard claw released."

"Engage wildcats," the captain ordered.

"Port cat in."

"Starboard in."

"Kill brakes."

"Port brake gone."

"Starboard gone."

Anthony raised his forearm to his mouth and gave dear Lorelei a kiss. "Okay, boys—let's reel Him in."

"Port motor on," said Chickering.

"Starboard on," said Ramsey.

Spewing black smoke, belching hot steam, the wildcats began to turn, raveling up the great steel chains. One by one, the links rose out of the sea, dripping foam and spitting spray. They slithered through the chocks, arched over the devil's claws, and dropped into the whelps like skee-balls scoring points.

"I need lead lengths, gentlemen. Call 'em out."

"Two thousand yards on the port chain," said Chickering.

"Two thousand on the starboard," said Ramsey.

"Marbles, let's get under way! Forty rpm's, if you please!"

"Aye! Forty!"

"Fifteen hundred on the port chain!"

"Fifteen hundred on the starboard!"

Anthony and the chief mate had been up all night poring over Rafferty's *U.S. Navy Salvor's Handbook*. With a tow this prodigious, a gap of more than eleven hundred yards would render the *Val* unsteerable. But a short leash, under nine hundred yards, could mean trouble too: if she suddenly slowed for any reason—a snapped shaft, a blown boiler—the cargo would plow into her stern through sheer momentum.

"Fifty rpm's!" Anthony ordered.

"Fifty!" said Rafferty.

"Speed?"

"Six knots!"

"Steady, Weisinger!" Anthony told the quartermaster.

"Steady!" the AB echoed.

The chains kept coming, over the windlasses and through the hatches, filling the cavernous steel lockers like performing cobras returning to their wicker baskets after a hard day's work.

"One thousand yards on the port chain!"

"One thousand on the starboard!"

"Speed?"

"Seven knots!"

"Brakes!" screamed Anthony into the walkie-talkie.

"Port brake on!"

"Starboard on!"

"Sixty rpm's!"

"Sixty!"

Both windlasses stopped instantly, screeching and smoking as they showered the afterdeck with bright orange sparks.

"Disengage wildcats!"

"Port cat gone!"

"Starboard gone!"

"Hook claws!"

"Port claw hooked!"

"Starboard hooked!"

Something was wrong. The carcass's speed had doubled, eight knots at least. Briefly Anthony imagined some supernatural jolt galvanizing the divine nervous system, though the real explanation, he suspected, lay in a sudden conjunction of the Guinea Current and the Southeast Trades. He lowered the binoculars. The Corpus Dei surged forward, crushingly, inexorably, spindrift flying from its crown as it bore down on the tanker like some primordial torpedo.

The prudent tactic was obvious: unlock the cats, free the chains, hard right rudder, full speed ahead.

But Anthony hadn't been hired to play it safe. He'd been hired to bring God north, and while he didn't relish the thought of presiding over the *Valparaíso*'s second collision in two years, either this damn rig worked or it didn't. "Marbles, eighty rpm's!"

"Eighty?"

"Eighty!"

"Eighty!" said the mate.

"Speed?"

"Nine knots!"

Nine, good: faster, surely, than the oncoming corpse. He studied the chains. No slack! No slack, and the ship was moving! "Quartermaster, ten degrees left rudder!" Lifting the binoculars, laughing into the wind, the captain studied His vast shining brow. "Course three-five-zero!"

"Three-five-zero!" said Weisinger.

Anthony pivoted toward the bow. "All engines ahead full!" he shouted to Rafferty, and they were off—off like some grandiose water-skiing act, off like some demented rendition of Achilles dragging Hector around the walls of Troy, off like some absurdist advertisement for Boys Town, USA, the angelic youngster bearing his crippled brother on his back (*He ain't heavy, Father, He's my Creator*)—off, towing Jehovah.

Part two

Teeth

As THE BURDENED *Valparaíso* crawled north through the Gulf of Guinea, Cassie Fowler realized that her desire to see their cargo destroyed was more complicated than she'd initially supposed. Yes, this body threatened to further empower the patriarchy. Yes, it was a terrible blow to reason. But something else was going on, something a bit more personal. If her dear Oliver could actually bring off such a spectacular feat, successfully applying his brains and wealth toward God's obliteration, he would emerge in her eyes as a hero, second only to Charles Darwin. She might even, after all these years, acquiesce to Oliver's longstanding proposal of marriage.

On July 14, at 0900, Cassie went to the radio shack and made her pitch to Lianne "Sparks" Bliss. They must send Oliver a secret fax. Immediate and total sabotage was required. The future of feminism hung in the balance.

Not that she didn't love Oliver as he was: a sweet man, a committed atheist, and probably the best president the Central Park West Enlightenment League had ever had—yet also, Cassie felt, a castaway like herself, shipwrecked on the shores of his own essential uselessness, not just a Sunday painter but a Sunday human being. How better for a person to acquire some self-respect than to save Western Civilization from a return to misogynist theocracy?

"The future of feminism?" said Lianne, nervously fingering her crystal pendant. "Are you serious?"

"Deadly," said Cassie.

"Yeah? Well, nobody except Father Thomas is allowed to contact the outside world. Captain's orders."

"Lianne, this damn body is *exactly* what the patriarchy has been waiting for—evidence that the world was created by the male chauvinist bully of the Old Testament."

"Okay, but even if we *did* send a message, would your skeptic friends believe you?"

"Of course my skeptic friends wouldn't believe me. They're skeptics. They'd have to fly over, take pictures, argue among themselves . . ."

"Forget it, sweetie. I could get booted out of the Merchant Marine for something like this."

"The future of feminism, Lianne . . ."

"I said forget it."

The next morning, Cassie tried again.

"Century after century of phallocratic oppression, and finally women are gaining some ground. And now—bang—it's back to square one."

"Aren't you overreacting a bit? We're gonna *bury* the thing, not put it on fucking *Oprah*."

"Yeah, but what's to prevent somebody from happening on the tomb in a year or two and spilling the beans?"

"Father Thomas talked to an angel," said Lianne defensively. "There's obviously a cosmic necessity behind this voyage."

"There's a cosmic necessity behind feminism, too."

"We shouldn't go tampering with the cosmos, friend. We absolutely shouldn't."

For the rest of the day, Cassie made a point of avoiding Lianne. She had presented her case fully, outlining the ominous political implications of a male Corpus Dei. Now it was time to let the arguments sink in.

How different all this was from Cassie's previous voyage. On the *Beagle II* you periodically knocked off your feet, thrown from your bunk, plunged into nausea: you knew you were at sea. But the *Valparaíso* felt less like a ship than like some great metal island rooted to the ocean floor. To get any sense of motion, you had to climb down into the forward lookout post, a kind of steel patio thrust out over the water, and watch the stem plates smashing through the waves.

On the evening of July 13, Cassie stood in the bow, sipping coffee, savoring the sunset—a breathtaking spectacle to which the tubby AB on duty, Karl Jaworski, seemed oblivious—and imagining the androgynous marvels that lay perhaps two miles beneath her feet. *Hippocampus guttulatus*, for instance, the sea horse, whose males incubated the eggs in special ventral pouches; or groupers, all of whom began life as females (half destined to undergo a sex change at adulthood); or the wonderfully subversive lumpfish, a species whose maternal instincts resided exclusively within the fathers (it being they who oxygenated the eggs during incubation and subsequently guarded the fry). To her right, beyond the horizon, spread the wide sultry delta of the Niger River. To her left, likewise hidden by the planet's curve, lay Ascension Island. A suffocating heat arose, clothing her in equatorial steam, and she resolved to escape to the *Valparaíso*'s congenial little movie theater. True, she'd seen *The Ten Commandments* before—most recently Oliver's laserdisc of the 35th Anniversary Collector's

Edition—so it wouldn't have much dramatic impact, but at the moment air-conditioning mattered more than catharsis.

She took the elevator to level three, opened the door to the theater, and plunged into the gloriously cool air.

As it happened, Cassie harbored a special affection for *The Ten Commandments*. Without it, she would never have written her angriest play, *God Without Tears* (a prophetic title, she now realized), a one-act satire on the many bowdlerizations Cecil B. DeMille and company had committed in transferring Exodus, Leviticus, Numbers, and Deuteronomy to the screen. She'd been particularly severe with DeMille's unwillingness to consider the moral implications of the Ten Plagues, with his failure to record the injustices the Hebrews had suffered at their Sponsor's hands as they wandered in the wilderness (Yahweh striking down the people who disparaged Canaan, firebombing those who complained at Hormah, sending serpents against the ones who grumbled on the road from Mount Hor, visiting a pestilence upon everybody who backslid at Peor), and with his glaring omission of the speech Moses had made to his generals following the subjugation of the Midianites: "Why have you spared the life of all the women? These were the very ones who perverted the sons of Israel! Kill all the male children! Kill also all the women who have slept with a man! Spare the lives only of the young girls who have not slept with a man, and take them for yourselves!" Paired with *Runkleberg*, *God Without Tears* had run for two weeks at Playwrights Horizons on West Forty-second Street, a bill that drew a rave review in *Newsday*, a pan in the *Village Voice*, and an Op-Ed letter of condemnation in the *Times*, written by Terence Cardinal Cooke himself.

Whatever its artistic shortcomings, DeMille's homage to God's omnipotence fully acknowledged the bladder's limits. The movie had an intermission. After an hour and forty minutes, as Moses began his audience with the Burning Bush, the urge to urinate arose. Cassie decided to hold out. She couldn't remember exactly when the hiatus came, but she knew it was imminent. Besides, she was enjoying herself, in a perverse sort of way. The urge worsened. She was about to leave *in medias res*—Moses heading back to Egypt with the aim of liberating his people—when the music swelled, the image faded, and the curtains closed.

Two women were ahead of her, almond-eyed Juanita Torres and asthmatic An-mei Jong, waiting to use the single-toilet ladies' room. There she stood, mulling over her theory that the patriarchy derived in large measure from urinary flexibility, the male's enviable ability to pee on the run, when a deep, familiar voice intruded.

"Want some?" said Lianne, extending a large, half-empty bag of popcorn. "Vegetarian style—no butter."

Cassie grabbed a handful. "Seen this movie before?"

"My Sunday school class went in the mid-sixties, some sort of revival. 'Beauty is but a curse to our women.' Yech. If it weren't for Follingsbee's popcorn, I'd leave."

A breach, thought Cassie. A chink in Lianne's armor. "Watch what they do with Queen Nefretiri in Part Two."

"I don't like what they do with *any* of the women."

"Yeah, but watch what they do with Nefretiri—DeMille and the patriarchy, watch what they do. Notice how, whenever Pharaoh commits some atrocity, chasing after the Hebrews with his chariots and so on, it's because Nefretiri put him up to it. Same old story, right? Blame the woman. The patriarchy never sleeps, Lianne."

"I can't send your boyfriend a fax."

"I understand."

"They could take away my FCC license."

"Right."

"I *can't* send it."

"Of course you can't." Cassie took a greedy helping of Follingsbee's popcorn. "Watch what they do with Nefretiri."

July 16.

Latitude: 2°6'N. Longitude: 10°4'W. Course: 272. Speed: 9 knots when the Southeast Trades are with us, 3 in a headwind, 6 on average. Slow—much too slow. At this rate, we won't cross the Arctic Circle before August 25, a full week behind schedule.

More bad news. The promised predators have finally caught our scent, and at 6 knots we can't outrun them. We're killing a dozen sharks on nearly every watch, and almost as many Liberian sea snakes and Cameroon vultures, but they keep on coming. When I sit down to write the official chronicle of this voyage, I'll dub these bloody days the Battle of the Guinea Current.

"Why don't they show their Creator a little more respect," I ask Ockham, "like the porpoises and manatees did last week?"

"Respect?"

"He *made* them, right? They owe Him everything."

"In partaking of such a meal," says Ockham, "quite possibly they *are* showing Him respect."

Our afterdeck groans, our windlasses creak, our chains rattle. We sound like Halloween. God forbid a link should break. Once, when I was third mate on the *Arco Bangkok*, ferrying napalm into the Gulf of Thailand, I saw a towline snap in two, whip across the poop deck, and cut the bos'n in half. Poor bastard lived for a good three minutes afterward. His last words were, "What are we doing in Vietnam, anyway?"

This morning I sent Dad a fax. I told him I've gotten the *Valparaíso* back and am now working for Pope Innocent XIV. "If it's okay with you," I wrote, "I'll be dropping by Valladolid on my return trip."

The snowy egrets loathe me, Popeye. The sea turtles scream for my blood.

At least once a day, I make a point of ferrying myself over

to God, picking up a bazooka or a harpoon gun, and joining the battle. It helps the crew's morale. The work is dangerous and exhausting, but they're acquitting themselves well. I think they see our cargo as one of those things worth fighting for, like honor or the American flag.

Every evening, beginning around 1800 hours, Cassie Fowler drinks coffee in the forward lookout post. I've pretended to bump into her three times already. I think she's catching on.

To what uncharted places did your passion for Olive Oyl take you, Popeye? Did you ever imagine lying with her on the fo'c'sle deck at the height of a monsoon, making furious love as the hot rain slicked your naked bodies? Did your creators ever animate such a moment for you, just to give you the thrill?

When the deckies think I'm not looking, they plunder the Corpus Dei, scraping off bits and pieces from the hairs, pimples, warts, and moles, then mixing them with potable water to make a kind of ointment.

"What's it for?" I ask Ockham.

"Whatever ails them," he replies.

An-mei Jong, the padre explains, swallows the stuff by the spoonful, hoping to relieve her asthma. Karl Jaworski rubs it on his arthritic joints. Ralph Mungo sticks it on an old Korean War wound that keeps acting up. Juanita Torres uses it for menstrual cramps.

"Does it help?" I ask Ockham.

"They say it does. These things are so subjective. Cassie Fowler calls it the placebo effect. The deckies call it glory grease."

If I smear some glory grease on my forehead, Popeye, will the migraines go away?

"Shark off the starboard knee! Repeat: shark off the starboard knee!"

Neil Weisinger rose from his bed of holy flesh, set his WP-17 exploding-harpoon gun upright inside a kneecap pore, and pressed the SEND button on his Matsushita walkie-talkie. The heat was unbearable, as if the Guinea Current were about to boil. Had he not slathered his neck and shoulders with glory grease, they would surely have blistered by now. "Course?" he radioed the bos'n, Eddie Wheatstone, currently on lookout.

"Zero-zero-two."

In his dozen or so voyages as a merchant mariner, Neil had performed many hateful duties, but none so hateful as predator patrol. While washing toilets was degrading, cleaning ballast tanks disgusting, and chipping rust tedious beyond words, at least these jobs entailed no immediate threat to life and limb. Twice already, he'd taken the elevator up to the chief mate's quarters, determined to lodge a formal complaint, but on both occasions his courage had deserted him at the last minute.

Clipping the Matsushita to his utility belt, right next to the WP-17's transmitter, Neil raised his field glasses to his eyes and looked east. From his present station he couldn't see Eddie—too much distance, too much mist—but he knew the bos'n was there all right, standing on the lee side of a starboard toe and surveying the choppy bay created by God's half-submerged legs.

He hit SEND. "Bearing?"

"Zero-four-six. He's a twenty-footer, Neil! I've never seen so many teeth in one mouth before!"

Lifting the harpoon gun from its pore, Neil marched across the wrinkled, spongy beach that stretched for sixty yards from His knee to the ocean. Water reared up, a high spuming wall eternally created and re-created as the great patella cut its way through the Atlantic. "Operation Jehovah," the captain was forever calling this peculiar tow, evidently unaware that for a Jew like Neil the word *Jehovah* was vaguely offensive, the secret and unspeakable YHWH contaminated with secular vowels.

He scanned the churning rollers. Eddie was right: a twenty-foot hammerhead shark, swimming coastwise like some huge organic mallet bred to nail the divine coffin shut. Balancing the WP-17 on his shoulder, Neil cupped the telescopic sight against his eye and plucked the walkie-talkie from his belt.

"Speed?"

"Twelve knots."

"We aren't required to do this," Neil informed the bos'n. "I'll bet you anything it's against union rules. We simply aren't required. Range?"

"Sixteen yards."

Curious, he mused, how each predator had staked out its own culinary territory. From on high came the Cameroon vultures, swooping down like degenerate angels as they laid claim to the corneas and tear ducts. From below came the Liberian sea snakes, ruthlessly devouring the succulent meat of the buttocks. The surface belonged to the sharks—vicious makos, malicious blues, crazed hammerheads—nibbling away at the soft bearded cheeks and picking at the tender webbing between the fingers. And, indeed, the instant Neil drew a bead on the hammerhead, it turned abruptly and swam west, fully intending to bite the hand that made it.

He tracked the shark via the telescopic sight, aligning the crosshairs with the hammerhead's cartilaginous hump as he looped his finger around the trigger. He squeezed. With a sudden throaty explosion the harpoon leapt from the muzzle. Rocketing across the sea, it struck the surprised animal in the brow and burrowed into its brain.

Neil took a large swallow of moist African air. Poor beast—it didn't deserve this, it had committed no sin. Even as the shark spun sixty degrees and headed straight for the knee, the AB felt nothing toward it save pity.

"Throw the switch, buddy!"

"Roger, Eddie!"

"Throw it!"

Singing with pain, spouting blood, the shark hurled itself on the fleshy shore, raging so furiously that Neil half expected it to sprout legs and come crawling after him. He clasped the harpoon gun against his fishnet shirt, reached toward the transmitter on his utility belt, and threw the switch.

"Run!" cried Eddie. "Run, for Christ's sake!"

Neil turned, sprinting across the squishy terrain. Seconds later he heard the warhead explode, the awful grunt of TNT crushing live tissue and vaporizing fresh blood. He looked back. The shock wave was wet and red, a bright sloshy blossom filling the sky with bulbous lumps of brain.

"You okay, buddy? You aren't hurt, are you?"

As Neil mounted the kneecap, the debris came down, a glutinous rain of shark thoughts, all the hammerhead's dead hopes and shattered dreams, spattering the AB's jeans and shirt.

"I swear, I'm goin' straight to Rafferty!" he wailed. "I'm gonna stick this harpoon gun right smack in his face and tell him I didn't sign on for this shit!"

"Settle down, Neil."

The hammerhead's blood smelled like burning hair. "My grandfather never had to blow up sharks!"

"In thirty-five minutes we're outta here."

"If Rafferty won't take me off this stupid duty, I'm gonna harpoon *him*! I'm not kiddin'! *Bang*, right between the eyes!"

"Think how good that shower's gonna feel."

And the truly strange thing, Neil realized, throbbing with freedom—the strange, astonishing, terrifying thing—was that he *wasn't* kidding.

"There's no more God, Eddie! Don't you get it? No God, no rules, no eyes on us!"

"Think about Follingsbee's Chicken McNuggets. I'll even slip you one of my Budweisers."

Neil propped his gun against the shaft of a particularly thick hair, leaned toward the barrel, and, wetting his sun-baked lips, kissed the hot, vibrant metal.

"No eyes on us . . ."

It was appropriate, Oliver Shostak felt, that the Central Park West Enlightenment League followed only a loose approximation of *Robert's Rules of Order*, for neither rules nor order had anything to do with the organization's raison d'être. People didn't understand that. Say "rationalist" to the average New Age chucklehead, and you conjured up unappetizing images: killjoys obsessed with rules, boors fixated on order, logic-mongers skating around on the surface of things, missing the cosmic essence. Phooey. A rationalist could experience awe as readily as a shaman. But it had to be quality awe, Oliver believed, awe without illusions—the sort of awe he'd felt upon intuiting the size of the universe, or sensing the unlikeliness of his birth, or reading the fax from the SS *Carpco Valparaíso* currently residing in his vest pocket.

"Let's get started," he said, signaling to the attractive young Juilliard student playing the harpsichord on the far side of the room. She lifted her hands from the keyboard; the music stopped in midmeasure, Mozart's deliciously intricate Fantasia in D Minor. No gavel, of course. No table, no minutes, no agenda. The eighteen members sat in an informal circle, submerged in the splendor of soft recamier couches and lush velvet divans.

Oliver had appointed the room himself. He could afford it. He could afford anything. Thanks to the near-simultaneous ascents of feminism, fornication, and several major venereal diseases, the planet was using latex condoms in unprecedented quantities, and in the late eighties his father's amazing invention, the Shostak Supersensitive, had emerged as the brand of choice. By the turn of the decade, astonishing quantities of cash had begun flowing into the family's coffers, an ever-rising tide of profit. At times it seemed to Oliver that his father had somehow patented the sex act itself.

He sipped his brandy and said, "The chair recognizes Barclay."

Deciphering Cassie's fax had been easy. It was in Heresy, the numerical code they'd invented in tenth grade to obscure the records of the organization they'd founded, the Freethinkers Club. (Besides Cassie and Oliver, the club had boasted only two other members, the lonely, homely, and hugely unpopular Maldonado twins.) *This is no joke. Come see for yourself. We are really towing . . .*

As the League's vice president rose, the entire membership drew to attention, not simply to hear Barclay's report but to bathe in his celebrity. In recent years the United States of America had managed to accommodate a full-time debunker—a counterweight to its twenty thousand astrologers, five thousand past-life therapists, and scores of scoundrels routinely cranking out bestsellers about UFO encounters and the joy of runes—and that debunker was golden-haired Barclay Cabot. Barclay, handsome devil, had media presence. The camera liked him. He'd done all the major talk shows, demonstrating how charlatans appeared to bend spoons and read minds when in fact they were doing nothing of the kind.

He began by reviewing the crisis. Two weeks earlier, the Texas legislature had voted to purge all the state's high schools of any curriculum materials that failed to accord so-called scientific creationism "equal time" with the theory of natural selection. Not that the Enlightenment League doubted the outcome of a showdown between the God hypothesis and Darwin. The fossils shouted evolution; the chromosomes screamed descent; the rocks declared their antiquity. What the League feared was that America's textbook publishers would simply elect to duck the whole issue and, readopting their spineless expedient of the forties and fifties, omit any consideration of human origins whatsoever.

Meanwhile, every Sunday, creationism would continue to be taught unchallenged.

In conspiratorial tones, Barclay outlined his committee's plan. Under cover of night, a small subset of the League, a kind of atheist commando unit, would crawl across the luxurious lawn of the First Baptist Church of Dallas—"the Pentagon of Christianity," as Barclay put it—and jimmy open a basement window. They would sneak into the church. Infiltrate the nave. Secure the pews. And then, unholstering their Swingline staplers, they would take up each Bible in turn and, before replacing it, neatly affix a thirty-page précis of *On the Origin of Species* between the table of contents and Genesis.

Equal time for Darwin.

What a bold scenario, thought Oliver, as audacious as the time they'd faked a materialization of the Virgin Mary on Boston Common, as nervy as when they'd upstaged an antiabortion rally in Salt Lake City by hiring the notorious rock group Flesh Before Breakfast to stand across the street singing "What a Drug We Have in Jesus."

"All in favor of the proposed counterattack . . ."

Seventeen *ayes* reverberated through the west lounge of Montesquieu Hall.

"All opposed . . ."

Inevitably, the League's recording secretary, cantankerous Sylvia Endicott, stood up. "Nay," she said, not so much speaking the word as growling it. "Nay and nay again." Sylvia Endicott: skepticism's oldest living warrior, the woman who in her radical youth had led a losing campaign to have IN GOD WE TRUST removed from the nation's coins and an equally unsuccessful fight to get a plaque installed on the Kansas City street corner where Sinclair Lewis had dared the Almighty to strike him dead. "You know my views on scientific creationism—O paragon of oxymorons. You know where I stand on Dallas Baptists. But come on, people. This so-called 'counterattack' is really just a *prank*. We're the children of François-Marie Arouet de Voltaire, for Christ's sake. We aren't the fucking Marx Brothers."

"The *ayes* have it," said Oliver. He'd never cared for Sylvia Endicott, who said pompous things like *O paragon of oxymorons* whenever she got the floor.

"When will we stop being a bunch of dilettantes and start playing hardball?" Sylvia persisted. "I can remember a time when this organization would've sued the Texas legislature for de facto censorship."

"You want to make a motion?"

"No, I want us to acquire some backbone."

"Any new business?"

"Backbone, people. Backbone!"

"Any new business?" said Oliver again.

Silence, even from Sylvia. The crone of reason sank back into her chair. The fire crackled merrily in the hearth. Throughout the city, the hot July evening simmered away, but within Montesquieu Hall an ingenious deployment of insulation and air conditioners was neatly simulating a frigid February night. It was Oliver's idea. He'd covered the costs. An extravagance? Yes, but why be wealthy if one didn't occasionally indulge a personal foible or two?

"*I* have some new business," said Oliver, reaching into his silk vest and taking out the troubling communiqué. "This fax is from Cassie Fowler, currently aboard the supertanker *Carpco Valparaíso* somewhere off the coast of Liberia. You can see the Carpco logo"—Oliver pointed to the famous stegosaurus—"right here on the letterhead. So the telegram her mother received last week was evidently authentic, and Cassandra is very much alive. That's the good news."

"And the bad?" asked comely, jewel-eyed Pamela Harcourt, the guiding light behind the League's feisty and unprofitable periodical, *The Skeptical Investigator* (circulation: 1,042).

"The bad branches into two possibilities." Oliver held up his index finger. "Either Cassandra is having a psychotic breakdown"—he added his middle finger to the illustration—"or the *Valparaíso* is towing the corpse of God."

"Towing the what?" Taylor Scott, a frail young man whose affection for the Enlightenment extended to wearing greatcoats and ruffles, flipped open his silver cigarette case.

"Corpse of God. It's evidently rather large."

Taylor removed a Turkish cigarette and slid it between his lips. "I don't understand."

"Two miles long, she says here. Humanoid, nude, Caucasian, male, and dead."

"Huh?"

"Corpus Dei. How can I be clearer?"

"Fiddlesticks," said Taylor.

"Horse manure," said Barclay.

"Cassandra assumed that would be our reaction," said Oliver.

"I should hope so," said Pamela. "Oliver, dear, what's this all about?"

"I don't *know* what it's all about." Brandy snifter in hand, Oliver rose and, stepping outside the ring of rationalists, slowly paced the perimeter. Under ordinary circumstances, the west lounge of Montesquieu Hall was his favorite place on earth, a soothing conjunction of mullioned windows, fabric-lined walls, eighteenth-century French *redouté* floral prints, and his own original oil paintings of famous freethinkers striking characteristic poses: Thomas Paine hurling a copy of *The Age of Reason* through a cathedral window, Baron d'Holbach offering Pope Leo XII a Bronx cheer, Bertrand Russell and David Hume playing chess with crèche figurines. (Two weeks earlier Oliver had added a self-portrait to the gallery, a gesture that might have seemed presumptuous had the painting not included a brutally truthful depiction of his faltering chin and ill-proportioned nose.) But tonight the lounge brought him no comfort. It seemed gloomy and damp, besieged by ignorant armies. "The tanker's on some sort of burial mission," he continued. "There's a tomb in the Arctic. Angels have been spotted. Look, I admit this all sounds utterly crazy, but Cassandra is inviting us to inspect the evidence."

"*Evidence?*" said Pamela. "How can there be *evidence?*"

"She proposes that we fly to Senegal, charter a helicopter, and reconnoiter the *Valparaíso*'s cargo."

"Why, oh, why, are you wasting our time like this?" Winston Hawke, an intense, nervous little man for whom the collapse of Soviet communism merely heralded the True Revolution to come, sprang to his feet. "The Baptists are taking over," cried the Marxist, "the yokels are on the march, the yahoos are at the gates, and *you're* giving us a lot of shit about a supertanker!"

"Let me make a motion," said Oliver. "I move that we dispatch a task force to Dakar before sundown tomorrow."

"I can't believe you're serious," said owlish Rainsford Fitch, a computer programmer who spent his nights hunched over his Macintosh SE-30, working out complicated mathematical disproofs of God's existence.

"Neither can I," said Oliver. "Would anyone like to second the motion?"

The League's treasurer, matronly Meredith Lodge, an IRS functionary whose lifelong ambition was to deliver a tax bill to the Mormon Church, popped open her ledger book. "Is this really the sort of enterprise we should be spending our money on?"

"I'll pay for everything." Oliver polished off his brandy. "Plane fares, helicopter rentals . . ."

"Pray tell," said Barclay, making no effort to stifle his smirk, "did the late Jehovah bequeath anything to His creatures?"

"I said, 'Would anyone like to second the motion?' "

"Ah, but of *course* He did," Barclay persisted. "We've all heard of God's will!" Appreciative guffaws rippled through the lounge. "I *do* hope He left me something nice. The Colorado River, maybe, or perhaps a small planet in Andromeda, or else—"

"Second the motion," interrupted Pamela, flashing a sturdy smile. "And while I'm at it, let me volunteer to head up the task force. I mean, what's the big deal, friends? What are we afraid of? We all know the *Valparaíso* isn't towing God."

Thank goodness for off-road vehicles, thought Thomas Ockham as, dropping the Jeep Wrangler into first gear, he guided it up the wrinkled, spongy slope of the forehead. An ordinary car—his Honda Civic, for example—would have been defeated by now, hung up on a pimple or mired in a pore. It all sounded like an announcement you'd see emblazoned outside some run-down Evangelical church in Memphis. TODAY'S SERMON: IT TAKES FOUR-WHEEL DRIVE TO REALLY KNOW THE LORD.

Lifting his hand from the gearshift lever, he accidentally brushed Sister Miriam's left thigh.

Initially she hadn't wanted to come along. "I'm not prepared to meet Him *that* way," she'd said, but then Thomas had pointed out that, if they were ever going to get beyond their grief, they would first have to confront the corpse directly, pimples, pores, moles, warts, and all. "The logic of the open casket," as he'd put it.

Struggling against a headwind, the corpse was riding low this morning, so low that the CB radio reports arriving from the torso sentries spoke of waves breaking against the nipples and a tidal pool swirling in the navel. To wit, the Wrangler wouldn't be making the full trip today—down the jaw, over the Adam's apple, across the chest and belly. Just as well. Forty-eight hours earlier Thomas had traveled the entire length, pausing briefly atop the abdomen to behold the great veiny cylinder floating between the legs (a truly unnerving sight, the scrotal sac undu-lating like the gasbag of some unimaginable blimp), and he was loath to repeat the experience with Miriam. It wasn't just that the sharks had wrought such terrible destruction, stripping off the foreskin like a gang of sadistic *mohel*s. Even if in good shape,

God's penis would still rank high among those vistas a priest and a nun could not comfortably share.

They crested the brow and started downward, bound for the deep, windswept gorge from which the great nose grew.

Technically, of course, His gonads made no sense; they might even be marshaled to dispute the corpse's authenticity. But such an objection, Thomas felt, smacked of hubris. If their Creator had once wanted (for whatever reasons) to reshape Himself in the image of His products, He'd have gone ahead and done so. "Let there be a penis," and there would be a penis. Indeed, the more Thomas thought about it, the more inevitable the appendage became. A God without a penis would be a *limited* God, a God to whom some possibility had been closed, hence not God at all. In a way it was rather noble of Him to have endorsed this most controversial of organs. Inevitably Thomas thought of Paul's beautiful First Letter to the Corinthians: "And those members of the body which we think to be less honorable, upon these we bestow more abundant honor . . ."

The Wrangler was ascending again, conquering the proboscis at five miles per hour. Miriam jammed one of her audiocassettes into the tape deck, realized she'd loaded it upside down, tried again. She pushed PLAY. Instantly the bombastic opening of Richard Strauss's *Also Sprach Zarathustra* erupted from the speakers, a fanfare popularized by Stanley Kubrick's *2001: A Space Odyssey*, the great eschatological movie she and Thomas had seen twenty-four years earlier on what the secular world would have termed a date.

While the genitalia held an intrinsic fascination for the priest, the things the *Val*'s cargo lacked likewise engaged his curiosity. There was no dirt under the fingernails, for example, no clay of Creation—more evidence for calling the corpse counterfeit, although the scouring action of the sea offered an equally likely explanation. The wrists exhibited no crucifixion marks: an instance of divine self-healing, Thomas surmised, although a Unitarian might legitimately seize upon this circumstance to rail against conventional Christianity's obsession with the Trinity. The flesh displayed none of the scorching that would normally result from a plunge through the earth's atmosphere; it was as if the carcass hadn't "fallen" in the literal sense but had materialized instead—or maybe He'd been *alive* during His descent, willfully exempting Himself from friction and allowing Himself to perish only upon hitting the Gulf of Guinea.

As they reached the summit, Miriam said, "It's a paradox, isn't it?"

"What do you mean?"

"How the fact of God steals away our faith in God."

Thomas killed the engine, then rotated the ignition key forward a notch so the cassette would keep playing. "The literalness of all this is most depressing, I'll grant you. But it's important to sense the mystery behind the meat. What is flesh, really? What is matter? Do we know? We don't. In its own way, carrion is as numinous as the Host."

"Maybe," said Miriam evenly. "Could be," she added without emotion. "Sure. Right. I want my belief back, Tom. I want to feel that old-time religion again."

Yanking the emergency brake with one hand, Thomas gave his friend's shoulder an affectionate squeeze with the other. "I suppose we could try believing in a God synonymous with something beyond this corpse—a God outside God. But Gabriel didn't allow us that option. He was a good Catholic, my angel. He understood the ultimate indivisibility of body and spirit."

The priest climbed out of the cab, laying his palm on the hot steel hood. A Wrangler's engine, a *Homo sapiens sapiens*, a Supreme Being—in each case, the soul of the thing could not be abstracted from the thing itself. Just as Einstein had demonstrated the fundamental equivalence of matter and energy, so did Thomas's church teach the fundamental equivalence of existence and essence. There was no ghost in the machine.

Pulling his Handicam from the rear compartment, the priest pivoted toward the great glassy lake of their cargo's left eye. Both irises were a vibrant cyan, the luxurious hue of unoxygenated blood. (And God said, "Let me have Scandinavian eyes.") He put the camera on STANDBY. Gradually the scene painted itself across the viewfinder screen: a frightened deckie on predator patrol, bazooka at the ready, standing by the shore of the watery cornea as he scanned the sky for Cameroon vultures. Beyond lay His great frozen smile, each visible tooth sparkling like a sunstruck glacier.

Teeth, eyes, hands, gonads—so much to contemplate, and yet Thomas also found himself pondering those parts presently hidden from view. Did the hair swirl clockwise, like a human's? Were the palms callused? Were the molars configured in a manner suggesting a particular diet? (Given the popularity of animal sacrifice in the Old Testament, it was unlikely He'd been a vegetarian.) Anything remarkable about the buttocks evoked so enigmatically in Exodus 33:23?

"Then, of course," called Miriam above *Also Sprach Zarathustra*, "there's the question of why. Any theories, Tom?"

He pulled the Handicam's trigger, preserving God's sightless gaze and grinning rictus on half-inch videotape. "I plan to organize my thoughts tonight and send them to Rome. In my gut I feel it was an empathic death. He died from a bad case of the twentieth century."

Miriam offered a nod of assent. "We've killed Him a hundred million times in recent memory, haven't we? And we never even bothered to hide the bodies."

What a supple, sensuous mind, he thought. " 'Hide the bodies,' " he echoed. "Would it be all right if I quoted you in my fax to Cardinal Di Luca?"

"I'd be flattered," the nun said, smiling spectacularly. Like God, she had perfect teeth: no surprise, really, the poverty of Carmelites being strictly genteel, poverty with a dental plan.

Scrambling out of the passenger seat, Miriam circumvented the tarry surface of a blackhead and ambled confidently to his side. Her getup, he admitted—pith helmet, dungarees, safari jacket sealed tightly with bone buttons—aroused in him a certain prurience. All during his youth, Thomas had harbored a vague notion that, lifting the edge of a nun's habit, you'd find nothing there. How wrong he'd been. The denim clung to her hips, thighs, and calves, outlining her like the drifting snow into which the dying Claude Rains had fallen at the climax of *The Invisible Man*.

" 'The madman sprang into their midst and pierced them with his glances,' " she said, reciting a famous passage from *Die Fröhliche Wissenschaft*. " 'Where has God gone?' he cried. 'I shall tell you. We have killed Him—you and I. We are all His murderers.' "

" 'But how was this done?' " said Thomas, continuing the passage. They couldn't get away from Nietzsche today: *Zarathustra* on the tape deck, *Die Fröhliche Wissenschaft* on their tongues. " 'How were we able to drink up the sea?' " He shut off the Handicam. " 'Who gave us the sponge to wipe away the entire horizon?' "

They returned to the Wrangler, drove down the western nasal slope, and improvised a path through the whiskers of the left cheek. On its fringes, the beard had become a kind of fishing net, a vast natural web the seafaring apostles might have envied, jammed with entangled groupers, porpoises, and marlin. The Wrangler bucked and lurched but stayed on course, looping steadily eastward into the mustache.

Twin caverns rose before them, the great yawning tunnels through which their cargo had once breathed and sneezed.

"To be honest"—Miriam stared into the moist depths—"I'm learning more than I care to."

"Quite so," said Thomas, grimacing. Marshes of mucus, boulders of dried snot, nose hairs the size of obelisks: this was not the Lord God of Hosts they'd grown up with. "But we can't leave yet." He swung the steering wheel hard over and, putting the Wrangler in reverse, eased the rear bumper against the high escarpment running between upper lip and right nostril. Leaning out the window, he wiped the sea spray from the rearview mirror, a saucer-sized disk jutting into space on rusted aluminum struts. "A test," he explained.

"I suppose there's always hope."

"Always," Thomas muttered without conviction.

Together they studied the glass, watching it with the same rapt intensity of the prophet Daniel beholding MENE, MENE, TEKEL, UPHARSIN materialize upon the wall. The merest cloud would have satisfied them—the slightest smudge, the feeblest hint of fog.

Nothing. The surface remained mockingly clear, obscenely pristine. God, the mirror said, was dead.

Miriam took Thomas's hand, pressing it so firmly between her palms that the blood crowded into his fingertips. "Then, of course, there's the toughest question of all."

"Yes?"

"Now that we know He's gone, really gone, making no judgments, preparing no punishments, now that we truly *know* these things"—the nun offered a diffident little grin—"why should we fear to sin?"

July 26.

Latitude: 25°8′N. Longitude: 20°30′E. Course: 358. Speed: 6 lousy knots. We're rounding the great bulge of northwest Africa, tracing in reverse those audacious voyages of exploration Prince Henry the Navigator dispatched from Portugal beginning in 1455. If dear old Dad was Christopher Columbus in a previous life, perhaps I used to be Prince Henry. When the benighted monarch died, his friends stripped him down and found he was wearing a hair shirt.

My plan is amazingly clever. Ready, Popeye? I'm going to blow the ballast. All of it: the 60,000 tons we picked up in New

York Harbor, the 15,000 (so far) with which we've been compensating for spent bunker fuel. And then—here's the brilliant part—we're going to trim the *Val* with His blood.

Think of it. One simple, standard pumping operation, no longer than 5 hours, and we'll have reduced our towing load by 15 percent. According to Crock O'Connor, we can run both engines at a steady 85 rpm's after that, maybe even 90.

Count on Father Ockham to object.

"After we blow the ballast, we'll be at the corpse's mercy," he asserted, ever the physics professor. "A strong wind, and the thing could drag us a hundred miles off course."

"It'll be like a transfusion," I explained. "As the water goes shooting out of the ballast tanks, the blood'll come pouring into the cargo tanks. We'll remain in trim the whole time."

"You mean you're going to drain our Creator's liquid essence into those filthy cargo tanks?"

I figured I should tell him the truth, even though I could see where he was heading. "Yes, Thomas, that's one way to put it."

"We'll have to clear it with Rome."

"No, we won't."

"Yes, we will."

The Vatican got back to us in less than an hour.

"The synod has reached a consensus," said somebody named Tullio Cardinal Di Luca. "Under no circumstances may His blood be defiled with secular oil. Before the transfusion, you must scrub the cargo tanks thoroughly."

"*Scrub* them?" I moaned. "That'll take two days!"

"Then we'd better start right now," said the padre, simultaneously smiling and frowning.

Eat more yogurt, Neil Weisinger's physician had advised him upon appraising the cramps, diarrhea, and general misery that had settled in his gut shortly after his twentieth birthday. Yogurt,

Dr. Cinsavich had explained, would increase his acidophilus count and aid his digestion. Until that moment, Neil hadn't even realized that his intestines housed bacteria, much less that the bugs performed a welfare function. And so he tried the yogurt cure, and while it didn't work (he was in fact suffering from lactose intolerance, a condition he eventually conquered by abstaining from dairy products), he nevertheless came away with an intense respect for his internal ecosystem.

Four years after his visit to Dr. Cinsavich, as Neil climbed into number two center tank aboard the SS *Carpco Valparaíso*, he found himself identifying fiercely with the microbial proletariat teeming inside him. It was germs' work, this thankless and malodorous business of scouring the ship's innards, preparing them to receive God's blood. Although the washing machine had done a good job, pulverizing the largest tarballs and flushing them away, there was still a considerable residue to harvest, gluey blobs of asphalt clinging to the ladders and catwalks like immense wads of discarded chewing gum. Gradually he descended—hand under hand, Leo Zook by his side—below the hawsepipes and the Plimsoll line, past the churning surface of the sea, deeper, ever deeper, into the hull. They scrubbed as they went, scooping up the gunk with their ladles and plopping it into a huge steel mucking bucket dangling beside them on a chain. Whenever the bucket became full, they broadcast the news via walkie-talkie to Eddie Wheatstone on the weather deck, and he winched the load aloft.

Grandfather Moshe, no doubt, would have found redemption in this drudgery. The old man actually liked crude oil. "Oil's a fluid fossil," he'd once lectured his ten-year-old grandson as they stood on the Baltimore docks watching a supertanker glide across the horizon. "Memories of the Permian, messages from the Cretaceous, crushed and cooked and turned to jam. That ship's a pail of history, Neil. That ship carries liquid dinosaurs."

Having Zook along only made things worse. In recent days

the Evangelical's piety had taken a truly ugly turn, degenerating into full-blown anti-Semitism. True, his mind was in upheaval, his soul in torment, his worldview in flames. But that was no excuse.

"Please understand, I don't think *you're* in any way responsible for this terrible thing that's happened," said Zook, sweat leaking from beneath his hard hat and trickling down his freckled face.

"That's mighty gracious of you," said Neil with a sneer. His voice reverberated madly in the great chamber, echoes of echoes of echoes.

"But if I had to point a finger, which is not my style, but if I had to point, all I could say is, 'Your people killed God once before, so maybe they did it *this* time too.'"

"I don't want to hear this shit, Leo."

"I'm not talking about you personally."

"Oh, yes, you are."

"I'm talking about Jews in general."

During their first hour in the tank, the midday sun lit their path, the bright golden shafts slanting through the open hatchway, but fifty feet down they had to switch on the electric lamps bolted atop their hard hats. The beams shot forward a dozen feet and vanished, swallowed by the darkness. Neil hacked a wad of mucus into his throat. He spit. A goddamn underwater coal miner, that's what he was. How had this happened to him? Why had his life come to so little?

At last they reached the bottom—a grid of high steel walls flung outward from the keelson, dividing the tank into twenty gloomy bays, each the size of a two-car garage. Neil unhooked the bucket and took a deep breath. So far, so good: no hydrocarbon stink. Groping toward his utility belt, he snapped up the walkie-talkie.

"You with us, bos'n?" he radioed Eddie.

"Roger. How's the weather down there?"

"Swell, I think, but be ready to bail us out, okay?"

"Gotcha."

Mucking bucket at the ready, Neil began the inspection, crawling from compartment to compartment via the two-foot-long culverts cut into the bulkheads, Zook right behind. Bay one proved clean. Bay two held not a smudge. You could eat your lunch off the floor of three and blithely lick the walls of four. Five was the purest space yet, home to the washing machine itself, a conical mountain of pipes and nozzles rising over twenty feet. In six they finally found something worth removing, a glop of paraffin cleaving to a handgrip. They ladled it into the bucket and pressed on.

It happened the instant Neil stepped into bay seven. At first there was just the odor—the ghastly aroma of a ruptured gas bubble, drilling into his nose. Then came the tingling in his fingertips and the patterns in his head: silvery pinwheels, red mandalas, shooting stars. His stomach unhooked itself, plunging downward.

"Gas!" he screamed into the walkie-talkie. No doubt the malignant sphere had been waiting there for months, crouching in the prison of its own surface, and now the beast was out, popped free by Neil's footfalls. "Gas!"

"Jesus!" wailed Zook.

"Gas!" Neil screamed again. "Eddie, we got gas down here!" He looked skyward. The hatchway drifted two hundred feet above his head, shimmering in the corrupted air like a harvest moon. "Drop the Dragens, Eddie! Bay seven!"

"Jesus Lord God!"

"Gas! Bay seven! Gas!"

"God!"

"Stay put, guys!" came Eddie's voice, crackling out of the walkie-talkie. "The Dragens are coming!"

Both sailors were weeping now, tear ducts spasming, cheeks running with salt water. Neil's flesh grew bumpy and numb. His tongue itched.

"Hurry!"

Zook tucked his thumb against his palm and uncurled his fingers. One . . . two . . . three . . . four.

Four. It was something you learned during seamanship training. A man gassed at the bottom of a cargo tank has four minutes to live.

"They're coming," said the Evangelical, choking on the words.

"The Dragens," Neil agreed, reaching uncertainly into the side pocket of his overalls. His hands had taken on lives of their own, trembling like epileptic crabs.

"No, the horsemen," Zook gasped, still holding up his fingers.

"Horsemen?"

"The four horsemen. Plague, famine, war, death."

As Neil tore the Ben-Gurion medal free, a hot stream of half-digested Chicken McNuggets coursed up his windpipe. He vomited into the mucking bucket. What ship was this? The *Carpco Valparaíso*? No. The *Argo Lykes*? No. The rogue freighter on which Chief Mate Moshe Weisinger had borne fifteen hundred Jews to Palestine? No, not a merchant vessel of any sort. Something else. A floating concentration camp. Birkenau with a rudder. And here was Neil, trapped in a subsurface gas chamber as the *Kommandant* flooded it with Zyklon-B.

"Death," he echoed, dropping the Ben-Gurion medal. The bronze disc bounced off the rim of the bucket and clanked against the steel floor. "Death by Zyklon-B."

"Huh?" said Kommandant Zook.

Neil's brain was airborne, hovering outside his skull, bobbing around on the end of his spinal cord like a meat balloon. "I know your game, Kommandant. 'Lock those prisoners in the showers! Turn on the Zyklon-B!' "

Like spiders descending on silvery threads, a pair of Dragen rigs floated down from the weather deck. Caught in the beam of Neil's hard-hat lamp, the oxygen tanks glowed a brilliant orange. The black masks and blue hoses spun wildly, intertwining. Lunging forward, he flexed his unfeeling fingers and began loosening the rubbery knot.

"Zyklon *what?*" said Zook.

Neil freed up a pear-shaped mask. Frantically he strapped it in place. He reached out, arched his fingers around the valve, rotated his wrist. Stuck. He tried again. Stuck. Again. It moved! Half an inch. An inch. Two. Air! Closing his eyes, he inhaled, sucking the sweetness through his mouth—nose—pores. Air, glorious oxygen, an invisible poultice drawing the poison from his brain.

He opened his eyes. Kommandant Zook sat on the floor, skin pale as a mushroom, lips fluted in a moan. One hand held his mask in place. The other rested atop the tank, curled over the valve like a gigantic tick in the act of siphoning blood.

"Help me."

It took Neil several seconds to grasp Zook's predicament. The Nazi was completely immobile, frozen by some dreadful combination of brain damage and fear.

"Plague," said Neil. Dragging his oxygen tank behind him, he hobbled to Zook's side.

"P-please."

Freedom rushed through Neil like a hit of cocaine. YHWH wasn't watching. No eyes on Neil. He could do whatever he felt like. Open the *Kommandant*'s valve—or cut his hose in two. Give him a shot of oxygen from the functioning rig—or spit in his face. Anything. Nothing.

"Famine," said Neil.

The *Kommandant* stopped moaning. His jaw went slack. His eyes turned dull and milky, as if made of quartz.

"War," Neil whispered to Leo Zook's corpse.

From his breast pocket he drew out his Swiss Army knife. He pinched the spear blade, rotated it outward. He clenched the red handle; he stabbed; the blade pierced the rubber as easily as if it were soap. Laughing, reveling in his freedom, he carved a long, ragged incision along the axis of the Nazi's hose.

"Death."

Neil crouched beside the suffocated man, drank the delicious oxygen, and listened to the slow, steady thunder of the retreating horsemen.

Plague

For Oliver Shostak, learning that the illusory deity of Judeo-Christianity had once actually inhabited the heavens and the earth, running reality and dictating the Bible, was hands-down the worst experience of his life. On the scale of disillusionment, it far outranked his deduction at age five that Santa Claus was a mountebank, his discovery at seventeen that his father was routinely screwing the woman who boarded the family's Weimaraners, and the judgment he'd suffered on his thirty-second birthday when he'd asked the curator of the Castelli Gallery in SoHo to exhibit the highlights of his abstract-expressionist period. ("The great drawback of these paintings," the stiff-necked old lady had replied, "is that they aren't any good.") But the fruits of Pamela Harcourt's recent expedition could not be denied: a dozen full-color photographs, each showing a large, male, grinning, supine body being towed by its ears northward through the

Atlantic Ocean. The 30 × 40 blowups hung in the west lounge of Montesquieu Hall like ancestral portraits—which, in a manner of speaking, they were.

"Our labors of late have been, if I may speak mythologically, Herculean," Barclay Cabot began, his haggard face breaking into a yawn. "Our itinerary included stops in Asia, Europe, the Middle East . . ."

Oliver fixed on the blowups. He loathed them. No feminist forced to sit through a Linda Lovelace film festival had ever felt more offended. Yet he refused to admit defeat. Indeed, on receiving Pamela's dire bulletin from Dakar he'd swung into action immediately, deputizing Barclay to form an ad hoc committee and lead it on a frantic journey around the world.

Winston Hawke finished off a petit four, wiping his hands on his Trotsky sweatshirt. "After eighty-four hours of unbroken effort, our team has reached a sobering conclusion."

Rising, Barclay slipped a sheet of legal paper out of his waist-coat pocket. "By presenting yourself as the agent of a foreign government eager to prevent its financial resources from falling into the wrong hands . . ."

"Its own people, for example," said Winston.

". . . you can, these days, obtain almost any tool of mass destruction that catches your fancy. To be specific"—Barclay perused the legal paper—"the French Ministry of Defense was prepared to rent us a *Robespierre*-class attack submarine equipped with eighteen forward-launched torpedoes. The Iranian State Department proposed to sell us the nine million gallons of Vietnam-surplus napalm it acquired from the American CIA in 1976, plus ten F-15 Eagle fighter jets with which to dispense it. The Argentine Navy offered us a two-month lease on the battleship *Eva Perón*, and if we'd closed the deal on the spot, they'd have thrown in six thousand rounds of ammunition for free. Finally, as long as we agreed to keep the source a secret, the People's Republic of China would've given us what they called a 'package deal' on a tactical nuclear weapon and the delivery system of our choice."

"Every one of these offers fell through the minute the merchants learned we did not in fact represent a sovereign state." Winston selected a second petit four. "It's immoral and destabilizing, they said, for private citizens to possess such technologies."

"The sole dissenter from this policy was itself a private institution, the American National Rifle Association," said Barclay. "But the things they wanted to sell us—four M110 howitzers and seven wire-guided TOW missiles—are useless for our purposes."

Oliver groaned softly. He'd been hoping for a more encouraging report: not simply because he wished to impress Cassandra, whose fax had clearly contained a subtext—*prove yourself*, she was saying between the lines, *show me you're a man of substance*—but also because he truly wanted to spare his species a millennium of theistic ignorance and mindless superstition.

"So we're licked?" asked Pamela.

"There is one ray of hope," said Winston, devouring the tiny cake. "This afternoon we spoke with—"

The Marxist stopped in midsentence, stunned by the ascent of Sylvia Endicott, a surge so abrupt it was as if the springs of her Empire chair had suddenly popped free. "Have I missed something?" the old woman demanded in a low, liquid hiss. "Did I fail to attend a crucial meeting? Was I out of town during an emergency session? When, exactly, did we agree on this sabotage business?"

"We never put it to a formal vote," Oliver replied, "but clearly that's the consensus in the room."

"Not in *this* part of the room."

"What are you saying, Sylvia?" snarled Pamela. " 'Sit back and do nothing'?"

"The Svalbard tomb can hardly be a secure place," Meredith

Lodge hastened to add. "Hell, I suspect it's vulnerable as Cheops's pyramid."

"Obliteration's the only answer," said Rainsford Fitch.

Scowling profoundly, Sylvia shuffled to the bust of Charles Darwin stationed by the fireplace.

"Assuming for a moment the *Valparaíso* is really towing what Cassie Fowler says it's towing," she began, "shouldn't we have the collective courage, if not the simple decency, to admit we've been *wrong* all these years?"

"Wrong?" said Rainsford.

"Yes. Wrong."

"That's a rather extreme word," said Barclay.

"It's probably time to amend our charter," said Taylor Scott, puffing on a Turkish cigarette, "but we shouldn't throw the baby out with the bathwater. The theistic world was a nightmare, Sylvia. Have you forgotten the Renaissance witch hunts?"

"But we're not being *honest*."

"The trial of Galileo? The massacre of the Incas?"

"I haven't forgotten those things, nor have I forgotten the scientific curiosity that is the *sine qua non* of this organization." Sylvia tightened her woolen shawl, her primary protection against the ersatz winter raging through Montesquieu Hall. "We should be *studying* this corpse, not sweeping it under the rug."

"Let's look at it from another angle," said Winston. "Yes, some sort of large entity is currently being hauled toward the Arctic, and for all we know this entity hung the stars, spun the earth, and molded Adam out of clay. But does that mean it's *God*? The unmoved mover? The first and final cause? The be-all and end-all? It's *dead*, for Christ's sake. What kind of Supreme Being goes belly up like that?"

"A fake Supreme Being," said Rainsford.

"Exactly," said Winston. "A fake, a fraud, a phony. The problem, of course, is that such logic will never impress the credulous masses. A relic like this becomes yet another confirmation of their faith. Ergo, for the good of all, in the name of reason, this God-who-isn't-God must be removed."

"Winston, you appall me." Arms akimbo, Sylvia aimed her blighted corneas directly at the Marxist. "Reason, you said? 'The name of reason'? This isn't *reason* you're doling out—it's atheist fundamentalism!"

"Let's not play with words."

Sylvia tore off the shawl, hobbled into the foyer, and yanked open the front door. "Ladies and gentlemen, you leave me no other choice!" she foamed as the July heat wafted into the frigid lounge. "Honor dictates but one course for me—I must resign from the Central Park West Enlightenment League!"

"Lighten up, Sylvia," said Pamela.

The old woman stepped into the steamy night. "Got that, you intellectual pharisees?" she called over her shoulder. "I'm quitting—forever!"

Oliver's innards contracted. His throat grew dry. Sylvia, goddamn it, had a point.

"The sack of Jerusalem!" wailed Winston as the door slammed shut.

"The siege of Belfast!" howled Rainsford.

"The slaughter of the Huguenots!" screamed Meredith.

A point—but that was *all* Sylvia had, Oliver decided, a mere rational argument, and meanwhile the woods were burning.

"Let's hear about that ray of hope," said Pamela.

Barclay strode to the hearth, warming his hands over the roiling flames. "You've probably never heard of Pembroke and Flume's World War Two Reenactment Society, but it's pretty much what the name implies—a couple of ambitious young impresarios who buy up mothballed B-17s and battleships and such. They hire hungry actors, unemployed merchant sailors, and discharged Navy fliers, then travel around simulating the major encounters between the Axis and the Allies."

"Last summer, Pembroke and Flume put on their version of

Rommel's Africa campaign, substituting the Arizona desert for Tunisia," said Winston, joining Barclay by the fire. "The winter before, they did the Ardennes counteroffensive in the Catskills. This year, as it happens, is the fiftieth anniversary of the Battle of Midway, so they've got a Hollywood crew working up on Martha's Vineyard, reconstructing the entire base out of Styrofoam and plywood. On August first, dozens of classic Japanese warplanes will take off from three-quarter-scale fiberglass facsimiles of the carriers *Akagi, Soryu, Hiryu*, and *Kaga*, then bomb the base to smithereens. The next day, all four Jap flattops will be sunk by a squadron of dive bombers from the vintage American carrier *Enterprise*—the pride of Pembroke and Flume's collection."

"Which is actually something of a cheat," said Barclay. "The *Yorktown* and the *Hornet* also sent planes, but Pembroke and Flume are operating on a budget. On the other hand, they do use live bombs. The audience gets its money's worth."

"Bread and circuses," said Winston, sneering. "Only in late-capitalist America, eh?"

"The relevant fact is this: once they're done with Midway, Pembroke and Flume have no immediate prospects," said Barclay. "They'll be eager to let us hire 'em."

"Hire 'em to do what?" asked Meredith.

"Restage the battle all over again—with fresh ammunition. Between their dive bombers and their torpedo planes, we're pretty sure they can deliver enough TNT to scuttle Van Horne's cargo."

A quick, delicious thrill shot through Oliver as, rising from his méridienne daybed, he marched across the Aubusson carpet to the bust of Darwin. He liked this Midway business. He liked it very much. "What'll they charge us?"

"They quoted a few rough figures at lunch," said Winston, scanning a ragged 3×5 card. "Salaries, food, gasoline, bombs, lawyers, insurance riders . . ."

"And the bottom line?"

"Gimme a minute." Winston's index finger danced along the keyboard of his pocket calculator. "Sixteen million, two hundred and twenty thousand, seven hundred and fifty dollars."

"Think we can get 'em down to fifteen?" asked Oliver, sliding his thumb across the marble furrows of Darwin's frown. Not that it mattered. If his sister could squander her trust fund collecting Abraham Lincoln memorabilia and his brother could piss away his making cornball biographical movies about major-league baseball stars, Oliver was not about to balk at financing so worthy a project as this.

"Damn good chance of it," Winston replied. "I mean, these clowns really *need* us. They practically lost their shirts on Pearl Harbor."

July 28.

Midnight. Latitude: 30°6'N. Longitude: 22°12'W. Course: 015. Speed: 6 knots. Wind: 4 on the Beaufort. Heading north across the Cape Verde Abyssal Plain, the Canaries to starboard, the Azores dead ahead, Ursa Minor directly above.

This afternoon, in preparation for the blood transfer, we tried piercing His right carotid artery with a series of interconnected chicksans—"the world's biggest hypodermic needle," as Crock O'Connor put it. A disaster. Ten feet below the epidermis, He becomes hard as iron. Easier to rupture a football with a banana.

Assuming there's no mutiny in the meantime, we'll try again tomorrow.

You think I'm kidding about a mutiny, Popeye? I'm not.

Something strange is happening aboard the *Carpco Valparaíso.* Every time Bud Ramsey organizes a poker game, one of the players cheats and the whole affair turns into a bloody brawl. Graffiti's been appearing on the bulkheads faster than I can order it sandblasted away: JESUS IS COMING IN HIS PANTS, and worse.

(I'm not a religious man, but I won't have that kind of crap on my ship.) The deckies are constantly smoking near the cargo bays, thus breaking the first rule of oil-tanker safety.

Marbles Rafferty informs me that not an hour goes by without somebody pounding on his door to report a theft. Wallets, cameras, radios, knives.

I told our bos'n, Eddie Wheatstone, he'd either learn to hold his liquor or I'd clap him in irons. So this morning, what does the idiot do? Gets roaring drunk and smashes up the rec-room pinball machine, thereby obliging me to jam his ass in the brig.

Able Seaman Karl Jaworski insisted he gave Isabel Bostwick "nothing but a friendly good-night kiss." Then I talked to the woman, a wiper, and she showed me her cuts and bruises, and after that two others came forward, An-mei Jong and Juanita Torres, with similar marks and similar complaints about Jaworski. I stuck him in the cell next to Wheatstone.

Until 48 hours ago, nobody had ever died on a vessel under my command.

Leo Zook. An AB. Poor bastard caught a lethal dose of hydrocarbon gas while cleaning out number 2 center tank. Now here's the really troubling part. The hose of his Dragen rig was cut to pieces, and when Rafferty arrived on the scene, Zook's mucking partner—Neil Weisinger, that nervy kid who manned the helm during Beatrice—was crouching beside the body holding a Swiss Army knife.

Whenever I stand outside Weisinger's cell and ask him to tell what happened, he just laughs.

"The corpse is taking hold," is how Ockham explains our situation. "Not the corpse per se, the *idea* of the corpse—that's our great enemy, that's the source of this disorder. In the old days," says the padre, "whether you were a believer, a nonbeliever, or a confused agnostic, at some level, conscious or unconscious, you felt God was watching you, and the intuition kept you in check. Now a whole new era is upon us."

"New era?" I say.

"Anno Postdomini One," he says.

The Idea of the Corpse. Anno Postdomini One. Sometimes I think Ockham's losing it, sometimes I think he's dead right. I hate locking up my own crew, especially with His carotid artery still unbreached and the sharks running so thick, but what other choice do I have? I fear that we're a plague ship, Popeye. Our cargo's gotten inside us, sporing and spawning, and I'm no longer certain who's towing whom.

A profound sense of regret fell upon Thomas Ockham as, dressed in his Fermilab sweatshirt and Levi Strauss jeans, he descended the narrow ladder to the *Valparaíso*'s makeshift brig. This, he decided, is how he should have spent his life—collar off, moving among the rejected and the jailed, siding with the world's outcasts. Jesus hadn't wasted His time worrying about superstrings or some eternally elusive TOE. The Master had gone where needed.

Lower than the pump room, lower even than the engine flat, the cells were strung along an obscure starboard passageway crowded with shielded cables and perspiring pipes. Thomas advanced at a crouch. The three prisoners were invisible, locked behind riveted steel doors improvised from boiler plates. Slowly, haltingly, the priest moved down the row, past the vandal Wheatstone and the lecher Jaworski, pausing before the case he found most disturbing, Able Seaman Neil Weisinger.

Twenty-four hours earlier, Thomas had contacted Rome. "In your opinion, does our current ethical disarray trace to some palpable force generated by the process of divine decay," ran his fax's final sentence, "or to some subjective psychological effect spawned by theothanatopsis, that is, to the Idea of the Corpse?"

To which Tullio Di Luca had replied, "How much travel time do you estimate will be lost to this development?"

Outside the cell, Big Joe Spicer sat on an aluminum folding chair, a flare pistol strapped menacingly to his shoulder and a *Playboy* centerfold lying open on his lap.

"Hello, Joe. I'm here to see Weisinger."

Spicer scowled. "Why?"

"A troubled soul."

"Nah, he's happy as a clam at high tide." The second mate jabbed a dull brass skeleton key into the lock, twisting it suddenly like a race-car driver starting his engine. "Listen. The kid makes any threatening gestures"—he patted the flare pistol—"you let out a holler, and I'll come set his face on fire."

"I don't see you at Mass anymore."

"It's like fucking, Father. You gotta be up for it."

Stepping inside the cell, Thomas nearly gagged on the smell, a noxious brew of sweat, urine, and chemically treated feces. Naked to the waist, Weisinger lay atop his bunk, staring upward like a victim of premature burial contemplating the lid of his coffin.

"Hello, Neil."

The kid rolled over. His eyes were the dull matted gray of expired light bulbs. "Whaddya want?"

"To talk."

"About what?"

"About what happened in number two center tank."

"You got any cigarettes?" asked Weisinger.

"Didn't know you were a smoker," said Thomas.

"I'm not. You got any?"

"No."

"Sure could use a cigarette. A Jew-hater died."

"Zook hated Jews?"

"He thinks we murdered Jesus. God. One of those people. What day is this, anyway? You lose all sense of time down here."

"Wednesday, July twenty-ninth, noon. Did you kill him?"

"God? Nope. Zook? Wanted to." Weisinger climbed off his bunk and, staggering to the bulkhead, knelt beside his cistern, a battered copper kettle filled with water the color of Abbaye de Scourmont ale. "Ever known a moment of pure, white-hot clarity, Father Tom? Ever stood over a suffocating man with a Swiss Army knife clutched in your fist? It clears all the cobwebs out of your brain."

"You cut Zook's hose?"

"Of course I cut his hose." The kid splashed his doughy chest with handfuls of dirty water. "But maybe he was already dead, ever think of *that*?"

"Was he?" asked Thomas.

"What difference would it make?"

"Big difference."

"Not these days. The cat's away, Tommy. No eyes on us. The Tablets of the Law: *fizz, fizz*, gone, like two Alka Seltzers dissolving in a glass of water. Be honest, don't *you* feel it too? Don't you find yourself dreaming of your friend Miriam and her world-class tits?"

"I won't pretend things haven't gotten confusing around here." Thomas gritted his teeth so hard a tingling arose in his right middle ear. His musings concerning Sister Miriam had indeed been intense of late, including the features specified by Weisinger. He'd even, heaven help him, given them names. "I'll admit the Idea of the Corpse threatens this ship." Wendy and Wanda. "I'll admit we're in the throes of Anno Postdomini One."

"*Fizz, fizz*—I can think any damn thought I want. I can think about picking up a Black and Decker needle gun and drilling my Aunt Sarah's eyes out. I'm free, Tommy."

"You're in the brig."

Weisinger dipped a Carpco coffee mug into the cistern and, raising the water to his lips, drank. "You wanna know why I scare you?"

"You don't scare me." The kid terrified Thomas.

"I scare you because you look at me and you see that *anybody* here on the *Val* could find the freedom I've got. Joe Spicer out there could find it. Rafferty could find it. Sure you don't have a cigarette?"

"Sorry." Thomas sidled toward the door and paused, transfixed by the steel rivets; they were pathological and obscene, boils on the back of some leprous robot. Maybe he wasn't cut out for this sort of work. Maybe he'd better stick with quantum mechanics and his meditations on why God died. He looked at Weisinger and said, "Does it help, talking with me like this?"

"O'Connor could find it."

"Does it help?"

"Haycox could find it."

"Anytime you get the urge to talk, just have Spicer send for me."

"Captain Van Horne could find it."

"I really want to help you," said the priest, rushing blindly out of the cell.

"Even you could find it, Tommy," the kid called after him. "Even you!"

As the shabby and foul-smelling taxi pulled up to 625 West Forty-second Street, Oliver realized they were only a block away from Playwrights Horizons, the theater where his personal favorite among Cassie's plays, *Runkleberg*, had premiered on a double bill with his least favorite, *God Without Tears*. Lord, what a sexy genius she was. For her he would do anything. For Cassandra he would rob a bank, walk on burning coals, blow God to Kingdom Come.

Viewed from the sidewalk, the New York offices of Pembroke and Flume's World War Two Reenactment Society looked like just another Manhattan storefront, indistinguishable from a dozen such establishments occupying the civilized side of Eighth Avenue, that asphalt DMZ beyond which the sex shops and peep shows had not yet advanced. The instant the three atheists entered, however, a curious displacement occurred. Stumbling into the dark foyer, attaché case swinging at his side, Oliver felt as if he'd tumbled through time and landed in the private chambers of a nineteenth-century railroad magnate. A Persian rug absorbed his footfalls. A full-length, gilt-edged mirror rose before him, flanked by luminous cut-glass globes straight from the age of gaslight. A massive grandfather clock announced the hour, four P.M., tolling with such languor as to suggest its true purpose lay not in keeping time but in exhorting people to slow down and savor life.

They were met by a tall, swan-necked woman in a Mary Astor fedora and a sky blue business suit with padded shoulders, and while she was obviously too young to be Pembroke and Flume's mother, she treated the atheists less like clients than like a gang of neighborhood boys who'd come over to play with her own children. "I'm Eleanor," she said, leading them into a small paneled office, blessedly air-conditioned. Posters decorated the walls. PEMBROKE AND FLUME PRESENT *BATTLE OF THE BULGE* (the four *T*s formed by the muzzles of tank cannons) . . . PEMBROKE AND FLUME PRESENT *ATTACK ON TOBRUK* (cut into the battlements of a fortified harbor) . . . PEMBROKE AND FLUME PRESENT *FIGHT FOR IWO JIMA* (written in blood on a sand dune). "I'll bet you fellas would like something cold and wet." Eleanor ambled over to an early-forties Frigidaire icebox and opened the door to reveal a slew of classic labels: Ruppert, Rheingold, Ballantine, Pabst Blue Ribbon. "New beer in old bottles," she explained. "Budweiser, in fact, from the bodega around the corner."

"I'll take a Rheingold," said Oliver.

"Pabst for me," said Barclay.

"Ah, the pseudo-choices of late capitalism," said Winston. "Make mine a Ballantine."

"Sidney and Albert are in the back parlor, listening to their favorite program." Eleanor removed the beers, popping the caps with a hand-painted Jimmy Durante opener. "Second door on the left."

As Oliver entered the parlor in question—a dark, snug sanc-tum decorated with pinup photos of Esther Williams and Betty Grable—a high, attenuated male voice greeted him: ". . . where they discovered that Dr. Seybold had perfected his cosmo-tomic energizer. Listen now as Jack and Billy investigate that lonely stone house known as the Devil's Castle."

Two pale young men sat on opposite ends of a green velvet sofa, holding Rupperts and leaning toward a Chippendale coffee table on which rested an antique cathedral radio, its output ev-idently being supplied by the adjacent audiocassette player. No-ticing their visitors, one man slipped a cigarette from a yellowing pack of Chesterfields while the other stood up, bowed politely, and shook Barclay's hand.

On the radio, a teenaged boy said, "Great whales and little fishes, Jack! Can you imagine some foreign nation having all that electrical energy for nothing? We'll be reduced to a pauper country!"

Barclay made the introductions. Because the moniker "Pem-broke and Flume" seemed to suggest a cinematic comedy team whose trademarks included the physical disparity between its members—Abbott and Costello, Laurel and Hardy—Oliver was taken aback by the impresarios' similarity to each other. They could have been brothers, or even fraternal twins, a notion un-derscored by the matching red-and-black-striped zoot suits hang-ing from their elongated frames: Giacometti bodies, Oliver, the artist, decided. Both men had the same blue eyes, gold fillings, and blond pomaded hair, and it was only through concentrated effort that he distinguished Sidney Pembroke's open, smiling countenance from the more austere, vaguely sinister visage of Albert Flume.

"I see Eleanor found you some brews," said Pembroke, ejecting the cassette. "Good, good."

"What were you listening to?" asked Winston.

Jack Armstrong, the All-American Boy."

"Never heard of it."

"Really?" said Flume with a mixture of disbelief and disdain. "You're not serious."

Whereupon the partners threw their arms across each other's shoulders and sang.

> *Wave the flag for Hudson High, boys,*
> *Show them how we stand!*
> *Ever shall our team be champions,*
> *Known throughout the land!*

"There are better programs, of course," said Flume, lighting his cigarette with a silver-plated Zippo. *"The Green Hornet:* 'He hunts the biggest game of all—the public enemies who try to destroy our America!'"

"And *Inner Sanctum*, if you've got really strong nerves," said Pembroke.

Flume faced Oliver squarely, taking a long drag on his Chesterfield. "I'm told your organization wishes to purchase our services."

"I was quoted a figure approaching fifteen million."

"Were you, now?" said Flume cryptically. Obviously the dominant partner.

"Could you tell us more about the target?" asked Pembroke eagerly. "We don't have a clear picture yet."

Oliver's blood froze. Here it was, the moment when he must explain why obliterating a seven-million-ton corpse that didn't belong to any of them was a necessary course of action. Opening his attaché case, he removed an 8 × 10 color photo and balanced it atop the radio cabinet.

"As you know," he began, "the Japanese have always been self-conscious about their height."

"The Japs?" said Flume, looking perplexed. "Indeed."

So far, so good. "According to the Freudian interpretation of World War Two, they sought to expand horizontally in compensation for their genetic inability to expand vertically. As scholars of that particular conflict, you're undoubtedly familiar with this theory."

"Oh, yes," said Pembroke, even though Oliver had invented it the previous Tuesday.

"Well, gentlemen, the stark fact is that, at the beginning of this year, a team of Japanese scientists over in Scotland found a way to expand vertically. By exploiting the latest breakthroughs in genetic engineering, they've grown the Asian of the future—the gigantic humanoid creature whose prototype you see in this picture. You with me?"

"Sounds like a rejected *Green Hornet* script," said Flume, coiling the gold chain of his zoot suit around his index finger.

"They call it Project Golem," said Barclay.

"Most golems are Jewish," said Winston. "This one's Japanese."

"The Japs are in *Scotland*?" said Pembroke.

"The Japs are everywhere," admonished Flume.

"Thus far they've failed to endow their golem with life," said Winston, "but if they ever *do*—well, you can imagine the danger such a megaspecies would pose for the environment, not to mention the free enterprise system."

"Jack Armstrong would shit his knickers," said Barclay.

"Luckily, the coming weeks afford us a perfect opportunity to stop Project Golem in its tracks," said Oliver. "Ever since the hot weather hit, the scientists have been looking for a way to freeze the prototype before it putrefies. Then, last Wednesday, they resolved to hook it up to the supertanker *Valparaíso* and tow it above the Arctic Circle."

"*Valparaíso*—that's not a Jap name," said Pembroke.

"Neither is 'Rockefeller Center,'" said Winston.

"I don't understand why private enterprise must redress this matter," said Flume. "The United States of America boasts the largest navy in the world. Much larger than Sid's and mine."

"Yeah, but you can't use the American Navy without Congressional approval," said Barclay.

"The CIA?"

"Good people, but we'd never mobilize 'em in time," said Oliver.

"This is clearly a job for concerned businessmen like ourselves," said Winston. "Vigilante capitalism, eh?"

"I'm not a mystical sort of fella," said Barclay, "but I feel it's no accident your ship is named *Enterprise*."

Oliver took a hearty swallow of beer. "So, what do you think?"

Pembroke shot his partner a pained glance. "What do we think, Alby?"

Flume flicked his cigarette ashes into a pewter tray shaped like Dumbo the Flying Elephant. "We think it sounds pretty fishy."

"Fishy?" said Oliver, peeling the label off his Rheingold bottle.

"Fishy as the hold of a Portuguese trawler."

"Oh?"

"We think this thing you want out of the way might be a Jap golem, and then again it might not be." Flume took a drag, blew a smoke ring. "We also think this: money talks. You mentioned fifteen million. That's a good start. A darn good start."

"It's more than a *start*," grunted Oliver.

"Indeed. The thing is . . ."

"All right—sixteen."

"The thing is, you're not asking us to do a normal reenactment. In some ways, this is the real McCoy." Flume blew two rings this time, one inside the other. "Wars have a way of going over budget."

"A single strike might not be enough to remove the target," Pembroke elaborated. "The planes might have to return to *Enterprise* and rearm."

"Final offer," said Oliver. "This is it. Tops. Ready? Seventeen million dollars. For that kind of money, you could stage a goddamn musical of my eighth-grade civics text on the back of the moon and keep it running for ten years."

Had the impresarios been dogs, Oliver decided, their ears would have shot straight up and stayed there.

"Overlord," said Flume in a hushed and reverent voice.

"What?" said Oliver.

"Operation Overlord. An old dream of ours."

"You know—Normandy," said an equally respectful Pembroke.

"D-Day," said Flume. "I mean, if you're serious about seventeen million dollars, really serious, no strings attached, then, with a certain amount of luck—like maybe the job turns out to be a cakewalk, you know, a one-strike affair—well, we'd probably have enough left over for a D-Day. All of it. The diversionary bombings, the amphibious landing, the sweep through France. A risky venture, sure, but I predict it'll turn a profit, don't you, Sid?"

"Enough to finance Stalingrad, I should imagine," said Pembroke.

"Or Arnhem, eh?" said Flume. "Forty thousand Allied paratroopers dropping out of the sky like sleet."

"Or maybe even Hiroshima," said Pembroke.

"No," said Flume firmly.

"No?"

"No."

"Poor taste?"

"Execrable."

"World War Two," sighed Pembroke. "We'll never see its like again."

"Let's get one thing straight," said Oliver. "You can't just damage the golem—it's got to vanish without a trace."

"Korea was a crummy stalemate," Pembroke persisted.

"We expect you to blast the tow chains apart," said Oliver, "and send the sucker straight into the Mohns Trench."

"Vietnam had potential," said Flume, "but then the hippies got their hands on it."

"Don't even *talk* to us about Operation Desert Storm," said Pembroke.

"A lousy video game," said Flume.

"A goddamn mini-series," said Pembroke.

"Do you understand me?" said Oliver. "The *Valparaíso's* cargo must disappear."

"No problem," said Flume. "Only we follow U.S. Navy usage 'round here, okay? No 'the' before a ship's name. It's *Valparaíso*, not 'the' *Valparaíso*. *Enterprise*, not 'the' *Enterprise*. Got that?"

Hovering over the photo, Pembroke jabbed his index finger into the carcass's chest. "Why's it grinning like that?"

"If you were that big," said Barclay, "you'd grin too."

"Any reason to suspect we won't get a clear shot at it?" asked Flume. "When Scout Bombing Six sank *Akagi*, Commander McClusky had to put up with all sorts of crap—fighter planes, screening vessels, flak. *Valparaíso* isn't carrying any Bofors guns, is she?"

"Of course not," said Winston.

"No destroyer escort?"

"Nothing like that."

"Oh," said Pembroke, sounding vaguely disappointed. "I think we should use TBD-1 Devastator torpedo planes, don't you, Alby?"

"They'd clearly be the most effective against a target of this sort," said Flume, nodding. "On the other hand . . ." Gripped by a sudden reverie, the impresario closed his eyes.

"On the other hand . . . ?" said Winston.

"On the other hand, it was SBD-2 Dauntless dive bombers that actually blew *Akagi* out of the water."

"So while the Devastators would work the best . . . ," said Pembroke.

"The Dauntlesses would be more historically accurate," said Flume.

"I'd vote for the Devastators," said Oliver.

"A tough call either way. Shall we leave it to the admiral, Sid?"

"Good idea."

Flume stubbed out his cigarette in the Dumbo tray. "Naturally this has to be a hit-and-run operation. I figure if *Enterprise* hunkers down, say, a hundred and fifty miles west of the target, the Nips'll never know where the planes came from."

"The last thing we want is for Japan to be pissed at Alby and me," Pembroke explained. "We're gonna need their full cooperation for Guadalcanal."

"Swing by Shields, McLaughlin, Babcock, and Kaminsky on Wednesday, and they'll give you a rough draft to shoot past your lawyers," said Flume. "It'll probably take a couple weeks to nail down all the details—payment schedules, representations and warranties, the indemnity picture . . ."

"You mean—we've got ourselves a deal?" said Winston eagerly.

"Seventeen million?" said Flume, raising his Ruppert.

"Seventeen million," Oliver confirmed, lifting his Rheingold.

Two vintage beer bottles came together, clanking in the hot Manhattan air.

"You know what I think we should do right now?" said Pembroke. "I think we should bow our heads and pray."

A silken breeze blew across the *Valparaíso*'s stem as Cassie climbed down the ladder and, like Juliet stepping onto her balcony, joined Able Seaman Ralph Mungo in the forward lookout post. The cool air caressed her flesh. Slowly the sweat evaporated from her face. By morning, thank God, they'd be across the thirty-third parallel, the wretched North African summer forever behind them.

Puffing on a Marlboro, Mungo stared out to sea. The waxing moon hung low, fixed in the starry sky like a luminous slice of cantaloupe. Cassie set her flip-top coffee Thermos on the rail, reached into her shorts pocket, and removed the encrypted fax Lianne had intercepted that afternoon up in the radio shack.

Oliver's love letters, with their mawkish poems illustrated by pornographic sketches, had never truly touched Cassie, but these words cut to her core. Decoding them, she'd experienced something primal, the same variety of awe that Darwin, Galileo, and a handful of others must have felt upon realizing they were shaping the course of intellectual history. True, the particulars were troubling: despite her affection for all things theatrical, she did not like placing reason's fate in the hands of any organization that would call itself Pembroke and Flume's World War Two Reenactment Society. (These men did not sound like the saviors of secular humanism; they sounded like a couple of lunatics.) What Cassie found so moving was Oliver's rationality, the fact that he'd correctly interpreted the body as a menace and immediately swung into action. His insistence on security struck her as particularly astute. Intuitively he'd sensed that if the Vatican got wind of an impending attack, they'd either reroute the mission or erect defenses the Reenactment Society could never hope to penetrate. "This will be my only communiqué," he'd written near the end.

Expect air strike at 68°11'N, 2°35'W, 150 miles east of launch point, Jan Mayen Island. In restaging Midway, planes will sever tow chains, breach target, and send our troubles to bottom of Mohns Trench. . . .

Leaning over the rail, she accorded the fax the same treatment she'd inflicted on the blisteringly negative review the *Village Voice* had given her play about Jephthah, the warrior in the Book of Judges who immolated his own daughter by way of keeping a bargain with God. "Authentic satire is to puerile sniggering as a firecracker is to a soda cracker, a distinction to which a young author named Cassie Fowler is evidently oblivious . . ."

Good old Oliver. He'd always stuck by her—hadn't he?— even when she was a struggling playwright and he a leftist ne'er-do-well painting grim urban landscapes while waiting for his trust fund to kick in. There she'd be, sitting in the basement of some Broome Street saloon or Avenue D hockshop, one of those scuzzy roach reserves that had the nerve to call themselves off-Broadway theaters (any farther off, and she'd have been in Queens), watching a disastrous rehearsal of *Runkleberg* or *God Without Tears*, and suddenly Oliver would appear, even if it was three A.M., bringing her black coffee and sweet rolls, telling her she was the Lower East Side Jonathan Swift.

No sooner had Cassie tossed the bits of paper into the Portugal Current than Anthony Van Horne himself descended into the lookout post, dressed in his tattered Mets baseball jacket and John Deere visor cap. A spasm of guilt shot through her. This man had saved her life, and here she was, plotting to abort his mission.

"You're in luck, sailor—I'm taking over your watch," Van Horne told Ralph Mungo. A large purple bruise, frosted with glory grease, spread outward from the old AB's right eye. "That okay with you?"

"Aye-aye, sir." Saluting, grinning, Mungo threw his cigarette butt overboard and scooted up the ladder.

"Stargazing?" the captain asked Cassie.

"Something like that." Raising the Thermos to her lips, she took a big swallow of jamoke. It was the fifth time she'd run into him here. She suspected she was being pursued—a flattering thought, but the last thing she needed just then was her adversary developing a crush on her. "I've decided to rename the constellations." She pointed heavenward. "It's time for a wholly American mythology, don't you think? Look, there's the Myth of the Family. There's Equality. There's One Nation Under God with Liberty and Justice for All."

"You hate our cargo, don't you?"

Cassie nodded. "That's why I hang out here—the farthest I can get from Him without ending up in the water. And what about you, Captain? Do you hate our cargo?"

"I never knew Him." The captain yawned; the reflex took hold of him, rippling through his face and shoulders. "I only know it's good to be at sea again."

"You're exhausted, sir."

"We've been trying to siphon His blood into the tanks—a way to get us moving faster—but His neck won't accept the chicksans." Another elaborate yawn. "The worst of it's . . . I'm not sure what word to use. The *anarchy*, Cassie. Notice that AB's black eye? He got it in a brawl. It's been a week of fistfights, attempted rapes, possibly even a murder. I've had to put three men in the brig."

An odd combination of dread and annoyance crept over Cassie. "Murder? Jesus. Who died?"

"Deckie named Zook—he got gassed in a cargo bay. Ockham says we're in thrall to the corpse. Not the corpse itself, the Idea of the Corpse. With God out of the picture, people have lost their main reason to be moral. They can't help experimenting with sin."

As she always did in the presence of intellectually untenable arguments, Cassie thrust her left hand into her pocket and pinched her inner thigh through the fabric. "Can't help it? Gimme a break, Anthony. The whole thing's an *alibi*. A clever alibi, but an alibi. These sailors of yours—want my opinion? They're seizing on the carcass to rationalize their crimes. God's death is so *convenient*."

"I think it goes deeper than that." Reaching into his baseball jacket, Anthony produced a sheet of beige paper covered with smeary black characters, and for one awful instant Cassie imagined he meant to confront her with a copy of Oliver's communiqué. "Do me a favor, Doc. Read this. It's from my father."

The letter was handwritten on Exxon Shipping stationery: a cramped, feathery scrawl that struck her as oddly feminine.

> *Dear Anthony:*
>
> *You say you want to visit, but that's not a very good idea. Tiffany gets easily flustered by guests, and you probably intend to bring up a lot of old grievances, like the . . .*

"This seems awfully personal."
"Just read it."

> *. . . parrot business. My idea of a relaxing retirement—can you believe it?—includes not having my firstborn dropping by and screaming at me.*
>
> *Don't think I wasn't pleasantly surprised to receive your letter. You're a good sailor, son. Flappable, but good. You deserved to get the* Val *back, though I can't imagine what the Vatican needs with a ULCC.*
>
> *Hauling holy water, are you?*
>
> *Love,*
> *Dad.*

"So, what do you make of it?" asked Anthony.

"Who's Tiffany?"

"My stepmother. Major airhead. What's he telling me?"

A humbling sense of her own parochialism crept over Cassie. So far in her life, the worst burdens she'd had to bear were rotten reviews in the *Voice* and deadhead students in her classes, nothing remotely comparable to a hostile father, an unbreachable neck, or a supertanker crew lapsing into vice. "I'm no psychologist . . . but when he says you have grievances against him, maybe he's really saying he has grievances against you."

"Of *course* he has grievances against me. I dishonored him at Matagorda Bay. I dragged the family name through an oil slick."

"What's this 'parrot business'?"

Anthony snorted, grimaced, and put on his mirrorshades.

"For my tenth birthday, Dad brought back a scarlet macaw from Guatemala."

"Order *Psittaciformes*. Family *Psittacidae*."

"Yeah. Beautiful bird. She arrived speaking Spanish. 'Vaya con Dios.' '¿Qué pasa?' I tried teaching her 'See you later, alligator,' but it didn't stick. I named her Rainbow. So, four months later, what does Dad do? He decides Rainbow's costing us too much in parrot food and vet bills, and she's noisy besides, messy too, so he drives me and the bird across town to a pet store, and he goes up to the counter, and he says, 'If anybody comes in and wants this miserable beast, I'll split the take with you, fifty-fifty.' "

"How mean."

"There's a pattern here, actually. I'm eleven—okay?—and the thing I most want for Christmas is a Revell plastic model kit of the USS *Constitution*, one to the forty-second scale, two hundred and thirty separate pieces, real canvas for the sails. Dad buys me the kit all right, but he won't let me put it together. He says I'll screw it up."

"So he does it himself?"

"Yeah, and here's the weird part. He gets some glass blower in Wilmington to seal up my ship in a big blue water-cooler bottle. So I can't touch it, right? I can't hold the *Constitution* or play with it. It isn't really mine." Anthony took back the fax, wadded it up, and stuffed the ball in his jacket. "The problem is that I *need* the bastard."

"No, you don't."

"He's the one who can wash the oil away."

"Matagorda Bay?"

"Yeah. I won't be free till Dad looks right at me and says, 'Good job, Anthony. You laid His bones to rest.'"

"Oh, come on."

"I got it straight from Raphael's lips."

"I don't care whose lips you got it from." A completely irrational theory, Cassie decided as she drained the last of her jamoke. "It doesn't add up." The breeze turned nasty, clawing at her cheeks, biting her fingers. She pulled the zipper tab of Lianne's windbreaker as high as it would go. "I need some of Follingsbee's hot cocoa."

The captain cocked his head. Aries lay reflected in both lenses of his mirrorshades. "Birds fly through my dreams."

"Birds? Parrots, you mean?"

"Egrets, herons, ibises—dripping oil. I take showers, but it doesn't help. Only my father . . . you understand?"

"No. I don't. But even if I *did* . . . well, what if your dad regards absolution as just another present? What if he gives you a clear conscience and then—bang—he takes *that* away too?"

"He wouldn't."

"The man who sent you that fax"—Cassie indicated the bulge in Anthony's jacket—"is not a man you can trust." She started up the ladder, retreating not so much from the cold as from this confused, frightening, peculiarly alluring man, this captain who dreamed of oiled egrets. "Know something, sir? When we get back to New York, I'm going to buy you a scarlet macaw."

"I'd like that, Doc."

"Know something else?" She paused on the topmost rung. "It's perfectly okay to hate our cargo. It's really quite okay."

August 3.

On this day in 1924, my *Mariner's Pocket Companion* notes, "Joseph Conrad, author of *Lord Jim, Typhoon*, and other classics of the sea, died in Bishopsbourne, England."

I'll start with the good news. For reasons best known to themselves, the predators have thrown in the towel. When it comes to the vultures and snakes, my guess is that we've sailed too far beyond their territories. As for the sharks—well, who knows what goes on in those antique minds?

This morning I had Rafferty gather up all the antipredator matériel, remove the shells and charges, and secure the empty weapons in the fo'c'sle hold. We no longer need the stuff, and in the present anarchic atmosphere I can easily imagine the deckies making murderous use of a harpoon gun or a bazooka.

Once again we tried screwing chicksans into His right carotid artery, and once again we failed, but that's not the really bad news.

The fights and thefts continue, but that's not the really bad news either.

The really bad news is the weather.

Dead reckoning places us 50 miles south of the Azores. It's hard to know for sure, because the Marisat signals aren't getting through, and we can't see more than 20 yards in any direction. Fog I can deal with, but this is something else, a stew so thick it's blinded both our radars. Forget the sextants.

An hour ago I explained our options to Ockham. Either we break radio silence and ask the Portuguese Coast Guard where the hell we are, or we slow to a crawl to avoid ramming into the Azores.

"You mean like four knots?"

"I mean like three knots."

"At that speed, we won't beat the deadline," noted the padre.

"Correct."

"His neurons will die."

"Yeah, if He's got any left."

"What's your preference?" Ockham wanted to know.

"Raphael never mentioned neurons," I replied.

"Neither did Gabriel. You want us to slow down?"

"No, I want us to save His brain."

"So do I, Anthony. So do I."

At 1355 we broke radio silence. In our hearts we both knew it wouldn't work. The damn fog devoured everything we put out: shortwave broadcasts, CB signals, fax transmissions.

Got to go, Popeye. Got to drop us back to 10 rpm's. My present migraine is the worst ever, despite generous applications of glory grease. It's like my brain is dying, cell by cell by cell, shutting down along with His.

Again, the music of Strauss—*Salomé* this time, a hundred operatic voices filling the Jeep Wrangler's cab as Thomas drove into the soggy depths of the navel. The route was dangerous, an ever-narrowing gyre cloaked in glutinous fog, but the Wrangler cleaved to the path, carrying Jesuit and Carmelite through the omphalogical terrain like a burro bearing tourists into the Grand Canyon.

The trip, he would admit, was an act of desperation, a last-ditch effort to discredit the body in question, for only by invalidating the corpse per se could he hope to invalidate the Idea of the Corpse and thus—perhaps—end the plague now raging aboard the *Valparaíso*. At first blush, of course, their cargo's navel held no more teleological meaning than its warts ("Let there be a bellybutton," and there was a bellybutton), and yet something about this particular feature, with its clear implications of a previous generation, had aroused in Thomas an uncharacteristic optimism. Did a navel not herald a Creator's Creator? Did it not bespeak a God before God?

Within minutes they were at the bottom, a half-acre of flesh mottled with chunks of coral, swatches of algae, and an occasional dead crab. Thomas rotated the ignition key, shutting off the engine along with *Salomé*. He inhaled. The fog filled his lungs like steam rising from a Mesozoic swamp. In a move the priest found perplexing, Sister Miriam leaned over and aggressively rotated the ignition key, restoring *Salomé* to life.

He unhooked his seat belt, climbed out of the cab, and made his way across the damp, briny basin. Dropping to his knees, he ran his palm along the epidermis, searching for some clue that an umbilicus had once towered, sequoialike, from this spot—evidence of a proto-Deity, sign of a pre-Creator, proof of an unimaginable placenta floating through the Milky Way like an emission nebula.

Nothing. Zero. Not a nub.

He'd expected as much. And yet he persisted, massaging the terrain as if attempting some eschatological variety of cardiopulmonary resuscitation.

"Any luck?"

Until that moment, he hadn't realized Miriam was beside him.

Or naked.

What astonished him was how detailed she was, how wonderfully particularized. The blue veins spidering across her breasts, the wiry twists and turns of her pubic hairs, the cyclopean gaze of her navel, the tampon string dangling between her legs like a fuse. Her pimples. Her freckles. Her birthmarks, pores, and scabs. This wasn't Miss November. This was a woman.

So Weisinger had called it right. Anyone, even Miriam, could find the freedom that travels in God's wake. "No luck," Thomas replied nervously, lifting his palm from the cavity's floor. A loud *glunk* escaped his throat. "I don't f-feel a thing."

"What we're really talking about, of course," said Miriam, sucking in a deep breath, "is Gnosticism." Her clothes—dungarees, khaki work shirt, underwear, all of it—lay puddled at her feet. Stepping uncertainly forward, she called to mind Botticelli's Venus emerging from her seashell, a humanoid and endlessly desirable scallop.

"True." Sweat circled Thomas's neck. He popped open his saturated collar. "We're praying our cargo will t-turn out to be the D-Demiurge," he continued, unbuttoning his black shirt.

"We're hoping it's not God at all."

"Except Gnosticism's a heresy," the priest noted, climbing out of his Levi's. "No, worse than a heresy: it's *depressing*. It reduces us to st-stifled spirits trapped in evil flesh."

A furious drumming poured from the Wrangler's speakers.

"The Dance of the Seven Veils," Miriam explained nervously, wiggling her epic hips. Wendy and Wanda were on the move, flouncing in hypnotic oscillations. "The trumpets and trombones speak up next, and then it becomes a waltz. Have you ever waltzed naked in God's navel, Tom?"

The priest removed his shirt and Jockey shorts. "Never."

Trumpets shrieked, trombones bleated, a lone tuba blared. At first Thomas simply watched, wearing nothing but his bifocals. He imagined he was Herod Antipas, beholding the impossibly sensual dance that, in a paroxysm of pedophilia, he'd commissioned from his nubile stepdaughter, Salomé, never guessing that her price would be John the Baptist's head. And Miriam's movements were indeed sensual—not lewd, not lascivious, but sensual, like the Song of Solomon, or Bathsheba's ablutions, or the Magdalene washing the Lord's dusty feet.

Taking his friend's hand, he encircled her fine, substantive waist. They waltzed: awkwardly at first, clownishly, in fact, but then some buried engram took over, some latent feeling for rhythm and form, and he guided her across the rubbery floor with bold, sweeping strides. The strange fog hung everywhere, blankets of mist wrapping their spinning bodies in a thick, delicious warmth. Something stirred in his mothballed loins. No erection followed. No lust consumed him. He was glad. This dance went deeper than loins, well beyond lust, back to some ancient, presexual existence they shared with sponges and amoebas.

"Nobody's watching," noted Miriam.

Their bodies pressed tightly together, like hands clasped in prayer. "We're alone," Thomas corroborated. So true, so pathetically true; they were orphans in Anno Postdomini One, beyond good and evil. It was like living inside a naughty joke. *How much fun do priests have? Nun.* He felt soiled, wicked, damned, ecstatic.

A tremor caressed their bare feet.

"The High Court's adjourned," said Miriam.

A second tremor, twice the intensity of the first.

"The bench has been eaten by worms."

A fearsome quaking shook the navel.

They separated, throwing their arms out for balance. Confusion swept through Thomas. Resurrection? Their dancing was so sinful it had roused God from His coma?

"What's happening?" gasped Miriam.

Typhoon? Tidal wave? "I don't know. But I think this is the wrong place to be right now."

They dressed hurriedly and incompletely, Thomas pausing briefly to observe an act he'd never seen before, the odd yogic posture by which a woman snaps on her brassiere. The flesh beneath their feet jiggled like a field of aspic. Explosions rattled the air. Spray splashed into the gorge. It seemed as if the entire Corpus Dei were aquiver, seized by some posthumous epileptic fit.

Shoes and socks in hand, they dashed back to the Wrangler, climbed inside, and, silencing *Salomé*, zoomed away.

"Whirlpool?" asked Miriam.

"Possibly."

"Waterspout?"

"Could be."

Gunning the engine, Thomas guided the Wrangler to the surface of the belly and, heedless of the blinding fog, started along the midriff. Veering east, he stopped. The *Juan Fernández*, thank heaven, was where they'd left her, tied to the rubber wharf Rafferty had moored to the starboard armpit shortly before the tow began. Abandoning the Wrangler, they climbed down the Jacob's ladder, crawled on hands and knees across the rolling pier, and vaulted into the launch.

"How do you feel?" Thomas asked, settling behind the steering wheel.

"Guilty." Miriam cast off. "We sinned, didn't we? We gazed upon each other's nakedness."

"We sinned," he agreed, twisting the ignition key. The engine turned over and held. "You're beautiful, Miriam."

"So are you."

He brought the *Juan Fernández* about and, opening the throttle all the way, piloted her across the submerged elbow. The passage along the cheek was choppy and treacherous, and it took them nearly fifteen minutes to gain open water. Dead ahead lay the supertanker, deckhouse shrouded in fog, hull pitching and rocking as if making passionate love to the sea.

"And how does guilt feel?" asked Thomas, steering the launch along a course defined by the starboard tow chain.

"Bad," she replied.

"Bad," he agreed.

"Guilt does not feel as bad," she added, after some thought, "as dancing feels good."

At which juncture—defying logic, denying gravity, snubbing

Newtonian physics—the *Valparaíso* began to rise. Locking the steering wheel with his elbows, Thomas tore off his bifocals and wiped the condensation with his sleeve. He repositioned them. Yes, it was truly happening, an entire ULCC moving toward heaven, great sheets of seawater spilling from her hull and keel. He groaned. In the new, normless universe, what arcane force was struggling to be born? What had God's death wrought?

Now came the answer. An island: a six-mile sprawl of ragged coves and crimson cliffs pushing free of the Gibraltar Sea like a breaching whale, carrying the tanker with it. Huge waves poured from the ascending mass, spewing foam and flotsam as, flowing south, they broke against the divine cranium.

"Oh, hell," said Miriam. "Oh, bloody, bloody hell."

A sudden *crack* echoed across the Portugal Current, like the hatching of some gigantic egg: God's earbones snapping, Thomas realized, a sound no human being had ever heard before.

When at last the newborn island halted—leaving the *Valparaíso* beached, the corpse adrift, and every chart of the Gibraltar Sea obsolete—Miriam took the priest's knobby, trembling hand. "Jesus, Tom, we *lost* Him."

"We lost Him," he agreed.

"We found Him, and now we've lost Him. What does it mean? Is it our fault?"

"*Our* fault? I hardly think so."

"But we sinned," said the nun.

"Not on *this* scale," he said, pointing toward the errant land mass.

Whereupon Thomas Wickliff Ockham, S.J., his God gone, his self-respect shattered, threw himself against the steering wheel and wept.

Island

Anthony couldn't stop laughing. Ever since they'd steamed out of New York Harbor, he realized, the universe had been casting about for some particularly cruel and elaborate joke to play on him, and now it had finally found one. Thrust an absurd little island out of the Gibraltar Sea. Beach Van Horne's ship. Steal his cargo.

Hilarious.

The bridge was buzzing. Upon deducing that the *Val* was aground, nearly everyone above the rank of AB had instinctively gone looking for his captain, demanding that he explain this bizarre upwelling, though the tanker's master was as mystified as his crew. Now they all stood amid the control consoles and radar scopes—officers, engineers, chief steward, pumpman—fidgeting like a congregation of millennialists awaiting the end of the world. Anthony could feel their hostility. He sensed their disgust. He knew what they were thinking. Never again, each mariner was promising himself. Never again shall I sail with Anthony Van Horne.

"I'm assumin' I should I kill the engines," said Dolores Haycox, the mate on duty, leaning toward the joysticks.

Until that moment, Anthony hadn't realized the propellers were still moving, spinning ineffectually in space. "Kill 'em," he said, snickering.

"No need to hold the wheel, right?" asked James Echohawk, the AB at the helm.

"Right," said the captain, giggling.

"What's so fuckin' funny?" asked Bud Ramsey.

"You wouldn't get it."

"Try me."

"The universe."

"Huh?"

Choking down his laughter, Anthony grabbed the PA mike. "Now hear this! Now hear this! As you can see, sailors, we're in quite a jam!" His amplified words boomed across the weather deck and vanished into the mist-shrouded dunes beyond. "It'll take at least three days, maybe four, to dig ourselves out of here, after which we'll find the body, reconnect"—he struggled to believe himself—"and get this show on the road again!"

The immediate problem, he realized, was not freeing the *Val* but simply climbing down and inspecting the damage. They were imprisoned in their own ship, cut off like the plastic *Constitution* his father had sealed up in the water-cooler bottle. On all sides, the tanker's stranded hull plunged toward the wet sands, a drop no mere gangway or Jacob's ladder could begin to plumb.

"Hey, any of you guys ever hear of such a thing?" moaned Charlie Horrocks. "An island comin' outta nowhere like this, any of you ever even *hear* of it?"

"Not me," said Bud Ramsey.

"It's unprecedented," said Big Joe Spicer. "Even on a weird-ass voyage like this, it's totally unprecedented."

"Maybe Father Thomas could give us an explanation," said Lianne Bliss. "He's a genius, right? Where's Father Thomas?"

"Any more shit happens on this trip," said Sam Follingsbee, "I'm gonna go outta my mind."

"You *really* think we'll be able to dig ourselves free?" asked Crock O'Connor, rubbing the ancient steam burn that covered his brow.

Good question, Anthony decided. "Of course I do." The captain ran his index finger along the apex of his broken nose. "Faith can move mountains, and so can the United States Merchant Marine."

"Want my opinion?" asked Marbles Rafferty. "Our only hope is for this damn thing to go sliding back down where it came from, suddenly, in a great big *whoosh*, exactly the way it arrived."

"Yeah? Well, I wouldn't count on *that*," said Dolores Haycox. "If you ask me, it's here to stay, and we are too, stuck on our own private paradise."

"Private paradise," Anthony repeated. "Then we've got the right to name it." He curled his palm around Echohawk's beefy arm. "The next entry in the quartermaster's log goes like this: 'At 1645 hours, the *Valparaíso* ran aground on Van Horne Island.'"

"How modest of you," said Rafferty.

"I'm not naming it after *me*. My father spent his entire life trying to find an uncharted island. A major asshole, dear old Dad, but he deserves this."

Anthony lifted his angel feather from the breast pocket of his pea jacket and scratched his itching forehead with the quill. *Chains*, he thought. Yes. Chains. The tow chains were impossibly fat, but an anchor lead would make a perfect ladder. Flipping on the intercom, he raised the engine flat and instructed Lou Chickering to send somebody forward with instructions to drop the port kedge.

"Crock told me we're high and dry," Chickering protested. "Fetched up on an atoll, right?"

"Something like that."

" 'Fraid we'll drift?"

"Just lower the goddamn anchor, Lou."

Rafferty inserted a Pall Mall between his lips. "If you like, Captain, I'd be happy to head up an exploration party."

It was the logical next step, but Anthony knew that he himself must be the first man to take the measure of his father's world. "Thanks, Marbles, but I'm reserving that particular job for yours truly. It's a personal matter. Expect me back late tonight."

"Maintain present course?" asked the chief mate, deadpan.

"Maintain present course," said Anthony without batting an eye.

He rode the elevator to level three, visiting first his cabin and then the main galley as he provisioned himself for the conquest of Van Horne Island: food, water, compass, flashlight, bottle of Monte Alban mescal complete with pickled Oaxacan worm. Descending to the weather deck, he pedaled O'Connor's trail bike along the catwalk, entered the fo'c'sle, and crawled into the damp, sewery reaches of the hawsepipe.

The climb down the anchor chain was treacherous and painful—the links were slippery, the coarse metal scraped his palms—but within fifteen minutes Anthony stood on the island's spongy surface.

Scaly and gritty, red as claret, the stuff composing the surrounding dunes looked more like flecks of rust than like the brown-sugar sands one normally encountered along the 35th parallel. The deadness of the place unnerved him. It seemed not so much an island in the Gibraltar Sea as a meteor hewn from the crust of some singularly inert and sterile planet.

The *Val*'s wounds were ugly and deep. The lower half of her rudder was bent about ten degrees. Her keel was serrated like a carving knife. Her port shaft had sprung loose, and the propeller itself stood upright in a dune like the blades of a sinking windmill. Heavy damage, no question, but not so heavy that a smart skipper couldn't compensate through some astute maneuvers and a few tricks of the trade. It all came down to the hull, the ship's one truly vital organ. Anthony stared at the barnacle-encrusted plates; he rubbed them with his fingers, brushed them with his feather. A ragged seam ran for sixty yards along the starboard side like a surgical scar, evidence of her fateful encounter with Bolivar Reef, but the weld looked unscathed—indeed, the entire hull looked whole. Assuming they could in fact manage to dig the tanker loose, she would almost certainly float.

He stepped back. Like the Ark come to rest on Ararat, the tanker sat atop a mountain of sand, mud, coral, stones, and shells. The Vatican flag hung limply on its halyard. The tow chains drooped impotently off the stern, hit the dunes, and trailed away into the sea. Slipping on his mirrorshades, Anthony scanned the cove, hoping their cargo had miraculously drifted into the shallows, but he saw nothing except jagged rocks and clots of fibrous fog.

He drew the compass from his canvas knapsack, oriented himself, and marched north.

The farther Anthony went, the more obvious it became that Van Horne Island had lain beneath a major deep-sea dump site. Ascending from the ocean floor, the island had brought with it the trash of half a continent. This was Italy's garbage can, England's dustbin, Germany's cesspool, France's chamber pot.

Cupping a palm over his mouth and nose, he rushed past a huge mound of chemical waste, hundreds of 55-gallon drums stacked up in a kind of post-industrial Aztec pyramid. A mile beyond lay the remains of over a thousand automobiles, their gutted chassis piled side by side like skeletons flanking the promenade of a charnel house. Next came the appliances: blenders, toasters, refrigerators, ranges, microwaves, dishwashers—all randomly discarded yet collectively forming an oddly coherent setting, a backdrop for some post-theistic sitcom featuring an aging and demented Donna Reed brooding alone in her kitchen, plotting to poison her family.

Dusk descended, stealing the island's warmth and turning its red sands black. Anthony zipped up his jacket, drew the bottle of Monte Alban from his knapsack, and, taking a long, hot swallow, pressed on.

An hour later, he found himself among the gods.

Four, to be exact: four granite idols over fifteen feet high, each commanding a different corner of a muddy flagstone plaza. Anthony gasped. Strange enough that Van Horne Island even existed, much less that the place had once hosted a human community—the Atlantic's answer, perhaps, to that cheerless tribe that had made its home on Easter Island. To the north rose the graven image of a plump imbiber, lifting a goatskin container high above his parted lips and releasing a torrent of wine. To the east a fat-cheeked glutton, his belly the size of a wrecking ball, attempted to ingest an entire live boar in one grand gulp. To the south a goggle-eyed opium eater wolfed down a bouquet of poppies. To the west a sodomy aficionado, possessed of an erection so enormous he appeared to be riding a seesaw, made ready to copulate with a female manatee. Wandering among the idols, Anthony felt as if he'd been transported into the past, back to a time when the major sins were celebrated—no, not celebrated, exactly: it was more as if sin hadn't been invented yet, and people simply did as their drives demanded, not worrying too much about any hypothetical Supreme Being's opinion of such behaviors. The gods of Van Horne Island made no laws, passed no sentences, asked for no sympathy.

As night settled over the pantheon, Anthony switched on his flashlight. In the center of the plaza a ponderous marble slab rested atop the disembodied forepaws of a stone lion. The captain sprayed his flashlight beam across the altar's surface. Mud. Crushed oyster shells. A grouper skeleton. Blood gutters.

Beyond, a high free-standing wall displayed a series of lurid instructional friezes. It was, Anthony realized, a kind of user's guide to the altar, including the best way to position the victim, the proper angle at which to insert the knife, and the correct method for scooping out the contents of a human abdomen.

According to the friezes, the island's gods were connoisseurs of entrails. Once lifted from their sloshy abodes, the duodena, jejuna, and ilea had evidently been transferred to clay tureens and set before the idols like steaming bowls of linguine. A jagged, star-shaped fragment from one such tureen lay at Anthony's feet. He stomped on it with a mixture of fear and disgust, as if squashing a roach. Thus far on the voyage he'd failed to work up much affection for their cargo, that sour old smiler, that grinning judge, but Judeo-Christian monotheism suddenly seemed to him a major step forward.

Weariness crept through the captain's bones. Drawing out his Monte Alban, he took a big gulp, then swept the trash from the slab and climbed on top. Another gulp. He stretched out, lay down. Another. In Anno Postdomini One, a man could drink as much as he pleased.

Anthony yawned. His eyelids drooped. Lemuria, Pan, Mu, Dis, Atlantis: to be a merchant sailor was to have heard of a dozen lost worlds. Going by the *Val*'s position alone—north of the Madeiras, east of the Azores, just beyond the Pillars of Hercules—Atlantis was the most likely candidate, but he knew it would take more than mere geography to make him rename his father's island.

He awoke to the sound of a shout—a booming cry of "Anthony!"—and for an instant he thought the drunkard, glutton, opium eater, or sodomite had come to life and was calling to him. Sunlight suffused the temple, its hot rays slashing through the fog. He unbuttoned his pea jacket.

"Anthony! Anthony!"

Rising from the slab, he realized he was hearing Ockham's professorial voice. "Padre!"

Dressed in his Fermilab sweatshirt and Panama hat, the priest stood panting in the sodomite's shadow. He looked dazed, shell-shocked, as might any man of his vocation beholding the gritty particulars of bestiality.

"We were on the corpse when the earbones snapped," said Ockham. "Most terrible noise I ever heard, the crack of doom. Somehow we made our way to the *Juan Fernández*."

"Thomas, I'm happy to see you," said Anthony, touching the priest's arm with the empty Monte Alban bottle. With decadence rampant among the crew and stone gods rising from the seabed, it was good to be with someone who'd heard of the Sermon on the Mount. "Everything's falling apart, and there you are, a port in a storm."

"Yesterday I danced naked in God's navel."

Anthony shuddered and gulped. "Oh?"

"With Sister Miriam." The priest seized the neck of his sweatshirt and peeled the sticky cotton from his chest. "A slip. The Idea of the Corpse. I'm in control now. Really."

"Father, what's going on? This island makes no sense."

"Miriam and I discussed the problem over dinner."

"Come up with anything?"

"Yeah, but it's pretty wild. Ready? I don't suppose you keep up with so-called chaos theory . . ."

"I don't."

". . . but one of its key concepts is the 'strange attractor,' the phenomenon that evidently underlies turbulence and other seem-ingly random events. As the *Val* and her cargo traveled north, they may have generated a unique variety of turbulence, and the body—this is just a guess—the body became a strange attractor. Now, here's the crux. The old, pagan order would be particularly energized by an attractor of this sort. Understand? As the Corpus Dei passed overhead, this world was naturally drawn to it, eager to assert itself once again. You follow me?"

"You're saying His body acted like a magnet?"

"Exactly. A metaphysical magnet, pulling down preternatural mists from heaven even as it sucked up a pagan civilization from the ocean floor."

"Why didn't something like this happen way back in the Gulf of Guinea?"

"Presumably no pagan civilizations lie at the bottom of the Gulf of Guinea."

"I've heard Atlantis used to be somewhere around here."

"Plato to the contrary, I'm quite certain Atlantis never existed."

"Then we'll keep calling it Van Horne Island."

Marching up to the glutton, Anthony pondered the peculiar combination of terror and rhapsody sculpted onto the doomed boar's face. Chaos theory . . . strange attractors . . . metaphysical magnets. Jesus.

"We won't let this place defeat us, right?" said the captain. "Maybe our ship's beached and our cargo's lost, but we'll still put up a fight. We'll get the deckies to dig us a canal."

"No," said Ockham. "Not possible." His tone was leaden and portentous. "They quit, Anthony."

"Who quit?"

"The crew."

"What?"

"It happened around midnight. They sprang Wheatstone, Jaworski, and Weisinger from the brig, then rigged up a gantry and unloaded a lot of stuff over the side—galley gear, video projectors, some heavy machinery, most of our food . . ."

"I don't believe I'm hearing this."

"Plus maybe a dozen crates of smuggled liquor and about two hundred six-packs."

"And then?"

"They took off. They're gone, Anthony."

"Gone?" In the warm, bloody folds of the captain's cerebrum, a migraine began taking root. "Gone where?"

"I last saw them heading north across the dunes."

"Officers too? Engineers?"

"Spicer, Haycox, Ramsey."

"Who stayed?"

"Miriam, of course, plus Rafferty, O'Connor, our castaway, our radio officer—"

"Cassie stayed? Good."

"Her way of repaying us, I suppose."

"Anybody else?"

"Chickering. Follingsbee. Counting me, you've got eight people on your side."

"Mutiny," said Anthony, the word turning to dung in his mouth.

"Desertion, more like."

"No, mutiny." Gripping the empty mescal bottle by the neck, he smashed it against the glutton's left knee, launching the pickled worm into the air. Bastards. He'd show them. It was one thing to break every law known on land and quite another to violate the first commandment of the sea. Turn against your captain? You might as well eat lye, fire a laser at a mirror, write the Devil a bad check. "What do they think they can accomplish with this shit?"

"Hard to say."

"We're gonna hunt 'em down, Thomas."

"Spicer mentioned one goal."

"Hunt 'em down and hang 'em from the kingposts! Every last mutineer! What goal?"

"He said they'd be giving their prisoners—quote—'the punishment they deserve.'"

When Cassie iearned that Big Joe Spicer, Dolores Haycox, Bud Ramsey, and most of the crew had gone berserk, looting the

tanker and fleeing across the sands, a rage rushed through her
such as she'd not known since the *Village Voice* had called her
Jephthah play "the sort of theatrical evening that gives sophomoric
humor a bad name." Without a crew, there was no way to free
the ship; without a ship, no way to catch the carcass and resume
the tow; without a tow, no way for Oliver's mercenaries to locate
and sink their target. Meanwhile, the damn thing was bobbing
around in the Gibraltar Sea, where any fool could stumble on it.
Perhaps any fool *had* stumbled on it. For all Cassie knew, a bunch
of Texas fundamentalists were busy hauling the Corpus Dei
toward Galveston Bay, intending to make it the centerpiece of a
Christian theme park.

What most frustrated her was the feebleness of the deserters'
reasoning, the way they were exploiting God's body to justify
their spurious embrace of anarchy. "They're using it as an *excuse*,"
she complained to Father Thomas and Sister Miriam. "Why can't
they see that?"

"I suspect they *can* see it," said the priest. "But they love their
newfound freedom, right? They need to keep on following it,
all the way to the edge."

"It's the logic of Ivan Karamazov, isn't it?" said Miriam. "If
God doesn't exist, everything is permitted."

The priest knitted his brow. "One also thinks of Schopenhauer. Without a Supreme Being, life becomes sterile and meaningless. I hope Kant had it right—I hope people possess some
sort of inborn ethical sense. I seem to recall him rhapsodizing
somewhere about 'the starry skies above me and the moral law
within me.'"

"*Critique of Practical Reason*," said Miriam. "I agree, Tom.
The deserters, all of us, we've got to make Kant's leap of faith—
his leap *out* of faith, I should say. We must get in touch with
our congenital consciences. Otherwise we're lost."

Thomas and Miriam, Cassie decided, enjoyed a rapport and
an affection—indeed, a passion—many married couples would

have envied. "I made that leap years ago," she said. "Take a hard-nosed look at Part Two of *The Ten Commandments*, and you'll see that God knows nothing of goodness."

"Well, I certainly wouldn't go that far," said Miriam.

"I would," said Cassie.

"I know you would," said Father Thomas dryly.

"It's not like Kant was an *atheist*," added the nun, setting her exquisite teeth in a grim smile.

As the day wore on, Cassie inevitably found herself thinking of *God Without Tears*, her one-act deconstruction of *The Ten Commandments*. God knew nothing of goodness, goodness knew nothing of God—it was all so wrenchingly obvious, yet over three-quarters of the ship's company had succumbed to the Idea of the Corpse. Maddening.

Her dream that night carried her off the island, over the Atlantic, and back to New York City, where she found herself sitting front row center at Playwrights Horizons, attending the premiere of *God Without Tears*. Up on the stage, the glow of a spotlight caught the prophet Moses crouching at the base of a Dead Sea sand dune, fielding questions from an unseen interviewer who wanted to know all about "the legendary unexpurgated version of DeMille's motion picture masterpiece."

The audience consisted entirely of the *Valparaíso*'s officers and crew. To Cassie's left sat Joe Spicer, petting a creature that alternated between being a Norway rat and a horseshoe crab. To her right: Dolores Haycox, methodically tying knots in a Liberian sea snake. Behind her: Bud Ramsey, smoking a Dacron mooring line.

Moses hikes up the dune and caresses the Tablets of the Law, which stick out of the sand like the ears on a Mickey Mouse cap.

INTERVIEWER

Is it true DeMille's original cut was over seven hours long?

MOSES

Uh-huh. The exhibitors insisted he trim it back to four. (*holds up fistful of motion picture film*) During the last decade, I've managed to collect bits and pieces from nearly every lost scene.

INTERVIEWER

For example?

MOSES

The Plagues of Egypt. The release prints included blood, darkness, and hail, but they were missing all the really interesting ones.

The spotlight shifts to two elderly, working-class Egyptian women, Baketamon and Nellifer, potters by trade, pulling clay from the banks of the Nile.

INTERVIEWER

Tell me about the frogs.

BAKETAMON

It was hard to know whether to laugh or to cry.

NELLIFER

You'd open your unmentionables drawer and—pop—one of them little fuckers would jump in your face.

BAKETAMON

Don't let anyone tell you God hasn't got a sense of humor.

INTERVIEWER

Which plague was the worst?

BAKETAMON

The boils, I'd say.

NELLIFER

The boils, are you kidding? The locusts were far worse than the boils.

BAKETAMON

The mosquitoes were pretty bad, too.

NELLIFER

And the flies.

BAKETAMON

And the cattle getting murrain.

NELLIFER

And the death of the firstborn. A lot of people *hated* that one.

BAKETAMON

Of course, it didn't touch Nelli and me.

NELLIFER

We were lucky. Our firstborns were already dead.

BAKETAMON

Mine died in the hail.

INTERVIEWER

Frozen?

BAKETAMON

Beaned.

NELLIFER

Mine had been suffering from chronic diarrhea since he was a month old, so when the waters became blood—*zap*, kid got dehydrated.

BAKETAMON

Nelli, your mind's going. It was your *second*born who died when the waters became blood. Your *first*born died in the darkness, when he accidentally drank that turpentine.

NELLIFER

No, my *second*born died much later, drowned when the Red Sea rolled back into its bed. My *third*born drank the turpentine. A mother remembers these things.

INTERVIEWER

I was certain you'd be more bitter about your ordeals.

NELLIFER

Initially we thought the plagues were unjust. Then we came to understand our innate depravity and intrinsic wickedness.

BAKETAMON

There's only one good Person in the whole universe, and that's the Lord God Jehovah.

INTERVIEWER

You've converted to monotheism?

BAKETAMON

(*nodding*) We love the Lord our God with all our heart.

NELLIFER

All our soul.

BAKETAMON

All our strength.

NELLIFER

Besides, there's no telling what He might do to us next.

BAKETAMON

Fire ants, possibly.

NELLIFER

Killer bees.

BAKETAMON

Meningitis.

NELLIFER
I've got two sons left.

BAKETAMON
I'm still up a daughter.

NELLIFER
The Lord giveth.

BAKETAMON
And the Lord taketh away.

NELLIFER
Blessed be the name of the Lord.

Cassie scanned the audience. Shimmering halos of pure reason hovered above Joe Spicer, Dolores Haycox, and Bud Ramsey, igniting their faces with skepticism's holy glow. The Enlightenment, she sensed, was about to prevail. As *God Without Tears* progressed, the *Valparaíso* deserters would inevitably come to apprehend and reject the fatal fallacy on which they were predicating their rebellion.

The spotlight swings back to Moses atop the sand dune.

INTERVIEWER
When you went up on Mount Sinai, Jehovah offered you a lot more than the Decalogue.

MOSES
DeMille shot everything, Marty, all six hundred and twelve laws, each one destined for the cutting-room floor.

A rear-projection screen descends, displaying an excerpt from The Ten Commandments. *God's animated forefinger is busily etching the Decalogue on the face of Sinai. As the last rule is carved—*THOU SHALT NOT COVET—*the frame suddenly freezes.*

GOD

(*voice-over*) Now for the details. (*beat*) When you go to war against your enemies and the Lord your God delivers them into your power, if you see a beautiful woman among the prisoners and find her desirable, you may make her your wife.

INTERVIEWER

I have to admire DeMille for using something like that. Deuteronomy 21:10, right?

MOSES

You got it, Marty. He was a much gutsier filmmaker than his detractors imagine.

GOD

(*voice-over*) When two men are fighting together, if the wife of one intervenes to protect her husband by putting out her hand and seizing the other by the private parts, you shall cut off her hand and show no pity.

INTERVIEWER

"Private parts"? DeMille used *that?*

MOSES

Deuteronomy 25:11.

GOD

(*voice-over*) If a man has a stubborn and rebellious son, his father and mother shall bring him out to the elders of the town, and all his fellow citizens shall stone the son to death.

MOSES

Deuteronomy 21:21.

INTERVIEWER

And here I'd always thought DeMille was afraid of controversy.

MOSES
> One ballsy mogul, Marty.

INTERVIEWER
> Damn theater chains.

MOSES
> (*nodding*) They think they own the world.

Joe Spicer jumped to his feet, hurled down his horseshoe crab, and said, "Mates, we've been committing a serious epistemological error!"

"Schopenhauer was cracking walnuts in his ass!" agreed Dolores Haycox, tossing aside her Liberian sea snake. "Life's meaning doesn't come from God! Life's meaning comes from life!"

"Captain, you gotta forgive us!" pleaded Bud Ramsey.

At which point Cassie woke up.

August 6.

Ockham wasn't kidding. The bastards cleaned us out. Until we can get a fishing party together, we'll be eating whatever stuff they dropped or didn't want in the first place.

I'm burning up, Popeye. I'm ablaze with migraine auras and shimmering visions of what I'll do to the mutineers once I catch them. I see myself keelhauling Ramsey, the *Val*'s barnacled bottom scraping off his skin like a galley grunt peeling a potato. I see myself cutting Haycox into neat little cubes and tossing them into the Gibraltar Sea, snacks for sharks. And Joe Spicer? Spicer I'll tie to a Butterworth plate, whipping him till the sun glints off his backbone.

Welcome to Anno Postdomini One, Joe.

At 1320 Sam Follingsbee handed me an inventory: 1 bunch

of bananas, 2 dozen hot dogs, 3 pounds of Cheerios, 5 loaves of bread, 4 slices of Kraft American cheese . . . I can't go on, Popeye, it's too depressing. I told the steward to work out a rationing system, something that will keep us functioning for the rest of the month.

"And after that?" he asked.

"We pray," I replied.

Although the mutineers broke into the fo'c'sle hold and made off with all the antipredator weapons, they didn't think to loot the deckhouse locker, so they're without shells for the bazookas and harpoons for the WP-17s. When it comes to serious firepower, we have effectively disarmed each other. Unfortunately, they also ripped off two decorative cutlasses from the wardroom, six or seven flare pistols, and a handful of blasting caps. Given this arsenal and their superior numbers, I see no way to attack their camp and win.

So we sit. And wait. And stew.

Sparks keeps trying to raise the outside world. No luck. I can deal with a grounding, a food shortage, maybe even a mutiny, but this endless fog is making me nuts.

At 1430 Ockham and Sister Miriam filled their knapsacks and set off north across the dunes, looking for the bastards. "We're assuming Immanuel Kant had it right," the padre explained. "There's a natural moral law—a categorical imperative—latent within every person's soul."

"If we can make the deserters understand that," said Miriam, "they may very well recover."

Know what I think, Popeye? I think they're about to get themselves killed.

They found the deserters by their laughter: whoops of primitive delight and cries of post-theistic joy blowing across the wet sands. Thomas's heart beat faster, rattling the miniature crucifix sandwiched between his chest and sweatshirt.

Straight ahead, a range of high, damp dunes sizzled in the sun. Side by side, Jesuit and Carmelite ascended, pausing halfway up to drink from their canteens and mop the perspiration from their brows.

"No matter how far they've sunk, we must offer them love," Sister Miriam insisted.

"We've been there ourselves, haven't we?" said Thomas. "We know what havoc the Idea of the Corpse can wreak." Reaching the summit, he lifted Van Horne's binoculars to his eyes. He blenched, transfixed by a sight so astonishing it rivaled Miriam's recent Dance of the Seven Veils. "Lord . . ."

A marble amphitheater sprawled across the valley floor, its facade broken by arched niches in which resided eight-foot-high statues of nude men wearing the heads of bulls, vultures, and crocodiles, its main gate guarded by a sculpted hermaphrodite happily engaged in a singularly dexterous act of self-pleasuring. Built to accommodate several thousand spectators, the arena now held a mere thirty-two, each deserter stuffing his face with food while watching the gaudy entertainment frantically unfolding below.

In the center of the rocky field, the *Val*'s Toyota forklift truck careened in wild circles, its steel prongs menacing a terrified mariner dressed only in tennis shoes and black bathing trunks. Inevitably Thomas thought of the last time he'd seen the forklift in action, the night he and Van Horne had watched Miriam transport a paddock of fresh eggs across the galley. It seemed now as if this very truck had, like the crew, fallen into depravity, seized by some technological analogue of sin.

He twisted the focusing drive. The threatened sailor was Eddie Wheatstone, the alcoholic bos'n Van Horne had jailed for destroying the rec-room pinball machine. Sweat glazed the bos'n's face. His eyes looked ready to burst. Thomas panned, focused.

Joe Spicer sat behind the steering wheel, dressed in a Michael Jackson T-shirt and khaki shorts, holding a can of Coors: sensitive Joe Spicer, the Merchant Marine's most civilized officer, the man who brought books to the bridge, now mesmerized by the Idea of the Corpse. Pan, focus. Near the portcullis cowered blubber-bellied Karl Jaworski, the ship's notorious lecher, in cotton briefs and Indian moccasins. Neil Weisinger, clad in nothing but a jockstrap, lay curled up beside the north wall like a catatonic.

The mismatch between Wheatstone and Spicer was outrageous. True, the bos'n was armed—in his right hand he grasped a stockless anchor from the *Juan Fernández*—but no matter which way he dodged, the forklift kept pace with him, its prongs slashing the foggy air like the tusks of a charging elephant. Wheatstone grew wearier by the minute; the priest could practically see the lactic acid fouling the poor man's blood, byproduct of his muscles' hopeless attempt to burn up all their sugar.

"It's even worse than we imagined," said Thomas, passing the binoculars to his friend. "They've gone over to the gods."

Miriam focused on the field and shuddered. "Is this the future, Tom—vigilante vengeance, public executions? Is this the shape of the post-theistic age?"

"We've got to have faith," he said, taking back the binoculars.

Miraculously, Wheatstone now seized the initiative. As a bestial cry broke from his lips—a howl such as Thomas had last heard at an exorcism—the bos'n set the anchor twirling above his head, apparently aiming to puncture a tire. He released the rope. The anchor flew, hit the forklift's right prong, and flipped into the mud. Applause erupted from the pagans, appreciation for a futile gesture well done.

Seconds later, they were urging Spicer to retaliate.

"Get him, Joe!"

"Run the bastard down!"

"Go!"

"Go!"

"Go!"

Laughing maniacally, Spicer pulled a cargo net from the forklift's rear compartment and neatly dropped it over the terrified bos'n. Wheatstone tripped, falling face down. The more he fought, the more entangled he became, but it was only after he began sliding forward—body bouncing across the sharp rocks, forehead cutting through the mud like a plow making a furrow—that Thomas noticed the Dacron mooring line running from the cargo net to the rear bumper.

"Tom, he's gonna kill that man!"

Round and round Spicer towed his prey, as if enacting some grotesque parody of the *Val*'s mission. Wheatstone screamed. He kicked and flailed. He started coming apart, his liquid constituents leaking through the interstices of the cargo net like squashed tomatoes permeating the bottom of a grocery bag.

When it became clear that Wheatstone was dead, two husky ordinaries rushed onto the field, cut the mooring line, and flung the bos'n's trussed body toward the portcullis.

The pagans jumped to their feet and cheered.

"Yay, Joe!"

"Way to go!"

"Yay, Joe!"

"Way to go!"

Priest and nun raced into the valley, whimpering in dismay, wet sand grabbing at their boots. Together they passed through the main gate and entered the world beneath the tiers, a maze of slimy, silty tunnels in which plunder from the *Val*—bazookas, refrigerators, footlockers, diesel generators, video-game consoles—lay about like beached jetsam. Daylight beckoned. A ramp appeared. They charged into the open air.

A river of wine flowed down the marble steps; abandoned sausages festered under the seats; gnawed pizza slices and half-eaten apples rotted in the heat. As Karl Jaworski ran across the arena—ran, literally, for his life—Thomas and Miriam ascended a dozen rows and paused, panting, between Charlie Horrocks, his features buried in a huge slice of watermelon, and Bud Ramsey, his lips locked around a bottle of Budweiser. It took Thomas several seconds to realize that Dolores Haycox and James Echohawk, stretched out on the seats directly in front of him, were engaged in energetic sexual congress.

"Hiya, Father Tom!" said Ramsey. Beer foam flecked his chin. "Afternoon, Miriam."

"Great party, huh?" said Horrocks, emerging from his watermelon chunk.

Haycox and Echohawk groaned in unison, groping toward orgasms of an intensity that, in the previous era, they could probably only have imagined.

To Horrocks's left, Karl Jaworski's three victims—robust Isabel Bostwick, svelte An-mei Jong, exotic Juanita Torres—sat huddled together, blowing kisses toward Spicer. Bostwick licked a Turkish taffy. Jong guzzled a bottle of Cook's champagne. Dressed only in bra and panties, Torres shook a pair of pompoms she'd improvised by ripping up her Menudo T-shirt and tying the shreds to needle guns.

Despite the vivid frenzy on the field—despite the horrific fact that Spicer had somehow maneuvered Jaworski against the south wall and was now driving straight for him—it seemed to Thomas that what the arena really contained was a kind of Barthian *Nichtige*: an ontological nothingness where once God's grace had been, its blind gravity devouring all goodness and mercy like a black hole feasting on light. Jaworski dropped to his knees. Spicer lowered the forklift prongs accordingly. In a choral display of utter joy, Bostwick, Jong, and Torres rose in a body and together shouted, "Kill!"

Thomas could see what was about to happen. He begged God that it wouldn't.

"Kill!"

"Kill!"

Even as the entreaty took shape on the priest's lips, the left forklift prong struck Jaworski squarely, slipping into his abdomen as smoothly as the spear of Longinus entering the crucified Savior.

"Bull's-eye!" squealed Jong as Jaworski, impaled, ascended.

"No!" howled Thomas. "No! No!"

"Calm down, man," said Ramsey. "Don't have no fuckin' cow."

Spicer backed up. Jaworski, screaming in agony, hung suspended from the prong, wriggling like a beetle on a hatpin.

"No!" moaned Miriam.

"Right on!" yelled Torres.

"Mazel tov!" shouted Bostwick.

Brow knitted in a thoughtful frown, Spicer operated the lift controls, working the prong ever deeper as he raised the skewered man up and down, up and down. Jaworski gripped the wet steel shaft, bathing his hands in his own blood as he attempted, bravely but hopelessly, to free himself.

"Spicer, Spicer, he's our man!" cried Bostwick. "If he can't do it, no one can!"

An urge to vomit grew in Thomas, wrenching his stomach and burning his windpipe, as the same ordinaries who'd previously disposed of Wheatstone slid Jaworski's corpse off the prong and casually dumped it in the mud. Miriam, weeping, took her friend's hand, digging her thumbnail so deeply into his palm she drew blood. He beat back his nausea through force of will.

"Go, go, Joe, Joe!" shouted Torres, swishing her pom-poms. "Go, go, Joe, Joe! Go, go, Joe, Joe!"

Anchor at the ready, Neil Weisinger stumbled toward the center of the field. Spicer, downshifting, gave chase.

"Stop this!" cried Miriam. She sounded, Thomas had to admit, more like a teacher disciplining a kindergarten than like the voice of reason evoking the spirit of Immanuel Kant. "Stop this right now!"

Spicer threw his net.

He missed.

The kid retreated, anchor swinging at his side, his bare feet splashing through the mud. Gushing black exhaust, the forklift bore down on him at five, ten, fifteen miles an hour. Spicer elevated the prongs to the height of Weisinger's belly.

"Go!"

"Go!"

The kid stopped, turned, waited.

"Kill!"

"Kill!"

And suddenly the anchor was airborne, arrowing straight for the driver's seat.

"Go!"

"Go!"

Acting on instinct, Spicer swerved—the same pathetic impulse, Thomas guessed, by which a soldier walking into a hail of grapeshot will raise his arms to fend off the balls.

"Kill!"

"Kill!"

The anchor landed between the second mate's legs. Shrieking with pain, he released the steering wheel and groped toward his crotch.

"Go!"

"Go!"

The forklift hit the wall at over thirty miles per hour, a collision of such force it threw Spicer from the cab and sent him somersaulting through the air. The two hundred and thirty pound man landed on his feet. His femurs shattered audibly. He collapsed, stabbed by his own bones, and began flopping around in the sand.

"Weisinger, Weisinger, he's our man! If he can't do it, no one can!"

The kid wasted no time. Retrieving the anchor from the

forklift seat, he dashed across the arena and hunched over Spicer. He scanned the crowd. At first Thomas assumed Weisinger merely wanted to savor the moment—where, when, and under what other circumstances could an able-bodied seaman receive a standing ovation?—but then he realized the kid was waiting for a sign.

In a weirdly synchronous gesture, thirty-two hands shot forward, thumbs up.

With equally uncanny coordination, thirty-two wrists rotated.

Thumbs down.

"Neil, no!" cried Thomas, gaining his feet. "It's me, Neil! It's Father Thomas!"

"Don't do it!" shouted Miriam.

Weisinger got to work, chopping relentlessly with the anchor, mooring himself to Spicer.

An enormous bare-chested sailor turned toward Thomas, exuding the sickly sweetness of whiskey. Black beard, bad skin, a face like the granite glutton on the far side of the island. Thomas recognized him as a demac named Stubby Barnes. The man had come to Mass twice. "Hey, you oughta settle down, Father. You too, Sister." The demac's right hand cradled an empty bottle of Cutty Sark. "I mean no disrespect, but this ain't your party!"

"No, *you* settle down!" wailed Thomas.

"Take it easy." Stubby Barnes lifted the bottle high over his head.

"No, *you* take it easy!"

"We can do whatever we want, man," Barnes insisted, letting the Cutty Sark fly.

"Listen to your congenital conscience!"

The bottle struck Thomas squarely, a pound of glass crashing into his temple. He felt warm blood rolling down his face, tickling his cheeks, and then he felt nothing at all.

August 7.

It goes from bad to worse. Yesterday at 0915 Ockham and Sister Miriam came stumbling back to the ship, the padre bleeding from a nasty head wound. Their news knocked me for a loop. The mutineers have executed Wheatstone and Jaworski in some sort of crazy rodeo. Joe Spicer's dead too, killed when Able Seaman Weisinger turned the tables on him.

If you want my opinion, Spicer got what he deserved.

Ever try mescal, Popeye? It has all the kick of spinach, I promise you, and it dulls the pain. Somehow the bastards missed my supply. I've given the creatures in the remaining bottles names. Caspar, Melchior, Balthazar—the Three Wise Worms.

I shouldn't drink, of course. I'm vulnerable. Dad's probably an alky, and somewhere along the line I had a wino aunt who burned down her house, plus a rummy cousin who shot the mailman for bringing the wrong size welfare check. But what the hell—this is Anno Postdomini One, right? It's the era when anything goes.

We have exactly 10 days to get Him to the Arctic.

Last night I polished off the first bottle, leaving Caspar beached like the *Val*, after which I went a bit berserk. Stuck a lighted Marlboro in my palm, puked my guts out, climbed down the anchor chain and rolled around in the sand. I woke up beside the keel, sober but numb, clutching an aluminum soup ladle to my breast.

It was Cassie who found me. What a pathetic creature I must've seemed, beard clogged with rust, clothes soaked in mescal. She guided me back up the chain, led me to the main galley, and began doling out aspirin and coffee.

"I didn't crash into this island," I insisted, as if she'd said I had.

"This island crashed into you."

"Am I repulsive, Doc? Am I downright disgusting? Do I smell like Davy Jones's jockstrap?"

"No, but you ought to shave off that beard."

"I'll consider it."

"I've always hated beards."

"Yeah?"

"It's like kissing a Brillo pad."

The word *kissing* lingered in the air. We both noticed it.

"I think I'm going crazy," I told her. "I tried digging us out with a soup ladle."

"That's not crazy."

"Oh?"

"Crazy would've been if you'd used a teaspoon."

And then, with a flirtatious toss of her head, or so it seemed, she left me alone with my hangover.

As Thomas entered the empty arena, mirages made of late-afternoon heat arose, twisting and shimmering above the bloody sand. The forklift truck sat inertly in the southeast corner, right prong clean, the left tarnished with Karl Jaworski.

Van Horne and Miriam had both been appalled by the idea of a second mission to the deserters—"Lord, Tom," the nun had said, "they'll execute *you* next time"—but Thomas's sense of duty demanded not only that he bury the dead but that he once again try to help the living find the Kantian moral law within.

Like a conquistador planting the Spanish flag in the New World, he thrust his steel spade into the ground. Ten yards away, Jaworski's punctured body lay festering in the shadow of the sculpted hermaphrodite. Beyond, the netted remains of Eddie Wheatstone lay across the eviscerated carcass of Joe Spicer. A mere twenty-four hours had elapsed since their executions, but the decomposition process was fully under way, filling the priest's nostrils with an acid stench.

Licking sweat from his lips, he retrieved the spade and got busy. The sand, though heavy, was as easily dislodged as new-fallen snow, and the job went effortlessly—so effortlessly, he decided, that should rationality ever descend upon Van Horne Island, then excavating the stranded *Valparaíso* might prove more feasible than he'd supposed. One hour later, a mass grave yawned in the center of the field.

He dumped in the corpses, prayed for their souls, and shoveled back the sand.

Following the deserters' trail out of the amphitheater was no problem. Cigarette butts, beer-can tabs, wine-bottle corks, peanut shells, orange rinds, and banana peels marked the way. Inevitably Thomas thought of Hansel and Gretel, dropping their pebbles so they'd be able to rejoin their tractable father and malicious stepmother. Even a dysfunctional family, apparently, was better than none at all.

The route took him through typical terrain—past decaying appliances and discarded 55-gallon drums, past mounds of automobile tires clumped together like gigantic charred bagels—and then, suddenly, it appeared: the wall.

It was huge, sixty feet from foundation to battlements, assembled from the purest marble, each block bleached white as bone. Spidery characters decorated the gateway, the forgotten phonemes of some long-unspoken tongue. He entered.

Music screamed in the city's heart—amplified guitars, high-tech keyboards. It seemed to Thomas not so much a song as a warning, the sort of sound with which a city might alert its citizens to incoming nuclear warheads. Mud lay everywhere, thick brown seabed pies drooping from the cornices and oozing off the balconies. Cloaked in the omnipresent mist, the temples, shops, and houses were in a sorry state, their roofs crushed by the weight of the Gibraltar Sea, their facades erased by underwater currents.

But could natural processes alone account for this destruction, or had God, too, had a hand in it? Was this another of those wicked cities the Almighty had elected to eradicate personally, sister to Babylon, kin to Gomorrah?

Ringed by fluted columns, a vast public building loomed over the priest, its gaping bronze doors carved with bas-relief images of the island's four reigning deities. He climbed the steps, entered the vaulted foyer, and started down the mud-carpeted hallway beyond. The music, louder now, assaulted his brain. Moving past the rooms, he imagined he was wandering through one of those hands-on museums to which upscale parents liked to drag their children, though here the exhibits were strictly for adults. One space, to judge from the mosaics, had been an opium den. Another, a masturbation booth, frescoed with antediluvian center-folds. There was a cubicle for pederasty. For bestiality. Sadomasochism. Necrophilia. Incest. Obsession after obsession, perversion upon perversion, a Museum of Unnatural History.

The hall turned a corner, opening onto a flagstone courtyard bordered by airy arcades and packed with the *Valparaíso* deserters, most of them naked. Such an astonishing range of skin tones, thought Thomas: ivory, pink, bronze, saffron, fawn, flaxen, dun, cocoa, sorrel, umber, ochre, maple sugar. It was like gazing upon a jar of mixed nuts, or a Whitman's Sampler. Many of the sailors had painted themselves, sketching sinuous arrows and coiled serpents on their bodies with mashed grapes, the juices running down their limbs like purple sweat. Wall to wall, the courtyard vibrated with a combination binge, bacchanal, orgy, brawl, and disco tourney, with many revelers participating in all five possibilities—drinking, eating, fornicating, fighting, dancing—simultaneously. Marijuana smoke mingled with the fog. Strobelights brightened the dusk. Along the southern arcade, Ralph Mungo and James Echohawk dueled with the decorative cutlasses they'd stolen from the wardroom, while a few yards away eight men stood in a circle, each plugged into another, a carousel of sodomy.

Crushed beer cans and empty liquor bottles littered the ground. Scores of spent condoms lay about like an infestation of giant planaria, a fact from which Thomas drew a modicum of hope: if the revelers were sane enough to worry about pregnancy and AIDS, they might be sane enough to ponder the categorical imperative. Arms undulated, hips shimmied, breasts swayed, penises swung—the sybaritic aerobics of Anno Postdomini One.

"Hiya, Tommy!" Neil Weisinger strode over, an unlit cigarette parked in his mouth, gleefully ripping a barbecued chicken in two. "Didn't expect to see *you* here!" he said drunkenly.

"That music . . ."

"Scorched Earth, from Sweden. The album's called *Chemotherapy*. You should see their stage act. They read entrails."

Dominating the courtyard was a polished obsidian banquet table, its surface supporting not only four enormous hams and two sides of beef but a diesel generator, a CD player, and an RCA Colortrak-5000 video projector spraying concupiscent images on a white bedsheet hanging wraithlike inside the northern arcade. Thomas had never seen Bob Guccione's notorious *Caligula*, but he guessed that's what the movie was. The camera dollied along the main deck of a Roman trireme on which nearly everyone was rutting.

"Helluva party, huh?" said Weisinger, waving half the bisected chicken in Thomas's face. The air reeked of semen, tobacco, alcohol, vomit, and pot. "Want some dinner?"

"No."

"Go ahead. Eat."

"I said no."

The kid displayed a bottle of Löwenbrau. "Beer?"

"Neil, I saw you in the amphitheater Tuesday."

"I really nailed Spicer, didn't I? Got him like some nervy goyische cowboy roping a steer."

"An immoral act, Neil. Tell me you understand that."

"This looks like just another Löwenbrau bottle," said

Weisinger, "but it's much, much more than that. Washed up on the beach yesterday. Inside was a message. Ask me what message."

"Neil . . ."

"Go ahead. Ask."

"What message?"

" 'Thou shalt have whatever other gods thou feels like,' it said. 'Thou shalt covet thy neighbor's wife.' Sure you don't wanna beer?"

"No."

" 'Thou shalt bugger thy neighbor's ass.' "

Everywhere Thomas looked, food was being squandered on a grand scale. Huge untended caldrons sat atop driftwood fires, rapidly reducing entire wheels of cheddar, Muenster, and Swiss to an inedible tar. Five sailors from the engine crew and five from the deck crew battled it out with what seemed like the *Valparaíso*'s entire stock of fresh eggs. Charlie Horrocks, Isabel Bostwick, Bud Ramsey, and Juanita Torres ripped the lids off vacuum-packed cans and merrily showered themselves with clam chowder, vegetable soup, baked beans, chocolate topping, and butterscotch sauce. They licked each other like mother cats grooming their young, the residue spilling down their flesh and disappearing amid the flagstones.

Weaving through the tangle of bodies, Thomas made his way to the banquet table. He studied the metal plate on the generator: 7500 WATTS, 120/240 VOLTS, SINGLE-PHASE, FOUR-STROKE, WATER-COOLED, 1800 RPMS, 13.2 HP—the only piece of rational discourse in the entire museum. The music was at a fever pitch, bandsaws dying of cancer. He shut off the CD player.

"What'd ya do *that* for?" wailed Dolores Haycox.

"Turn it back on!" screamed Stubby Barnes.

"You must listen to me!" Thomas leaned toward the Color-trak-5000, currently projecting Malcolm McDowell working his greased fist into a wincing man's anus, and pushed EJECT.

"Put the movie back on!"

"Start the music!"

"Fuck you!"

"Caligula!"

"Listen to me!" Thomas insisted.

"Scorched Earth!"

"Caligula!"

"Scorched Earth!"

"Caligula!"

"You're using the corpse as an excuse!" the priest shouted. "Schopenhauer was wrong! A Godless world is not ipso facto meaningless!"

The food came from every point of the compass—barrages of boiled potatoes, salvos of Italian bread, cannonades of grapefruit. A large, scabrous coconut grazed Thomas's left cheek. A pomegranate smashed into his shoulder. Eggs and tomatoes exploded against his chest.

"There's a Kantian moral law within!"

Someone restarted *Caligula*. Under the persuasion of a Roman senator's wife's tongue, a large erect penis not belonging to the senator released its milky contents like a volcano spewing lava. Thomas rubbed his eyes. The erupting organ stayed with him, hovering in his mind like a flashbulb afterimage as he fled the Museum of Unnatural History.

"Immanuel Kant!" cried the despairing priest, rushing through the city streets. He reached under his Fermilab shirt and squeezed his crucifix, as if to mash Christ and Cross into a single object. "Immanuel, Immanuel, where are you?"

Famíne

VIEWED THROUGH THE frosted window of the twin-engine Cessna, Jan Mayen Island appeared to Oliver Shostak as one of his favorite objects in the world, the white lace French brassiere he'd given Cassie for her thirtieth birthday. Corresponding to the cups were two symmetrical blobs, Lower Mayen and Upper Mayen, masses of mountainous terrain connected by a natural granite bridge. Raising his field glasses, he ran his gaze along the Upper Mayen coastline until he reached Eylandt Fjord, a groove so raw and ragged it suggested the aftermath of a bungled tooth extraction.

"There it is!" Oliver called above the engines' roar. "There's Point Luck!" he shouted, giving the bay the name by which Pembroke and Flume insisted it be called.

"Where?" asked Barclay Cabot and Winston Hawke in unison.

"There—to the east!"

"No, that's Eylandt Fjord!" corrected the Cessna's pilot, a weatherbeaten Trondheim native named Oswald Jorsalafar.

No, thought Oliver—Point Luck: that hallowed piece of the Pacific northwest of Midway Island where, on June 4, 1942, three American aircraft carriers had lain in wait to ambush the Japanese Imperial Navy.

He panned the field glasses back and forth. No sign of the *Enterprise*, but he wasn't surprised. Only by Pembroke and Flume's best-case scenario would they have already made the crossing from Cape Cod to the Arctic Ocean. Most likely they were still south of Greenland.

Jan Mayen's sole airstrip lay along the eastern fringe of its only settlement, a scientific-research station grandiosely named Ibsen City. As the Cessna touched down, the prop wash set up a tornado of snow, ice, volcanic ash, and empty Frydenlund beer bottles. Oliver paid Jorsalafar, tipped him generously, and, shouldering his backpack, joined the magician and the Marxist on the cold march west.

In the pallid rays of the midnight sun, Ibsen City stood revealed as a collection of rusting Quonset huts and dilapidated clapboard houses, each set on a gravel foundation lest it sink into the illusory ground called permafrost. Reaching the central square, Oliver, Barclay, and Winston made for the Hedda Gabler Inn, a split-level motel grafted onto a tavern fashioned from a corrugated-aluminum airplane hangar. A neon sign reading SUN-DOG SALOON flashed in the tavern window, a beacon on the tundra.

The inn's manager, Vladimir Panshin, a Russian expatriate with the raw, earthy look of a Brueghel peasant, didn't buy the atheists' claim to be disaffected jetsetters seeking those exotic, exciting places the travel bureaus didn't know about. ("Whoever told you Jan Mayen is exciting," said Panshin, "must get an orgasm from flossing his teeth.") But ultimately his suspicions didn't matter. He was more than happy to book the atheists into the Gabler and sell them the half pound of Gouda cheese (five American dollars), the gallon of reindeer milk (six dollars), and the dozen sticks of caribou jerky (one dollar each) they'd need for the next day's trek.

Oliver slept badly that evening—Winston's cyclonic snoring combined with the challenge of digesting overpriced ptarmigan stew—rousing himself the next morning only with the aid of the Gabler's strongest coffee. At eight o'clock, Jan Mayen time, the atheists trudged past the city limits and entered the trackless tundra beyond.

After an hour's hike they paused for lunch, spreading out their picnic on the narrow neck of rock marking the way to Upper Mayen. The cheese was moldy, the milk sour, the jerky tough and gritty. Inevitably Oliver imagined Anthony Van Horne's cargo fashioning this particular isthmus: the gigantic hands reaching down from heaven, pinching the island in the middle. The vision alarmed and depressed him. What would the scientists back in Ibsen City do if they ever found out that their elaborate theories of uniformitarianism and plate tectonics were fundamentally meaningless? How would they react upon learning that the *real* answer to the geomorphic riddle was, of all things, divine intervention?

Crossing into Upper Mayen, the three men followed a pumice-covered path through the foothills of the Carolus Mountains, a journey made entertaining by a particularly dazzling performance from the aurora borealis. Had Oliver brought his art supplies along, he would have tried painting the phenomenon, laboring to capture on canvas its diaphanous arcs, ethereal swirls, and eerie crimson flickers.

At last Eylandt Fjord lay before them, a smooth expanse of steel blue water irregularly punctuated by gigantic chunks of floating pack ice. Oliver's great fear was that the *Enterprise* would be delayed and they would have to camp on the tundra, so his mood brightened considerably when he saw her lying at anchor, four PBY flying boats tethered to her stern. His joy did not last.

The carrier looked old, feeble, small. She *was* small, he knew: smaller than the *Valparaíso* by half, smaller than God by a factor of twenty. The five dozen warplanes strapped to her flight deck did not seem remotely equal to the task at hand.

Barclay worked his portable semaphore, sending bursts of electric light across the fjord. G-O-D-H-E-A-D, the code name for their campaign.

The *Enterprise* replied: W-E-A-R-E-C-O-M-I-N-G.

The atheists scrambled down the cliff face, a treacherous descent through slippery patches of moss, jagged chunks of pumice, and a thorny, mean-spirited plant that tore their mukluks and bloodied their ankles. They reached the beach simultaneously with the carrier's barge: a wooden inboard motorboat sporting a canvas canopy over her helm and flying a historically accurate 48-star flag. Dressed in a *Memphis Belle* bomber jacket, Sidney Pembroke sat on the foredeck, waving a mittened hand.

"Welcome to Point Luck!" Condensed breath gushed from Pembroke's mouth. Even with the Arctic air flushing his cheeks, he still looked anemic. "Hop aboard, men!"

"There's plenty of piping hot Campbell's tomato soup back on *Enterprise!*" called Albert Flume, also bloodless, from behind the wheel. "Mmm, mmm, good!" He'd traded his zoot suit for the saboteur look: vicuña vest, blue crewneck sweater, black watch cap, like Anthony Quinn in *The Guns of Navarone.*

Wrapping a calfskin bombardier's glove around the throttle, Flume eased the motor into neutral. Beside him stood a granite-jawed, swag-bellied man wearing the unassuming khaki uniform or an American naval officer in the process of winning World War Two. Admirals' stars decorated his shoulders.

Oliver waded into the shallows, wincing as the icy water gushed through the rips in his mukluks, and climbed over the transom, Barclay and Winston right behind. The Navy man ducked out from under the canopy and smiled, an unlit briar pipe clamped between his teeth.

"You must be Mr. Shostak," said the admiral, subjecting

Oliver to a strenuous handshake. "Spruance here, Ray Spruance. I use your dad's brand of rubber all the time. Boy, I'll bet this AIDS thing's been a real boon to your family, right? It's an ill wind that blows nobody good."

Oliver grimaced and said, "These are my colleagues—Barclay Cabot, Winston Hawke."

"Pleasure's all mine, fellas."

"What's your actual name?" asked Winston, beating back a smirk.

"Doesn't matter, Mr. Hawke. For the next two weeks, I'm Raymond A. Spruance, rear admiral, U.S. Navy, charged with the tactical side of this operation."

"As opposed to the strategic?" asked Oliver. He was beginning to understand how these idiots thought.

"Yep. Strategy's Admiral Nimitz, back at Pearl Harbor."

"Where's Nimitz really?"

"New York," said Flume.

"We're not *paying* him, are we?" asked Oliver.

"Of course we're paying him." Putting the motor in gear, Flume guided the barge away from the beach.

"Why are we paying him if he's not doing anything?"

"He *is* doing something."

"What?"

"Ray just told you. Strategy."

"But we *know* the strategy."

"Look, boys," said Spruance's portrayer, whipping the briar pipe from his mouth, "if I couldn't picture old Chesty Nimitz back at Pearl, planning our strategy, I wouldn't have the heart to go through with this."

"But he's *not* at Pearl," said Oliver. "He's in New York."

"We could send him to Pearl if you wanted," said Flume, "but it'd cost you a pretty penny."

Biting his tongue, Oliver said nothing.

"You know, I'd never heard of vigilante capitalism until

Sidney and Albert told me about it"—Spruance offered the atheists a sly, conspiratorial wink—"but I must say, I'm impressed."

"Some folks think we're out of line," said Winston, "but that won't stop us from doing our patriotic duty."

"Hey, you needn't persuade *me*," said Spruance. "For *years* I been sayin' the Nips are a bigger threat to America right now than they ever were in '42."

As Flume piloted them across the fjord, Pembroke climbed off the foredeck, wiped a dollop of eider-duck guano from his bomber jacket, and drew up beside Winston. "So how do you like Task Force Sixteen?" Pembroke asked, pointing toward the *Enterprise*.

"I see only one ship," said Winston.

"Well, it's a task force to *us*," said Pembroke in an aggrieved tone. "Task Force Sixteen. We've got *Enterprise*, her barge, four PBYs . . ."

"Right."

"A task force, yes?"

"You bet."

"Things go okay on Martha's Vineyard?" asked Barclay.

"Beautiful," said Pembroke. "A sell-out crowd."

"We watched it all from Dad's cabin cruiser," said Flume. "A regular ringside seat."

"Alby brought along the most amazing picnic."

"Everything's better with the Battle of Midway raging all around you."

"Potato salad's better. Chocolate cake's better."

"Except *Soryu*—wouldn't you know it?—she didn't sink," said Flume, carefully maneuvering the barge alongside the carrier.

"Oh?" said Oliver.

"Yeah, she stayed afloat even after McClusky unloaded one of his eggs right down her aft smokestack," said Spruance. "Hey, don't get worried, son. We'll be dropping fifty times more TNT on your golem than we did on *Soryu*." The admiral vaulted athletically from the barge to the gangway. "Best torpedoes and demolition bombs in the whole damn navy. State-of-the-art ordnance."

Disembarking, Oliver followed Spruance up the wobbly stairs, a route that took them directly past an open hangar bay. A middle-aged sailor in an ensign's uniform stood hunched over the fuselage of a TBD-1 Devastator, tinkering with the engine.

"The way we figure it," said Oliver, calling above the growl of the pack ice, "the *Valparaíso* won't cross the circle till five or six days from now."

"Okay, but we'd better start sending patrols out right away, just to make sure," said Spruance. "Our PBYs will get the job done. State-of-the-art reconnaissance."

"Any danger of the *Val* slipping past us?"

Spruance looked Oliver in the eye. The Arctic wind tousled the admiral's dapple-gray hair. "A PBY is the finest search plane of its day, Mr. Shostak. Understand? The finest of its day."

"What day?"

"Nineteen forty-two."

"But it's nineteen *ninety*-two."

"That's a matter of opinion. Anyway, we got brand-new radar equipment on *Enterprise*'s bridge."

"State-of-the-art radar?" Oliver was feeling better now. The Devastator was a truly fearsome-looking machine. It radiated a kind of technological haughtiness, metal's contempt for flesh.

"State-of-the-art radar," echoed Ray Spruance's portrayer with an emphatic thumbs-up. "Panasonic all the way."

A low, steady growl. A sharp, gut-deep ache. Hunger? wondered Neil Weisinger, cracking into consciousness. Yes, that was the word, *hunger*.

Freeing himself from the knot of sleeping, snoring bodies,

the young AB glanced at his digital watch. August 10. Wednesday. Nine A.M. Damn, he'd been asleep two whole days. His eyes itched. His bladder spasmed. Slowly he picked his way through the wreckage—the Miller Lite cans and Cook's champagne bottles, the chicken bones and eggshells, the raunchy CDs and X-rated videocassettes—and, after walking stark naked through the southern arcade, peed copiously on a lovely bucolic fresco depicting a herd of rams gang-banging a buxom shepherdess.

"Quite a blowout," groaned Charlie Horrocks, joining Neil at the improvised urinal.

"The social event of the season," mumbled Neil. Lord, it was glorious being a pagan. The choices were so simple. Vodka, rum, or beer? Oral, anal, or vaginal?

"Somebody's been playin' football with my head," said the pumpman.

"Somebody's been playin' billiards with my balls," said Neil. Their revels, clearly, had ended, though whether this was because even pagans grow weary of pleasure or because the party had run out of fuel (no more beer in the kegs, soup in the kettles, bread in the baskets, jism in the testes), the AB couldn't say. "What's for breakfast?"

"Beats me."

In the western arcade, a large and resonant stomach grumbled. Another took up the cry. A third joined in. A choral gurgling filled the air, as if the museum were honeycombed with defective storm drains. Stumbling aimlessly toward the banquet table, Neil grew suddenly aware of how encrusted he was, how wide the variety of dried substances clinging to his skin and matting his hair. He felt like an extension of the island itself, a repository for waste.

"I could eat a cow," said Juanita Torres, slipping into a silk chemise.

"A herd of cows," said Ralph Mungo. "A *generation* of cows."

But there were no cattle on Van Horne Island.

"Hey, we got ourselves a problem here," said Dolores Haycox, the ranking officer among the deserters now that Joe Spicer had been disemboweled with a stockless anchor. She spoke tentatively, as if uncertain whether to assume command or not. Should she elect to do so, Neil decided, she'd best put on some clothes. "I think we ought to, you know, talk," rasped the third mate.

Potable water, everyone agreed, wasn't an issue: the omnipresent fog continually deposited gallons of dew in the city's various cisterns and gutters. Food was a different matter. Even with stringent rationing, there probably weren't enough provisions left to satisfy their appetites for more than a day.

"Jeez . . . I feel so *stupid*," said Mungo.

"Stupid, stupid, stupid," said Torres.

"Stupid as an ox," said Ramsey.

"If we dwell on the past," said Haycox, slinging a tattered canvas seabag around her waist, "we'll go mad."

Ramsey wanted them to start scouring the island immediately. Despite its seeming sterility, he argued, the place might very well harbor a few stranded crustaceans or an edible species of kelp. But the revelers had seen far too many acres of lifeless mud and barren sand to work up much enthusiasm for this idea.

Horrocks suggested they go back to the *Valparaíso* and beg for a portion of whatever scraps they might have overlooked while looting the ship. This scenario sounded promising until James Echohawk pointed out that, if any such supplies existed, the loyalists had no reason to be generous with them.

It was Haycox who offered genuine hope. They must fashion a raft from the banquet table, she argued, and send it east. After reaching civilization—Portugal, most probably, though maybe Morocco was nearer—its crew would hunt out the authorities and arrange for a rescue ship to be dispatched. If the raft proved incapable of such a journey, her crew would return forthwith to Van Horne Island, laden with the deep-sea fish they were certain to catch along the way.

On Haycox's orders the deserters got dressed and spent the morning scavenging. They cut the fat from hambones, dug pulp out of apricot pits, clawed bits of egg from shell fragments, pried globs of Chef Boyardee ravioli from steel cans, and chiseled nuggets of pizza from the flagstones. Once the museum itself was picked clean, the mariners retraced their steps to the amphitheater, following the path of their prodigality, gathering up each orange rind and banana peel as if it were a priceless gem.

Entering the arena, Neil was momentarily bewildered to realize that the corpses of Wheatstone, Jaworski, and Spicer were nowhere to be seen, but then he noticed a mound of mud in the center of the field, evidence that someone—Father Thomas, quite likely—had buried them. An unholy odor rose from the grave, so intense it instantly killed any notion of solving the incipient famine through the ingestion of former shipmates.

By 1530 the pagans were back in the city, sorting through the day's harvest. It came to a little over thirty pounds, which Haycox divided into two equal stockpiles, storing the first in a seabag—bait, she explained—and parceling out the second on the spot. Greedily Neil grabbed his allotment, a conglomeration of apple cores, Concord grapes, and frankfurter stubs welded together with Turkish taffy and melted cheddar cheese. Staking out a shady spot beneath the banquet table, he sat down, lit a Marlboro, and puffed.

He stared at his meal. A sharp moan broke from his larynx. This wasn't food. It was a travesty of food, a cruel impersonation of food, tormenting him the way a dead child's voice torments its parents.

He devoured the ration in four big bites.

"I got a job for you."

Neil looked up. Dolores Haycox stood over him, her stocky form now swathed in a beige Exxon jumpsuit.

"We need pontoons," she said, handing Neil a set of battery-powered needle guns. "Four of 'em."

"Aye-aye."

"Take Mungo, Jong, and Echohawk. Locate some fifty-five-gallon drums. Good ones. Drain 'em."

He took a drag on his Marlboro. "Gotcha."

"We're gonna get out of this mess, Weisinger."

"You bet, Captain Haycox."

After a half-hour's hike across a mud flat riddled with aerosol cans and disposable diapers, Neil and his three shipmates reached the nearest chemical dump, a dark, viscous swamp where dozens of 55-gallon drums lay about like chunks of pineapple suspended in Jell-O. Most of the drums were fractured and leaking, but before long Mungo spotted a cluster that the dumpers, in an effort to either appease their consciences or cover their asses, had evidently sealed against saltwater corrosion. The sailors switched on their needle guns and got to work, chipping the rust from the caps with the radical caution of neurosurgeons severing frontal lobes: each cap had to be loosened but must not suffer damage in the process.

As Neil freed up his cap, two disquieting images arrived.

Leo Zook, suffocating.

Joe Spicer, bleeding.

Summoning all his pagan powers, the full force of Anno Postdomini One, he tore their livid faces from his mind.

He unplugged the drum, laid it on its side, and watched in appalled fascination as something that resembled black mucus and smelled like burning sulfur flowed forth. He screwed the cap on tight. Within minutes, Mungo, Jong, and Echohawk were emptying out their respective drums: a sudden rush of stinking yellow goo, a steady stream of putrid brown syrup, a slow trickle of acrid purple pus.

Like Sisyphus rolling his stone, Neil began pushing his drum across the mud flat, his companions following, and by sundown all four pontoons were safely within the city's walls.

The deserters rose at dawn, carrying the banquet table to the beach and lashing the pontoons in place with wires and fan belts scrounged from the nearest auto graveyard. By 0800 the vessel, christened *Cornucopia*, was ready for sea. Captain Haycox assumed a commanding position in the bow, right beside the freshwater casks. Echohawk, the designated first mate, manned the tiller. Ramsey and Horrocks settled down amidships, their fists wrapped firmly around two jumper cables whose clamps had been twisted into fishhooks. Mungo and Jong took up a corroded pair of Datsun bumpers and began paddling.

Standing on the beach, Neil watched the *Cornucopia* smash through the breakers and vanish into the dark waters beyond. As fog engulfed the raft, he turned and joined the solemn little march back to the city.

For the next two days, Neil and his mates remained in the museum, lolling in the muddy yard like fourteenth-century Londoners in thrall to the Black Death. They spoke in grunts. They dreamed of food. Not simply the aquatic delicacies promised by Captain Haycox's mission (lobster bisque, pollack chowder, marlin pie), not simply imitation franchise food from Follingsbee's galley, but good old-fashioned sailors' fare as well: hardtack, cracker hash, midshipman's muffins, strike-me-blind. The fog thickened. Prayers drifted heavenward. Tears fell. Neil figured that each mariner's reasoning was not unlike his own. Yes, Haycox and her crew might break the covenant, blithely fishing their way to Portugal and never bothering to save their stranded mates, but to do so would constitute betrayal on a cosmic scale. There is honor among the starving, the AB sensed. An unfathomable fraternity binds those who seriously contemplate cutting off their own toes and chewing the raw flesh from the bones.

"I hate you," muttered Isabel Bostwick. "I hate all of you. You . . . you *men*, you and your slime. It's a real fine line between a consensual orgy and a rape, that's one thing I've learned on this trip, a *real* fine line."

"I didn't see you worryin' about any fine lines during the *party*," said Stubby Barnes.

"I'd better not be pregnant," said Juanita Torres.

"If we don't stop talking," said Neil, "we're gonna lose our strength."

On the morning of the third day, the *Cornucopia*'s little company staggered into the museum. Their faces looked scored and deflated, as if painted on expiring helium balloons. The news was doubly bad. Not only did an impassable barricade of waterspouts and maelstroms surround Van Horne Island, but her bays and inlets were as bereft of fish as the dusty seas of the moon.

"We ate only our fair share," said Haycox, setting the bait bag on the flagstones.

One by one, the sailors who'd stayed behind came forward, each thrusting a hand into the bag and drawing out his due measure. Neil's portion consisted of half a Three Musketeers bar on which sat eleven raisins, a cherry LifeSaver, and five sugar-coated Alpha-Bits, K, T, A, S, E. He couldn't help noticing that the letters, rearranged, spelled STEAK.

August 17.

Course: nowhere. Speed: 0 knots.

They came back 24 hours ago, weak, dizzy, and frightened, stumbling out of the fog like, as Ockham put it, "a bunch of extras from *Night of the Living Dead*." I've never seen such a scraggly gang of sailors in my life. Led by their phony captain, Dolores Haycox, they threw down their weapons—bazookas, harpoon guns, flare pistols, blasting caps, decorative cutlasses—and collected in the shadow of the hull.

Their arrival proved no surprise to Ockham. On his return from the city, he told me their provisions would be gone by the 9th, so frantic was their bacchanal. Assuming the padre calculated correctly, the mutineers held out for over a week after eating their last morsel.

Impressive.

The minute I saw them, I ordered the anchor raised, locking the bastards out. It's like some crazy inverse siege—the trapped defenders eating, the outside army starving. I am not a cruel man. I am not Captain Bligh. But if I don't feed Rafferty and my other loyalists the last of our reserves, they won't have the energy to keep taking the *Juan Fernández* on the trolling expeditions that are our last, best, and only hope. So far nobody's gotten more than two miles from shore before encountering a twenty-foot wall of turbulence, impossible for a small craft to penetrate. Within the navigable zone, though, we're certain to find fish.

Last night I ordered Follingsbee to do a new inventory, this time throwing in everything that remotely qualifies as food.

- 3 pounds Cheerios
- 2 pounds Sun Maid raisins
- 3 12-oz. tubes Colgate toothpaste
- 2 loaves Pepperidge Farm whole wheat bread
- 1 36-oz. can Libby's string beans
- 1 48-oz. jar Hellman's mayonnaise
- 1 12-oz. jar glory grease
- 4 12-oz. bottles Vick's cough syrup
- 1 pound popcorn (gleaned from the floor of our movie theater)
- 2 1-gallon cans Campbell's tomato juice
- 6 carrots
- 1 bunch broccoli
- 6 Oscar Mayer hot dogs (we'd better save most of these for bait)
- 607 communion wafers
- 311 acorn barnacles scraped from our rudder and hull (lucky thing we harvested these before the mutineers arrived)

76 goose barnacles (ditto)
1 banana
1 slice Kraft American cheese (we'll set this aside for
an emergency)

Sam's worked out our rations for the coming week. Curious
to know the menu aboard the luxury liner *Valparaíso*? Breakfast:
10 Cheerios, 4 ounces tomato juice. Lunch: 7 string beans, 2
communion wafers. Dinner: 2 acorn barnacles, 1 ounce bread, 1
carrot cube, 8 raisins. The captain, on occasion, will get a belt of
mescal.

A force-12 gale swept across Van Horne Island this morning,
driving squalls of rain before it. Did I imagine the accumulation
might be enough to lift us free? Of course I did. Did I picture
the winds blowing the fog away? I'm only human, Popeye.

The mutineers have decided to protect themselves from future
storms. Their homes are grotesque, twisted shanties cobbled together from Toyota doors and Volvo hoods, bulging out of the
sand like steel igloos.

"Please feed us," gasps their emissary of the moment, a demac
named Barnes, dressed only in hot pink bathing trunks. Evidently
he'd been a real porker before the famine. His vacated skin hangs
from his torso like blobs of wax dripping down the shaft of a
candle.

"We have nothing to spare," I call to him.

"I had a life," moans the demac. "Done things. Slung hash,
been to Borneo, fathered four boys, organized church picnics. I
had a life, Captain Van Horne."

Tomorrow, as it happens, is the OMNIVAC's deadline for
hauling God across the Arctic Circle. I can see His brain disintegrating, Popeye, each neuron entering oblivion with a sudden,
brilliant burst, like five billion flashbulbs firing at some apoca-
lyptic press conference.

During his first three days aboard the *Enterprise*, Oliver's favorite amusement was to stand in the forward lookout post and sketch the PBYs as they left on their daily reconnaissance patrols. Scooting along on their flat bottoms, weaving amid the pack ice, the four flying boats would suddenly retract their stabilizer floats and begin their clumsy ascents, fighting their way skyward like a flock of arthritic herons rising from a marsh.

By the end of the week, the PBYs had flown seventy-three separate missions without spotting anything resembling a supertanker towing a golem.

"Think she got sidetracked by a hurricane?" asked Winston.

"How the hell should I know?" replied Oliver.

"If the body's started to rot, it might be soaking up seawater," said Barclay. "A few thousand extra tons could cut Van Horne's speed in half."

"Maybe the problem's mechanical," said Winston. "Merchant ships are built to fall apart. That's how capitalism works."

As far as Oliver was concerned, none of these theories could begin to account for the *Valparaíso* being so woefully behind schedule. On the morning of August 22, he went to the cabin of Ray Spruance's portrayer and inquired whether the *Enterprise* had a fax machine.

"*Enterprise*, not 'the' *Enterprise*," said the admiral, chewing on the stem of his briar pipe. "Sure we got one, a Mitsubishi-7000."

"I want to send a message to our agent on the tanker."

"Since when do we have an agent on the tanker?"

"A long story. She's my girlfriend, Cassie Fowler. Something's obviously gone wrong."

"At this point, Mr. Shostak, any communication with *Val-*

paraíso would be a bad idea. Absolute radio silence figured crucially in the American victory at Midway."

"I don't give a fuck about Midway. I'm worried about my girlfriend."

"If you don't give a fuck about Midway, you don't belong on this ship."

"Jesus—do you people *always* have to live in the past?"

The admiral scowled, manifestly taken aback. He sucked on his pipe. "Yes, friend," he said at last, "as a matter of fact we *do* always have to live in the past, and if you'd give it a minute's thought, you'd want to live there too." Eyes flashing, Spruance paced compulsively around his cabin, back and forth, like a caged wolf. "Do you realize there was a time when the United States of America actually made sense? A time when you could look at a Norman Rockwell painting of a GI peeling potatoes for Mom and get all choked up and nobody'd laugh at you? A time when the Dodgers were in Brooklyn like they're supposed to be and there were no jigaboos shooting up our cities and every schoolday started with the Lord's Prayer? It's all gone, Shostak. People are scared of their own *food*, for Christ's sake. In the forties nobody ate yogurt or Egg Beaters or goddamn turkey franks."

"You know, Admiral, if you won't let me contact Cassie Fowler, I might just go out and hire a different set of mercenaries."

"Don't diddle me. I like you, friend, but I won't be diddled."

"I'm serious, Spruance, or whatever the hell your name is," snapped Oliver, pleased to be discovering unexpected reserves of impertinence within himself. "As long as I'm paying the piper, I'm also calling the tune."

It took Oliver over an hour to compose a fax that met the admiral's standards. The message had to convey curiosity about the *Valparaíso*'s position yet remain sufficiently ambiguous that if it fell into what Spruance insisted on calling "enemy hands," and if that enemy succeeded in cracking the code (it was in

Heresy), nobody would suspect the tanker's cargo had been targeted. "You are my heart's most valued occupant, dearest Cassandra," Oliver wrote, "though in which chamber you currently reside I cannot say."

At 1115 hours, the *Enterprise*'s radio officer, a scrawny Latino actor named Henry Ramírez, fed Oliver's letter into the Mitsubishi-7000. At 1116, a message popped onto the concomitant computer screen.

TRANSMISSION TERMINATED—ATMOSPHERIC DISTURBANCE AT RECEPTION POINT.

"Heavy weather?" asked Spruance's portrayer.

"There's no storm activity anywhere in the North Atlantic today," Ramírez replied.

An hour later, the radio officer tried again. TRANSMISSION TERMINATED—ATMOSPHERIC DISTURBANCE AT RECEPTION POINT. He made a third attempt an hour after that. TRANSMISSION TERMINATED—ATMOSPHERIC DISTURBANCE AT RECEPTION POINT.

But it wasn't really "atmospheric disturbance," Oliver decided; it was something far more sinister. It was the New Dark Ages, spilling across the globe, spreading their inky ignorance everywhere like oil gushing from the *Valparaíso*'s broken hull, and there was nothing, absolutely nothing, a mere rich atheist could do about it.

Cassie seized the compass binnacle, hugging it with the desperation of a wino bag lady steadying herself on a lamppost. She could no longer imagine what a clear head was like, couldn't remember a time when moving, breathing, or thinking had come easily. Clutching her inflamed belly, she stared at the twelve-mile radar. Fog, always fog, like the output of some demented cable station devoted to anomie and existential dread, the Malaise Channel.

And suddenly here was Father Thomas, holding out a cupped hand. A mound of Cheerios, doubtless from his own allotment, lay in his palm. His generosity did not surprise her. The day before, she'd seen him lean over the *Val*'s starboard rail and, in a benevolent and forbidden act, throw down a handful of goose barnacles for the poor moaning wretches in the shantytown.

"I don't deserve them."

"Eat," ordered the priest.

"I'm not even supposed to be on this voyage."

"Eat," he said again.

Cassie ate. "You're a good person, Father."

Sweeping her bleary gaze past the twelve-mile radar, the fifty-mile radar, and the Marisat terminal, she focused on the beach. Marbles Rafferty and Lou Chickering were climbing out of the *Juan Fernández*, having just returned from another manifestly disastrous sea hunt. They jumped into the breakers and, collecting their trolling gear, waded ashore.

"Not even an old inner tube," sighed Sam Follingsbee, slumped over the control console. "Too bad—I got an incredible recipe for vulcanized rubber in cream sauce."

"Shut up," said Crock O'Connor.

"If only they'd found a boot or two. You should taste my *cuir tartare*."

"I said shut up."

Lifting the late Joe Spicer's copy of *A Brief History of Time* from atop the Marisat, Cassie slipped it under the cowhide belt she'd borrowed from Lou Chickering. Miraculously, the book seemed to ease her stomach pains. She limped into the radio shack.

Lianne Bliss sat faithfully at her post, her sweaty fist clamped around the shortwave mike. ". . . the SS *Carpco Valparaíso*," she muttered, "thirty-seven degrees, fifteen minutes, north . . ."

"Any luck?"

The radio officer tore away her headset. Her cheeks were

sunken, eyes bloodshot; she looked like an antique photograph of herself, a daguerreotype or mezzotint, gray, faded, and wrinkled. "Occasionally I hear something—bits of sports shows from the States, weather reports from Europe—but I'm not gettin' through. Too bad the deckies aren't here. Big news. The Yankees are in first place." Lianne put her headset back on and leaned toward the mike. "Thirty-seven degrees, fifteen minutes, north. Sixteen degrees, forty-seven minutes, west." Again she removed her headset. "The worst of it's the moaning, don't you think? Those poor bastards. At least we get our communion wafers."

"And our barnacles."

"The barnacles are hard for me. I eat 'em, but it's hard."

"I understand." Cassie brushed the sea goddess on Lianne's biceps. "The last time I was in a jam like this . . ."

"Saint Paul's Rocks?"

"Right. I behaved shamefully, Lianne. I prayed for deliverance."

"Don't worry about it, sweetie. In your shoes I'd have done the same thing."

"There are no atheists in foxholes, people say, and it's so true, it's so fucking *true*." Cassie swallowed, savoring the aftertaste of the Cheerios. "No . . . no, I'm being too hard on myself. That maxim, it's not an argument against atheism—it's an argument against foxholes."

"Exactly."

A cold gray tide washed through Cassie's mind. "Lianne, there's something you should know."

"Yeah?"

"I think I'm about to faint."

The radio officer rose from her chair. Her mouth moved, but Cassie heard no words.

"Help . . . ," said Cassie.

The tide crested, crashing against her skull. She slipped down slowly, through the floor of the radio shack . . . through the superstructure . . . the weather deck . . . hull . . . island . . . sea.

Into the green fathoms.

Into the thick silence.

"This is for you."

A deep voice—deeper, even, than Lianne's.

"This is for you," said Anthony again, handing her a stale slice of American cheese, its corners curled, its center inhabited by a patch of green mold.

She blinked. "Was I . . . unconscious?"

"Yeah."

"Long?"

"An hour." The Exxon tiger grinned down from Anthony's T-shirt. "Sam and I agreed that the first person who passed out would get the emergency ration. It's not much, Doc, but it's yours."

Cassie folded the slice into quarters and, pushing the ragged stack into her mouth, gratefully wolfed it down. "Th-thanks . . ."

She rose from the bunk. Anthony's cabin was twice as large as hers, but so cluttered it seemed cramped. Books and magazines were scattered everywhere, a *Complete Pelican Shakespeare* on the bureau, a stack of *Mariners' Weather Log*s on the washbasin, a *Carpco Manual* and a *Girls of Penthouse* on the floor. A spiral notebook lay on his desk, its cover displaying an airbrushed portrait of Popeye the Sailor.

"You'll have some, won't you?" asked Anthony, flashing her a half-empty bottle of Monte Alban. MEZCAL CON GUSANO, the label said. Mescal with worm. Without waiting for a reply, he sloshed several ounces into two ceramic Arco mugs.

"It's hell being a biologist. I know too much." As the pains started up again, Cassie pressed her palm against the *Brief History of Time* belted to her stomach. "Our fats were the first to go, and now it's the proteins. I can practically feel my muscles coming apart, cracking, splitting. The nitrogen floats free, spilling into our blood, our kidneys . . ."

The captain took a protracted sip of mescal. "That why my urine smells like ammonia?"

She nodded.

"My breath stinks too," he said, handing her an Arco mug.

"Ketosis. The odor of sanctity, they used to call it, back when people fasted for God."

"How soon before we . . . ?"

"It's an individual sort of thing. Big fellas like Follingsbee, they're likely to last another month. Rafferty and Lianne—four or five days, maybe."

The captain drained his mescal. "This voyage started out so well. Hell, I even thought we'd save His brain. It's hash by now, don't you think?"

"Quite likely."

Settling behind his desk, Anthony refilled his mug and retrieved a brass sextant from among the nautical charts and Styrofoam coffee cups. "Know something, Doc? I'm just tipsy enough to say I think you're an incredibly attractive and altogether wonderful lady."

The remark aroused in Cassie a strange conjunction of delight and apprehension. A door to chaos had just been opened, and now she'd do best to fling it closed. "I'm flattered," she said, taking a hot gulp of Monte Alban. "Let's not forget I'm practically engaged."

"I was practically engaged once."

"Yeah?"

"Yeah. Janet Yost, a bos'n with Chevron Shipping." The captain sighted Cassie through his sextant; a lascivious grin twisted his lips, as if the instrument somehow rendered her blouse transparent. "We bunked together for nearly two years, running the glop down from Alaska. Once or twice we talked about a wedding. Far as I'm concerned, she was my fiancée. Then she got pregnant."

"By you?"

"Uh-huh."

"And . . . ?"

"And I freaked out. A baby's no way to start a marriage."

"Did you ask her to get an abortion?"

"Not in so many words, but she could tell that's where I stood. I'm not fit for fatherhood, Cassie. Look at who I've got for a model. It's like a surgeon learning his business from Jack the Ripper."

"Maybe you could've . . . hunted around, right? Gotten some guidance."

"I *tried*, Doc. Talked to sailors with kids, walked uptown to F.A.O. Schwarz and bought a Baby Feels-So-Real, you know, one of those authentic-type dolls, so I could take it home and hold it a lot—I felt pretty embarrassed buying the thing, I'll tell you, like it was some sort of sexual aid. And, hey, let's not forget my trips to Saint Vincent's for purposes of studying the newborns and seeing what sort of creatures they were. You realize how easy it is to sneak into a maternity ward? Act like an uncle, that's all. None of this shit worked. To this day, babies scare me."

"I'm sure you could get over it. Alexander did."

"Who?"

"A Norway rat. When I forced him to live with his own offspring, he started taking care of them. Sea horses make good fathers too. Also lumpfish. Did Janet get the abortion?"

"Wasn't necessary. Mother Nature stepped in. Before I knew it, we'd lost the relationship too. An awful time, terrible fights. Once she threw a sextant at me—that's how my nose got busted. After that we made a point of staying on separate ships. Maybe we passed in the night. Didn't hear from her for three whole years, but then, when the *Val* hit Bolivar Reef, she wrote to me and said she knew it wasn't my fault."

"Was it your fault?"

"I left the bridge."

Gritting her teeth, Cassie placed both her hands against *A*

Brief History of Time and pushed. "We ever gonna find food out there?"

"Sure we are, Doc. I guarantee it. You okay?"

"Woozy. Abdominal pains. I don't suppose you have any more cheese?"

"Sorry."

She stretched out on the rug. Her brain had become a sponge, a *Polymastia mamillaris* dripping with Monte Alban. A mescal haze lay between her psyche and the world, hanging in space like a theatrical scrim, backlit, imprinted with twinkling stars. A scarlet macaw flew across the constellations—the very bird she'd promised to buy Anthony once they were home—and suddenly it was molting, feather by feather, until only the bare, breathing flesh remained, knobby, soft, and edible.

The minutes tocked by. Cassie nodded off, roused herself, nodded off . . .

"Am I dying?" she asked.

Anthony now sat beside her, his back against the desk, cradling her in his bare, sweaty arms. His tattooed mermaid looked anorectic. Slowly he extended his palm, its lifeline bisected by three objects resembling thick, stubby pretzel sticks.

"You won't die," he said. "I won't let anybody die."

"Pretzels?"

"Pickled mescal worms. Caspar, Melchior, Balthazar."

"W-worms?"

"All meat," he insisted, languorously lifting Caspar—or maybe it was Melchior, or possibly Balthazar—to her mouth. The creature was flaxen and segmented: not a true worm, she realized, but the larva of some Mexican moth or other. "Fresh from Oaxaca," he said.

"Yes. Yes. Good."

Gently, Anthony inserted Caspar. She sucked, the oldest of all survival reflexes, wetting the captain's fingers, saturating his larva. Satisfaction beamed from his face, a fulfillment akin to what a mother experiences while nursing—not bad, she decided, for a man who'd panicked at his girlfriend's pregnancy. She worked her jaw. Caspar disintegrated. He had a crude, spiky, medicinal flavor, a blend of raw mescal and *Lepidoptera* innards.

"Tell me what you told me before," said Cassie. "About my being—how did you put it?—'a wonderfully attractive . . .'"

He fed her Melchior. "An incredibly attractive . . ."

"Yeah." She devoured the larva. "That."

Now came Balthazar. "I think you're an incredibly attractive and altogether wonderful lady," Anthony informed her for the second time that day.

As Cassie chewed, a mild sense of well-being took hold of her, transient but real. The wheat of General Mills, the cheese of Kraft, the worms of Oaxaca. She licked her lips and drifted toward sleep. Faith did not exist aboard the *Carpco Valparaíso*, nor hope either, but for the moment, at least, there was charity.

Whatever the cause of the *Valparaíso*'s failure to appear in Arctic waters, Oliver couldn't help noticing that the World War Two Reenactment Society was profiting heavily from the delay. According to the contract the Enlightenment League had signed with Pembroke and Flume, each sailor, pilot, and gunner had to receive "full combat pay" for every day he served aboard the carrier. Not that the men didn't earn it. Their commanders worked them around the clock, as if there were a war on. But Oliver still felt resentful. His money, he decided, was like Cassie's large chest. All during high school, she'd never known for certain why she was constantly being asked out—or, rather, she *had* known, and she didn't like it. A person should be valued for what he gave, Oliver believed, not for what he possessed.

The short, homely man portraying Lieutenant Commander Wade McClusky, the officer in charge of Air Group Six, required both his squadrons to fly two practice missions a day, dropping wooden bombs and Styrofoam torpedoes on the icebergs of Tromso Fjord. Meanwhile, the fellow playing the carrier's skipper, a burly Irishman with a handlebar mustache, made his men keep the flight deck completely clear of ice and snow, even during those hours when the warplanes weren't flying their milk runs. For Captain George Murray's beleaguered sailors, combat duty aboard the *Enterprise* was like living in some suburbanite hell, a world where your driveway was six hundred feet long and needed shoveling even in the middle of summer.

An hour after the ninetieth straight PBY mission failed to find the *Valparaíso*, Pembroke and Flume summoned Oliver to their cabin. During World War Two, these spacious quarters had functioned as the wardroom, but the impresarios had converted it into a two-bedroom suite featuring a parlor furnished with an eye to late-Victorian ostentation.

"The crew's getting itchy," Albert Flume began, guiding Oliver toward a plush divan reminiscent of the couch in Delacroix's *Odalisque*.

"Our pilots and gunners're going nuts." Sidney Pembroke unwrapped a facsimile of a Baby Ruth candy bar circa 1944. "If something doesn't happen soon to improve morale, they'll be asking to go home."

"To wit, we'd like to start granting the boys shore leave."

"At full combat pay."

Oliver glowered and clenched his fists. "Shore leave? Shore leave to where? Oslo?"

Flume shook his head. "No way to get 'em there. The PBYs are tied up with reconnaissance, and we can't hire bush pilots without attracting attention."

"We hopped over to Ibsen City last night," said Pembroke. "Dull place on the whole, but that Sundog Saloon has possibilities."

Oliver scowled. "It's nothing but an old airplane hangar."

"We'll give it to you straight," said Pembroke, merrily devouring his candy bar. "Assuming you're willing to bankroll us, Alby and I intend to turn the Sundog into a classic-type USO Club. You know, a home away from home, a place for the boys to get a free sandwich, dance with a pretty hostess, and hear Kate Smith sing 'God Bless America.'"

"If it's entertainment your people want," said Oliver, "Barclay does a damn good magic act. Last year he was on the *Tonight* show, debunking faith healers."

"Debunking faith?" Flume opened the refrigerator, removed a Rheingold, and popped the cap. "What is he, an atheist?"

"No, nothing like that."

"We don't mean to disparage your friend's abilities," said Pembroke, "but we're envisioning something more along the lines of Jimmy Durante, Al Jolson, the Andrews Sisters, Bing Crosby . . ."

"Aren't those people dead?"

"Yeah, but it's not that hard to come up with impersonators."

"We'll also be importing a string of attractive young women to work the room," said Flume. "You know, nice girl-next-door types handing out cigarettes, offering to dance, and maybe allowing a stolen kiss or two."

"No bimbos, of course," said Pembroke. "Wholesome, aspiring actresses who know there's more to life than topless bars and wet T-shirt contests."

"Right now it's three A.M. in Manhattan," said Flume, "but if we get on the phone 'round suppertime we'll be able to reach the relevant talent agencies."

"You actually think the average New York actor will drop whatever he's doing and catch the first plane to Oslo?" said Oliver.

"I do."

"Why?"

"Because for the average New York actor," said Flume, swallowing Rheingold, "getting paid a scale wage to impersonate Bing

Crosby on an obscure island in the Arctic Ocean is the closest he's come to a job in years."

August 27.

In my entry of July 14, I told you what I heard, saw, and felt when I first laid eyes on our cargo. For sheer exhilaration, Popeye, it was nothing compared to my second epiphany.

At 0900 I was standing outside the wheelhouse, binoculars raised, watching the mutineers lying about in the streets of their shantytown. Until that moment, I hadn't realized what a difference our feeble rations make. We, at least, can move.

A gamey fragrance wafted across the bridge wing. Then: a low, deep drumming. I pivoted toward the beach.

And there it was, the glorious promontory of His nose, rising in the distance like Mount Sinai itself. My migraine vanished. My blood jumped. The drumming continued, the steady *boom-boom-boom* of surf crashing inside His armpits.

Whether this amazing break ultimately traces to rogue winds, maverick currents, chaos theory, or some posthumous form of divine intervention, I can't really say.

I only know He's back.

After considerable soul-searching and much mental agony, Thomas decided to start with the bosom. Given its vastness, he reasoned, mutilating this feature would constitute a lesser violation than an equivalent assault on the brow or cheeks. Even so, he was not at peace. Situational ethics had always given him pause. Were the *Valparaíso* not cut off from the outside world, Thomas would certainly have faxed Rome, soliciting the cardinals' official views on deophagy.

The eight loyalists and their captain made the crossing in the *Juan Fernández* and, maneuvering past the starboard ribs, landed on the inflatable wharf. Shouldering their various backpacks and seabags, they fought their way up the Jacob's ladder, and, led by Van Horne, began the dizzying hike east across the collarbone and south along the sternum. Pots and pans swung from the loyalists' belts like gigantic jail keys, clanging in counterpoint to the thunder booming from His armpits.

At last they reached the edge of the areola, a red, rubbery pasture dominated by the tall, pillarlike form of the nipple. Thomas stopped, turned, removed his Panama hat. He bade his congregation sit down. Everyone obeyed, even Van Horne, though the captain kept his distance, secluding himself in the shadow of a mole.

Opening his knapsack, Thomas drew out the sacred hardware: candlesticks, chalice, ciborium, silver salver, antependium (the pride of his collection, pure silk, printed with the Stations of the Cross). The congregation awaited the sacrament eagerly but respectfully—all except Van Horne and Cassie Fowler, who both looked highly annoyed. Eight communicants, Thomas thought with a wry smile, the most he'd ever had at a *Valparaíso* Mass, either before or after His death became known aboard the tanker.

Sister Miriam reached into her seabag and removed the altar: a situational-ethics altar, he had to admit, for in truth it was a Coleman stove fueled by propane gas. While Miriam unfolded the aluminum legs and dug them into the soft epidermis, Thomas spread out the antependium like a picnic blanket, fastening the corners with candlesticks.

"Can't he move any faster?" grumbled Fowler.

"He's doing his best," snapped Miriam.

As Sam Follingsbee handed the nun a battery-powered carving knife, Crock O'Connor gave her one of the waterproof chain saws he'd used to open God's eardrums, and she in turn passed these tools to Thomas. In the interest of speed, he elected to dispense with the normal preliminaries—the Incensing of the Faithful, the Washing of the Hands, the Orate Fratres, the Reading of the Diptychs—and move straight to the matter of deconsecration. But here he was stuck. There was no antidote for transubstantiation in the missal, no recognized procedure for turning the divine body back into daily bread. Perhaps it would be sufficient simply to reverse the famous words of the Last Supper, "Accipite et manducate ex hoc omnes, hoc est enim corpus Meum." *Take and eat ye all of this, for this is My body.* Very well, he thought. Sure. Why not?

Thomas hunkered down. He yanked the starter cord. Instantly the chain saw kicked in, buzzing like a horror-movie hornet. Clouds of black smoke poured from the engine housing. Groaning softly, the priest lowered the saw, firmed his grip, and stabbed his Creator.

He jerked the saw away.

"What's the matter?" gasped Miriam.

It simply wasn't right. How could it be right? "Better to starve," he muttered.

"Tom, you *must*."

"No."

"Tom."

Again he lowered the saw. The spinning teeth bit into the flesh, releasing a stream of rosy plasma.

He raised the saw.

"Hurry," rasped Lou Chickering.

"Please," moaned Marbles Rafferty.

He eased the smoking machine back into the wound. Languidly, reluctantly, he dragged the blade along a horizontal path. Then a second cut, at right angles to the first. A third. A fourth. Peeling away the patch of epidermis, he inserted the saw clear to the engine housing and began his quest for true meat.

"Pleni sunt caeli et terra gloria Tua," Miriam recited as she primed the altar. *Heaven and earth are full of Thy glory.* Opening a box of Diamond kitchen matches, she ignited a stick, cupped the vulnerable flame, and lit the right-hand burner. "Hosanna in excelsis." Instinctively they were opting for the grand manner, Thomas realized: an old-style Eucharist, complete with the Latin.

The fog hissed as it hit the little fire. Miriam seized Follings-bee's eighteen-inch iron skillet and set it atop the burner.

"Meum corpus enim est hoc," muttered Thomas, cutting and slashing as he desacralized the tissues, "omnes hoc ex manducate et accipite." As heavy magenta blood came bubbling to the surface, Miriam took the chalice, knelt down, and scooped up several pints. "Omnes eo ex bibite et accipite," said the priest, filtering the holiness from the blood. He kept working the saw, at last freeing up a three-pound swatch of flesh.

It had to be this way. No other choice existed. If he didn't do it, Van Horne would.

Shutting off the vibrating blade, he carried the fillet to the altar and dropped it into the skillet. The meat sizzled, pink juices rushing from its depths. A wondrous scent arose, the sweet aroma of seared divinity, making Thomas's mouth water.

"It's done," seethed Cassie Fowler. "It's fucking *done.*"

"Patience," snarled Miriam.

"Christ on a raft . . ."

Sixty seconds passed. Thomas grabbed the spatula and flipped the fillet. A matter of balances: he must heat the thing long enough to kill the pathogens, but not so long as to destroy the precious proteins for which their bodies screamed.

"What's next?" snorted Van Horne.

"The Fraction of the Host," said Miriam.

"Screw it," he said.

"Screw you," she said.

Sliding the spatula under the meat, Thomas transferred it to the silver salver. He took a breath and, switching on the carving knife, divided the great steak into nine equal portions, each the size of a brownie. "Haec commixtio," he said, slicing a tiny bit off his own share, "corporis et sanguinis Dei"—with the particle he made the Sign of the Cross over the chalice and dropped it in—"fiat accipientibus nobis." *May this mingling of the body and blood of God be effectual to us who receive it.* "Amen."

"Stop stretching it out," gasped Fowler.

"This is sadistic," whined Van Horne.

"If you don't like it," said Miriam, "find another church."

Squeezing his portion between thumb and forefinger, feeling the sticky warmth roll across his palm, Thomas raised it to his lips. He opened his mouth. "Perceptio corporis Tui, Domine, quod ego indignus sumere praesumo, non mihi proveniat in condemnationem." *Let not the partaking of Thy body, O Lord, which I, though unworthy, presume to receive, turn to my condemnation.* He sank his teeth into the meat. He chewed slowly and gulped. The flavor astonished him. He'd been expecting something manifestly classy and valuable—London broil, perhaps, or milk-fed veal—but instead it evoked Follingsbee's version of a Big Mac.

And the priest thought: of course. God had been for everyone, hadn't He? He'd belonged to the fast-food multitudes, to all those overweight mothers Thomas was forever seeing in the Bronxdale Avenue McDonald's, ordering Happy Meals for their chubby broods.

"Corpus Tuum, Domine, quod sumpsit, adhaereat visceribus meis," he said. *May Thy body, O Lord, which I have received, cleave to my inmost parts.* He felt a sudden, electric surge, though whether this traced to the meat itself or to the Idea of the Meat he couldn't say. "Amen."

Myriad sensations gamboled among Thomas's taste buds as, silver salver in hand, he approached Follingsbee. Beyond the burgerness lay something not unlike Kentucky Fried Chicken, and beyond that lay intimations of a Wendy's Triple.

"Father, I feel real bad about this," said the plump chef.

"I'm sure you could've cooked it better. Don't tell the stewards' union."

Follingsbee winced. "I used to be an altar boy, remember?"

"It's perfectly okay, Sam."

"You promise? It seems sinful."

"I promise."

"It's okay? You sure?"

"Open your mouth."

The chef's lips parted.

"Corpus Dei custodiat corpus tuum," said Thomas, inserting Follingsbee's portion. *May God's body preserve thy own.* "Eat slowly," he admonished, "or you'll get sick."

As Follingsbee chewed, Thomas moved down the line— Rafferty, O'Connor, Chickering, Bliss, Fowler, Van Horne, Sister Miriam—laying a share on each extended tongue. "Corpus Dei custodiat corpus tuum," he told them. "Not too fast," he warned.

The communicants worked their jaws and swallowed.

"Domine, non sum dignus," said Miriam, licking her lips. *Lord, I am not worthy.*

"Domine, non sum dignus," said Follingsbee, eyes closed, savoring his salvation.

"Domine . . . non . . . sum . . . dignus," groaned the radio officer, shuddering with self-disgust. For a committed vegetarian like Lianne Bliss, this was obviously a terrible ordeal.

"Domine, non sum dignus," said Rafferty, O'Connor, and Chickering in unison. Only Van Horne and Fowler remained silent.

"Dominus vobiscum," Thomas told the congregation, stepping onto the areola.

Under the captain's direction the loyalists drew out their machetes, stilettos, and Swiss Army knives and set to work, systematically enlarging the original indentation as they carved out additional fillets for their mates back in the shantytown, and within an hour they had flensed the corpse sufficiently to fill every pot and pan.

"He smells ripe," said Van Horne, pinching his nostrils as he joined Thomas on the areola.

"If not rotten," said the priest, watching Miriam cram a bloody fillet into the ciborium.

"You know, I probably believe in Him more strongly right now than I ever did when He was alive." The captain dropped his hand, letting his nostrils spring open. "It's an absolute miracle, don't you think?"

"I don't know what it is." Fanning himself with his Panama hat, Thomas turned toward the communicants.

"Either that, or His body got caught on the crest of the Canary Current, entered the North Atlantic Drift . . ."

"Ite," Thomas announced in a strong, clear voice.

". . . and then came 'round full circle."

"Missa est."

"So what do you think, Father? A miracle, or the North Atlantic Drift?"

"I think it's all the same thing," said the dazed, exhausted, satiated priest.

Feast

WILD APPLAUSE AND delirious cheers greeted Bob Hope as, dressed in baggy green combat fatigues and a white golfing cap, he stepped onto the stage of the Midnight Sun Canteen. The spotlight caught his famous and complex nose, limning its beloved contours.

"I'm sure havin' a swell time here on Jan Mayen Island," the comedian began, waving to his audience: a hundred and thirty-two Navy pilots and gunners—most of them wearing chocolate brown bomber jackets with black fur collars—plus two hundred and ten sailors in white bucket hats and blue neckerchiefs. "You all know what Jan Mayen is." He tapped the floor mike, producing an amplified *thock*. "Shangri-La with icicles!"

Appreciative howls. Delighted guffaws.

Oliver, sitting alone, did not laugh. He polished off his second Frydenlund beer of the evening, burped, and slumped down farther in his chair. Some terrible tragedy, he was sure, had overtaken Cassandra and the *Valparaíso*. Typhoon, maelstrom, tsunami—or maybe the force was human, for surely there were institutions other than the Central Park West Enlightenment League that wished to get God's carcass out of the way, institutions that wouldn't hesitate to sink a supertanker or two in the process.

Albert Flume and his partner ambled up to Oliver's table. "May we join you?"

"Sure."

"Another beer?" asked Sidney Pembroke, pointing to the pair of empty bottles.

"Yeah, why not?"

"Last night I slept in the barracks along with the boys," said Bob Hope. Hands in pockets, he hunched toward the mike. "You know what barracks are. That's two thousand cots separated by individual crap games."

A Hope classic. The pilots, gunners, and sailors nearly fell out of their chairs.

"Alby, we done good," said Pembroke.

"Definitely one of our better productions," said Flume. "Hey, girl-o'-my-dreams!" he called toward a pretty, honey-blonde hostess as, hips swaying, she carried a plate of ham sandwiches across the room. "Bring our friend Oliver here a Frydenlund!"

The impresarios' pride was in fact justified. In a mere three days they'd managed to turn the Sundog Saloon into a forties USO club. Except for the availability of beer, the Midnight Sun Canteen was entirely authentic, right down to the fluted public-address speakers on the girders, the SERVICEMEN ONLY sign above the front door, and the LOOSE LIPS SINK SHIPS and NIMITZ HAS NO LIMITS posters on the walls. At first Vladimir Panshin had resisted the transformation, figuring his usual clientele would be irate, but then he realized that for every Ibsen City scientist who stayed away at least two Reenactment Society members would take his place.

The refurbishing had cost Oliver nearly eighty-five thousand dollars, most of it going to the carpenters and electricians they'd ferried over from Trondheim, but that sum was nothing compared to the sizable percentage of his bank account Pembroke and Flume had consumed in procuring the talent. The New York office of Actors Equity had sent two dozen ingenues and chorus girls, all of them more than willing to put on cocktail aprons and flirt with a bunch of middle-aged schizophrenics who thought they were fighting World War Two. From the William Morris Agency had come Sonny Orbach and His Harmonicoots, sixteen septuagenarian musicians who, when sufficiently plastered on Frydenlund, became a veritable reincarnation of Glenn Miller's band. But the impresarios' real coup was tracking down the amazingly gifted and chronically obscure Kovitsky Brothers: Myron, Arnold, and Jake, aka the Great American Nostalgia Machine—borscht-circuit mimics whose repertoire extended beyond such obvious choices as Bob Hope and Al Jolson into the rarefied world of female impersonation. Myron did a first-rate Kate Smith, Arnold a credible Marlene Dietrich, Jake a passable Ethel Merman and a positively uncanny Frances Langford. Fusing their falsettos in tight, three-part harmony, the Kovitsky Brothers could make you swear you were hearing the Andrews Sisters singing "Don't Sit Under the Apple Tree (with Anyone Else but Me)."

Oliver looked at his watch. Five P.M. Damn. Commander Wade McClusky's portrayer should have reported in well over an hour ago.

"You know, I recently figured out that all General Tojo wants is peace," said Hope. "A piece of China, a piece of Australia, a piece of the Philippines . . ."

By his own account, Wade McClusky was a crackerjack target spotter. While still an ensign, he'd become known as the man who could pick out a camouflaged aircraft factory from three miles up, though Oliver was unclear on whether it was the real McClusky, the real McClusky's portrayer, or the real McClusky's portrayer's fictionalized version of the real McClusky who boasted this talent. In any event, ten hours earlier the stalwart leader of Air Group Six had taken personal charge of the reconnaisance operation, assuming command of the PBY flying boat code-named "Strawberry Eight." An auspicious development, Oliver felt. So why wasn't McClusky back yet? Was the *Valparaíso* armed with Bofors guns after all? Had Van Horne shot Strawberry Eight out of the sky?

Hope motioned for the gorgeous and curvaceous Dorothy Lamour—Myron Kovitsky in wig, makeup, evening gown, and latex breasts—to join him on stage. Smiling, blowing kisses, Lamour slithered across the canteen, accompanied by choruses of wolf whistles.

"Just wanted you boys to see what you're fighting for." Another Hope classic. "Yesterday, Crosby and I were—"

"Attention, everyone! Attention!" A breathless voice broke from the loudspeakers, popping and fizzing like a draught of Moxie encountering an ice cube. "This is Admiral Spruance on *Enterprise*! Great news, men! Barely four hours ago, sixteen army B-25s took off from the carrier *Hornet* under the command of Lieutenant Colonel James H. Doolittle and dropped over fifty demolition bombs on the industrial heart of Tokyo!"

Whoops and applause resounded through the Midnight Sun Canteen.

"The extent of the damage is not known," Spruance's portrayer continued, "but President Roosevelt is calling the Doolittle raid 'a major blow to enemy morale'!"

The war reenactors stomped their feet. Bewildered but eager to please, the hostesses set down their sandwich trays and cheered.

"That is all, men!"

When the tumult died away, the spotlight pivoted toward the northeast corner, just as Sonny Orbach and His Harmonicoots, in full evening attire, launched into a spirited imitation of Glenn Miller's "Pistol Packin' Mama." Leaping up, the Midnight Sun

Canteen's patrons began jitterbugging—with each other, with their hostesses, and, in the case of one fantastically lucky tail gunner, with Dorothy Lamour herself.

At the next table over, a perky redheaded hostess was busy earning her salary, sharing a Coca-Cola with a chunky sailor in his early forties.

". . . not supposed to ask where you're going," the hostess was saying as Oliver tuned in their conversation.

"That's right," the sailor replied. "The Japs have spies everywhere."

"But I *can* ask where you're from."

"Georgia, ma'am. Little town called Peach Landing."

"Really?"

"Newark, actually."

"Golly, I never met anyone from Georgia." The hostess batted her eyes. "Got a girl, sailor?"

"Sure do, ma'am."

"Carry her picture with you, by any chance?"

"Yes, ma'am." With a sheepish grin the sailor pulled his wallet from his bell-bottoms and, slipping out a small photograph, handed it to the hostess. "Her name's Mindy Sue."

"She looks real sweet, sailor. Does she blow you?"

"What?"

At 1815 hours, the unmistakable roar of a PBY flying boat's Pratt and Whitney engines passed over the Midnight Sun Canteen, rattling the Frydenlund bottles. A delicious anticipation flooded through Oliver. Surely this was Wade McClusky, heading for the nearest fjord in Strawberry Eight. Surely the *Valparaíso* had been spotted.

Glenn Miller followed "Pistol Packin' Mama" with "Chattanooga Choo-Choo," then the spotlight swung back to the stage for the Andrews Sisters singing "The Boogie-Woogie Bugle Boy of Company B." (At some point Myron had sneaked off and changed costumes.) Next came Bing Crosby crooning "Pack Up

Your Troubles in Your Old Kit Bag," after which Hope sauntered over to his buddy. Swaying back and forth, the two of them offered their famous rendition of "Mairzy Doats."

"Speaking of mares," said Flume as Hope and Crosby welcomed Frances Langford on stage, "did you know our subs used to carry buckets of horse guts along on their missions?"

Oliver wasn't sure he'd heard correctly. "Buckets of . . . ?"

"Horse guts. Sometimes sheep guts. That way, whenever the Nazis dropped their depth charges, the sub commander could send the stuff to the surface, and the enemy would think he'd scored a hit!"

"What an amazing war," said Pembroke, sighing with admiration.

"I'm in the mood for love," sang Frances Langford.

"Baby, you came to the right place!" a randy sailor shouted.

"Simply because you're near me . . ."

The front door flew open, and a small gale swept through the Midnight Sun Canteen. Blue with cold, Wade McClusky's craggy portrayer strode inside and marched over to Oliver's table. Ice crystals glittered on his flight jacket. Snow sat on his shoulders like a prodigious case of dandruff.

"Jeez, am I glad to see *you*!" shouted Oliver, slapping the group leader on the back. "Any luck?"

Smiling, blowing kisses, Frances Langford launched into her signature tune, "Embraceable You."

"Gimme a lousy minute." McClusky pulled a pack of Wrigley's spearmint from his flight jacket, then slid a stick into his mouth like a doctor inserting a tongue depressor. "Hey, cutie!" he called to the redheaded hostess, who was still drinking Coke with the chunky sailor. "We'll take a Frydenlund over here!"

"Embrace me, my sweet embraceable you," sang Frances Langford. "Embrace me, my irreplaceable you . . ."

"You know, there's a wonderful story connected with that number," said Pembroke. "Miss Langford was visiting a field hospital in the African desert. There'd been a big tank battle earlier that week, and some of the boys were shot up pretty bad."

"Hope suggested she give 'em a song," said Flume, "so naturally Frances trotted out 'Embraceable You.' And when she looked toward the nearest bed—well, you'll never guess what she saw."

"Did you find the *Valparaíso?*" Oliver demanded. "Did you find the golem?"

"I didn't find a goddamn thing," said McClusky, accepting his beer from the hostess.

"She saw a soldier without any arms," said Pembroke. "Both of 'em had been burned off. Isn't that a wonderful story?"

The late-afternoon breeze lifted nuggets of rust from the dunes, hurling them over the starboard bulwark and scattering them across the weather deck like buckshot. Anthony donned his mirrorshades and, peering through the sandstorm, studied the approaching procession. His stomach, filled, purred contentedly. Like pallbearers transporting a small but emotionally burdensome coffin—the coffin of a pet, a child, a beloved dwarf—Ockham and Sister Miriam carried an aluminum footlocker down the catwalk. Descending to the deck, they set the box at Anthony's feet. They opened it.

Packaged in wax paper, sixty sandwiches lay in neat ranks, files, and layers. Closing his eyes, Anthony inhaled the robust fragrance. Follingsbee's great breakthrough had occurred less than an hour after the inverse Eucharist, when he'd discovered that their cargo's epidermis could be mashed into a paste possessing all the best qualities of bread dough. While Rafferty and Chickering had fried the patties, Follingsbee had baked the buns. In Anthony's view, the fact that he'd be giving his crew not just meat but a facsimile of their favorite cuisine all but guaranteed the mutiny's end.

The captain leaned over the rail. Today's emissary from the shantytown was an elderly, cod-faced man, stripped to the waist and wearing black bicycle pants. He sat motionless amid the thick mist and swirling rust, arms outstretched in a gesture of entreaty, ribs bulging from his shriveled torso like bars on a marimba.

"What's your name?" Anthony called to the starving man.

"Mungo, sir." The sailor rose and stumbled backward, slumping against the tanker's thrown propeller like a leprechaun crucified on a gigantic shamrock. "Able Seaman Ralph Mungo."

"Find your shipmates, Mungo. Tell 'em to report here at once."

"Aye-aye."

"Give 'em a message."

"What message?"

" 'Van Horne is the bread of life.' Got that?"

"Aye."

"Let's not get carried away," said Ockham, cupping his palm around Anthony's shoulder.

"Repeat it," Anthony ordered the sailor.

"Van Horne is the bread of life." Mungo pushed off from the orphan screw. Gasping for breath, he staggered away. "Van Horne is the bread . . ."

Twenty minutes later the mutineers appeared, flopping and crawling across the foggy dunes, and soon the lot of them sat clustered around the propeller. The allegory pleased Anthony. Above: he, Captain Van Horne, master of the *Valparaíso*, splendid in his dress blues and braided cap. Below: they, abject mortals, groveling in the muck. He wasn't out to torment them. He had no wish to steal their wills or claim their souls. But now was the time to bring these traitors to heel once and for all, now was the time to bury the Idea of the Corpse in the deepest, darkest hole this side of the Mariana Trench.

Anthony drew a package from the footlocker. "This soup kitchen's like any other, sailors. First the sermon, then the sandwich." He cleared his throat. " 'When evening came, the disciples went to Him and said, "Send the people away, and they can go to the villages to buy themselves some food." ' " He'd spent the noon-to-four watch paging through Ockham's *Jerusalem Bible*, studying the great precedents: the manna from heaven, the water from the rock, the feeding of the five thousand. " 'Jesus replied, "Give them something to eat yourselves." But they answered, "All we have is five loaves and two fish." ' "

Tearing off his Panama hat, Ockham squeezed Anthony's wrist. "Cut the crap, okay?"

So far Follingsbee had wrung four distinct variations. The steward's own favorite was the basic hamburger, while Rafferty found the Filet-o-Fish unbeatable (seafood flavor derived from areola tissue) and Chickering preferred the Quarter Pounder with Cheese (curds cultivated from divine lymph). Nobody much liked the McNuggets.

" 'Breaking the loaves, He handed them to His disciples,' " Anthony persisted, " 'who gave them to the crowds.' " He hurled the sandwich over the side. " 'They all ate as much as they wanted . . .' "

The Filet-o-Fish arced toward the mutineers. Reaching up, Able Seaman Weisinger made the catch. Incredulous, he unwrapped the wax paper and stared at the gift. He rubbed the bun. He sniffed the meat. Tears of gratitude ran down his face in parallel tracks. Crumpling the paper into a ball, he tossed it aside, raised the sandwich to his mouth, and swept his lips along the breaded, juicy fibers.

"Eat," Anthony commanded.

Placing one index finger under his nose, Weisinger hooked the other over his lower teeth and pried his jaw open. He inserted the Filet-o-Fish, bit off a large piece. He swallowed. Gulped. Shuddered. A retching noise issued from his throat, like a ship scraping bottom. Seconds later he vomited up the offering, marring his lap with a sticky mixture of amber fat and sea green bile.

"Chew it!" called Anthony. "You aren't scarfing down peanuts in a fucking waterfront dive! *Chew* it!"

Weisinger broke off a modest morsel and tried again. His jaw moved slowly, deliberately. "It's *good*!" rasped the AB. "It's so *good*!"

"Of course it's good!" shouted Anthony.

"Where'd you get it?" asked Ralph Mungo.

"All good things come from God!" cried Sister Miriam.

Anthony drew a Quarter Pounder with Cheese from the locker. "Who is your captain?" he screamed into the wind.

"You are!" cried Dolores Haycox.

"You are!" insisted Charlie Horrocks.

"You are!" chimed in Ralph Mungo, Bud Ramsey, James Echohawk, Stubby Barnes, Juanita Torres, Isabel Bostwick, Anmei Jong, and a dozen more.

Quarter Pounder in hand, Anthony thrust his arm over the rail. "Who is the bread of life?"

"You are!" cried a chorus of mutineers.

He waved the sandwich around. "Who can forgive your sins against this ship?"

"You can!"

Springing sideways, Sister Miriam grabbed the Quarter Pounder from Anthony and tossed it into the air. Like a tight end catching a forward pass, Haycox snagged the package, instantly ripping away the wax paper.

"You had no right to do that," Anthony informed the nun. "You're just a passenger, for Christ's sake."

"I'm just a passenger," she agreed. "For Christ's sake," she repeated, curling her lower lip.

Ockham rummaged around in the locker, drawing out four hamburgers and four boxes of McNuggets. "You each get two!"

he shouted, chucking the packages over the rail. "Eat slowly!"

"*Very* slowly," said Miriam, throwing down six Filets-o-Fish.

The sky rained godsend. Half the packages were caught in midair, half hit the sands. Anthony was impressed not only by the orderliness with which the mutineers retrieved the fallen meat but by the fact that no sailor took more than his or her share.

"They fear me," he observed.

"You proud of that?" asked Ockham.

"Yes. No. I want my ship back, Thomas."

"How does it feel, being feared? Heady stuff?"

"Heady stuff."

"That all?"

"All right, I'll be frank—sure, I'm tempted to have my ass kissed. I'm tempted to become their god." Anthony fixed on Ockham. "If *you* had my power," said the captain, voice dripping with sarcasm, "no doubt you'd use it only for good."

"If I had your power," said the priest, closing the footlocker, "I'd try not to use it for anything at all."

August 28.

I saved them, Popeye, and for the moment I am their god. It's not really me they worship, of course—it's the Idea of the Quarter Pounder. No matter. They still do whatever I say.

Their thirst is fearsome, but they don't stop excavating. The sun shines without mercy, burning through the mist and frying their backs and shoulders, but they keep at it, pausing only long enough to wolf down sandwiches or apply protective coatings of glory grease to their skin.

"They've discovered the categorical imperative," Ockham tells me.

"They've discovered the full belly," I correct him.

I am their god, but Sister Miriam is their savior. Canteen in hand, she moves from digger to digger. Inevitably she evokes Debra Paget working the brick pits in *The Ten Commandments*, giving water to the Hebrew slaves.

Cassie may be a cynic and an egghead, but she's certainly doing her part toward getting us out of here, dispensing water alongside Miriam and sometimes even digging herself. Furtively I watch. Until the day I die, I shall retain the image of a beauteous, raven-haired woman in cut-off jeans and a Harley-Davidson T-shirt, shoveling out the *Carpco Valparaíso*.

When we first went on this diet, we all assumed it would change us in some way. Has it? Hard to say. I've seen nothing truly astonishing so far, no big jump in anybody's reading speed or knot-tying skills. While our bowel movements have been remarkably pale and coherent—it's like shitting soap—that's hardly a miracle. (Sparks points out you can get the same result from macrobiotic food.) True, the deckies have tons of energy, a phenomenal amount, but Cassie insists there's nothing supernatural going on. "His flesh is acting like Dumbo's magic feather," she says, "enabling us to tap our own latent powers."

With Spicer and Wheatstone both gone, we've had to reapportion the duties. Dolores Haycox seems completely rehabilitated, and so we've made her our second mate, bumping James Echohawk up to third. The new bos'n is Ralph Mungo. I'm inclined to stick Weisinger back in the brig, but Ockham is convinced that Zook died before the kid ripped his hose, and right now we need every available pair of hands.

While Rafferty's people disassemble the mountain, O'Connor's men repair the damage, smoothing the keel with scrap-metal patches and straightening the port shaft by banging it with a sledgehammer. It turns out the thrown propeller has a seven-foot fissure running through one blade, but the backup screw seems fine, and that's the one we'll be mounting.

This morning Rafferty and Ockham made exploratory dives. Their report was encouraging. Just as we suspected, the anvil bones snapped in both His ears, but the padre says we can almost certainly get a firm grip on the stirrups.

Okay, I'll admit it: His brain is surely mush by now. I keep telling myself this doesn't matter. The angels wanted a decent burial, that's all. Just a decent burial.

During the past twenty-four hours, Sam Follingsbee has gone way beyond McDonald's, finding amazingly creative ways to prepare the fillets. He's frustrated that so many spices and condiments got gobbled up during the famine, but he's a wiz at making do. The local sand, for example, has a decidedly peppery flavor. The body itself supplies other essentials: wart fragments for mushrooms, mole scrapings for garlic cloves, tear duct chunks for onions. Most astonishing of all, by combining a fresh-water condenser and a microwave oven into a contraption that causes rapid fermentation, our chef can now distill His blood into something that tastes exactly like first-class burgundy.

The names Sam gives his dishes—Dieu Bourguignon, Domine Gumbo, Pater Stroganoff, Mock Turtle Soup—don't begin to convey how filling and delicious they are. Believe me, Popeye, no human palate has ever known such wonders.

Dieu Bourguignon

20 lbs. meat, cubed	*7 cups stock*
42 small onions, sliced	*3 lbs. mushrooms, sliced*
14 cups burgundy	*7 cloves garlic*

Marinate meat in wine and stock for 4 hours. Remove meat, reserve marinade. Brown onions in 3 heavy skillets, remove and reserve. Brown meat in same skillets. Add marinade, bring to a boil, cover, and simmer 2 hours. Return onions to skillets, add mushrooms, garlic cloves, and simmer, covered, 1 hour more. Serves 35.

For all this, the poor steward frets about our nutrition. He's been trying everything he can think of, extracting selenium, iodine, and other minerals from the Gibraltar Sea and mixing them into the recipes, but it's not enough. "All we're really getting is fat and protein," he tells me. "Folks recovering from a famine need Vitamin C, sir. They need Vitamin A, the B-complex, calcium, potassium . . ."

"Maybe we could mine His liver," I suggest.

"Thought of that. To get there, you'd have to cut through eighty-five yards of the toughest flesh on the planet, a three-week dig at least."

There hasn't been an outbreak of scurvy on an American merchant ship since 1903, Popeye, but that happy fact may be about to change.

When the dinner bell finally rang—a low blast from the *Valparaíso's* foghorn, like a shofar heralding Rosh Hashanah— Neil Weisinger took a long, hard look at his hands. He barely recognized them. Blisters speckled his palms like clutches of tiny red eggs. A white callus covered the root of each finger.

He jabbed his spade into the wet sand, seized his Bugs Bunny lunch box, and sat down. His back ached. His arms throbbed. All around him, sweaty deckies opened their various boxes and buckets and removed their McNuggets, Quarter Pounders, and Filets-o-Fish, devouring them with piggish zeal. They were proud of themselves. They deserved to be. In a mere four and a half days they'd dismantled a three-hundred-thousand-ton mountain and brought the world's largest oil tanker back down to sea level.

Neil glanced toward the cove. The setting sun sparkled in their cargo's starboard eye. Mist cloaked the archipelago of His toes. Languidly the tide rolled in, soughing beneath the *Valparaíso's* hull and splashing against her keel. He imagined the moon as a kind of loving mother, gently drawing a blanket of surf across the island's southern shore, and he continued to imagine this tender scene as, picking up his lunch box, he began his bold little march away from the ship.

Slipping a hand into his pants pocket, Neil ran his finger along the grooved edge of his grandfather's Ben-Gurion medal. At any moment, he knew, his courage might desert him. Nerves shot, he would return and join his mates in fleeing this wretched place. But he kept on walking, past the crimson dunes and the 55-gallon drums, the rusting Volvos and the rotting Goodyear tires, following the shrouded shoreline.

Ahead, a classic Mediterranean fig tree stood perched on a sandy knoll, and the instant Neil saw the fruited branches he resolved to venture no farther. This was it—his own private Burning Bush, the place where he would at last encounter YHWH's unknowable essence, the vantage from which he would finally behold the God of the four A.M. watch. He ascended the knoll and caressed the trunk. Cold, coarse, hard. A rock. His fingertips continued exploring. Branches, bark, leaves, fruit: rock, all of it—a tree become stone, like Lot's wife turned to salt. No matter. The thing would serve its purpose.

A man said, "Astonishing."

Neil spun around. Father Thomas stood beside him, dressed in black jeans and a yellow windbreaker, sweat dribbling from beneath his Panama hat.

"What happened to it?" Neil asked.

"The Gibraltar Sea's full of minerals—that's how Follingsbee's been seasoning our meals. I suspect they petrified the fibers."

Neil peeled off his fishnet shirt and, mopping his brow, looked south. The moon was performing its hydraulic miracle, flooding the cove with tidewater and levitating the tanker inch by inch. "Can you keep a secret, Father? When the *Val* leaves tonight, I'll be standing by this fig tree."

"You aren't coming with us?" Father Thomas frowned, tangling his bushy eyebrows.

"It's what a Christian would call an act of contrition."

"Leo Zook was dead before you took out your knife," the priest protested. "And with Joe Spicer—self-defense, right?"

"There's a picture in my head, Father, a scene I keep playing over and over. I'm in number two center tank, and all that's needed is for me to reach out and open Zook's oxygen valve. A simple twist of the wrist, that's all." Neil hugged the immortal trunk. "If only I could go back and *do* it . . ."

"Your brain was full of hydrocarbon gas. It was wrecking your judgment."

"Maybe."

"You couldn't think straight."

"A man died."

"If you stay here, *you'll* die."

Neil plucked a stone fig. "Maybe so, maybe not."

"Of course you'll die. You can't eat that thing, and we're taking God with us."

"You really think our cargo is God?"

"Difficult question. Let's discuss it on the ship."

"Ever since I can remember, my Aunt Sarah's been saying I'm trapped inside myself—'Neil the hermit, hauling his private cave around with him wherever he goes'—and now I'm really going to become one, a hermit just like . . ."

"No."

". . . like Rabbi Shimon."

"Who?"

"Shimon bar Yochai. At the end of the second century, Rabbi Shimon climbed into a hole in the ground and stayed there, and what do you think finally happened to him?"

"He starved to death."

"He partook of the Creator's unknowable essence. He encountered *En Sof*."

"You mean he saw God?"

"He saw God. The true, formless, nameless God, the God of the four A.M. watch, not King Kong out there."

"For all we know, this crazy island might suddenly sink back where it came from." Father Thomas doffed his Panama hat and raked a withered hand through his hair. "Chaos is . . . chaotic. You'd drown like a rat."

Neil walked his fingers along the stone bark. "If He forgives me, He'll deliver me."

"An action like this—it's *irresponsible*, Neil. There are people back home who care about you."

"My parents are dead."

"What about your friends? Your relatives?"

"I have no friends. My aunts can't stand me. I adored my grandfather, but he died—what?—six years ago."

The priest harvested a rock. He tossed it into the air, caught it, tossed it, caught it. "I'll be honest," he said at last. "This *En Sof* of yours—I want to know it too, I really do." He put his hat back on, snugging the brim all the way to his eyebrows. "Sometimes I think my church made a fatal error, turning God into a man. I love Christ, truly, but He's too easily imagined."

"Then I've got your blessing?"

"Not my blessing, no. But . . ."

"What?"

"If this is what your conscience demands . . ."

Sighing, Father Thomas extended his right arm. Neil reached out. Their bruised fingers intertwined. Their battered palms connected.

"Good-bye, Able Seaman Weisinger. Good-bye and good luck."

Neil sat down beside the immortal trunk. "God be with you, Father Thomas."

Turning, the priest descended the knoll and marched back toward the whispering surf.

Two hours later, Neil had not moved. The night wind cooled his face. Stars peeked through the fog like candles shining behind frosted windows. Moonlight spilled down, glazing the breakers, transforming the dunes into mounds of sparkling gems.

Lunch box in hand, Neil climbed the tree, progressing branch by branch, as if scaling a mainmast. As he settled into a high crook, both of the *Valparaíso's* engines started up, their hisses and chugs echoing across Van Horne Island, and within minutes she was sailing out of the harbor. The tow chains tightened, their links grinding together like the wisdom teeth of some immense insomniac dragon. The ship kept moving, all ahead full. Panic seized the AB. It was not too late. He could still give himself a reprieve, charging down to the beach and screaming for the tanker to stop. If worse came to worst, he could even try swimming after her.

His stomach muscles spasmed. His digestive juices burbled. Drawing out his Ben-Gurion medal, he rubbed his thumb across the old man's profile. There, that was better, yes, yes. Any day now, any hour now, the tree would grow warm—warmer— hot—begin smoking—catch fire.

And it would not be consumed.

Neil Weisinger opened his Bugs Bunny lunch box, removed a Quarter Pounder with Cheese, and ate it very, very slowly.

Part three

Eden

On the second of September, at 0945 hours, the *Carpco Valparaíso* steamed free of the fog. The vibrant, piercing clarity of the world—the sparkle of the North Atlantic, the azure glow of the sky, the brilliant white feathers of the passing petrels—made Thomas Ockham weep with joy. This was how the blind beggar must have felt when, told by Christ to visit the Pool of Siloam and wash the muddy spittle from his eyes, he suddenly found he could see.

At 1055 Lianne Bliss's fax machine kicked in, spewing out what Thomas took to be the latest in a series of hysterical transmissions from Rome, this one distinguished primarily by its being the first to get through. Why had Ockham cut off communication? the Vatican wanted to know. Where was the ship? How was the Corpus Dei? Good questions, legitimate questions, but Thomas was reluctant to reply. While the sudden upwelling of a lost pagan civilization was hardly something he could have anticipated or prevented, he sensed that Rome would nevertheless find some way to blame him—for Van Horne Island, the intolerable delay, their cargo's dissolution, everything.

At first neither Thomas nor anyone else on board realized how radically the corpse had soured. Their innocence remained intact as late as September 4, when the tanker crossed the 42nd parallel, the latitude of Naples. Then the wind shifted. It was a stench that went beyond mere olfaction. After burrowing into everyone's nostrils and sinuses, the fumes next sought out the remaining senses, wringing tears from the sailors' eyes, burning their tongues, scouring their skin. Some deckies even claimed to *hear* the terrible odor, wailing across the sea like the voices of the sirens enticing Ulysses's crew to its doom. Whenever a party of stewards crossed over in the *Juan Fernández* to harvest edible fillets from amid the burgeoning rot, they had to take Dragen rigs along, breathing bottled air.

Ironically, the softening of the flesh meant that Van Horne was finally able to get his chicksans into a carotid artery: a pathetic gesture at this point, but Thomas understood the captain's need to make it. On September 5, at 1415, Charlie Horrocks and his pump-room gang began the great transfusion. Although they'd never sucked cargo on the run before, in less than six hours Horrocks's men had managed to shoot eighty-five thousand gallons of salt water out of the ballast tanks and into the sea while simultaneously channeling as much blood into the *Valparaíso*'s cargo bays.

And it worked. From the very first, the ship began running at a steady nine knots, a third faster than at any time since the start of the tow.

The officers kept their watches faithfully. The deckies chipped and painted conscientiously. The stewards collected fillets dutifully. But only when the sailors started responding to their obligations with their customary grumpiness, only when the *Val*'s companionways began ringing with profane complaints and hair-raising curses, did Thomas grow confident that normalcy had returned to the ship.

"It's over," he told Sister Miriam. "It's finally over. Thank God for Immanuel Kant."

"Thank God for God," she replied tartly, biting into a Quarter Pounder with Cheese.

As Labor Day dawned, cold and overcast, the priest saw that he could no longer deny, either to himself or to Rome, how woefully behind schedule Operation Jehovah had fallen. Indeed, their cargo was now so malodorous that he wondered, half seriously, if this sign of their misadventure could have spread eastward across the ocean, all the way to the gates of the Vatican. His fax was frank and detailed. They were two thousand miles from the Arctic Circle. The ship had gone aground on an uncharted Gibraltar Sea island (37 north, 16 west), trapping them on a mountain of rust for twenty-six days. During this interval, not only had the ethical relativism seeded by the Idea of the Corpse blossomed into total chaos, but putrefaction and neurological disorganization had doubtless befallen the body itself. Yes, the Kantian categorical imperative was now keeping everyone in line, and, yes, the captain's transfusion scheme had boosted their speed significantly, but neither of these happy facts could begin to compensate for the hiatus on the island. Only when it came to the famine did Thomas censor himself, declining to specify the source of their salvation. Pope Innocent XIV, he felt, was not yet ready for Sam Follingsbee's recipe for Dieu Bourguignon.

The synod took only one day to absorb, debate, and act upon the bad news. On September 8, at 1315, Di Luca's reply poured forth.

Dear Professor Ockham:
  What can we say? Van Horne has failed, you have failed, Operation Jehovah has failed. The Holy Father is

devastated beyond words. According to the OMNIVAC-2000, not only is the divine mind now lost, the concomitant flesh has been corrupted too. By the time the freezing process begins, the degeneration will be so profound as to dishonor Him Whose remains we were elected to salvage. At this point, clearly, a different strategy is indicated.

We have decided to suffuse the Corpus Dei with a liquid preservative, a procedure the OMNIVAC believes will go smoothly, Van Horne having already siphoned off 18 percent of the blood.

Toward this end, Rome has chartered a second ULCC, the SS Carpco Maracaibo, *filling her hold with formaldehyde in the port of Palermo and dispatching her west across the Mediterranean. The* Maracaibo's *officers and crew have been advised they're on a mission to commandeer a prop from a planned motion picture of unconscionably pornographic content, thereby forestalling production. We don't need your friend Immanuel Kant to tell us such a ploy is morally ambiguous, but we feel the body's true identity is already known to far too many individuals.*

Upon receiving this message, you shall direct Van Horne to come about and revisit the island on which he bestowed his surname, there to rendezvous with the Maracaibo. *I shall be on board, ready to supervise the formaldehyde injections and subsequent conveyance of the body to its final resting place.*

Sincerely,
Tullio Di Luca, Msgr.
Secretary of Extraordinary
Ecclesiastical Affairs

Beyond the rude and uninformed finger pointing of the first paragraph, this letter actually pleased Thomas. Wonder of wonders: it looked as if he'd be getting a second chance to argue Neil Weisinger out of his suicidal penance, a matter that had been weighing on him ever since they'd left Van Horne Island. No less appealing was the thought of dumping the whole sordid, smelly business of Operation Jehovah into Di Luca's lap. At the moment Thomas wanted nothing more than to go home, settle into his musty Fordham office (how he missed the place, its miniature Foucault pendulum, framed fractal photographs, bust of Aquinas), and start teaching a new semester of Chaos 101.

"He's gotta be kidding," said Van Horne after reading Di Luca's communiqué.

"I think not," said Thomas.

"Do you realize what this man's asking?" Lifting Raphael's feather from his desk, Van Horne weaved it back and forth through the God-choked air. "He's asking me to give up my command."

"Yes. I'm sorry."

"Looks like *you're* getting the boot too."

"No regrets, in my case. I never wanted this job."

Van Horne settled behind his desk and, opening a drawer, removed a corkscrew, two Styrofoam cups, and a bottle of burgundy. "Too bad you told Di Luca we blew the ballast. He'll factor that into his calculations when he starts chasing us." The captain twisted the corkscrew home with the same authority he'd brought to the problem of hoving chicksans into their cargo's neck. "Luckily, we've got a good head start." Yanking out the cork, Van Horne sloshed a generous amount of Château de Dieu into each cup. "Here, Thomas—it drives away the stink."

"Am I to understand you intend to disobey Di Luca's orders?"

"Our angels never said anything about an embalming."

"Nor did they say anything about strange attractors, inverse Eucharists, or ballasting the *Val* with blood. This voyage has been full of surprises, Captain, and now we're obliged to turn the ship around."

"And never learn why He died? Gabriel said you'd have to go the whole nine yards, remember?"

"I'm no longer interested in why He died."

"Yes, you are."

"I just want to go home."

"The bottom line is this: I don't trust your friends in Rome"—Van Horne neatly ripped Di Luca's fax in half—"and, what's more, I suspect you don't trust them either. Drink your wine."

Thomas, wincing, lifted the cup to his lips. He sipped. A chill spiraled through him, head to toe. He felt as if he were experiencing the fate that Poe had contrived for the protagonist of "The Pit and the Pendulum," except in this case the bisection was occurring along the prisoner's axis. Only after his third sip did the half of Thomas beholden to Holy Mother Church overcome the half that shared the captain's suspicions.

"Did you know Seaman Weisinger stayed behind?" Thomas asked.

"Rafferty told me."

"The kid thinks he's going to have a major religious experience."

"A major starvation experience."

"Exactly."

"We aren't turning around," said Van Horne.

"When the cardinals hear you've gone renegade, they'll become irrational—you realize that, don't you? They'll—Lord only knows. They'll send the Italian Air Force after you with cruise missiles."

Van Horne gulped his burgundy. "What makes you think the cardinals will hear I've gone renegade?"

"You have your responsibilities, I have mine."

"Jesus, Thomas—do I have to ban you from the radio shack?"

"That isn't your prerogative."

"Let's make it official. Okay? From this moment on, the shack's off limits to you. Make that the whole damn bridge. If I catch you sending Di Luca so much as a fucking chess move, I'll lock you in the brig and throw the key over the side."

An icy knot congealed in Thomas's stomach. "Anthony, I must say something here. I must say that I've never had an enemy in my whole life, but today, I fear, you have become my enemy." He grimaced. "As a Christian, of course, I must attempt to love you just the same."

Van Horne poked his index finger through the bottom of his Styrofoam cup. "Now let *me* say something." He flashed the priest a cryptic grin. "When the cardinals obtained your services, Thomas Ockham, they got a much better man than they deserved."

September 9.

Latitude: 60°15'N. Longitude: 8°5'E. Course: 021. Speed: 9 knots. Sea temperature: 28° Fahrenheit. Air temperature: 26° and falling.

Thank God for the Westerlies, wafting out of Greenland like Grant took Richmond and driving away the stench. I can breathe again, Popeye. I can see clearly, hear distinctly, think straight.

Even though my decision to muzzle Ockham and hijack the body was made in the thick of the stink, I'm sure I did the right thing. Assuming we can maintain our 9 knots, we'll have dropped our load and started for Manhattan before Di Luca's even crossed the circle. If the man wants to play taxidermist after that, fine.

Yesterday Sam Follingsbee put it to me: either we get some vitamins into the crew, or we start converting the officers' wardroom into a sick bay. So I changed course—reluctantly, as you might imagine—and by 1315 the *Val* was within 2 miles of Galway Harbor and its world-famous grocery shops.

"Would you like to be dropped off here?" I asked Cassie, fervently hoping she'd pass up the offer. "You could probably get a plane out of Shannon Airport before sundown."

"No," she replied without hesitation.

"Won't your bosses be pissed?"

"This voyage is the most interesting thing that's ever happened to me," she said, taking my hand and giving it an unchaste squeeze (or so it felt), "and I need to see it through."

The chief steward himself led the expedition. At 1345 he and his pastry chef, Willie Pindar, set out in the *Juan Fernández*, their pockets stuffed with shopping lists and American Express travelers' checks.

A few minutes after Sam left, a fiberglass cutter with a gold harp on her side appeared, poking around our tow chains like an Irish wolfhound sniffing its littermate's balls. The skipper got on his bullhorn and demanded a meeting, and I couldn't see any choice about it. With the Vatican out hunting us in the *Maracaibo*, I wasn't about to irritate the rest of militant Christendom as well.

Commander Donal Gallogherm of the Irish Republican Coast Guard turned out to be one of those big, blowsy sons-of-the-old-sod that Pat O'Brien used to play in the movies. He came up to the bridge with his exec, sprightly Ted Mulcanny, and between the two of them they made me homesick—not for the actual New York City, but for the New York City of Hollywood legend, the New York of warmhearted Irish cops whacking their nightsticks across the rumps of Dead End Kids. And at base that's what these clowns were: a couple of Irish cops patrolling their watery beat from Slyne Head to Shannon Bay.

"Impressive vessel you got here," said Gallogherm, striding around the wheelhouse like he owned the place. "Took over our whole radar screen."

"We're a bit off course," said Dolores Haycox, the mate on duty. "Damn Marisat—always crashing."

"That's an awfully strange flag-o'-convenience you be flyin'," said Gallogherm.

"You've seen it before," I told him.

"That so? Well, you know what Mr. Mulcanny and I are thinkin'? We're thinkin' there's a major irregularity about this tramp tanker of yours, and so we'll be needin' to see your Crude Petroleum Right o' Passage."

"Crude Petroleum *what?*" I said, wishing I'd run their cutter down when I'd had the chance. "Phooey."

"You don't *have* one? It's a strict requirement for bringin' a loaded supertanker through Irish territorial waters."

"We're in ballast," Dolores Haycox protested.

"Like hell you are. You're at the top of your Plimsoll line, sailor girl, and if you don't produce a Crude Petroleum Right o' Passage posthaste, we'll be obliged to detain you in Galway."

"Say, Commander," I asked, catching on, "might you happen to have one of those 'Crude Petroleum Rights of Passage' on your cutter?"

"Not sure. What about it, Teddy?"

"Only this mornin' I noticed just such a document flutterin' about on my desk."

"Is it . . . available?" I asked.

Gallogherm flashed me a majority of his teeth. "Well, now that you be mentionin' it . . ."

"Dolores, I believe we have a stack of—what do you call them?—American Express travelers' checks in our safe," I said.

"The price bein' eight hundred American dollars," said Gallogherm.

"The price being six hundred American dollars," I corrected him as the mate went off to fetch the checks.

"You mean *seven* hundred?"

"No, I mean six hundred."

"You mean six hundred and fifty?"

"I mean six hundred."

"I'm sure you do," said Gallogherm. "Then, of course"—he

pinched his nostrils—"there's the large and fragrant matter of that sewage you got in tow."

"Smells like an Englishman," said Mulcanny.

I knew exactly how to bamboozle them. "Actually, Commander, it's the dead and rotting carcass of God Almighty."

"The what?" said Mulcanny.

"You've a scandalous sense of humor," said Gallogherm, more amused than offended.

"The Catholic God or the Protestant?" asked Mulcanny.

"Teddy, lad, can't you recognize a joke when you hear one?" Gallogherm gave me a conspiratorial wink. "So, what we've got here is an ambitious sea captain who's gone and converted his supertanker to a free-lance garbage scow, am I right? And just where might this ambitious captain be intendin' to make his dump?"

"'Way up north. Svalbard."

Haycox returned in time to hear Gallogherm say, "In any event, it's your Solid Waste Right o' Passage we'll be needin' to see."

"Don't overplay your hand, Commander."

"Solid Waste Rights o' Passage normally run six hundred American dollars, but this week they be goin' for a mere five."

"No, this week they're going for a mere four. What's more, if you two pirates don't stop jerking us around, I guarantee it won't be long before this scam of yours ends up on page one of the *Irish Times*."

"Don't you presume to be judgin' me, Captain. You've no notion of what I've seen in this life. Ireland's a nation at war. You've no notion of what I've seen."

Grimly I signed and recorded $1,000 worth of travelers' checks. "Here's your lousy toll," I said, greasing Gallogherm's palm.

"A pleasure it's been to do business with you."

"Now get the fuck off my ship."

At 1600, Follingsbee and Pindar appeared with the groceries. If you factor in Gallogherm's shakedown money, each orange cost us about $1.25, and the rest was equally outrageous. At least it's quality stuff, Popeye—juicy yams, crisp cabbages, robust Irish potatoes. You'd envy us our spinach.

Midnight now. A choppy beam sea. Ursa Minor high above. Before us lie the Faeroes, 80 miles distant as the petrel flies, and then it's open water all the way to Svalbard. Rafferty was just on the intercom, telling me the forward searchlight has picked out "an iceberg shaped like the Paramount Pictures logo."

We're steaming for the frigid Norwegian Sea, trimmed with blood, all ahead full, and I'm feeling like a master again.

Beer mug in hand, Myron Kovitsky shuffled up to the piano stool, sat down, and, pressing his Jimmy Durante nose in place, began pounding the keys. He scratched his schnozzola and raised his gravel voice, singing to the tune of "John Brown's Body."

> *We was flyin' in our bombers at one*
> *hundred fuckin' feet,*
> *Da weather fuckin' awful, fuckin' rain and*
> *fuckin' sleet;*
> *Da compass it was swinging fuckin' south and*
> *fuckin' north,*
> *But we made a fuckin' landing in da Firth of*
> *fuckin' Forth.*

Durante stopped playing and showed the crowd a big loopy grin. The men of the *Enterprise* shuffled uncomfortably in their seats. No one applauded. Oliver cringed. Undaunted, Durante took a slug of Frydenlund and launched into the chorus.

Ain't da Navy fuckin' awful?
Ain't da Navy fuckin' awful?
Ain't da Navy fuckin' awful?
We made a fuckin' landing in da Firth of
      fuckin' Forth.

Rising from the stool, Durante said, "Goodnight, Mrs. Calabash, wherever you are!"

Hard times had befallen the Midnight Sun Canteen. Bored to death and sick of the cold, the Great American Nostalgia Machine had started adulterating its repertoire with off-color songs that, despite their historical authenticity, were clearly nothing Jimmy Durante, Bing Crosby, or the Andrews Sisters would have ever performed in public. The hostesses were tired of pretending to have crushes on the pilots and sailors, and the pilots and sailors were tired of the hostesses being tired of them. As for Sonny Orbach and His Harmonicoots, they had quit the scene entirely, off reincarnating Glenn Miller's band at a bar mitzvah in Connecticut, a long-standing commitment they'd insisted on honoring despite Oliver's offer to double their wages. Those servicemen who still felt the urge to dance were forced to settle for either Myron Kovitsky's feeble piano-playing skills or Sidney Pembroke's Victrola rasping out Albert Flume's original 78-rpm records of Tommy Dorsey, Benny Goodman, and the real Glenn Miller.

Oliver had to admit it: his grand crusade was on the verge of collapse. By sitting around doing nothing for three weeks, Pembroke and Flume had amassed enough in retainer fees to stage a first-rate D-Day, and while the notion of sinking a Jap golem still appealed to them, they were far more anxious to get home and locate a reasonable facsimile of Normandy. And even if Oliver *could* somehow convince everybody to stay at Point Luck until a PBY recon flight spotted the *Val*, it was quite possible that, because of the dreadful Arctic weather, Admiral Spruance would refuse to give the go-ahead. Flaps and landing gear were sticking during the milk runs. Gas lines were clogging. The flight deck was freezing faster than Captain Murray's men could clear it: an unbroken sheet of ice as vast as the mirror of the Hubble telescope.

Oliver spent these gloomy days at the bar, doodling randomly in his sketch pad as he tried to come up with reasons it was okay for them not to obliterate the Corpus Dei after all.

"Fellas, I got a question for you," he said, putting the final touches on a caricature of Myron Kovitsky. "This campaign of ours—is it truly justified?"

"What do you mean?" asked Barclay, deftly shuffling a pack of playing cards.

"Maybe the body should be left alone," said Oliver. "Maybe it should even be brought to light, like Sylvia Endicott insisted the night she quit." Rotating on his bar stool, he placed himself face to face with Winston. "A disclosure might even spark your True Revolution, right? Once everybody knows He's cashed it in, they'll leave their churches and start building the workers' paradise."

"You don't know very much about Marxism, do you?" Winston arranged two dozen stray Frydenlund bottle caps into a hammer and sickle. "Until they're given something better to replace it with, the masses will never abandon religion, corpse or no corpse. Once social justice triumphs, of course, the God myth will vanish"—he snapped his fingers—"like that."

"Oh, come off it." Barclay made the queen of spades vault magically from the pack. "Religion will always exist, Winston."

"Why do you think that?"

Al Jolson wandered drunkenly onstage.

"One word," said Barclay. "Death. Religion solves it, social justice doesn't." Turning toward Oliver, he caused the jack of hearts to leap into his friend's lap. "But what does it matter, eh? I hate to be blunt, Oliver, but I think it's pretty damn likely Cassie's ship has been lost at sea."

As Oliver winced, Jolson began singing a cappella:

Oh, I love to see Shirley make water,
She can pee such a beautiful stream.
She can pee for a mile and a quarter,
And you can't see her ass for the steam.

At which instant Ray Spruance's portrayer's static-laden voice exploded from the loudspeakers. "Attention, everyone! This is the admiral! Good news, boys! Initial dispatches from the Coral Sea indicate that Task Force Seventeen has badly damaged the Japanese carriers *Shohu* and *Shokaku*, thereby preventing the enemy from occupying Port Moresby!"

A solitary sailor clapped. A lone flier said, "That's nice."

"He's leaving out a few details," said Wade McClusky's portrayer, joining the three atheists at the bar. "He's afraid to mention we lost *Lexington* in that particular battle."

"Truth: the first casualty of war," said Winston.

"Attention!" continued Spruance. "Attention! All men attached to Task Force Sixteen will report to the ship immediately! This is not a drill! All men from Scout Bombing Six, Torpedo Six, and *Enterprise* will report immediately!" Spruance suddenly shifted to a jovial, folksy tone. "Strawberry Ten's just spotted the enemy, boys! That Jap golem's in Arctic waters, and now we're gonna bushwhack the sucker!"

"Hey, comrades—you hear that?" squealed Winston.

"We've done it, guys!" shouted Barclay. "We've got irrationality by the balls!"

Oliver hugged his sketch pad, kissing his caricature of Myron Kovitsky. The *Valparaíso* was afloat! Cassandra was alive! He pictured her standing on one of the tanker's bridge wings, scanning the sky for the promised squadrons. I'm on my way, darling, he thought. Here comes Oliver to save your *Weltanschauung*.

McClusky strode to Pembroke's Victrola and, detaching the huge conical speaker, held it to his mouth like a megaphone. "Well, boys, you heard the admiral! Let's get off our duffs and show them Nips they got no right to mess with the natural economic order of things!"

So now it was here, that bittersweet juncture each man had awaited with supreme patience, the moment when he must seek out his favorite hostess and bid her *au revoir*. Choking back tears half-crocodile and half-genuine, the sailor nearest Oliver clasped the hand of his best girl—a chubby woman with pigtails and dimples—and solemnly vowed to write her every day. The hostess, in turn, gave the sailor Oliver's money's worth, assuring him she would carry their brief encounter in her heart forever. Throughout the Midnight Sun Canteen, phone numbers were exchanged, along with fleeting kisses and sentimental tokens (brooches and locks of hair from the women, tie clips and aviation badges from the men). Even Arnold Kovitsky got into the mood, striding up to the mike and transforming himself into Marlene Dietrich singing "Lili Marlene."

The servicemen trembled and wept, stunned by the sheer hypnotic beauty of it all: the song, the farewells, the call to arms.

A blond, apple-cheeked flier whose name badge read BEESON turned to McClusky and raised his hand.

"Yes, Lieutenant Beeson?"

"Commander McClusky, sir, is there time for one last fox-trot?"

"Sorry, sailor, Uncle Sam needs us right now. Battle stations, men!"

September 14.

Latitude: 66°50′N. Longitude: 2°45′W. Course: 044. Speed: 7 knots. Sea temperature: 23° Fahrenheit. Air temperature: 12° and falling.

At 0745 two momentous events occurred. The *Valparaíso* crossed the Arctic Circle, and I shaved off my beard. A major

operation. I had to borrow a pair of butcher's shears from Follingsbee, and after that I went through a half dozen of Ockham's
disposable razors.

Ice enshrouds our cargo, a smooth crust running head to toe
like the casing on a sausage. By the time we reach Kvitoya, His
meat will be solid as marble.

"See, the putrefaction's stopped, just like our angels predicted," I said, striding up to Ockham. "We don't need the
Vatican's damn formaldehyde."

The padre was standing on the afterdeck, watching the pump-
room gang glide around on His sternum. Ice-skating has become
the crew's principal recreation of late, eclipsing both stud poker
and Ping-Pong. Their gear is jerry-built—cutlery affixed to hiking boots—but it works fine. For extra protection against the
cold, they coat their hands, feet, and faces with glory grease.

Ockham looked me in the eye and smiled, obviously relieved
that I'd just placed us back on speaking terms. "Someone should
contact Rome and tell them He's finally stable," he said as Bud
Ramsey fell squarely on his ass. "Surely you'd prefer not to have
Di Luca out chasing us in the *Maracaibo*."

I couldn't argue with the man's logic, and I even allowed
him to compose the message. (He did this in his cabin. They'll
be selling earmuffs in hell before I let Ockham on the bridge
again.) At 1530 Sparks faxed the good news to Rome, and at
1538 a second communiqué went out, this one to sunny Spain.
It was only a dozen words long. "Expect me in Valladolid next
month whether you want me or not," I told my father.

We're getting very near the end, Popeye.

After tonight's dinner, Follingsbee's best batch of stroganoff
yet, the steward said he wanted me to see the results of a "scientific
experiment" he'd been working on ever since our stop in Ireland.
He led me outside—what a wonderland our weather deck has
become, ice hanging from the catwalks in great crystalline webs,
frost shimmering on the pipes and valves—and into the depths

of number 4 ballast tank, chattering all the way about the joys of home agronomy. We hadn't gone 20 feet before my nostrils were quivering with pleasure. Lord, such a marvelous scent: utter ripeness, Popeye, sheer fecundity. I switched on my flashlight.

At the bottom of the tank lay a brightly colored garden, its vegetables grown bulbous beyond the wildest fantasies of Hieronymus Bosch, its fruits so fat they practically screamed aloud to be plucked. Gnarled trees lurched out of the darkness, their branches bent by apples the size of volleyballs. Asparagus spears reared up from the floor like some bizarre species of cactus. Broccoli flourished beside the keelson, each stalk as tall and thick as a mimosa tree. Vines drooped from the ladders, their dark purple grapes clustered together like Godzilla's lymph nodes.

"Sam, you're a genius."

The steward doffed his cream-puff hat and took a modest bow. "Seeds all came from them groceries we bought in Galway. Soil's a mixture of skin and plasma. What gets me is how *fast* everything grew, in subfreezing temperatures yet, and without a single ray of sunshine. You sow an orange pip, and ten hours later—bingo!"

"So half the credit belongs to . . ."

"More than half. He makes great compost, sir."

When this voyage is finally over, Popeye, there's only one thing I'm going to miss, and that's the food.

Cassie's parka, borrowed from Bud Ramsey, was stuffed with grade-A goose down; her socks, from Juanita Torres, were 100 percent virgin wool; her gloves, from Sister Miriam, contained pure rabbit fur. But the cold still penetrated, eating through each protective layer like some voracious Arctic moth. The thermometer on the starboard wing stood at negative eight degrees, and that didn't include the windchill factor.

Lifting her field glasses, she focused on the glistery, snow-capped nose. Far beyond, a steady stream of charged solar particles spilled forth, countless electrons and neutrons entering the earth's magnetic field and colliding with rarefied atmospheric gases. The resulting aurora filled the entire northern sky: a luminous blue-and-green banner flapping in eerie silence above the rolling waves and the wandering pack ice.

What she most admired about Anthony Van Horne, the fact that made him always *there* these days, always flitting about in her brain, was his obsessiveness. At last she'd met someone as stubborn as she. Snapshots from a sea odyssey: Anthony killing a tiger shark with a bazooka, quelling a mutiny with fast food, persuading his sailors to move a mountain. Just as Cassie would stop at nothing to destroy God, so the captain would stop at nothing to protect Him. It was truly intense, erotic almost, this strange, unspoken bond between them.

The question, of course, was whether Oliver's admirable project still existed. Pure logic said the slender threads binding the interests of the Central Park West Enlightenment League to those of the World War Two Reenactment Society had been completely severed during the *Valparaíso*'s long imprisonment on Van Horne Island. Yet Cassie knew Oliver. She understood his utter, passionate, tedious devotion to her. The more she thought about it, the more convinced she became that he'd found some way to keep the alliance alive. Any day now, any hour now, the Age of Reason would be visited upon the Corpus Dei.

The *Valparaíso*'s chart room, surprisingly, was no warmer than her bridge wings. As Cassie stepped inside, her vaporous breath drifted across the Formica table and hovered above a map of Sardinia, creating a massive cloud formation over Cagliari. Luckily, someone had undertaken to compensate for the defective heating ducts by bringing in a Coleman stove. She fired it up and got busy, scanning the wide, shallow drawers until she noticed one labeled ARCTIC OCEAN. She opened it. The drawer

contained over a hundred bodies of ice-choked water—Greenland's Scoresby Sound, Norway's Vestfjord, Svalbard's Hinlo-
penstreten, Russia's East Siberian Sea—and only after thumbing
halfway through the pile did she come upon a chart depicting
both the Arctic Circle and Jan Mayen Island.

Expect air strike at 68°11'N, 2°35'W, Oliver's fax had said, *150
miles east of launch point . . .*

Pivoting toward the Formica table, she unfurled the map. It
was dense with data: soundings, anchorages, wrecks, submerged
rocks—the geographic equivalent of an anatomy text, she decided, earth's most intimate particulars laid bare. She picked up
a ballpoint pen and did the math on a stray scrap of Carpco
stationery. Wary of the icebergs, Anthony had recently cut their
speed from nine knots to seven. Seven times twenty-four: they
were covering 168 nautical miles a day. Calibrating the dividers
against the bar scale, ten miles tip to tip, she walked them from
the *Val*'s position—67 north, 4 west—to the spot specified by
Oliver. Result: a mere 280 miles. If her optimism was not mis-
placed, the attack lay fewer than forty-eight hours in the future.

"Searching for the Northwest Passage?"

She hadn't heard him come in, but there he was, dressed in
a green turtleneck sweater and frayed orange watch cap. He was
clean-shaven, shockingly so. In the bright neon glow his chin lay
wholly revealed, its dimple winking at her.

"Homesick," she replied, pitching the dividers into the Norwegian Sea. "I figure we're a good four days from Kvitoya." She
rubbed each arm with the opposite hand. "Wish that damn stove
worked better."

Anthony slipped off his cap. "There are remedies."

"For homesickness?"

"For cold."

His arms swung apart like the doors to some particularly
cozy and genial tavern, and with a nervous laugh she embraced
him, pressing against his woolly chest. He massaged her back,

his palm carving deep, slow spirals in the space between her shoulder blades.

"You shaved."

"Uh-huh. Feeling warmer?"

"Hmmm . . ."

"Can you keep a secret?"

"It's been known to happen."

"The Vatican's ordered us to turn around and head south."

"South?" Panic shot through Cassie. She tightened her grip.

"We're supposed to rendezvous with the SS *Carpco Maracaibo* back in the Gibraltar Sea. She's got formaldehyde in her cargo bays."

"Those angels ordered Him *frozen*, not embalmed," she protested.

"That's why we're holding steady."

"Ahh . . ." Cassie relaxed, laughing to herself, cavorting internally. *Holding steady*—wonderful, perfect, straight into the clutches of the Enlightenment.

He kissed her cheek, softly, tenderly: a brotherly kiss, noncarnal. Then her brow, her eyes. Jaw, ear, cheek again. Their lips met. She pulled away.

"This isn't a good idea."

"Yes, it is," he said.

"Yes, it is," she agreed.

And suddenly they were connecting again, hugging fiercely, meshing. They kissed voraciously, mouths wide open, as if to swallow one another. Cassie shut her eyes, reveling in the liquidity of Anthony's tongue: a life-form unto itself, member of some astoundingly sensual species of eel.

Disengaging, the captain said, "The stove gets hotter, you know . . ."

"Hotter," she echoed, catching her breath.

He crouched over the Coleman and adjusted the fuel control, turning the flame into a roiling red mass, a kind of indoor aurora borealis. Opening the INDIAN OCEAN drawer, he whipped out a large, laminated map and spread it on the floor like a picnic blanket. "Madagascar's the best place for this sort of thing," he explained, winking at her. Slowly, lasciviously, the chart room heated up.

"You're wrong," said Cassie playfully, shedding her parka. She rifled the SULU SEA drawer and grabbed a portrait of the Philippines. "Palawan's much more erotic." She released the map, and it glided to the floor like a magic carpet landing in thirteenth-century Baghdad.

"No, Doc." Scanning the drawer called FRENCH POLYNESIA, he removed the Tuamotu Archipelago. "It's really Puka-Puka."

"This one," she giggled, pulse racing as she extracted Majorca from the BALEARIC ISLANDS drawer.

"No, Java here."

"Sulawesi."

"Sumatra."

"New Guinea."

They locked the door, turned off the overhead lights, and lay down amid the patchwork of scattered landfalls. Cassie exposed her neck; his lips roamed up and down the length of her jugular, planting kisses. Groaning softly, rolling toward the Caymans, they undressed each other, adrift in the warm waters of the Bartlett Deep. The tensor lamp cast harsh shadows across Anthony's shaggy legs and great simian chest. As they glided into the Bahia de Alcudi, Cassie went to work with her mouth, sculpting his ardor to full potential, until it seemed the figurehead of some grand priapic frigate.

They floated north, entering the cold, jolting Mozambique Channel, just off Madagascar, and it was here that Anthony drew a Shostak Supersensitive from his wallet and put it on. Wrapping her legs around the small of his back, she piloted his jacketed cock where it wanted to go. Smiling, he plied her salty waters: Anthony Van Horne, a ship with a mission. She inhaled. He exuded an amazing fragrance, an amalgam of musk and brine shot through with all the rubbery, suckered things God and natural selection had wrought from the sea. This, she decided, was how the Galápagos Islands would have smelled, had she gotten there.

By the time he came, they had journeyed all the way past the Mindoro Strait to the bright, steamy beaches of China's Hainan Island.

Withdrawing, he said, "I guess I feel a little guilty."

"Oliver?"

He nodded. "Making love to a lady with her boyfriend's condom . . ."

"Father Thomas would be proud of you."

"For fornicating?"

"For feeling guilty. You've got a Kantian conscience."

"It's not a *painful* sort of guilt," he hastened to add, sliding his index and middle fingers inside her. "It's not like how it feels to blind a manatee. I'm almost enjoying it."

"Screw Matagorda Bay," Cassie whispered, reveling in his touch. The Coleman hissed and growled. She dripped with all the planet's good and oozy things, with chocolate sauce and clarified butter, melted cheese and maple syrup, peach yogurt and potter's slip. "Screw guilt, screw Oliver, screw Immanuel Kant." She felt like a bell, a wondrous organic *Glocke*, and before long she would peal, oh, yes, just as soon as this gifted carillonneur, so attentive to her clapper . . .

"Screw them," he agreed.

Her orgasm occurred in the Gulf of Thailand.

It lasted over a minute.

As Anthony worked his condom free, the little sack leaked, adding its contents to the lovely mess of sweat and juices now rolling toward the shores of Hainan. "The thing I've always noticed about Chinese sex," he said, pointing to the tidal wave and grinning, "is that you feel like doing it again an hour later."

"An hour? That long?"

"Okay, twenty-five minutes." The captain cupped his hand around her left breast, hefting it like a housewife evaluating a grapefruit. "You want to know the key to my father, Doc?"

"Not really."

"His fixation on Christopher Columbus."

"Let's forget about Dad for a while, okay?"

Gently, Anthony squeezed the gland. "This is what Columbus thought the world looked like."

"My left breast?"

"Anybody's left breast. As the years went on, it became clear he hadn't come anywhere near circling the globe—the earth was obviously four times bigger than he'd guessed—but Columbus still needed to believe he'd reached the Orient. Don't ask me why. He just had a need. Next thing anybody knew, he'd made up this crazy theory that the world was really shaped like a woman's breast. He *had* gone most of the way around, only he'd done so at the nipple"—Anthony ran his finger along the edge of Cassie's areola, tickling her—"whereas everyone else was measuring the circumference much farther south." His fingers wandered downward. "So my father, in the end, has a fool for an idol."

"Jesus, Anthony—he can't be *all* bad. Nobody's *all* bad, not even God."

The captain shrugged. "He taught me my trade. He gave me the sea." A sardonic chuckle broke from his lips. "He gave me the sea, and I turned it into a cesspool."

Cassie grew suddenly tense. Part of her, the irrational part, wanted to keep this despairing sailor in her life long after the *Valparaíso* put to port. She could picture them chartering their own private freighter and setting off together for the Galápagos. The other part knew that he would never, ever be free of Matagorda Bay, and that any woman who let herself become entangled with Anthony Van Horne would end up treading the same malignant oil in which he himself was drowning.

For the next fifteen minutes, the captain pleasured her with his tongue—not an eel this time but a wet, fleshy brush, painting the mansion of her body. None of this will make a difference, she swore as he drew out a second Supersensitive. Even if I fall in love with him, ran Cassie's silent vow, I'll continue to make war on his cargo.

War

"GIVE ME PANTS that en-*trance*," chanted Albert Flume as he herded Oliver, Barclay, and Winston into the *Enterprise*'s rusting passenger elevator.

"Shoulders Gibraltar, shiny as a halter." Sidney Pembroke pushed the button labeled HANGAR DECK.

"A frantic cape," said Flume.

"Of antic shape," said Pembroke.

"Drape it."

"Drop it."

"Sock it."

"And lock it at the pocket!"

"Navy code?" asked Barclay as the rickety car descended into the hull.

"Zoot-suit slang," Pembroke replied. "Golly, I miss the forties."

"You weren't even alive in the forties," said Barclay.

"Yeah. Golly, I miss 'em."

The forward hangar bay was astonishingly hot, a phenomenon that evidently traced to the seven kerosene stoves roaring and snorting along the amidships bulkhead. Sweat popped onto Oliver's brow, rolling downward and stinging his eyes. Instinctively he stripped, taking off his Karakorum parka, cashmere scarf, cowhide gloves, and Navy watch cap.

"Tactics." Removing his *Memphis Belle* bomber jacket, Pembroke swept his bare arm across the cavernous bay.

"Exactly." Flume pulled off his blue crewneck sweater. "Strategy's the soul of war, but never underestimate the power of tactics."

The bay was jammed to the walls, plane stacked against plane, their wings folded like the arms of defeated infantrymen bent in surrender. Dressed in shorts and T-shirts, maintenance crews bustled about, chocking wheels, popping out instrument panels, poking around inside engines. A few yards away, two nervous-looking sailors rolled back the steel door to the powder magazine, gently picked up a 500-pound demolition bomb, and set it on a hand-operated trolley.

"American carrier planes are traditionally stored on the flight deck," said Pembroke.

"As opposed to the Jap convention of keeping 'em on the hangar deck," said Flume.

"By bringing both squadrons below, Admiral Spruance has thawed every rudder, flap, and gas line."

"Come dawn, he's gonna start all the engines down here. Imagine: starting your engines in your hangar bays—what a brilliant tactic!"

The bomb handlers dollied their charge across the bay and, as if returning a baby to the womb, stuffed it into the fuselage of an SBD-2 Dauntless.

"Say, you folks *are* planning to come, aren't you?" asked Flume.

"Come?" said Oliver.

"To the battle. Ensign Reid's agreed to fly us out in Strawberry Eleven."

"This isn't my sort of thing," said Barclay.

"Oh, you *must* come," said Pembroke.

"Marx never cared for battles," said Winston. "I don't either, especially."

"What about you, Oliver?"

The Enlightenment League's president took out his monogrammed linen handkerchief and wiped the perspiration from his forehead. If he worked at it, he could easily have discouraged himself, conjuring up fantasies of Strawberry Eleven crashing into an iceberg or being blown apart by a stray demolition bomb. But the final truth was this: he wanted to be able to tell Cassandra he was there, right there, when the Corpse of Corpses went into the Mohns Trench.

"I wouldn't miss it for the world."

The next morning at 0600, Spruance's pilots and gunners crowded into the carrier's stuffy, smoke-filled briefing room. Oliver immediately thought of the Episcopalian services to which his parents had periodically dragged him back home in Bala Cynwyd, Pennsylvania; there was the same weighty silence, the same restless reverence, the same mood of people getting ready to receive the lowdown on matters of life and death. The hundred and thirty-two war reenactors sat at rigid attention, parachute packs balanced on their laps like hymnals.

Ramrod straight, chest puffed out, Spruance's portrayer slipped his briar pipe between his teeth, ascended the podium, and, grabbing the sash cord, unfurled a hand-drawn overhead view of the body in question, cryptic grin included. "Our objective, gentlemen: the insidious Oriental golem. Code name, 'Akagi.'" The corpse was sketched with its limbs spread-eagled, evoking da Vinci's famous *Vitruvian Man*. "Nimitz's strategy calls for a series of coordinated strikes against two separate targets." Lifting the pointer from the chalk tray, the admiral jabbed it into the Adam's apple. "Our torpedo squadron will concentrate on this area here, Target A, hitting the region between the second and third cervical vertebrae and creating a rupture descending from the epidermis to the center of the throat. If we've calculated correctly, Akagi will then begin shipping water, much of it flowing down the windpipe and into the lungs. Meanwhile, Scout Bombing Six will drop its payloads on the midriff, systematically enlarging this depression here—Target B, the navel—until the abdominal cavity is breached." Clamping his pointer under his arm like a riding crop, Spruance faced the air group's leader. "We'll attack in alternating waves. Toward this end, Commander McClusky, you will divide each squadron into two sections. While one section's over its designated target, the other will be getting refueled and rearmed back here on Mother Goose. Questions?"

Lieutenant Lance Sharp, a paunchy, balding man with a tiny smear of brown mustache on his upper lip, raised his hand. "What sort of resistance might we expect?"

"The PBYs report a total absence of fighter planes and AA artillery on both *Valparaíso* and the golem. However, let's not forget who constructed this sucker. I calculate the enemy will launch a fighter umbrella of between twenty and thirty Zeroes."

Lieutenant Commander E. E. Lindsey, a tense Virginian who bore a startling resemblance to Richard Widmark, spoke up next. "Will they really launch a fighter umbrella?"

"That's basic carrier tactics, mister."

"But will they *really?*"

"They launched a hell of a fighter umbrella on June 4, 1942, didn't they?" Spruance chomped on his pipe. "Well, no, they won't *really* launch a fighter umbrella," he added, more than a little annoyed.

"Question about technique, Admiral," said Wade McClusky. "Shall we dive-bomb, or would glide-bombing be best?"

"If I were you, given the inexperience of my pilots, I'd opt for glide-bombing."

"My pilots aren't inexperienced. They're perfectly capable of dive-bombing."

"They weren't experienced in '42." Spruance slid his pointer along the left breast. "And be sure to come in from the east. That way the AA gunners'll be blinded by the sun."

"*What* AA gunners?" asked Lindsey.

"The Jap AA gunners," said Spruance.

"This is the Arctic, sir," said McClusky. "The sun rises in the south, not the east."

For a moment Spruance looked confused, then a smile to match Akagi's spread across his face. "Say, let's take advantage of that! Attack from the south, and dive-bomb the hell out of 'em!"

"Don't you mean, glide-bomb the hell out of 'em?" said McClusky.

"Your boys can't dive-bomb?"

"They couldn't in '42, sir. They can today."

"I think you should dive-bomb, don't you, Commander?"

"I do, sir," said McClusky.

Spruance lanced his pointer into Akagi's right side. "Okay, boys, let's show those slant-eyed bastards how to fight a war!"

At 0720, Ensign Jack Reid's handsome, toothy portrayer guided Oliver, Pembroke, Flume, and the burly actor playing Ensign Charles Eaton into the barge and ferried them out to Strawberry Eleven. Reid eased himself into the pilot's seat. Eaton assumed the copilot's position. After hunkering down in their machine-gun blisters, Pembroke and Flume swapped their parkas for matching mauve flak jackets, then slipped on their headsets, opened an aluminum cooler, and began removing the raw materials of a picnic: checkered tablecloth, paper napkins, plastic forks, bottles of vintage Rheingold, Tupperware containers filled with treats from the *Enterprise*'s galley. Within minutes the PBY flying boat was moving, climbing toward the gauzy midnight sun. Field glasses in hand, Oliver crawled through the unoccupied compartments, eventually settling on the mechanic's station; it was a cramped space, mottled with rust and flaking paint (poor Sidney and Albert, he thought, they could never really recover the forties, only its disintegrating remains), but the large window afforded a sweeping vista of sea and sky. For better or worse, this coign of vantage also lay within hearing distance of the impresarios.

"Look, Captain Murray's turning *Enterprise* into the wind," Pembroke told Oliver as the carrier swung slowly east.

"Standard procedure for launching a squadron," Flume elaborated. "With such a short runway, you want lotsa wind under everybody's wings."

Ensign Reid brought the PBY to two thousand feet, then leveled her off and looped around, giving his passengers a clear view of the flight deck. Dressed in green anoraks, a foul-weather crew scurried about, chopping the ice apart with pickaxes and pushing the fragments over the side with coal shovels. A yellow-suited firehose crew finished the job, aiming their nozzles at the runway and letting loose torrents of liquid de-icer.

"Here comes Torpedo Six," said Pembroke as, wings folded, two Devastators rode their respective elevators to the flight deck.

Taking care not to be swept overboard by the prop wash, a quartet of blue-suited plane handlers ran to the forward Devastator, 6-T-9, unchocking the wheels and spreading the wings, whereupon the pilot turned 180 degrees and taxied amidships. As the signal officer waved his batons, the pilot turned again, revved his engine, and sped down the runway, de-icer spewing from his wheels. Oliver half expected the plane to crash into the sea, but instead some God-made law took over—the Bernoulli effect, he believed it was called—lifting 6-T-9 off the bow and high above the waves.

"The Devastators need a head start over the dive bombers," Pembroke explained as 6-T-11 joined her airborne twin. Both planes circled the carrier, awaiting the rest of their section. "Slow devils, those Devastators. They were obsolete even before the first one rolled off the assembly line."

Oliver exhaled sharply, fogging the mechanic's window. "Obsolete? Oh?"

"Hey, not to worry, fella," said Pembroke.

"Your golem's good as dead," said Flume.

"And if worst comes to worst, we've always got Op Plan 29-67."

"Exactly. Op Plan 29-67."

"What's Op Plan 29-67?" asked Oliver.

"You'll see."

"You'll love it."

Two by two, the Devastators continued to arrive, taxiing, revving, taking off. By 0815 the entire first-strike section of Torpedo Six was aloft, fifteen planes arranging themselves into three V-shaped formations. A delicious inevitability hung in the air, a sense of Rubicons crossed and bridges burned, like nothing Oliver had experienced since he and Sally Morgenthau had relieved each other of their respective virginities following a Grateful Dead concert in 1970. My God, he'd thought at the time—my God, we're actually doing it.

"Let's hit the road, Ensign," Flume barked into his intercom mike. "We mustn't be late for the ball."

Turning the control yoke thirty degrees, Jack Reid's portrayer pushed back on the throttle. Oliver, pulse racing (actually doing it, actually doing it), put on his headset. Pembroke leafed through a wartime issue of *Stars and Stripes*. Flume opened a Tupperware container and removed a Spam-and-onion sandwich. Over the intercom, Ensign Eaton's portrayer whistled "Embraceable You." Strawberry Eleven flew alongside the sun, soaring at seventy knots above a range of mammoth icebergs as she chased Lieutenant Commander Lindsey's brave squadron east across the Norwegian Sea.

In his short but busy career as an able-bodied seaman, Neil Weisinger had helmed every sort of merchant ship imaginable, from reefers to Great Lakes freighters, bulk carriers to Ro-Ros, but he'd never before taken the wheel of anything so weird as the SS *Carpco Maracaibo*.

"Come right to zero-two-zero," commanded the officer on duty, Mick Katsakos, a swarthy Cretan in white bell-bottoms, an oil-stained parka, and a Greek fisherman's cap.

"Right to zero-two-zero," echoed Neil, working the wheel.

He'd certainly heard of such vessels, these Persian Gulf tankers outfitted with an eye to the political realities of the Middle East. When filled to her Plimsoll line, a Gulf tanker bore only half the load of a conventional ULCC, yet she displaced a third more water. A single glance at the *Maracaibo*'s silhouette was sufficient to explain this disparity. Three Phalanx 20mm cannon sat atop her fo'c'sle; six Meroka 12-barrel guns jutted from her stern; fifty Westland Lynx Mk-15 depth charges clung to her bulwarks. Missile-wise, the *Maracaibo* achieved the elusive ideal of multiculturalism: Crotales from France, Aspides from Italy, Sea Darts from Britain, Homing Hawks from Israel. Since adding a dozen Persian Gulf tankers to her shipping fleet, Carpco's stock had risen eleven points.

"Steady," said Katsakos.

"Steady," echoed Neil.

It was damn hairy, this business of maneuvering at high speed through the bergs and floes of the Norwegian Sea. Despite his second-mate status, Katsakos did not seem like a particularly smart or experienced sailor (the day before, he'd led them six leagues off course before noticing his error), and Neil did not really trust him to guide the tanker safely. Neil's fervent wish was that the *Maracaibo*'s captain himself would appear on the bridge and take over.

"Ten degrees left rudder."

"Ten left."

But the captain never appeared on the bridge—or anywhere else, for that matter. He was as aloof and inaccessible as the immaterial God whom Neil had failed to find during his self-imposed exile on Van Horne Island. At times he wondered whether the *Maracaibo* even had a master.

For the first three days, Neil's penance had gone well. The sun had been suitably hot, his hunger appropriately painful, his thirst fittingly intense (he'd allowed himself no more than a pint of dew every four hours). Perched in his petrified fig tree like some crazed, outcast, spiritually famished vulture, Neil had struggled to gain the universe's attention. "You appeared to Moses! You appeared to Job!" he'd cried into the fog, over and over until his tongue became so dry the words stuck to it like burrs. "Now appear to me!"

Looking out to sea, Neil had been astonished to behold a Persian Gulf tanker, gravid with cargo and lying at anchor in the very cove from which the *Valparaíso* had recently departed. An hour later, a Falstaffian man with bad skin appeared at the base of his tree, swathed in the island's eternal mist.

"And who might *you* be?" demanded the intruder in a musical Italian accent. Terra-cotta sand clung to his vinyl cassock, muting the bright red silk.

"Able Seaman Weisinger of the United States Merchant Marine," he mumbled, certain he was about to faint.

"Tullio Cardinal Di Luca of the Vatican. You may address me as Eminence. Are you with the *Carpco Valparaíso*?"

"Not anymore." A wave of vertigo. Neil feared he might fall from the tree. "I'm marooned, Eminence. Last time I saw the *Val*, she was headed for the Arctic."

"Strange. Your captain was ordered to return to this island. Evidently he's following his own star."

"Evidently."

"Was it Van Horne who marooned you?"

"I marooned myself."

"Oh?"

"To find God," Neil explained. The holes in Cardinal Di Luca's face suggested a child's connect-the-dots puzzle. What constellation would emerge if you drew a line from pock to pock? Ophiuchus, Neil guessed. Serpent Bearer. "The God beyond God. The God of the four A.M. watch. *En Sof*."

"You expect to find God in a tree?"

"Moses did, Eminence."

"Do you want a job, Able Seaman Weisinger?"

"I want to find God."

"Yes, but do you want a job? The *Maracaibo* departed before we could assemble a proper crew. I can offer you the position of quartermaster."

Hunger clawed at Neil's stomach. His gullet screamed for water. For all he knew, a few more hours of such suffering might be enough to inflame these branches with *En Sof*.

And yet . . .

"As far as the *Maracaibo*'s company is concerned," Di Luca continued, "Van Horne's cargo is a motion-picture prop. The Holy See aims to keep the film from getting made. Join us, Mr. Weisinger. Time-and-a-half for overtime."

The Lord, Neil decided, worked through many media, not just burning bushes and stone trees. YHWH dispatched angels, wrote on walls, poured dreams into prophets' heads. Perhaps He even used the Catholic Church from time to time. By sending Tullio Di Luca to this place, Neil realized with a surge of joy, the God of the four A.M. watch was almost certainly telling him to get on with his life . . .

"Right ten degrees."

"Right ten," echoed Neil.

"Steady."

"Steady."

Behind Neil a door squealed open. A pungent fragrance

wafted across the bridge, the sourness of human sweat mixed with the woodsy scent of a burning cheroot.

"What's your course, Katsakos?" A male voice, resonant and gruff.

The second mate stiffened. "Zero-one-four."

Neil turned. With his broad shoulders, ramrod spine, and leonine head emerging from the hood of a brilliant purple parka, the master of the *Maracaibo* looked aristocratic if not royal. Though scored with age, his face was astonishingly handsome, dark brown eyes shining from beneath a lofty brow, strong cheekbones flanking an aquiline nose.

"Speed?"

"Fifteen knots," said Katsakos.

"Bump her up to seventeen."

"Is that safe, Captain Van Horne?"

"When *I'm* on the bridge, it's safe."

"He called you Van Horne," Neil blurted out as Katsakos advanced the throttles.

"Quite so." The master of the *Maracaibo* puffed on his cheroot. "Christopher Van Horne."

"The last captain I shipped with was named Van Horne too. Anthony Van Horne."

"I know," said the old man. "Di Luca told me. My son's a good sailor, but he lacks—what shall we call it?—gumption."

"Anthony Van Horne . . . ," mused the second mate. "Wasn't he in charge when the *Valparaíso* spilled her cookies into the Gulf of Mexico?"

"I heard it was mostly Carpco's fault," said Neil. "An overworked crew, an understaffed ship . . ."

"Don't defend the man. Know what he's hauling now? A goddamn skin-flick prop, that's what." The captain stubbed out his cheroot on the twelve-mile radar. "Tell me, Mr. Weisinger, are you a sailor I can depend on?"

"I believe so."

"Ever held the wheel in a storm?"

"Last Fourth of July, I steered the *Val* through the heart of Hurricane Beatrice."

"Through the heart?"

"Your son wanted to get from Raritan Bay to the Gulf of Guinea in twelve days."

"That's insane," said the captain. His indignation, Neil felt, was tempered by a certain parental pride. "You made the deadline?"

"We stopped to rescue a castaway."

"But you *would've* made it?"

"Pretty likely."

"In just twelve days?"

"Yep."

Christopher Van Horne smiled, the wrinkled flesh rolling across his magnificent skull. "Listen, Seaman Weisinger, when we finally catch the *Val*, you're the man I want at the wheel." His voice dropped to a half whisper. "Unless I miss my guess, we'll be making some pretty tricky turns."

On the sixteenth of September, at 0915, as the *Valparaíso* hit the 71st parallel, Cassie Fowler realized that she was in love. Her discovery came during a moment of tranquility, as she and Anthony stood watching the tanker's hatchetlike prow push through the passage formed by two colossal bergs. Had it happened in the heat of sex (and there'd been plenty of that lately, an itinerant orgy staged wherever their impulses took them, from Anthony's cabin to the fo'c'sle locker to the bizarre garden Sam Follingsbee was cultivating below), she would have dismissed it as illusory, akin to the phenomenon that prompted dying people to mistake oxygen deprivation for the glow of heaven. But this emotion could be trusted. This felt real. Damn, it was confusing, loving the very man who'd been deputized to preserve the most malevolent counterfeminist artifact since Saint Paul's Letter to the Ephesians.

"The Arctic's a known quantity these days," said Anthony, "but you can't imagine all the grief and blood that went into mapping this part of the globe."

While Cassie's curiosity urged her to confess her passion then and there—would he laugh? panic? grow mute? say he was as crazy about her as she was about him?—her political convictions told her to wait. This morning, assuming she'd calculated correctly, Oliver would attack their cargo. She would be foolish to divide her loyalties by entertaining romantic protestations from Anthony at such an hour. If he did an effective job of conveying his love, she might even lose her nerve. Her worst-case scenario had her getting on the *Val*'s radio, contacting the *Enterprise*, and telling Oliver to scratch the mission.

"In the last century, your average armchair geographer believed there was an open, ice-free sea at the North Pole."

"Where'd they get *that* idea?" asked Cassie.

"Here in the Atlantic we've got our Gulf Stream—right?—and meanwhile the Japanese have their Kuroshio, their great Black Tide. The geographers imagined both currents flowing all the way north, melting the bergs and floes, then joining to form a vast warm ocean."

"There's nothing quite so pernicious as wishful thinking."

"Yeah, but such a *beautiful* wish. I mean, what captain wouldn't fall in love with a fantasy like that? Piloting your ship up the Bering Strait, finding a secret gateway in the ice, sailing across the top of the world . . ."

A burst of static drew Anthony's attention to the walkie-talkie clipped to his utility belt.

"Captain to the bridge!" screamed Marbles Rafferty. "We need you up here, sir!"

Anthony grabbed the radio, pressed SEND. "What's the problem?"

"Airplanes!"

"Airplanes?"

"Airplanes, Captain—from goddamn World War Two!"

"What the hell are you talking about?"

"Just get up here!"

Airplanes, thought Cassie, following Anthony as he abandoned the lookout post and started down the icy catwalk. Glory be, dear Oliver had actually brought it off. Before the day was out, if all went well, the New Dark Ages would no longer be crouching at the edge of human history, poised to claim center stage.

"Airplanes," grumbled Anthony, charging into the elevator car. "I don't need any fucking *airplanes* in my life right now."

"Their mission may be more benign than you suppose," said Cassie. As they rose to level seven, a peculiar thought possessed her. Might it be possible to win him over? If she mustered all her best arguments, might he come to see that locking this corpse forever out of history was far more important than sticking it in a tomb? "And *your* mission less so."

They disembarked, passed through the wheelhouse—An-mei Jong at the helm—and marched onto the starboard wing, where the eternally morose Marbles Rafferty stood peering aft through the bridge binoculars, grunting in dismay.

Cassie looked south. Three separate clusters of droning torpedo planes wove among the bergs, sweeping back and forth across the corpse's ice-glazed neck, while, several miles above sea level, a swarm of noisy dive bombers made ready to plunge toward the frozen omphalos. Wondrous vibrations surged through her, hymns of impending battle, pleasing for their own sake and pleasing for what they meant: despite her love for Anthony, despite the various moral and psychological ambiguities inherent in this crusade, she was not about to buckle.

Rafferty pressed the binoculars into Anthony's chest. "See what I'm talkin' about?" moaned the chief mate, pointing south as Anthony lifted the Bushnells and focused. "I think those are classic SBD-2 Dauntlesses over near the belly, and meanwhile we got ourselves a squadron of TBD-1 Devastators zooming 'round the throat—all of 'em built, I swear, Captain, all of 'em built in the late thirties. It's like some goddamn *Twilight Zone* episode!"

"Steady, sir?" called An-mei Jong from the wheelhouse.

"No—turn!" bellowed Anthony, cheeks reddening, eyes darting in all directions. "Left full rudder! We're 'taking evasive action!"

"You can't evade *this*," Cassie insisted.

"Marbles, get on the sticks! Flank speed!"

"Aye!"

As the mate sprinted into the wheelhouse, Anthony seized Cassie's forearm, squeezing so hard she felt the pressure through the goose-down stuffing. "What do you mean, I can't evade this?" he said.

"You're hurting me."

"Do you know where these planes are from?"

"Yep."

"Where?"

"Let go of my arm," Cassie insisted. He did. "Pembroke and Flume's World War Two Reenactment Society."

"Pembroke and who? What?"

"They're working for hire."

"Who hired them?"

"Some friends of mine."

"Friends of *yours*? Oliver, you mean?"

"Try to understand, Anthony—dead or alive, this body's a menace. If it ever becomes public, reason and women's equality go out the window. Entombment's not enough—it must be dumped in the Mohns Trench and left to decompose. Tell me you understand."

He faced her squarely, lips curled, teeth clenched. "Understand? *Understand?!*"

"I don't think that's asking too much."

"How could you betray me like this?"

"The patriarchy's been betraying my gender for the past four thousand years."

"How could you, Cassie? How *could* you?"

She looked him in the eye and said, "A woman's gotta do what a woman's gotta do."

For a moment Cassie's lover stood frozen on the bridge wing, immobilized by anger.

Checkmate, she thought.

He spun toward the wheelhouse. "Evasive action!" he yelled to Jong. "Left full rudder!"

"You already gave that order, sir!"

Locked in a tight V, five Devastators swung around from the west and flew straight for the neck, releasing their payloads as they drew within a thousand feet of the target. Swiftly, smoothly, the torpedoes made their runs, bubbly white lather spuming from their propellers. One by one, the warheads hit flesh and detonated, sending up fountains of boiling lymph and geysers of pulverized tissue. Cassie laughed: a long, low whoop of delight. At last she was getting it. *This* was why men took such trouble to arrange for fire and chaos in their lives—the rush of destruction, the imperial nonboredom of war, history's intoxicating grease. There were probably highs of equal caliber on earth, certainly less violent ones, but, oh, what lovely theater it made, what a hell of an opening night.

At last the tanker began her turn, carving a great crescent of foam in the Norwegian Sea, God inexorably following.

"Now hear this!" cried Anthony, grabbing the PA mike. "Now hear this—two squadrons of hostile warplanes are presently harassing our cargo! The *Val* herself is in no danger, and we're taking evasive action! Repeat: the *Val* is in no danger!"

Cassie released a contemptuous snort. He could call it evasive action if he liked, but at nine lousy knots the stiff was a sitting duck.

"I pulled you out of the sea!" Anthony brandished the binoculars, holding them before Cassie as if he meant to smash her across the face. "I fed you my mescal worms!"

She couldn't decide whether she was madder at Anthony or herself. How naive, how stupefyingly naive, to have imagined he might sanction her agenda. "Damn, I knew you'd miss the point, I just *knew* it." Tearing the binoculars from Anthony's hands, she aimed them at a PBY flying boat currently orbiting above their cargo's brow. For a brief instant Oliver materialized before her eyes—sweet, weak-chinned Oliver, sitting by a starboard window and looking like a roller-coaster rider on the verge of throwing up. "You know, Anthony, you're taking this attack much too personally. It's beyond your control. Relax."

"Nothing's beyond my control!"

At 0935 an echelon of six dive bombers struck, engines screaming as they peeled off and hurtled downward, lobbing their payloads against the stomach like a flock of blue-footed boobies defecating on Saint Paul's Rocks. With each direct hit, a ragged column of melted ice and vaporized skin shot skyward.

"What's going on here?" demanded a perplexed Father Thomas, striding onto the starboard wing in the company of an equally baffled Dolores Haycox.

"The Battle of Midway," Cassie replied.

"Jesus H. Christ," muttered Haycox.

"Is the Vatican behind it?" asked Father Thomas.

"*You* don't belong here!" shouted Anthony.

"I warned you not to mess with Rome," said the priest.

"Get out!"

"The Church can't take credit," said Cassie.

"Who, then?" asked Father Thomas.

"The Enlightenment."

"I said get out!" Anthony, sputtering, lurched toward the third mate. "I want to see Sparks—on the double!"

"Jesus H. Christ," said Haycox again, starting away.

The next two attacks occurred simultaneously, a V of torpedo planes methodically expanding the breach in God's neck while another echelon of dive bombers doggedly augmented His belly wound.

"I've never boasted a particularly sophisticated grasp of politics," Father Thomas confessed.

"This isn't politics," snarled Anthony. "It's feminist paranoia!" Again he squeezed Cassie's arm. "Has it occurred to you that if your little friends succeed, the body will drag us all down with it?"

"Don't worry—they'll be bombing the chains soon. Kindly remove your dung forks from my person."

Lianne strode onto the wing, face lit by a wide, meandering smile. "You rang, sir?"

"Those planes are destroying our cargo," wailed Anthony.

"So I see."

"I want you to raise the squadron leaders."

"Aye-aye."

"Hi, Lianne," said Cassie.

"Morning, sweetie."

"Shit, did *you* have a hand in this, Sparks?" asked Anthony.

Lianne winced. "I'll confess to harboring a certain sympathy for what those planes are trying to do, sir," she replied, sidestepping the question. "That body's bad news for women everywhere."

"Look on the bright side," Cassie told Anthony. "Normally you'd have to pay sixty dollars to see a Pembroke and Flume extravaganza."

"Raise those leaders, Sparks!"

Oliver hated the Battle of Midway. It was noisy, confusing, and manifestly dangerous. "Do we have to be so *close*?" he asked Ensign Reid over the intercom. The third Devastator attack had just gotten under way, five planes zooming across the deckhouse of the circling supertanker and lobbing their torpedoes straight into God's neck. As each payload exploded, Strawberry Eleven responded to the shock wave, twisting and rocking like a shot goose. "Why don't we watch"—Oliver extended a trembling index finger—"from over there? Over there by that big berg!"

"Don't listen to him, Ensign," said Pembroke, tearing into a pint of macaroni salad.

"Oliver, you gotta get into the spirit," said Flume, popping a deviled egg into his mouth.

"That's some golem, huh?" said Pembroke.

"Bet you could drive a Pershing tank down his urethra and not even scratch the fenders," said Flume.

"God, what a smile," said Pembroke.

As the last Devastator completed its run, happy chatter spilled from Strawberry Eleven's transceiver, five creatively fulfilled war reenactors singing their own praises.

"Powder river!"

"Golly, this is swell!"

"Got that baby comin' and goin'!"

"Hot-cha-cha!"

"The beers're on me, boys!"

Now the third Dauntless echelon moved into position, climbing swiftly to fifteen thousand feet. Through the haze of his fear, Oliver sensed that the raid was going well. He was particularly impressed by the forgotten art of dive-bombing, the skillful and reckless way the SBD pilots turned their planes into manned bullets, swooping out of the clouds, plunging headfirst toward the midriff, and, at the moment of payload release, pulling out just in time to avoid cracking up—a truly magnificent performance, almost worth the seventeen million dollars it was costing him.

The Dauntlesses peeled away and attacked, dropping their demolition bombs on the navel. Spewing flames and smoke, a seething orange tornado spun across God's abdomen.

"It's so beautiful!" gasped Pembroke.

"This is it, Sid—this is our masterpiece!" squealed Flume.

"We'll never top it, never, even if we do a D-Day!"

"I'm so *excited*!"

A husky female voice shot from Strawberry Eleven's transceiver. "*Valparaíso* to squadron leaders! Come in, squadron leaders!"

The head of Torpedo Six responded instantly. "Lieutenant Commander Lindsey here, United States Navy," he said in a tone at once curious and hostile. "Go ahead, *Valparaíso*."

"Captain Van Horne wishes to address you . . ."

The voice that now filled the PBY's cabin was so enraged Oliver imagined the transceiver tubes exploding, spraying glass into the cockpit.

"What the hell do you think you're doing, Lindsey?!"

"My patriotic duty. Over."

"Fuck you!"

"Fuck you! Over."

"You've got no right to destroy my cargo!"

"And you've got no right to destroy the American economy! I don't care how good your English is! Can't you Japs ever play fair? Over!"

"Japs? What're you talking about?"

"You know exactly what I'm talking about!" said Lindsey. "America first! Out!"

"Get back on the air, you dipshit!"

As the two squadrons turned west and headed for Point Luck, Strawberry Eleven circled the corpse, a slow, leisurely loop extending from nose to knees. The bellybutton, Oliver noted, was considerably larger now, a quarter-mile-wide crater into which the Norwegian Sea flowed like water spiraling into a bathtub drain. The neck sported a gaping cave, its portal a mass of shattered ice and shredded flesh. The only problem was that, in his admittedly inexpert judgment, God wasn't sinking.

"They did a great job with the bellybutton," said Pembroke.

"Navel warfare," said Flume, deadpan.

"Hey, that's a good one, Alby."

"Why isn't there more blood?" asked Oliver.

"Beats me," said Pembroke, polishing off the macaroni salad.

"Is it frozen?"

"Bombs would've thawed it."

"So where *is* it?"

"Probably it never had any," said Flume. "Blood's such complicated stuff—I'll bet even Mitsubishi can't make it."

As the PBY glided across the body's right nipple, her transceiver began broadcasting again. "Red Fox Leader to Mother Goose," said Lindsey. "Red Fox Leader to Mother Goose."

"Mother Goose here," said Admiral Spruance's portrayer aboard the *Enterprise*.

"We dropped our last egg ten minutes ago. Over."

"What about Scout Bombing Six?"

"Likewise disarmed. We're all headin' home for another batch. Over."

"How's it going?"

"Sir, the Japs might be listening in."

"No screening vessels, remember?" said Spruance. "No Bofors guns."

"Targets A and B were hit hard, sir," said Lindsey. "Real hard. Over."

"Was Akagi shipping water when you left her?"

"No, sir."

"Then we're shifting to Op Plan 29-67," said Spruance.

"Op Plan 29-67," echoed Lindsey. "Dandy idea."

"The second strike's taking off now, McClusky commanding from his Dauntless section. We can begin recovering your planes any time after 0945 hours. Over."

"Roger, Mother Goose. Out."

"*Now* will you tell me about Op Plan 29-67?" asked Oliver.

"An emergency strategy," explained Pembroke.

"*What* emergency strategy?"

"The swellest one ever," said Flume.

At 1120 a new wave appeared along the western horizon—three V-formations of torpedo planes coming in near sea level while three echelons of dive bombers rendezvoused from several miles up.

"Commander McClusky, Air Group Six, to Captain Van Horne on *Valparaíso*," came the actor's reedy voice from the PBY's transceiver. "You there, Van Horne? Over."

"This is Van Horne, asshole."

"Question, Captain. Is *Valparaíso* carrying a full complement of lifeboats?"

"What's it to you?"

"I'll assume that means *yes*. Over."

"Keep your paws off my cargo!"

"Captain, be advised that at 1150 hours we shall be implementing Op Plan 29-67, whereby *Valparaíso* comes under attack from a section of Devastators armed with Mk-XIII torpedoes. Repeat: at 1150, your ship comes under attack from a section of . . ."

Oliver lurched out of the mechanic's station and scrambled toward the machine-gun blisters. "McClusky said he's gonna hit the *Valparaíso*!"

"I know," said Pembroke, grinning.

"Op Plan 29-67," said Flume, winking.

"He can't hit the *Valparaíso*!" moaned Oliver.

"*Valparaíso*, not 'the' *Valparaíso*."

"He can't!"

"Shhh," said Pembroke.

"You have thirty minutes to abandon ship," said McClusky from the transceiver. "We strongly recommend you keep your officers and crew out of the water, which we estimate to be about twenty degrees Fahrenheit. You'll be rescued within two hours by the decommissioned aircraft carrier *Enterprise*. Over."

"Like hell I'm gonna abandon ship!" said Van Horne.

"Have it your way, Captain. Out."

"You can shove your torpedoes up your ass, McClusky!"

Pembroke ate a radish. "A desperate strategy," he explained, "but unavoidable under the circumstances."

"As the tanker sinks," Flume elaborated, chewing on a chicken thigh, "she'll drag the golem down with her, deep enough to swamp those wounds."

"After which the lungs and stomach will finally start to fill."

"And then—"

"Shazam—mission accomplished!"

Oliver grabbed Flume's shoulders, shaking the war reenactor as if attempting to rouse him from a deep sleep. "My girlfriend's on the *Valparaíso!*"

"Oh, sure," said Pembroke.

"Let go of me this instant," said Flume.

"I'm serious!" wailed Oliver, releasing Flume and rocking back on the balls of his feet. "Ask Van Horne! Ask him if he isn't carrying somebody named Cassie Fowler!"

"Hey, take it easy." Flume uncapped a Rheingold with a cast-iron Fred Astaire opener. "Nobody'll get hurt. We're giving the Japs *plenty* of time to save themselves. Want a beer? A Spam-and-onion sandwich?"

"You heard the captain! He's not gonna abandon ship!"

"Once he absorbs a hit or two, I'm sure he'll reconsider," said Pembroke. "It takes hours for a big boat like *Valparaíso* to go down—*hours.*"

"You people are insane! You're out of your fucking minds!"

"Hey, don't get pissed at *us*," said Flume.

"We're only doing what you hired us to do," said Pembroke.

"Contact Admiral Spruance! Tell him to call off the attack!"

"We *never* call off an attack," said Flume, swishing his index finger back and forth. "Have a nice cold Rheingold, okay? You'll feel much better." The impresario snatched up his intercom mike.

"Ensign Reid, I think it would be a bad idea if Mr. Shostak back here got his hands on our transceiver."

"Listen, fellas, I've been lying to you," groaned Oliver. "That body down there isn't a Jap golem."

"Oh?" said Pembroke.

"It's God Almighty."

"Right," said Flume with a snide smile.

"God Himself. I swear it. You wouldn't want to hurt *God*, would you?"

Flume sipped his beer. "Phew, Oliver, that's a pretty lame one."

At exactly 1150, just as McClusky had promised, a V of torpedo planes circled around and, ignoring Oliver's frantic protests, ran for the tanker, dropping their Mk-XIIIs and sailing over the deckhouse, concomitantly slashing the Vatican flag to ribbons. Like sharks on the scent of blood, the five torpedoes cut across the *Val*'s wake, passed under her starboard tow chain, grazed her stern, and kept on going. A minute later, they struck a berg and detonated, filling the air with glittering barrages of ice balls.

"Hah! Missed!" came Van Horne's voice from the transceiver. "You clowns couldn't hit a dead cat with a fly swatter!"

"Golly, I thought our boys were better trained than that," said Pembroke.

"They're not used to these low temperatures," said Flume.

Breathing a sigh of relief, Oliver looked out to sea—past the *Valparaíso*, past her cargo. A massive ship, encrusted with rockets and guns, was steaming onto the battlefield from the south.

"Hey, Oliver, what the heck is *that* thing?" demanded Flume.

"Don't ask me," the Enlightenment League's president replied, putting on his headset.

"You said there'd be no screening vessels!" whined Pembroke. "You explicitly said that!"

"I haven't the foggiest idea what that ship's doing here."

"Looks like one of them Persian Gulf tankers, Mr. Flume," said Reid over the intercom.

"That's what she is, all right," said Eaton. "A goddamn Persian Gulf tanker."

"Isn't that just like the nineties"—Reid banked Strawberry Eleven, flying her west across the tow chains—"showing up when you least expect 'em?"

"Missed!" cried Anthony, storming up and down the wheelhouse, glove wrapped firmly around the transceiver mike, its cable trailing behind him like an umbilicus. "Missed, suckers! You couldn't hit an elephant's ass with a canoe paddle! You couldn't hit a barn door with a water balloon!"

He didn't believe himself. He knew it was only through a happy accident that the first Devastator formation had launched all five of its fish without scoring a hit. Already a second V was looping around to the west, making ready to strike.

"Captain, shall we order the crew into life jackets?" asked Marbles Rafferty.

"Sounds like a good idea," said Ockham.

"Get the hell off the bridge," Anthony snapped at the priest.

Rafferty pounded his palm with his fist. "Life jackets, sir. Life jackets . . ."

"Life jackets," echoed Lianne Bliss.

"No," muttered Anthony, setting the mike atop the Marisat terminal. "Remember Matagorda Bay? A sixty-yard gash in her hull, and *still* she didn't sink. We can easily absorb a couple of obsolete torpedoes—I know we can."

"They've got *ten* left," noted Rafferty.

"Then we'll absorb ten."

"Anthony, you must believe me," said Cassie. "I never thought they'd come after your ship."

"War is hell, Doc."

"I'm truly sorry."

"I don't doubt it. Fuck you."

Remarkably, he could not bring himself to hate her. True, her duplicity was monumental, a betrayal to rank with that ignominious moment at Actium when Mark Antony had abandoned his own fleet in midbattle to go chasing after Cleopatra. And yet, at some weird, unfathomable level, he actually admired Cassie's plot. Her audacity turned him on. There was nobody quite so arousing, he decided, as a worthy opponent.

The door to the starboard wing flew open and Dolores Haycox charged onto the bridge, gripping a walkie-talkie. "Forward lookout reports approaching vessel, sir—a ULCC, low riding, bearing three-two-nine."

Anthony grunted. ULCC. Damn. Despite the blood transfusion, despite his quick and clever maneuvering through the bergs, he still hadn't managed to outrun the *Carpco Maracaibo*. He snatched up the bridge binoculars and, peering through the frosted windshield, focused. He gasped. Not only was the *Maracaibo* a ULCC, she was a Persian Gulf tanker, heavy with formaldehyde but coming on fast. Her thorny profile shifted east and steamed past a berg shaped like a gigantic molar, on a direct course for God's left ear.

"What's that, a battleship?" asked Ockham.

"Not quite," said Anthony, lowering the binoculars. "Your buddies in Rome are obviously serious about making me surrender the goods." He pivoted toward his chief mate. "Marbles, if we got uncoupled from our cargo, these Devastators would have no reason to target us, right?"

"Right."

"Then I propose we ring up the *Maracaibo* and ask her to shoot our chains apart."

Rafferty smiled, an event so rare that Anthony knew the plan was sound. "At worst, the skipper turns us down," noted the chief mate. "At best—"

"Oh, he'll say yes, all right," Ockham insisted. "Whatever Rome's ultimate ambitions may be, she has no wish to see this ship go under."

"Sparks, contact the *Maracaibo*," said Anthony, shoving the transceiver mike into Lianne Bliss's hand. "Get her skipper on the line."

"They shouldn't be attacking your ship like this," she said. "It isn't right."

Anthony was not surprised when, barely thirty seconds after Bliss ducked into the radio shack, the *Maracaibo* lashed out, shooting a Sea Dart guided missile toward the second Devastator formation. If Cassie's story was true, he reasoned, then the forces represented by the World War Two Reenactment Society and those represented by the Gulf tanker had not been privy to each other's machinations—but suddenly here they were, arriving simultaneously in the same unlikely sea, competing for the same unlikely prize.

"Hey, the *Maracaibo* can't do that!" screamed Cassie. "She's gonna kill somebody!"

"Looks that way," said Anthony dryly.

"This is murder!"

The instant the Devastators began their chaotic retreat, the V dissolving into five separate planes, Bliss piped the radio traffic onto the bridge.

"Scatter, boys!" screamed the formation leader. "Scatter! Scatter!"

"Christ, it's on your tail, Commander Waldron!" a flier shouted.

"Mother of God!"

"Bail out, Commander!"

Anthony raised his hand and saluted in the general direction of the Gulf tanker.

"Tell the *Maracaibo* this is just a reenactment!" screamed Cassie. "Nobody's supposed to be getting hurt!"

As Anthony tracked it with the binoculars, the lead torpedo plane shot straight across the *Val*'s weather deck, doggedly pursued by the near-sentient Sea Dart.

"Why's the missile so poky?" asked Anthony.

"A heat seeker, designed to lock on modern jet exhaust," Rafferty explained. "It'll take 'er a while to realize she's tracking an antique radial engine."

With an odd mixture of pure horror and indefensible fascination, Anthony watched the missile home in. An explosion brightened the steely sky, vaporizing the Devastator's two-man crew and disintegrating her fuselage, the thousand flaming shards flashing through the air like a migraine aura.

From the bridge speaker a flier screamed, "They got Commander Waldron! Waldron and his gunner!"

"Christ!"

"Just like in '42!"

"Lousy bastards!"

"Dirty Japs!"

"The *Maracaibo* doesn't answer," said Bliss, rushing out of the radio shack.

"Keep trying to raise her."

"She's stonewalling us, sir."

"I said keep trying!"

As Bliss returned to her post, two more missiles leapt from the *Maracaibo*, a svelte French Crotale and a delicate Italian Aspide, speeding toward the third Devastator formation. Seconds later came the roaring vermilion glare of the exploding Crotale, outshining the midnight sun and bursting the lead plane apart, followed by the shrieking, swirling, red-and-purple plumage of the Aspide, setting its target aflame. Four white parachutes blossomed above the Norwegian Sea, gently lowering their riders toward death by hypothermia.

"Holy shit, the crews bailed out," said Rafferty.

"God help them," said Ockham.

"No, *we'll* help them," said Anthony, snapping up the intercom mike and tuning in the bos'n's quarters. "Van Horne to Mungo."

"Mungo here."

"There're four men in the water, bearing two-nine-five. Drop a lifeboat, pick 'em up, give 'em hot showers, and stand by to rescue anybody else who jumps."

"Aye, Captain."

Once again Dolores Haycox popped in from the wing. "Starboard lookout reports torpedo wake approaching, sir, bearing two-one-zero."

Anthony raised his binoculars. Torpedo wake. Quite so. While Commander Waldron was being hunted down, one of his buddies had obviously gotten off a shot.

"Right full rudder!"

"Right full rudder!" repeated An-mei Jong, jerking the wheel forty degrees.

And then it happened. Before the tanker could answer to the helm, a horrid, toothy grinding reached the bridge, the slow-motion crunch of metal devouring metal, followed by a deep, ominous thud. Wall to wall, the wheelhouse shook.

"Delayed fuse," Rafferty explained. "Fish broke through our plates before goin' off."

"That good or bad?" asked Ockham.

"Bad. Damn things do twice the damage that way, like dum-dum bullets."

Seizing the PA mike, Anthony threw the switch. "Now hear this! We've just absorbed an Mk-XIII torpedo along our starboard quarter! Repeat: torpedo hit along starboard quarter! Remember, sailors, below decks the *Val* is divided into twenty-four watertight tanks—we're in no danger of foundering! Stand by to take on survivors from Mr. Mungo's party!"

"The *Maracaibo* still won't talk!" called Bliss from the radio shack.

"Keep trying!"

"Now what?" asked Rafferty.

"Now I go see if what I just told the crew is true."

No sooner had Anthony entered the elevator car and begun his descent when a second Mk-XIII drilled into the *Valparaíso* and exploded. The shock wave lifted the car back toward level seven. He dropped to his knees. The car plunged, the steel cables stopping its fall like elastic cords saving a Bungee jumper.

As Anthony ran outside, a third fish found its target, sending a metallic shudder along the *Val*'s entire hull. He dashed down the catwalk. The two guilty Devastators roared straight across the weather deck, fleeing the scene of their crime. An acrid fragrance filled the air, a blend of hot metal and burning rubber suffused with a hint of frying meat. The captain climbed down the amidships stairway, sprinted to the starboard bulwark, and leaned over the rail.

Déjà vu. "No!" It was all happening again, the whole impossible spill. "No! No!" The *Valparaíso* was leaking, she was bleeding, she was hemorrhaging her ballast into the Norwegian Sea. Blood, thick blood, gallon upon gallon of sizzling, smoking, pungent blood spreading outward from the wounded hull like the first plague of Egypt, staining the waters red. "No! No!"

Anthony looked west. A quarter mile away, Mungo and his lifeboat team rowed toward the torpedo crews: four benumbed war reenactors, treading water amid the billowing canopies and tangled lines of their parachutes.

Plucking the walkie-talkie from his waist, Anthony shouted, "Van Horne to Rafferty! Come in, Marbles!"

He looked down. Evidently a torpedo had blundered into Follingsbee's garden, for the Greenland Current now bloomed with huge broccoli stalks, sixty-pound oranges, and carrots the size of surfboards, the whole nutritious mess drifting on the crimson tide like croutons in gazpacho.

"Jesus—two more hits, right?" groaned Rafferty from the walkie-talkie. "What's it like down there?"

"Bloody."

"We sinking?"

"We're fine," Anthony insisted. His honest assessment, but also something of a prayer. "Call up O'Connor and make sure the boilers are okay. And let's get everybody into life jackets."

"Aye-aye!"

The captain pivoted north. A sickly blue aurora glimmered in the sky. Beneath the waves, a fourth torpedo made its run, heading straight for the prow.

"Stop!" he yelled at the obscene fish. "Stop, you!"

The torpedo hit home, and as the cargo bay burst open, releasing its holy stores, a disquieting question entered Anthony's brain.

"Stop! No! Stop!"

If the *Val* went down, was he supposed to go down with her?

"Get those bastards!" screamed Christopher Van Horne into the intercom mike. "Blow 'em out of the sky!" he ordered his first mate, a wiry Corsican named Orso Peche, presently stationed in the launch-control bunker amidships. The *Maracaibo*'s master spun toward Neil Weisinger. "Come right to zero-six-zero! They're trying to kill my son!"

Never before had Neil witnessed such sheer volcanic anger in a sea captain—in any man. "Right to zero-six-zero," he echoed, working the wheel.

The captain's misery was understandable. Of the entire squadron called Torpedo Six, only three armed planes still remained in the fight, but if even *one* of them kicked its load into the bleeding *Val*, she would surely die.

"All ahead full!"

"All ahead full," echoed Mick Katsakos at the control console. "What's that red stuff?"

"Ballast," Neil explained.

"Wish I had my camera."

An elegant little Aspide blasted from its launcher, tracking down and vaporizing its target just as the crew bailed out.

"One down, two to go," said Peche over the intercom.

"That is *quite* a body," said Katsakos. "Mmm-mmm."

"Never been another like it," said Neil.

Now, suddenly, a fourth man was on the bridge. Dressed in a waterproof alb, trembling with a fury that paled only in comparison with the captain's, Tullio Cardinal Di Luca waddled toward the console.

"Captain, you must stop shooting at those planes! You must stop it right now!"

"They're trying to kill my son!"

"I *knew* we hired the wrong man!"

For the tenth time since the *Maracaibo*'s arrival at the 71st parallel, the rugged old Spaniard named Gonzalo Cornejo popped out of the radio shack to announce that the *Valparaíso*'s communications officer was trying to get in touch.

"She's really—how do you say?—she's really driving me bugfuck."

"Like to talk back to her, would you?" asked the captain.

"Yes, sir."

"Tell the *Valparaíso* that Christopher Van Horne doesn't negotiate with pimps for the skin-flick industry. Got that, Gonzo? I don't talk to pimps." As Cornejo made a crisp about-face, the captain gave him a second order—"Pipe in the traffic, okay?"— then turned to Neil and said, "Ten degrees left rudder."

"Ten left," said Neil, wondering what sort of man would commit cold-blooded murder on his son's behalf but refuse to exchange two words with him over the radio.

"Captain, if you cannot resist the temptation to fire your

missiles, then we simply must leave," said Di Luca, face reddening. "Do you understand? I'm ordering you to turn this ship around."

"You mean retreat? Screw that, Eminence."

"The *cardinale* has a point," said Katsakos. "Maybe you noticed—these idiots still have six armed dive bombers over by the belly."

Even as the mate spoke, a Devastator pilot's agitated tones blasted from the bridge speaker. "Lieutenant Sharp to Commander McClusky. Come in, Commander."

"McClusky here," replied the leader of Air Group Six from his position above the omphalos.

"Sir, you got any eggs left?"

"One echelon's worth. We're about to unload 'em. Over."

"There's a Persian Gulf tanker on the field," said Sharp. "Any chance you could help us out?"

"Gulf tanker? Whoa! Spruance said there wouldn't be any screening vessels. Over."

"Guess he fibbed."

"We never done a Gulf tanker script, Sharp—nothin' that modern. Over."

"It's kickin' the shit out of us! We're down to just me and Beeson!"

"Christ. Okay, I'll see what we can do . . ."

Katsakos's golden Mediterranean skin acquired a decidedly greenish cast. "Sir, may I remind you we've got a full hold? If just *one* of McClusky's bombs connects, we'll go up like Hiroshima."

A prickly sensation overtook Neil, a tingling such as he'd not experienced since getting gassed inside the *Val*. The dive bombers were coming, bearing their deadly matches. "I should've stayed in Jersey City," he told Di Luca. "I should've waited for another ship."

"We can always come back later and make sure the *Enterprise* pulled your son and his crew from their lifeboats," said Katsakos. "As for now . . ."

"Anthony Van Horne won't be crawling into any goddamn lifeboat," said the captain. "He'll be going down with his ship."

"Nobody does that anymore."

"The Van Hornes do."

Sighting through the bridge binoculars, Neil saw McClusky's Dauntless echelon abandon the belly and begin a steady climb, evidently intending to circle around and attack the *Maracaibo* from the rear.

"Mr. Peche," said the captain into the intercom mike, "kindly target the approaching dive bombers with Crotales." He grabbed a swatch of the second mate's pea jacket, twisting it like a tourniquet. "Who on board can operate a Phalanx cannon?"

"Nobody," said Katsakos.

"Not you?"

"No, sir."

"Not Peche?"

"No."

"Then I'll fire it."

"I *insist* we turn around!" seethed Di Luca.

"Mr. Katsakos, I'm putting you in charge," said the captain, starting away. "Alter course as the situation requires, whatever gives me a clear shot at the tow chains—they're only targeting the *Val* so the body'll go down with her!"

Neil looked south. Two Crotales were flying across God's nose toward the maneuvering dive bombers. The warheads exploded simultaneously, hitting the echelon leader and the next plane in line an instant after their pilots and gunners bailed out. Trailing black oil, the first Dauntless crashed into the chin, shattering the encrusted ice and igniting the beard. Wingless, the second plane became a flaming sphere, roaring through the sky and falling into God's left eye like a cinder.

Neil focused on the beard, each whisker enveloped by a high, slender flame coiling around its shaft. He lowered his gaze. Christopher Van Horne stood on the fo'c'sle deck, his mountainous form hunched over the starboard Phalanx, his purple parka rippling in the Arctic wind.

"Steady," said Katsakos from the control console.

"Steady," echoed Neil.

As the blood spill splashed against the *Maracaibo*'s prow, her captain swerved the gun and aimed. A sudden puff of smoke appeared, haloing the muzzle. Fifty yards from the *Valparaíso*, a fountain of seawater shot into the air, dead center between the chains.

"Left ten," muttered Katsakos.

"Left ten."

Van Horne fired again. This time the shell hit home, turning the central link into a silvery flash of pulverized metal. As the chain flew apart, the segment nearer the cranium slithered into the ocean while its stubby counterpart swung toward the stern, clanging against the hull.

"Nice shooting, Captain!" cried the excited mate. "Steady!"

"Steady," said Neil.

"Dive bombers at twelve o'clock!" screamed Katsakos.

Another shell flew from the starboard Phalanx, disintegrating a link and neatly separating the *Val* from her cargo. Whether or not Christopher Van Horne saw the fruits of his marksmanship was unclear, for the instant the chain broke, a Dauntless dropped its payload barely fifty feet from the captain. The bomb detonated. Cannon, hatches, icicles, and chunks of bulwark sailed heavenward, borne on a pillar of fire. Within seconds the entire fo'c'sle was burning, gouts of black smoke swirling above the fractured deck like rain clouds poised to release India ink.

"No!" shrieked Katsakos.

"Holy shit!" groaned Neil.

"I *told* him to turn around!" sputtered Di Luca.

Flawlessly, the *Maracaibo*'s firefighting system sprang to life.

As the klaxon brayed across the Norwegian Sea, a dozen robot hoses appeared, rising from the bulwarks like moray eels slithering out of their lairs. Jets of frothy white foam shot from the nozzles.

"Oh, Christ!" screamed Katsakos as the flames gasped and died. "Oh, Lord!" he wailed. The foam subsided like an outgoing tide, leaving behind a mass of melted pipework and the fallen body of Christopher Van Horne. "Oh, God, they blew up the captain!"

When the *Maracaibo* went to war against Air Group Six, incinerating her torpedo planes and dive bombers with deadly guided missiles, the focus of Oliver's terror shifted from Cassie to himself. He was not embarrassed. It was Cassandra, in fact, who liked to dismiss so-called heroism as but one step removed from theistic self-delusion, and besides, at the moment his own peril clearly outclassed hers, the *Maracaibo* being likely to interpret Strawberry Eleven as yet another hostile plane and attack accordingly.

True, the Gulf tanker had just sustained a direct hit from a 500-pound demolition bomb. But instead of touching off either the tanker's cargo oil or her bunker fuel, the explosion had merely ignited her fo'c'sle deck—a localized conflagration soon brought under control by automated foam throwers—and before long she was enthusiastically targeting the two armed Devastators and three armed Dauntlesses remaining in the air.

"I can't stand this!" shouted Oliver.

"Scared, are you?" asked Flume, who did not himself seem particularly happy.

"You bet I'm scared!"

"Don't be ashamed if your bowels let go," said Pembroke,

likewise distraught. "During World War Two, almost a quarter of all infantrymen lost that kind of control in battle."

"At least, that's how many admitted to it," added Flume, nervously winding his headset cord around his wrist. "The actual percentage was probably higher."

Tow chains severed, the *Valparaíso* listed badly to starboard. Blood pooled along her hull. Even if she began to founder, Oliver reasoned, there'd be plenty of time for Cassie and her shipmates to get away in lifeboats—whereas if the *Maracaibo* opened fire on Strawberry Eleven, her crew and passengers would all, most probably, die.

"Van Horne must've been trimmin' her with blood," said Reid over the intercom. "Good way to lighten his load—right, Mr. Flume?"

Flume made no reply. His partner remained equally silent. As the *Maracaibo* took on the remnants of Air Group Six, the war reenactors sat rigidly in their machine-gun blisters and listened to the transceiver broadcasts, a radio horror show to put their beloved *Inner Sanctum* to shame.

"Missile at six o'clock!"

"Mayday! Mayday!"

"Bail out, everybody!"

"Help me!"

"Jump!"

"Shit!"

"Mommy! Mommy!"

"This isn't in my contract!"

Oliver felt like praying, but it was impossible to gather the requisite energy when the decayed, frozen, violated remains of the God he didn't believe in stretched so starkly before his eyes.

"Alby?"

"Yeah, Sid?"

"Alby, I'm not having any fun."

"I know what you mean."

"Alby, I want to go home."

"Ensign Reid," said Flume into his intercom mike, "kindly climb to nine thousand feet and set off for Point Luck."

"You mean—withdraw?"

"Withdraw."

"Ever walk out on one of your own shows before?" asked Reid.

"Just leave, Jack."

"Roger," said the pilot, pulling back on the control yoke.

"Alby?"

"Yeah, Sid?"

"Two of our actors are dead."

"Most of 'em bailed out."

"Two are dead."

"I know."

"Waldron's dead," said Pembroke. "His gunner too, Ensign Collins."

"Carny Otis, right?" said Flume. "I saw him at the Helen Hayes once. Iago."

"Alby, I think we done bad."

"Attention, Torpedo Six!" came Ray Spruance's portrayer's voice from the transceiver. "Attention, Scout Bombing Six! Listen, men, no matter how you slice it, we aren't being paid to mess with a Gulf tanker! Break off the attack and return to *Enterprise*! Repeat: break off attack and return! We weigh anchor at 1530 hours!"

From out of nowhere a crippled dive bomber arrived, sheets of flame flowing from her wings. The plane zoomed so close that Oliver could see the pilot's face—or, rather, he would have seen the pilot's face had it not been burned clear to the bone.

"It's Ensign Gay!" cried Pembroke. "They got Ensign Gay!"

"Please, God, no!" shouted Flume.

The runaway Dauntless headed straight for the flying boat's tail, shedding sparks and firebrands. Pembroke shrieked madly, moving his hands back and forth as if pantomiming a frenetic game of cat's cradle. Then, as Strawberry Eleven reached nine thousand feet, the bomber collided with her, snapping off the PBY's rudder, severing her starboard stabilizer, puncturing her fuselage, and pouring burning gasoline into the tunnel gunner's compartment, each individual disaster unfolding so rapidly that Oliver's single scream sufficed to cover them all. A mass of flames swept along the aft flooring and into the portside blister. Searing heat filled the cabin. Within seconds, Albert Flume's cotton trousers, aviator's scarf, and flak jacket were ablaze.

"Aaaiiii!"

"Alby!"

"Put me out!"

"Put him out!"

"God, put me out!"

"Here!" Charles Eaton's portrayer shoved a glossy red cylinder into Oliver's lap.

"What's this?" Oliver couldn't tell whether the tears flooding his eyes sprang from terror, pity, or the black smoke wafting through the mechanic's station. "What? What?"

"Read the directions!"

"Oh, Jesus!" screamed Flume. "Oh, sweet Jesus!"

"I think we lost our tail!" cried Reid over the intercom.

Oliver wiped his eyes. HOLD UPRIGHT. He did. PULL PIN. Pin? What pin? He made a series of desperate grabs—please, God, please, the *pin*—and suddenly he was indeed gripping something that looked like a pin.

"Put me out!"

"Put him out! Oh, Alby, buddy!"

STAND BACK 10 FEET AND AIM AT BASE OF FIRE. Oliver seized the discharge hose and pointed it toward Flume.

"We lost our tail!"

"Put me out!"

SQUEEZE LEVER AND SWEEP SIDE TO SIDE. A thick gray mist

gushed from the horn, coating the war reenactor in foul-smelling chemicals and instantly smothering the flames.

"It's gonna hurt!" groaned Flume as the PBY careened crazily, dropping toward the ocean. "It's really gonna hurt!"

"No tail!"

"Give me pants that en-*trance*! It's starting to hurt!"

Tearing off his headset, Oliver crawled past Flume's smoking, writhing form, lurched into the tunnel gunner's compartment, and began attacking the flames.

"Why does God permit this?" asked Pembroke of no one in particular.

"Shoulders Gibraltar, shiny as a halter!" screamed Flume, writhing in agony. "Oh, Jesus, it hurts! It hurts so much!"

Everyone tried to be polite.

Everyone struggled to avoid the subject.

But in the end Albert Flume's situation could not be denied, and right before Strawberry Eleven belly flopped into the Norwegian Sea, splitting into a dozen pieces, Pembroke turned to his best friend and said, in a soft, sad voice, "Alby, buddy, you don't have any arms."

Father

BY A MIRACLE OF the sort that in an earlier age Jehovah Himself might have wrought, the *Valparaíso* stayed afloat that afternoon, allowing the officers, crew, and rescued war reenactors to abandon her in an orderly fashion. There was even time to salvage certain crucial items: footlockers, musical instruments, fillets of Corpus Dei, a few jars of glory grease, some supervegetables from Follingsbee's garden, the *Ten Commandments* print. The *Valparaíso* was terminal, of course. Anthony knew it. A captain could always tell. No ingenious patching job or heroic pumping effort could save her. But what a fighter, he thought, what a tough old lady, ceding fewer than ten feet per hour to the bloodstained Norwegian Sea. By noon her weather deck lay completely buried, but her superstructure was still visible, rising out of the waves like a hotel perched on pylons.

At 1420, Anthony began ferrying the final group over the red ocean to the *Carpco Maracaibo*—a grim little party consisting of Cassie, Rafferty, O'Connor, Father Ockham, and Sister Miriam, each evacuee clutching a seabag. No one said a word. Cassie refused to look him in the eye. She had much to brood about, he knew, several reasons to be sad: the failure of her plot, the crash landing of her boyfriend's plane, the deaths of John Waldron and two other mercenaries. Were Anthony not himself benumbed and despondent, he might have actually felt sorry for her.

He parked the *Juan Fernández* beside a vulcanized rubber dock tied to the *Maracaibo*'s hull, waited until everyone had disembarked, then cast off.

"Where're you going?" Rafferty called after him.

"I forgot my sextant."

"Christ, Anthony—I'll buy you a sextant in New York!"

"My sister gave it to me!" he shouted toward the fading figures on the dock.

By 1445 Anthony was back at the wreck site, maneuvering the *Juan Fernández* alongside a first-floor window. He smashed the glass with the launch's stockless anchor and climbed over the sill. The elevator had shorted out, so he used the companionways instead. Reaching level seven, he entered the chart room, locked the door, and waited.

Brain lost.

Body lost.

Val lost.

There was no choice, really. He'd blown the mission. His second chance was gone.

He stared at the Formica table. The jumbled maps tormented him. Sulawesi, redolent of Cassie's midriff. Pago Pago, so evocative of her breasts. He lifted his gaze. Forward wall, the Mediterranean; aft wall, the Indian Ocean; port wall, the South Pacific; starboard wall, the North Atlantic. He was giving up so much, all these glorious tracts of sea and patches of shore, most of them despoiled and ravaged by the reigning species, yet all still painfully beautiful at the core. Let no man say Anthony Van Horne did not know what he was losing.

His migraine awoke. In a corner of the aura, an oiled egret rose from the chart of Matagorda Bay and flapped its matted wings. Seconds later, a pilot whale, glossy with Texas crude, wriggled out of the same poisoned sea, flopped onto the floor, and died. How would the end come? Would the ocean pour into the chart room and drown him? Or was the door sufficiently watertight that he would survive the descent into the Mohns Trench, only to perish when the impossible pressures hit the superstructure, crushing it like an egg under a jackboot?

A loud knock. Then four, rat-a-tat-tat. Anthony ignored them. His visitor persisted.

"Yeah?"

"It's Thomas. Open up."

"Get away!"

"Suicide's a sin, Anthony."

"In whose eyes? His? They went to jelly two weeks ago."

At least one of the losing admirals at Midway, he recalled, had done the honorable thing. Anthony hungered for the details. Had the poor defeated Jap chained himself to the helm? Had he changed his mind at the last minute but died anyway because nobody was around to unlock the manacle?

A new voice now. "Anthony, open the door. Something unbelievable has happened."

"Cassie, get out! You're on a sinking ship!"

"I just talked to the *Maracaibo*'s second mate, and he says her skipper is named Christopher Van Horne."

Anthony's migraine flared hotter than ever. "Get out!"

"Christopher Van Horne," she said again. "Your father!"

"My father's in Spain."

"Your father's a thousand yards to port. Open the door."

A dark laugh rose from the depths of Anthony's chest. Him? Dear old Dad? But of course, naturally, who *else* would the

Vatican have picked to hunt down the *Val* and steal her cargo? He wondered how they'd lured him out of retirement. Money, most likely. (Columbus had been greedy too.) Or had the old man been seduced by the opportunity to humiliate his son once again?

"He wants to see you, Katsakos says." Cassie sounded on the verge of tears.

"He wants to steal my cargo."

"He's in no shape to *steal* anything," Ockham insisted. "He was out in the open when that bomb hit the *Maracaibo*."

"He's hurt?"

"Sounds pretty bad."

"Is he *assuming* I'll come?"

"He's assuming you'll go down with your ship," said the priest. " 'The Van Hornes go down with their ships,' he told Katsakos."

"Then I mustn't disappoint him."

"Guess he knows you pretty well."

"He doesn't know me at all. Get back to the *Maracaibo*, both of you."

"He tried to save the *Val*," Cassie protested.

"I doubt that," said Anthony.

"Open the door. Why do you think he cut your chains?"

"To take my cargo away."

"To stop the torpedo strike. Why do you think he fired on the planes?"

"So they wouldn't sink our cargo."

"So they wouldn't sink *you*. Ask Katsakos. Open the door."

Anthony fixed on the starboard wall. He imagined God massaging the primordial continent, cleaving South America from Africa; he saw the new ocean, the Atlantic, pouring into the breach like amniotic fluid spilling from a ruptured birth sac. Was Cassie telling the truth? Had the old man's Midway tactics really been intended to save the *Val*?

"I lost God."

"Merely for the moment," said Ockham. "You'll finish this job yet."

"Your father loves you," said Cassie. "So do I, for that matter. Open the door."

"The *Val*'s doomed," said Anthony.

"Then you'll have to hitch Him to the *Maracaibo*, won't you?" said Ockham.

"The *Maracaibo*'s not mine."

"That needn't stop you."

Anthony opened the door.

And there she stood, eyes moist and sunken, lips chapped, a band of frost spread across her brow like a diamond tiara. Lord, what a perfect match they were: two strong-willed people preoccupied with seven million tons of carrion, though for very different reasons.

"You love me, Cassie?"

"Against my better judgment."

Taking his mirrorshades from the pocket of his parka, Anthony slipped them on and, turning, confronted Ockham with a dual reflection of his captain. "You really think we can resume the tow?"

"I've seen you pull bigger rabbits out of smaller hats," said the priest.

"Okay, but first I'm goin' to my cabin. I need some things. A Popeye the Sailor notebook . . ."

Ockham cringed. "Captain, the *Val*'s about to break apart."

"A brass sextant," said Anthony. "A bottle of burgundy."

"Be quick about it."

"The feather of an angel."

"I can certainly see the resemblance," said the agitated young man with the frozen stethoscope slung around his neck and the aluminum clipboard snugged against his chest. "The high fore-head, the heavy jaw—you're definitely your father's son."

"And my mother's . . ." Anthony climbed past a rack of empty Crotale missile launchers and stepped onto the *Maracaibo's* athwartships catwalk.

"Giuseppe Carminati," said the physician. His ensemble included an officer's cap with a red cross stitched above the brim and a ceremonial overcoat sporting gold buttons and epaulets, as if he'd just come from appearing in a Gilbert and Sullivan operetta about shipboard surgeons. "Your father's alive, but he can't be moved. Our quartermaster's attending him over by number three ballast tank. I believe you know the man. We picked him up in the Gibraltar Sea."

"Neil Weisinger?" asked Ockham eagerly.

Wrapping his glove around the frosty bulb of his stethoscope, Carminati turned toward the priest. "Correct. Weisinger." The physician smiled with the left side of his mouth. "Perhaps you remember me?"

"We've met?"

"Three months ago, in the Vatican screening room—I was Gabriel's attending physician." Carminati hugged himself. "I should be in Rome right now, listening to the Holy Father's heart. I don't function well in the cold."

"You got many casualties?" asked Anthony.

"Compared with the original Midway, no. Twenty-one cases of acute hypothermia, most of them complicated by lacerations and broken bones, plus a noncombatant observer who got badly burned when his PBY caught fire."

"Oliver Shostak?" asked Cassie in a fearful, repentant voice.

"Albert Flume," said Carminati, consulting his clipboard. "Shostak, it seems, has a dislocated shoulder. You know him?"

"An old boyfriend. Dislocated shoulder, that's all?"

"Superficial cuts, minor burns, treatable hypothermia."

"And some people say there's no God," muttered Anthony.

"Expect to lose anyone?" asked Ockham.

"No, though the actor portraying Lieutenant Commander John Waldron, a man named"—Carminati glanced at the list—"Brad Keating, was vaporized when a missile hit his torpedo plane. Ditto his gunner, Carny Otis in the role of Ensign Collins. Forty minutes ago we pulled a corpse from the sea: David Pasquali as Ensign George Gay. But for the fact that he'll be dead soon, Captain, your father would probably be facing a manslaughter indictment."

"Dead?" Anthony steadied himself on the Crotale rack. No, God, please, the bastard *couldn't* be checking out yet, not before shriving his son.

"Forgive my bluntness," said Carminati. "It's been a bad morning. I can promise you he's in no pain. The *Maracaibo* carries more morphine than bunker fuel."

"Anthony . . . I'm so sorry," said Cassie. "These people Oliver hired, they're obviously deranged. I never imagined . . ." The words froze in her throat.

The captain faced the bow, shouldered his knapsack, and marched down the *Maracaibo*'s central catwalk, passing over a vast tangle of valves and pipework spreading in all directions like exposed entrails. Reaching the fo'c'sle, he picked his way through the aftermath of the demolition bomb—buckled hatches, smashed bulwarks, melted Phalanx cannon—and, descending the ladder, started toward number three ballast tank.

Ever since the butane had gone into the gravy, Anthony had wondered exactly how he would behave when his father finally left the world. Would he snicker through the viewing? Pass out balloons at the funeral? Leave a lunger on the grave? He needn't have worried. The instant he beheld Christopher Van Horne's trapped and broken form, a flood of spontaneous pity poured through him.

Evidently the shock wave had lifted the old man from behind the Phalanx, flung him off the fo'c'sle, and dropped him beside the tank. There he lay, parka shredded, eyes closed, body imprisoned by an errant Hoffritz valve assembly, its ten-foot-long stem driven clear through the Butterworth plate, its huge circular handle—larger than a covered-wagon wheel—pressed tightly against his chest, pinning him to the starboard samson post in a dreadful parody of sitting. Fire had ravaged the sides of his face, exposing his beautiful cheekbones. His left leg, grotesquely bent, might have belonged to a castoff marionette, a puppet whose master had died for reasons not even the angels knew.

Neil Weisinger stood atop the plate, teeth chattering as he transferred fresh water from an insulated gallon jug to a cylindrical white Thermos bottle advertising *Indiana Jones and the Last Crusade*. "Good afternoon, sir," said the AB, saluting. "We got a team of licensed welders under the deck right now, cutting the stem loose."

"You're a two-time deserter, Weisinger." Anthony shed his knapsack.

"Not exactly, sir," said the AB, capping the bottle. A corrugated straw elbowed out of the lid. "I didn't break out of the brig—Joe Spicer kidnapped me."

"If somebody's a deserter," mumbled Christopher Van Horne, "he should be hauled off . . ."

Unzipping the knapsack, Anthony removed a liter of burgundy and gestured for the *Last Crusade* bottle.

". . . hauled off and shot."

Anthony dumped out the water and, in a small-scale recapitulation of the pump-room boys ballasting the *Val* with blood, filled the bottle to the brim. Kneeling, he placed one glove on the valve, the other on his father's shoulder. "Hello, Dad," he whispered.

"Son?" The old man's eyes flickered open. "That you? You came?"

"It's me. Hope you're not in pain."

"Wish I was."

"Oh?"

"I knew this guy once, a demac on the *Amoco Cádiz*, dying of bone cancer. You know what he said? 'When they give you morphine like there's no tomorrow, there isn't.'" An oddly seraphic grin spread across Christopher Van Horne's ashen face. "Tell Tiffany I love her. Got that? Old Froggy loves her."

"I'll tell her."

"You think she's a bimbo, don't you?"

"No, no." Like a firing-squad captain providing his prisoner with a last cigarette, Anthony pushed the corrugated straw between his father's lips. "Have some wine."

The old man sipped. "Good stuff."

"The best."

"No more beard, huh?"

"No more beard."

"You didn't go down with your ship." His tone was more curious than accusing.

"I've found the woman I want to marry. You'd like her."

"I really stuck it to those squadrons, didn't I?"

"She's got Mom's energy, Susan's spunk."

"Smeared 'em all over the sky."

Anthony withdrew the straw. "Something else you should know. That uncharted island in the Gibraltar Sea—I named it after you. Van Horne Island."

"Gave every damn Dauntless hell. More wine, okay?"

"Van Horne Island," said Anthony again, reinserting the straw. "You've finally got your own private paradise. Understand?"

"It's really shitty, dying. There's nothing good about it. Sure wish Tiff were here."

Sliding Raphael's feather from his knapsack, Anthony held it before the old man, its vane quivering in the wind. "Listen, Dad. Do you know what kind of feather this is?"

"It's a feather."

"What kind?"

"I don't give a fuck. Albatross."

"Angel, Dad."

"Looks like albatross."

"An *angel* hired me. Wings, halo, everything. This cargo I've been hauling, it's not a movie prop, it's God's dead body."

"No, *I'm* the one with the body, *I'm* the one, and now it's all wrecked. You left the bridge. Tiff's a real knockout, isn't she? Wonder what she sees in me. Half the time my dick doesn't even work."

"I'm going to get the job done. I'm going to haul our Creator to His tomb."

"You're not making a whole lot of sense, son. It's so weird, being crushed like this and not feeling anything. Angel? Creator? What?"

"All the bad things you ever did to me—Thanksgiving, locking up the *Constitution*—I'm ready to let them go." Anthony pulled off his gloves, holding his naked hands before his father. "Just tell me you're proud I drew this mission. Tell me you're proud, and you know I can finish it, and I should put the spill out of my mind."

"*Constitution?*"

As ice formed beneath his fingernails, Anthony slipped his gloves back on. "Look at me. Say, 'Put the spill out of your mind.' "

"What kind of stupid death is this?" Like crude oil seeping from a subterranean reservoir, blood rose to fill the old man's mouth, mingling with the wine; his words bubbled up through the pool. "Isn't it enough I shot your tow chains apart? Isn't that enough?" Tears came, rolling over his naked white cheekbones. "I don't know what you want, son. *Constitution?* Angel? Aren't broken chains enough?" The tears reached his jaw and froze. He shook violently, spasm after spasm of unfelt pain. "Take 'er over, Anthony." He grabbed the rim of the valve handle and tried to turn it, as if he were living back in 1954, a pumpman again, working the weather deck of the *Texaco Star*. "Take over the ship."

The pure hopelessness of the situation, the morbid comedy of it all, brought a sardonic smile to Anthony's lips, a grin to match his Creator's. For the first time ever, his father was offering him something that he wouldn't—couldn't—take back . . . only there was one small catch.

"She's not yours to give," said Anthony.

"Red sky at night—sailor's delight." The old man closed his eyes. "Red sky in the morning—sailors take warning . . ."

"Tell me Matagorda Bay doesn't matter anymore. The egrets forgive me. Say it."

"Mare's tails and mackerel scales . . . make tall ships carry low sails . . . red sky at night . . . sailor's delight . . . delight . . . delight . . ."

And then, with a feeling of profound and unutterable dissatisfaction, Anthony watched his father inhale, smile, spit blood, and die.

"May he rest in peace," said Weisinger.

Feather in hand, Anthony stood up.

"I didn't know him well," the AB continued, "but I could tell he was a great man. You should've seen him when those planes went after the *Val*. 'They're trying to kill my son!' he kept screaming."

"No, he wasn't a great man." Anthony slipped Raphael's feather into the topmost pocket of his parka, enjoying the feel of its gentle heat against his chest. "He was a great sailor, but he wasn't a great man."

"The world needs both, I suppose."

"The world needs both."

As Oliver Shostak eased himself over the side of the stainless steel rewarming tub and settled into the 110-degree water, he inevitably thought of an earlier avatar of secular enlightenment, Jean-Paul Marat, sitting in his bath day after day, enduring his diseased skin and dreaming the death of aristocracy. Oliver's shoulder throbbed, his ribs ached, but the sharpest pain was in his soul. Like Marat's revolution, Oliver's crusade had come to a wretched and humiliating end. At that moment, he harbored but one major ambition, a wish eclipsing both his desire to stop shivering and his urge to see Cassie, and that ambition was to be dead.

"Your prognosis is excellent," said Dr. Carminati, crouching beside Oliver. "But stay put, okay? If you move too much, the blood will flow to your extremities, cool off, and lower your temperature, and *that* could trigger lethal cardiac arrhythmia."

"Lethal cardiac arrhythmia," Oliver echoed dully, his teeth chattering like castanets. A most appealing idea.

"Your kilocalorie deficit is probably near a thousand right now, but I predict we'll normalize your core temperature in under an hour. After that, an Iceland Air-Sea Rescue helicopter will take you to Reykjavik General for observation."

"Was that really *God's* body the *Valparaíso* was towing?"

"I believe it was."

"*God's?*"

"Yes."

"It's hard to accept."

"Three months ago, the angel Gabriel died in my arms," said the young physician, starting away. "Since that moment, I've been open to all sorts of possibilities."

Steam rose on every side of the tub, obscuring the hypothermia victims lined up to Oliver's left and right. So efficient was health-care delivery aboard the *Maracaibo* that, once borne to the sick bay, they'd all been treated without delay: shoulders relocated, ribs taped, bones set, burns greased, gashes disinfected, lungs filled with warm, moist air from a heated Dragen tank. No amount of efficiency, however, could revive the faceless body that had passed through on a gurney shortly after their arrival. Oliver knew that he and the dead man had spoken several times in the Midnight Sun Canteen, but he could recall nothing specific from any of their exchanges. To Oliver he was merely another overpaid and anonymous war reenactor, currently engaged in his final performance, playing the corpse of Ensign George Gay.

Within twenty minutes, he felt warmer, but his mood remained bleak as ever. A woman's form appeared, swathed in steam. Charlotte Corday, he mused, come to stab Marat—he'd always adored Jacques-Louis David's painting—but instead of a dagger she wielded only a digital thermometer.

"Hello, Oliver. Good to see you."

"Cassandra?"

"They want me to take your temperature," she said, piercing the veil of mist.

"Listen, honey, I tried my darnedest. I really, really *tried*."

Bending beside the tub, she placed a quick, noncommittal kiss on his cheek. "I know you did," she said in a gratuitously condescending tone. Her face was gaunt, her demeanor cowed and diffident, and no doubt he appeared equally defeated to her. And yet, as she stood over him, pressing the tiny green button on the thermometer, he thought she'd never looked more beautiful.

"I tried my darnedest," he said again. "You gotta understand—I had no idea Spruance was planning to torpedo your tanker."

"I'll be blunt," said Cassie, easing the device between his lips. "I never really believed you'd hired the right people." The remark wounded Oliver—so severely that he almost bit off the thermometer bulb. (Jesus Christ, what did she expect on such short notice, the U.S. Seventh Fleet?) A faint ringing reached his ears, like the sound of a mouse's alarm clock. Cassie removed the thermometer and squinted at the little numerals. "Ninety-eight point two. Close enough. We'll let you walk around now."

"I tried my darnedest. Really."

"You don't need to keep saying that."

"Where's God?"

"Adrift," she replied, handing Oliver a white terry-cloth bath-robe and a beach towel imprinted with the Carpco stegosaurus. "He went east, I think. Quite possibly He's unsinkable. Oliver, we have to talk. Meet me in the snack bar."

"I love you, Cassandra."

"I know," she said evenly—ominously—and, whirling around, vanished into the mist.

As Oliver climbed out of the rewarming tub, a dizzying depression overcame him. He felt landlocked, marooned in the Age of Reason, and, meanwhile, way out to sea, nudging the horizon, there was his Cassandra, sailing into the post-Enlightenment, post-Christian, post-theistic future, moving farther and farther from him with each passing minute.

He dried off and, throwing on the bathrobe, limped through the ranks of dazed war reenactors, half of them sitting in re-warming tubs, the rest lying in bed. A ragged row of stitches ran down McClusky's left cheek. A turban of bandages sat atop Lieutenant Beeson's head. Burns dotted Lance Sharp's chest like abstract-expressionist tattoos. He pitied these eighteen men their snapped bones, their torn flesh, but he also felt betrayed by them. They should have made much bigger holes in God. They simply should have.

When Oliver first encountered the sorry spectacle of Albert Flume, he understood as never before what it meant for a man to lose his arms. Leg loss was a different matter. Leg loss was Captain Ahab, Long John Silver—a whole gallery of romantic heroes. But a man without arms simply looked like a mistake.

Pembroke stood by the bed, his forehead a mass of bruises, a gauze patch over his right eye. "This is all *your* fault," he told Oliver, gesturing toward his mutilated partner.

The impresario's arrogance stunned Oliver. "*My* fault?"

Flume stared at the ceiling and winced. Spirals of linen covered his stumps, giving the starkly truncated limbs the appearance of baseball bats whose handgrips had been wrapped in adhesive tape.

"You said there wouldn't be any screening vessels," whined Pembroke.

"You want a villain, Sidney?" asked Oliver, beating back his impulse to scream. "Try your buddy Spruance. Spruance and his Op Plan 29-67. Try that fool McClusky over there—he should've blown retreat the instant the *Maracaibo* showed up. Try *yourself*."

"*Maracaibo*, not 'the' *Maracaibo*."

"People around here are mumbling about lawsuits, extradition, manslaughter indictments," said Oliver. "I think we're in a lot of trouble, *all* of us."

"Don't be ridiculous. There weren't any *lawsuits* after Midway." Drawing a plastic comb from his bathrobe, Pembroke tidied up his friend's thick blond hair. "Jeez, I wish I could help you, Alby. I wish I could make Frances Langford appear right now and cheer you up."

"What'll *happen* to me?" moaned Flume.

"Nothing but the best therapy for you, buddy. You'll get wonderful mechanical arms—you know, like Harold Russell had."

"Harold Russell?" said Oliver.

"That double amputee who went into the movies," said Pembroke. "Ever see *The Best Years of Our Lives*?"

"No."

"Swell picture. Russell got an Oscar."

"I'll pay the bills," said Oliver, lightly brushing Flume's left stump. "No matter what those wonderful mechanical arms cost, I'll pay."

"I don't want wonderful mechanical arms," mumbled Flume. "Russell had to sell his Oscar."

"True," sighed Pembroke.

"Real arms."

"Hey, buddy, we're gonna stage one *hell* of a Guadalcanal, aren't we?"

"I don't want a Guadalcanal."

"No?" said Pembroke.

"I don't want a Guadalcanal, or an Ardennes, or a D-Day even."

"I understand."

"Arms."

"Sure."

"I keep trying to move my hands."

"Naturally."

"I can't move 'em."

"I know, Alby."

"I wanna play the piano."

"Right."

"Pitch pennies."

"Of course."

Time to leave, the Enlightenment League's president thought as Albert Flume voiced his wish to snap his fingers and twiddle his thumbs. Time to find Cassandra, Oliver decided as the armless impresario articulated his desire to wear a wristwatch, knit samplers, play with a yo-yo, raise the flag for Hudson High, and masturbate. Time to get on with the rest of what Oliver suspected was going to be a crushingly dull and utterly meaningless life.

A loaded bedpan, Thomas Ockham concluded, was a hopeless commodity. No fantasy could redeem it. Every time he bore one across the *Maracaibo*'s sick bay, he started out pretending it was a chalice, a ciborium, or the Holy Grail itself, but by the time he reached the bathroom he was carrying a bowl of turds. And so it happened that, when Tullio Di Luca demanded an emergency meeting to discuss the fate of the Corpus Dei, the priest was more than happy to forsake his duties and head for the elevator.

The *Valparaíso* group—Van Horne, Rafferty, Haycox, O'Connor, Bliss—was already in the wardroom when Thomas arrived, lined up along the far side of the table. Rafferty lit a Marlboro. O'Connor popped a cough drop. Dark concentric circles scored the captain's cheeks, as if his eyes were pebbles tossed into water. Gradually the *Maracaibo*'s staff filed in—Di Luca leading, then First Mate Orso Peche, Chief Engineer Vince Mangione, Communications Officer Gonzalo Cornejo, and Vatican Physician Giuseppe Carminati—each man looking more miserable and homesick than the one before him. Mick Katsakos, Thomas surmised, was up on the bridge, keeping the Gulf tanker a safe distance from the foundering *Valparaíso*.

"In my brief association with your father, I came to admire his seamanship and courage," said Di Luca, assuming the head of the table. "Your grief must be overwhelming."

"Not yet," grunted Van Horne. "I'll keep you posted."

Wincing at the captain's candor, Thomas seated himself beside Lianne Bliss and glanced through the nearest porthole. The *Val*'s deck island still towered above the choppy Norwegian Sea: the Rasputin of supertankers, he decided. Shoot her, poison her, bludgeon her, and still she clung to life.

Why had God died?

Why?

"The Vatican has a proposition for you," said Di Luca to Van Horne. "We are not certain why you absconded last week, but the Holy Father, a most generous man, is prepared to ignore your insubordination if you will take over the *Maracaibo*, subsequently doing as Rome wishes."

"History's ahead of you, Eminence," the captain replied. "Before he passed away, Dad bequeathed me this ship."

"He didn't have that right."

"I can't agree to follow Rome's orders till I know what they are."

"Step one: assume command. In the interests of efficiency"—
Di Luca swept his arm along the line of *Maracaibo* personnel—
"these men have all agreed to defer to your own officers. Step
two: pilot us to the motion-picture prop. Mr. Peche, do you still
have it on your radar screen?"

"Aye."

"Step three: anoint the prop fore to aft."

"Anoint it?" said Van Horne.

"With Arabian crude oil," Di Luca explained. "Step four: set
the prop on fire. Step five: transport us back to Palermo."

"On fire?" wailed Rafferty.

"What the fuck?" moaned O'Connor.

"No way," hissed Haycox.

"Ah, *now* we're talking!" cried Bliss, pointing her crystal
pendant toward Van Horne. "Hear that, sir? You're supposed to
burn the thing!"

"You said you were hauling formaldehyde, not Arabian
crude," Thomas protested.

Di Luca grinned feebly. "We're hauling oil," he admitted.

"You have your orders, Captain," said Bliss. "Now follow
them."

"You know perfectly well the body's meant to be entombed
at Kvitoya," Thomas reminded the cardinal. "You heard Gabriel's
wishes in person."

Di Luca pressed his palms to his bosom and smoothed his
waterproof cassock. "Professor Ockham, need I make the em-
barrassingly obvious point that Rome's liaison on this mission is
no longer you but myself?"

Thomas grew suddenly aware of his own blood. He felt his
plasma heating up. "Don't underestimate your man, Eminence.
Don't expect this Jesuit to lie down and die."

Leaning toward Van Horne, Di Luca picked up a glass ashtray, holding it out like Christ offering the first stone to the mob.
"The problem, Captain, is that Kvitoya provides no deterrents

to intrusion. Only a cremation can guarantee that, in the years to come, the corpse won't be exhumed and defiled."

"What does it matter if a movie prop gets defiled?" asked Peche.

"The angels seemed to think Kvitoya would be just fine," said Thomas. "So do I."

"Please be quiet," said Di Luca.

"Angels?" said Mangione.

"I *won't* be quiet," said Thomas.

Di Luca gave the ashtray a sudden twist, making it spin like a compass needle gone berserk. "Sir, is it not true that, once our Creator's death became common knowledge aboard the *Valparaíso*, a severe ethical breakdown occurred?"

"*Whose* death?" said Peche.

"Yes, but thanks to the meat, we're past that now," said Van Horne.

"Meat?" said Di Luca.

"When we fed the crew Quarter Pounders with Cheese, they regained their moral bearings."

"Quarter Pounders?"

"You don't want to know," said Rafferty.

"According to Father Ockham's fax of July twenty-eighth, there were thefts, attempted rapes, vandalism, quite possibly a murder." The cardinal arrested the whirling ashtray. "Now, sir, project such anarchy onto the planet at large, and you have chaos beyond comprehension."

"There's another way to look at it," said Van Horne. "Consider: our trip to the Gibraltar Sea was amazingly intense. We saw the corpse all the time, smelled it around the clock, killed its predators on every watch. Naturally the thing took hold of us. The whole world's never going to enter into such a close relationship with God."

"God?" said Mangione.

"The body must be obliterated," said Di Luca.

Thomas slammed his palm against the table. "Oh, come on, Tullio. Let's be honest, okay? Your heart was never in this project. If your OMNIVAC hadn't predicted a few surviving neurons, you'd have wanted a cremation straight away. But now the brain's beyond salvation, which means all your careers might be beyond salvation too, should the news ever get out. To which I say, 'Too bad, gentlemen. Swallow your pill. The Chair of Peter was never a tenure-track position.'"

"Father Thomas, I want you to leave this meeting," growled Di Luca. "Right now."

"Go fry an egg," said the priest. "From the Church's perspective this corpse might be a white elephant, but for Captain Van Horne and myself it's a sacred trust!"

"Get out!"

"No!"

The cardinal grew suddenly mute, absorbed in rapping the ashtray against the table, a steady, frustrated *thonk-thonk-thonk*.

"It's not a movie prop, is it?" said Peche.

"Not remotely," said O'Connor.

"Good God."

"Exactly," said Haycox.

Van Horne directed a wide, hostile smile toward Di Luca. "Step one: we steam over to our cargo. Step two: we lash Him to our stern. Step three: we restart the tow." He shifted his stare to Peche. "Assuming there are no objections . . ."

A sudden joy took hold of Thomas. How wonderful to be fighting, for once, on the same side as Van Horne.

"My mind's confused," asserted Peche, "but my heart, it knows how unforgivable it would be to burn this body."

Cornejo muttered, "If it's really what you say it is . . . if it's really, really *that* . . ."

"Who are we to go against angels?" said Mangione.

The captain reached into the pocket of his shirt, drawing out Raphael's angel feather and pointing it toward the first mate.

"Marbles, I want you to place our radio shack under armed guard. Any attempt by Monsignor Di Luca to enter should be resisted. While we're at it, let's be sure to blackball Sparks here and her buddy Dr. Fowler."

"Aye," said Rafferty.

Bliss clutched her crystal pendant and sneered.

"I assume you realize that, as of this moment, you're all in a lot of trouble with the Vatican," said Di Luca. "Rome receives regular dispatches from me. When I fail to report, they'll send another Gulf tanker after you. They'll send two—three—a whole armada."

"Never a dull moment," said Van Horne.

"You're making a tragic mistake, Captain. Worse than Matagorda Bay."

"I survived that. I'll survive this too." Van Horne aimed the feather directly at Dr. Carminati. "How soon before you lift the survivors out of here?"

"We expect the choppers in about twenty minutes. Give us an hour after that. I hope you realize I'm not about to join this outrageous mutiny of yours."

"*Mutiny*'s the word," said Di Luca.

Van Horne shifted the feather from the physician to the cardinal. "If I'm in rebellion against the Vatican, Eminence, then the Vatican's in rebellion against heaven." The captain closed his eyes. "I shall leave it for you to decide which is the more serious sin."

The half-dozen vending machines in the *Maracaibo*'s snack bar dispensed a wide variety of grotesqueries: Hostess Twinkies, Li'l Debbie Snack Cakes, Ring Dings—each item underscoring Oliver's creeping conviction that, with or without a Corpus Dei, Western civilization stood on the brink of collapse. Cassie occupied a contoured plastic chair adjacent to a small Formica table, nursing a Mountain Dew beneath the Lucite glow of the COLD DRINKS machine, an image that for Oliver recalled Degas's masterful *Glass of Absinthe.* To her right, PASTRY 'N SNACKS. To her left, CANDY 'N SWEETS. He approached HOT DRINKS, secured black coffee in a paper cup unaccountably decorated with playing cards, and joined her.

"I believe the Reenactment Society is going out of business," he said. "Midway finished it off."

"The past dies hard."

"I guess. Sure. You've always been a deeper thinker than me."

"It kicks and screams, but eventually it dies."

Oliver jammed his thumb into the scalding coffee, savoring the penitential pain. "Hey, Cassandra, we've had some terrific times together, haven't we? Remember Denver?" In some ways that particular Enlightenment League escapade—a colorful protest against the gigantic plywood Ten Commandments that the Fraternal Order of Eagles had erected on the capitol lawn—had been the high point of their relationship. In the park across the street he and Cassie had raised an equally formidable sign labeled WHAT GOD REALLY SAID and featuring a *nouvelle* decalogue they'd coauthored two days earlier between episodes of rapturous sex (they were field-testing the Shostak Supreme) in her apartment. "I'll bet if we work at it, we can remember them all. 'Thou shalt not make unto thee a graven image, except for Roman Catholics if they don't get tacky about it.' "

"I don't want to talk about Denver," said Cassie.

" 'Thou shalt not covet thy neighbor's manservant, nor his maidservant, nor question why thy neighbor has servants in the first place.' "

"Oliver, I'm in love with Anthony Van Horne."

And suddenly his hypothermia was back, stealing through his body organ by organ, turning them into frozen cuts of meat. "Shit." Charlotte Corday after all, stabbing him, murdering him. "Van Horne? Van Horne's the *enemy,* for Christ's sake." He closed his eyes and swallowed hard. "Have you . . . slept with him?"

"Yes."

"More than once?"

"Yes."

"What brand of condom?"

"Any answer to that question would be the wrong one."

Oliver licked his smarting thumb. "Has he asked you to marry him?"

"No."

"Good."

"I'm planning to ask *him*," she said.

"What do you see in a man like that? He's no rationalist, he's not one of us!"

In a move Oliver found at once intensely pleasurable and cruelly patronizing, Cassie stroked his forearm. "I'm sorry. I'm truly, truly sorry . . ."

"Know what I think? I think you've been seduced by the mystique of the sea. Hey, look, if this is the life you crave, fine, I'll buy you a boat. You want a sloop, Cassandra? A cabin cruiser? We'll sail to Tahiti, lie on the beach, paint pictures of the natives, the whole Gauguin bit."

"Oliver, it's over."

"It isn't."

"It is."

For the next minute neither of them spoke, their silence broken only by an occasional mechanical grunt from a vending machine. Oliver fixed on PERSONAL CARE, desirous of its wares, the Tylenol to assuage his headache, the Alka-Seltzer to settle his stomach, the Wilcox nail file to slit his wrists, the Shostak Supersensitives to facilitate his raging wish to have sex with Cassie one last time.

" 'Thou shalt not kill,' " he said. "Remember what we did with 'Thou shalt not kill'?"

"No."

"Me neither."

"Oliver . . ."

"My mind's a blank." A dull, metallic thumping filled the air. The Iceland choppers, Oliver realized, landing on the *Maracaibo*'s helipads. "Are you *certain* you can't remember?"

"I guess I've—I've . . . I'm not exactly sure what I mean. Blasphemy doesn't move me the way it used to."

"Come with me to Reykjavik, okay? You can catch a plane to Halifax tonight, a connecting flight to New York in the morning. With luck you'll be back teaching by Wednesday."

"Oliver, you're grasping at straws."

"Come with me."

"I can't."

"You can."

"No."

Oliver snapped his fingers. " 'Thou shalt not kill,' " he said, fighting tears, " 'except for communists, whom thou shalt kill with impunity.' "

September 16.

I assume you're grateful I rescued you, Popeye. Truth to tell, I'm glad to be here too. A lot of captains have gone down with their ships over the years, and I don't envy a single one of them.

Rafferty's worried that the target on the twelve-mile scope might be just another iceberg, but I'd know those holy contours anywhere. Assuming the chains are still in place, the best procedure will probably be to sling the ends around the Maracaibo's deck island and wire the lead links together. If the load's too much, of course, it'll tear the island loose and pull it overboard, dumping us all into the sea.

To earn a living, some men merely have to haul oil.

At 2015 the last of the Reykjavik choppers took off, bearing away Pembroke, Flume, and Oliver Shostak, along with those two fake ensigns who piloted the PBY. I had a notion to seek old Oliver out before he left, identify myself, and introduce his front teeth to the pit of his stomach, but then I decided stealing his girlfriend is revenge enough. Still, I'll never fully understand what he and Cassie have against our cargo. It seems to me a person ought to be thankful to his Creator. For now, though, none of my personal philosophical opinions matter. I've come to bury God, not to praise Him.

I'll give the *Val* till dawn. If she's not gone by then, I'll fire off an Aspide and put her out of her misery. After that I'll be sorely tempted to hunt down Spruance's carrier and send *her* to the bottom as well. But I'll resist, Popeye. Such vindictiveness would be wrong. "Once enthralled by the Idea of the Corpse," Ockham tells me, "a person must remain eternally vigilant, forever seeking the moral law within."

Under the midnight sun, despair acquires the intensity of sex, insomnia the vehemence of art. To the sailor who finds himself sleepless in the Arctic, wind has never felt sharper, salt air more pungent, a gannet's cry more piercing. As Anthony Van Horne wandered the central catwalk of the *Carpco Maracaibo*—icicles dangling everywhere, icebergs growling on all sides—he felt as if he'd become the hero of some vivid Scandinavian myth. He half expected to see the Midgard serpent cruising through the pink sea, swimming in circles around the dying *Valparaíso*, teeth flashing, eyes aflame, waiting for Ragnarok.

The old man lay on the fo'c'sle deck, wrapped in a canvas seabag like a statue of a Civil War general about to be unveiled.

"When you consider how much TNT and testosterone were on the scene this morning," said Cassie, tapping the corpse's head with her boot, "it's amazing only four people got killed." She smiled weakly. "How are you?"

"Tired," he said, unhitching the binoculars from around his neck. "Cold."

"Me too."

"We've been avoiding each other."

"True," she said. "Will my guilt ever go away?"

"You're asking the wrong man."

"Fucking Gulf tanker. I mean, who'd have figured on a *Gulf tanker* showing up?"

Bulky in their down parkas, graceless in their fur-lined boots, they pressed together like two bonded grizzly bears finding each other after a long hibernation.

"I hope you're not too sad," said Cassie, extending her sealskin mitten and gesturing toward the seabag.

"Reminds me of the time I got shot by a pirate in Guayaquil," said Anthony. "The pain didn't arrive all at once. I'm still waiting for something to hit."

"Grief?"

"Something. We had a few minutes together at the end."

"Did you talk about Matagorda Bay?"

"The man was on a morphine trip—hopeless. But even if he'd understood, he couldn't have helped me. The job's not done. The tomb's still empty."

"Lianne tells me the Vatican wants the corpse cremated."

"Did she also tell you we're forging ahead tomorrow?"

"To Kvitoya?"

"Yep."

"Wish you'd reconsider," said Cassie evenly. An oddly appealing, peculiarly sensual anger distorted her face. "The angels are dead. Your father's dead. God's dead. There's nobody left to impress."

"I'm left."

"Shit."

"Cassie, friend, wouldn't you say things have taken a pretty odd turn when the Holy Catholic Church and the Central Park West Enlightenment League want exactly the same thing?"

"I can live with that. Burn the sucker, honey. The world's women will thank you for it."

"I gave Raphael my word."

"The way I heard it," said Cassie, "Rome will dispatch more Gulf tankers if you don't play ball. Surely you don't want to be torpedoed again."

"No, Doc, I don't want that." Swerving toward the wreck, Anthony raised the binoculars and focused. "Of course, I could always send the Pope a fax saying the body's been torched."

"You could . . ."

"But I won't," said Anthony crisply. "There's been enough deception on this voyage." Black waves washed across the *Valparaíso*'s weather deck, hurling chunks of pack ice against the superstructure. "Doc, I'll make you a deal. If a Vatican armada intercepts us between here and Svalbard, I'll surrender our cargo without a fight."

"No showdowns?"

"No showdowns."

Cassie moved her mouth, working the frozen muscles into a smile. "I'll believe that when I see it."

With a deep gurgle and an unearthly groan, the *Valparaíso* began to spin, north to east to south to west, round and round, her bow falling sharply, stirring the Greenland Current into a frothy whirlpool as her ten-ton rudder, Ferris wheel–size propellers, and mammoth keel rose into the air. Level by level, companionway by companionway, the superstructure descended—cabins, galleys, wardroom, wheelhouse, stacks, mast, Vatican flag—sliding into the maelstrom as if into the mouth of some unimaginable grouper, portholes blazing brightly even after they slipped beneath the waves.

"Farewell, old friend." Anthony lifted his hand to his brow

and fired off a forceful salute. "I'll miss you," he called across the ice-choked sea. The gannets screeched, the wind howled, the watery jaws whooshed closed. "You were the best of them all," the captain told his ship as she began her final voyage, a slow, inexorable drop from the frothy surface of the Norwegian Sea to the inky blackness of the Mohns Trench, five thousand fathoms down.

Chíld

THE DIVINE FACE was still smoldering when the *Maracaibo* arrived on the scene, smoke wafting off His cheeks in thick black tendrils and drifting northwest toward Jan Mayen Island. Thousands of whisker stubs speckled the charred, exposed flesh of His lantern jaw, encircling the frosted lips and frozen smile, angling upward like the skeletal remains of a forest fire. God, Anthony saw, had become as beardless as he himself.

Despite the surplus of officers and seamen, it took the *Maracaibo*'s company all day to dredge up the severed chains, belt them around the superstructure, and splice the raw ends together. "Slow ahead," Anthony ordered. The chains tightened, grinding against the deckhouse walls, but the foundation held fast, and the Corpus Dei moved forward. At 1830 hours the captain gave the all-ahead-full, gulped down his four hundred and twenty-sixth cup of coffee since New York, and set his course for the Pole.

Anthony did not like the *Carpco Maracaibo*. It was all he could do to squeeze five knots out of her; even if the burdensome oil in her hold magically disappeared, he doubted she'd give him more than six. She had no soul, this tanker. The archangels had truly known what they were doing when they picked the *Valparaíso*.

The night the tow began, Cassie took up residence in Anthony's cabin, an environment made erotically tropical by the eighty-degree air Crock O'Connor was obligingly pumping in from the engine flat.

"I have to know something," she said, guiding Anthony's naked body onto the bunk. "If our Midway scheme had worked and God had gone under, would you have forgiven me?"

"That's not a fair question."

"True." She began arraying him in a decorator Supersensitive—the best-selling barber pole design, second in popularity only to the diamondback rattlesnake. "What's the answer?"

"I'd probably never have forgiven you," said Anthony, enjoying the way the sweat filled her cleavage like a river flowing through a gorge. "I know that's not the answer you wanted to hear, but . . ."

"But it's the one I expected," she confessed.

"Now *I* have to know something." He plugged her ear with his tongue, swizzling it around. "Suppose another opportunity came along for you to destroy my cargo. Would you take it?"

"You bet I would."

"You don't have to answer right away."

Laughing, Cassie unfurled the condom. "You're surprised?"

"Not really," he sighed. Slithering on top of her, he cupped her breasts like Jehovah molding the Andes. "You're a woman with a mission, Doc. It's what I love about you."

The next morning, while Cassie was out helping to chip ice from the central catwalk and Anthony lay in their bunk writing about the death of the *Valparaíso*, filling his Popeye journal with page after page of angry lamentation, a knock reverberated through the cabin. He rolled off the mattress, opened the door. Crock O'Connor stepped inside, accompanied by spindly little Vince Mangione, the latter gripping a brass birdcage, lifting it level with his face as if deploying a hurricane lantern against a moonless night.

Inside the cage, a parrot stood on a trapeze, making quick jabs with its beak in hopes of killing the mites under its wings. The bird turned its scarlet head, fixing on Anthony. Its eyes were like tiny oiled bearings. At first he thought some sort of resurrection had occurred, for the similarity between this macaw and his boyhood pet, Rainbow, was uncanny, but on further inspection he realized the present parrot lacked Rainbow's distinguishing marks—the peculiar hourglass shape on her beak, the small jagged scar on her right talon.

"Your father bought her in Palermo, right before we shipped out," Mangione explained, setting the cage on the bunk.

"The engine flat made a fine home—all that steam," said O'Connor. "But I'm sure she'll do fine in your cabin."

"Get her out of here," said Anthony.

"What?"

"I want nothing that belonged to my father."

"You don't understand," said Mangione. "He told me it was a present."

"A present?"

Despite the Thanksgiving humiliation, the bottled *Constitution*, the malign neglect—despite everything, Anthony was touched. At last the old man was trying to make amends, restoring to his son the gift he'd taken away forty years earlier.

"We don't know if your dad named her or not," said O'Connor.

"What do *you* call her?"

"Pirate Jenny."

"Leave her here," said Anthony, returning Pirate Jenny's

unblinking stare. A sudden queasiness came. He half expected the parrot to say something sardonic and wounding, like *Anthony left the bridge* or *Anthony fucked up*.

As O'Connor started out of the cabin, Pirate Jenny squawked but produced no vocables. "I'm bored," said the engineer, pausing in the jamb. He faced Anthony and frowned, crinkling the steam burn on his forehead. "The boilers around here are all on computers. There's nothing for me to *do*."

"The *Val* was an eyesore, hard to steer . . ."

"I know. I want her back."

"Me too, Crock. I want her back too. Thanks for the bird."

On September 21, a new variety of ice island appeared on the horizon, drifting southeast with the Greenland Current—glacier fragments so huge they made the Jan Mayen bergs seem like molehills. According to the Marisat, the *Maracaibo* was barely a day from her destination, but the prospect of journey's end brought Anthony no pleasure. Eight men had died; the *Val* was in the Mohns Trench; the divine brain was garbage; his father would never absolve him. And for all Anthony knew, a Vatican armada now lay at anchor inside the tomb, ready to pirate his cargo.

"Froggy loves Tiffany."

He was giving Cassie a backrub, pressing his palms against her beautiful flesh, vertebra after vertebra lined up like speed bumps, and for an instant he thought it was she who'd made the raspy little declaration.

"What?"

"Froggy loves Tiffany," the scarlet macaw repeated. "Froggy loves Tiffany."

The universe again, playing another of its outrageous jokes. Froggy loved Tiffany.

Anthony stifled a giggle. "It's all too perfect, wouldn't you say?"

"Perfect?" Cassie replied. "What?"

"Absolutely perfect. A masterpiece. The bastard's dead, and he's *still* taking back the things he gave me."

"Oh, come on—your *father*'s not doing anything. Mangione didn't understand the parrot was for Tiffany, that's all. There's no malice here."

"You think so?"

"Jesus Christ."

"I must admit, I'm actually rather impressed," said Anthony, struck by his mental picture of the old man sitting hour after hour in the engine flat, drilling the half-dozen syllables into the parrot's head. "Imagine how many times he had to say it, over and over . . ."

"Maybe he hired a deckie."

"No, Dad did the work, I'm sure. He loved that woman. Over and over and over."

"Froggy loves Tiffany," said Pirate Jenny.

"Cassie loves Anthony," said Cassie Fowler.

"Anthony loves Cassie," said Anthony Van Horne.

September 22.

The autumnal equinox. On this day in 1789, my *Mariner's Pocket Companion* informs me, 5 months after the mutiny on HMS *Bounty*, "Fletcher Christian and his crew sailed for the last time from Tahiti in search of a deserted island on which to settle."

Mr. Christian could've done a lot worse than where he ended up, Pitcairn's Island. He could've come here, for instance, to Kvitoya, surely the bleakest, coldest place south of Santa Claus's outhouse.

At 0920 we drew within sight of the coordinates Raphael gave me in the Manhattan Cloisters—80°6′N, 34°3′E—and, indeed, there it was, the Great Tomb, a waterborne mountain measuring nearly 16 miles across at its base and towering over

28,000 feet (the approximate height of Everest, Dolores Haycox noted), pinned between the deserted island and the beginning of what the charts call "unnavigable polar ice." As we bore down on the thing, weaving among the lesser bergs at 5 knots, the entire company gathered spontaneously on the weather deck. Most of the sailors dropped to their knees. About half crossed themselves. The shadow of the tomb spread across the water like an oil slick, darkening our path. Directly above, a shimmering gold ring ran around the sun, a phenomenon that prompted Ockham to get on the PA system and explain how we were seeing "light waves bending as they pass through airborne ice crystals." The sundogs appeared next: greenish, glassy highlights on either side of the ring, where the crystals were "acting like millions of tiny mirrors."

The sailors wanted no part of the padre's rationality, and I didn't either. This morning, Popeye, the sun wore a halo.

For an hour we cruised along the mountain's western face, probing, poking, seeking entrance, and at 1105 we spotted a trapezoidal portal. We came left 15 degrees, slowed to 3 knots, and crossed the threshold. Those angels knew their math, Popeye; their calculations were on the mark. Our cargo cleared the portal with a margin of perhaps 6 yards along each floating hand and not much more above the chest.

The *Maracaibo* steamed forward, her searchlights panning back and forth as she spiraled toward the core. For 20 miles we followed the smooth, slick, ever-curving passageway. It was like navigating the interior of a gigantic conch. Then, at last: the central crypt, its silvery walls soaring to meet a vaulted dome whose apex lay well beyond the reach of our beams.

No armada awaited. Rome may find us yet, of course; her ships could be gathering outside even as I write these words, barricading the exit. But right now we're free to conduct our business in peace.

Dead ahead, dark waves lapped against a mile-long ice shelf, its surface nearly level with our bulwarks, and the minute I saw the glistery, sculpted bollards I knew the angels had intended it as a pier.

At 1450 I sent a half-dozen ordinaries over in the launch. They had no trouble grabbing the mooring lines and making them fast, but docking the *Maracaibo* was still a damned dicey operation: deceptive shadows, crazy echoes, chunks of pack ice everywhere. By 1535 the bitch was tied up, both her engines cut for the first time since she left Palermo.

I ordered an immediate burial at sea. Cassie, Ockham, and I marched down the catwalk to the fo'c'sle deck, pried up the seabag with grappling hooks, and, after scavenging an anchor from the handiest lifeboat, carried poor old Dad to the starboard bulwark.

"I'm not sure how Dutch Presbyterians go about it," said Ockham, slipping a King James Bible from his parka, "but I know they're fond of this translation."

Loosening the drawstring, I removed my father's pale, crushed corpse. He was frozen solid. "A Pop-sicle," I muttered, and Cassie shot me a glance compounded of both shock and amusement.

Opening to First Corinthians, Ockham recited words I'd heard in a thousand Hollywood burial scenes.

" 'Behold, I show you a mystery: we shall not all sleep, but we shall all be changed, in a moment, in the twinkling of an eye, at the last trump: for the trumpet shall sound, and the dead shall be raised incorruptible . . .' "

Cassie and I wrapped the lifeboat anchor around Dad's waist and hoisted his iron-hard body onto the rail. The anchor hung between his legs like a codpiece. We pushed. He fell, crashing into the black lake. Even with the extra weight, he stayed on the surface for over a minute, drifting slowly toward God's brow.

"Farewell, sailor," I said, thinking how good it would feel to get back inside and savor a mug of Follingsbee's jamoke.

" 'Then shall be brought to pass the saying that is written: Death is swallowed up in victory,' " Ockham intoned as Dad dropped from view, legs first, then torso, head, and hair. " 'O death, where is thy sting?' " said the priest, and I found myself wondering whether the *Maracaibo*'s main pantry held any doughnuts. " 'O grave, where is thy victory?' "

And, in fact, it did.

Jelly, glazed, and sugar.

Cupping his gloves around the railing, Neil Weisinger joined the solemn little march down the gangway. Gingerly he crossed the slippery pier, one cautious step at a time. By 1715 the whole company stood on the ice, officers and crew alike, shuffling about in the harsh light, puffs of breath streaming from their mouths like dialogue balloons.

When Neil saw how the angels had prepared the crypt, a chill of recognition shot through him; he thought immediately of the Labor Day barbecue he'd attended two years earlier at the home of his neighbor, Dwight Gorka, a joyless celebration that reached its nadir when Dwight's cat, Pumpkin, was run over by a Federal Express truck. Responding instantly to his preschool daughter's grief, Dwight had nailed together a plywood coffin, dug a hole in the stiff Teaneck earth, and laid the poor cat to rest. Before her father shoveled back the dirt, little Emily packed the grave with all the things Pumpkin would need during his journey to cat heaven—his water dish (filled), a can of Friskies Fancy Feast (opened), and, most importantly, his favorite toy, a plastic bottle cap he'd spent many mindless feline hours batting around the house.

The north wall of the crypt featured six immense niches, each sheltering a product God had evidently held in high regard. The forward searchlight struck the colossal carcass of a blue whale, a form at once ponderous and sleek. The amidships beacon swept across the soaring hulk of a sequoia tree, limned the wrinkled remains of an African bull elephant, glinted off a stuffed marlin, ignited a family of embalmed grizzly bears, and, finally, came to rest on a frozen hippopotamus (quite possibly descended, Neil mused, from the hippos his grandfather had helped transport from Africa to France). Directly ahead, a cabinet constructed entirely of ice rose nearly twenty feet. He extended his sleeve, wiping frost and condensation from the transparent doors. He peered inside. Every shelf was jammed with items from the divine portfolio, bottle after bottle. Monarch butterfly . . . chunk of jade . . . divot blooming with Kentucky bluegrass . . . orchid . . . praying mantis . . . Maine lobster . . . human brain . . . king cobra . . . cricket . . . sparrow . . . nugget of igneous rock.

Spontaneously, the Mourner's Kaddish formed on Neil's lips. "Yitgadal veyitkadash shemei raba bealma divera chireutei . . ." *Let the glory of God be extolled, let His great name be hallowed, in the world whose creation He willed . . .*

Drawing up beside Neil, Cassie Fowler jerked a thumb toward the trophy cabinet. "God's greatest hits."

"You're not very religious, are you?"

"He may have been our Creator," she said, "but He was also something of a malicious lunatic."

"He may have been something of a malicious lunatic," he said, "but He was also our Creator."

The instant Neil spotted the altar—a long, low table of ice spread out beneath the blue whale—he was overwhelmed by a desire to use it. He was not alone in this wish. Somberly the officers and crew filed back up the gangway, returning twenty minutes later, tributes in hand. One by one, the deckies approached the altar, and soon it was piled high with oblations: a National steel guitar, a trainman's watch on a gold chain, a Sony Walkman, a Texas Instruments calculator, a packet of top-of-the-line condoms (the pricey Shostak Supremes), a silver whiskey flask, a five-string banjo, a shaving mug imprinted with a Currier and Ives skating scene, three bottles of Moosehead beer, a belt buckle bearing the sculpted likeness of a clipper ship.

A disturbing truth fell upon Neil as he observed James Echohawk offer up his 35mm Nikon. Years from now, enacting his love for the God of the four A.M. watch, Neil might actually start feeling good about himself. In buying Big Joe Spicer's sister a dress for her senior prom or funding a hip operation for Leo Zook's father, he might very well find inner peace. And the instant this happened, the minute he experienced satisfaction, he'd know he wasn't doing enough.

Anthony Van Horne came forward and, with a shudder of reluctance, laid down a Bowditch sextant replica that must have been worth five hundred dollars. Sam Follingsbee surrendered a varnished walnut case filled with stainless-steel Ginsu knives. Father Thomas arrived next, sacrificing a jeweled chalice and a silver ciborium, followed by Sister Miriam, who lifted a golden-beaded rosary from her parka and rested it on the stack. Marbles Rafferty added a pair of high-powered Minolta binoculars, Crock O'Connor a matched set of Sears Craftsman socket wrenches, Lianne Bliss her crystal pendant.

"I've been thinking," said Cassie Fowler.

Reaching into his wool leggings, Neil drew out his gift. "Veimeru: amein," he muttered. *And let us say: Amen.* "Yeah, Miss Fowler?"

"You're right—whatever else, we still owe Him. I wish I had an offering. I came aboard with nothing but an Elvis cup and a Betty Boop towel."

Neil placed his grandfather's Ben-Gurion medal on the altar and said, "Why not give Him your gratitude?"

In God's private tomb, Cassie Fowler soon learned, time did not exist. No tides foretold the dusk; no stars announced the night; no birds declared the break of day. Only by glancing at the bridge clock did she know it was noon, eighteen hours after she'd watched Neil Weisinger offer up his bronze medal.

Stepping out of the wheelhouse, melding with the small, sad party on the starboard wing, Cassie was chagrined to realize that everyone else wore more respectful clothing than she. Anthony looked magnificent in his dress whites. Father Thomas had put on a red silk vestment fitted over a black claw-hammer coat. Cardinal Di Luca sported a luxurious fur stole wrapped around a brilliant purple alb. In her shabby orange parka (courtesy of Lianne), ratty green mittens (donated by An-mei Jong), and scruffy leather riding boots (from James Echohawk), Cassie felt downright irreverent. She didn't mind snubbing their cargo— this was, after all, the God of Western Patriarchy—but she did mind feeding the cliché that rationalists have no sense of the sacred.

Raising the PA microphone to his fissured lips, Father Thomas addressed the company below, half of them assembled on the weather deck, the rest milling around on the pier. "Welcome, friends, and peace be with you." The cavernous crypt replayed his words, *be with you, with you, with you.* "Now that our Creator has departed, let it be known that we commend Him to Himself and commit His body to its final resting place—ashes to ashes, dust to dust . . ."

Anthony took up the deckhouse walkie-talkie, pressed SEND, and solemnly contacted the pump room. "Mr. Horrocks, the hoses . . ."

With the same spectacular efficiency it had displayed during the Battle of Midway, the *Maracaibo*'s firefighting system swung into action. A dozen hoses rose along the afterdeck and spewed out gallon upon gallon of thick white foam. Every bubble, Cassie knew, was holy, Father Thomas and Monsignor Di Luca having spent the morning in a frenzy of consecration. The purified lather arced through the air and splashed against His left shoulder, freezing solid at the instant of anointment.

"God Almighty, we pray that You may sleep here in peace until You awaken Yourself to glory," said Father Thomas. Cassie admired the skill with which the priest had adapted the classic rite, the subtle balance he'd struck between traditional Christian optimism and the brute facticity of the corpse. "Then You will see Yourself face to face and know Your might and majesty . . ."

Hearing her cue, she came forward, Father Thomas's Jerusalem Bible tucked under her arm.

"Our castaway, Cassie Fowler, has asked permission to address you," the priest told the sailors. "I don't know exactly what she intends to say"—an admonitory glance—"but I'm sure it will be thoughtful."

As she took up the mike, Cassie worried that she might be about to make a fool of herself. It was one thing to lecture on food chains and ecological niches before a class of Tarrytown sophomores and quite another to critique the cosmos before a mob of hardened and depressed merchant sailors. "In all of Scripture," she began, "it is perhaps the ordeal of Job that best allows me to articulate how rationalists such as myself feel about our cargo." Swallowing a frigid mouthful of air, she glanced down at the wharf. Lianne Bliss, standing beneath the blue whale, gave her an encouraging smile. Dolores Haycox, slumped against the sequoia, offered a reassuring wink. "Job, you may recall, demanded to know the *reason* for his terrible losses—possessions, family, health—whereupon the Whirlwind appeared and explained that justice for one mere individual was not the point." She leaned the Bible's spine against the rail and opened it near the middle. " 'Where were you when I laid the earth's foundations?' God asks, rhetorically. 'What supports its pillars at their bases? Who pent up the sea behind closed doors when it leapt tumultuous out of the womb?' " She extended her right mitten, indicating the frozen hippopotamus. " 'Now think of Behemoth,' " she said, still quoting God. " 'What strength he has in his loins, what power in his stomach muscles. His tail is as stiff as a cedar, the sinews of his thighs are tightly knit. His vertebrae are bronze tubing, his bones as hard as hammered iron . . .' " Pivoting ninety degrees, Cassie spoke to the Corpus Dei. "What can I say, Sir? I'm a rationalist. I don't believe the splendor of hippos is any sort of answer to the suffering of humans. Where do I even begin? The Lisbon earthquake? The London plague? Malignant melanoma?" She sighed with a mixture of resignation and exasperation. "And yet, throughout it all, You still remained You, didn't You? You, Creator: a function You performed astonishingly well, laying those foundations and anchoring those supporting pillars. You were not a very good man, God, but You were a very good wizard, and for that I, even I, give You my gratitude."

Accepting both the mike and the Jerusalem Bible from Cassie, Father Thomas ran through the rest of the modified liturgy. "Before we go our separate ways, let us take leave of our Creator. May our farewell express our love for Him. May it ease our sadness and strengthen our hope. Now please join me in reciting the words Christ taught us on that celebrated Mount in Judea: 'Our Father, which art in heaven, hallowed be Thy name. Thy kingdom come . . .' "

While the *Maracaibo*'s company prayed, Cassie scanned their smiling cargo, pondering its myriad misfortunes. The voyage had not been kind to God. Nearly a sixth of the right breast had been plundered for fillets. Demolition-bomb craters scarred the belly. Torpedo holes pocked the neck. The chin appeared to have been shaved with a blowtorch. Head to toe, the bites of predators and the ravages of ice alternated with vast swampy tracts of decay. A Martian happening upon the scene would never guess that the thing these mourners were entombing had once been their principal deity.

". . . and the power and the glory. Amen."

As Lou Chickering broke from the crowd and strode across the pier, tears sparkling in his eyes, Cassie recalled the many

times she'd heard his mellifluous baritone drifting upward from
the engine flat, reciting a soliloquy or belting out an aria. Reaching
the shore of the encapsulated bay, the gorgeous sailor threw back
his head and sang.

> *Swing low, sweet chariot,*
> *Comin' for to carry me home,*
> *Swing low, sweet chariot,*
> *Comin' for to carry me home.*

Now the entire company joined in, over a hundred voices
melding into a thunderous dirge that reverberated off the great
frozen dome.

> *I looked over Jordan, an' what did I see,*
> *Comin' for to carry me home?*
> *A band of angels comin' after me,*
> *Comin' for to carry me home.*

"All right, Professor Ockham, you win," said Di Luca, strok-
ing his stole. "This was all meant to be, wasn't it?"

"I believe so."

> *Swing low, sweet chariot,*
> *Comin' for to carry me home . . .*

"Tonight I'll compose a letter." The cardinal steadied himself
on the bridge rail. "I'll tell Rome the corpse was incinerated as
per the consistory's wishes—and then, with Van Horne's permission, I'll send it."

"Don't bother," said Father Thomas. "Three hours ago you
faxed the Holy Father just such a message."

"What?"

"I don't like situational ethics any more than you do, Tullio, but these are troubled times. Your signature's not hard to forge. It's fastidious and crisp. The nuns taught you well."

> *If you get there before I do,*
> *Comin' for to carry me home,*
> *Jes' tell my friends that I'm a-comin' too,*
> *Comin' for to carry me home.*

Cassie wasn't sure which aspect of this exchange disturbed her more: Father Thomas's descent into expedience, or her realization that Rome was not about to finish the job Oliver had so badly botched.

> *Swing low, sweet chariot,*
> *Comin' for to carry me home . . .*

The cardinal glowered but said nothing. Thomas kissed his Bible. Cassie closed her eyes, allowing the spiritual to coil through her unquiet soul, and by the time the last echo of the last syllable had died away, she knew that no being, supreme or otherwise, had ever received a more sonorous send-off to the dark, icy gates of oblivion.

The *Maracaibo* sailed southeast, crashing through the Arctic Ocean at a brisk sixteen knots as she headed toward the coast of Russia. For Thomas Ockham, the mood aboard the tanker was difficult to decipher. Naturally the sailors were delighted to be going home, but beneath their happiness he sensed acute melancholy and a grief past understanding. On the night of their departure from Kvitoya, a dozen or so off-duty deckies gathered in the rec room for a kind of eschatological hootenanny, and soon the entire superstructure was resounding with "Rock of Ages,"

"Kum-Ba-Yah," "Go Down Moses," "Amazing Grace," "A Mighty Fortress Is Our God," and "He's Got the Whole World in His Hands." The next day at noon, Thomas celebrated Mass as usual, and for the first time ever a whopping ninety percent of available Christians showed up.

As it turned out, the port of Murmansk boasted a deep-water mooring platform, the sort of rig that allowed a tanker to discharge her cargo directly into seabed pipes without entering harbor. Van Horne arranged the transaction over the ship-to-shore radio, and within four hours of hooking up, the *Maracaibo* had been pumped dry. Although the Russians could not comprehend why the Catholic Church was giving them eight million gallons of Arabian crude oil for free, they quickly stopped looking this gift horse in the mouth. Winter was coming.

On the morning of September 25, as the *Maracaibo* drew near the Hebrides, the urge to think overcame Thomas. He knew just what to do. Early in the voyage, he'd discovered that a supertanker's central catwalk was the perfect place for contemplation, as conducive to quietude as a monastery arcade. One slow march down its length and back, and he had effectively penetrated some great mystery—why existing TOE equations failed to accommodate gravity, why the universe contained more matter than antimatter, why God had died. A second such march, and he had ruthlessly generated a thousand reasons for calling his answer invalid.

Tall, choppy waves surrounded the *Maracaibo*. Walking aft, Thomas imagined himself as Moses leading the escaping Hebrews across the Red Sea basin, guiding them past the slippery rocks and bewildered fish, a cliff of suspended water towering on each side. But Thomas did not feel like Moses just then. He did not feel like any sort of prophet. He felt like the universe's stooge, a man who could barely solve a riddle on a Happy Meal box, much less derive a Theory of Everything or crack the conundrum of his Creator's passing.

A cosmic assassination?

An unimaginable supernatural virus?

A broken heart?

He looked to port.

The derelict bore the name *Regina Maris*: an old-style freighter with deckhouses both amidships and aft, dead in the water and drifting aimlessly through the Scottish mist like some phantom frigate out of *The Rime of the Ancient Mariner*. By 1400 Thomas was ascending her gangway, Marbles Rafferty right behind. The cold fog enshrouded them, turning their breath to vapor and roughening their skin with goose bumps.

As he stepped onto the main deck, Thomas saw that heaven's very remnants had figured in the *Regina*'s ill-starred run. Evidently she'd been manned by cherubs. Their gray, bloated corpses lay everywhere—dozens of plump miniangels rotting atop the fo'c'sle, putrefying by the kingposts, suppurating on the quarterdeck. Tiny feathers danced on the North Sea breeze like snowflakes.

"Captain, it's a pretty weird scene here," said Rafferty into the walkie-talkie. "About forty dead children with wings on their backs."

Van Horne's voice sputtered from the speaker. "Children? Christ . . ."

"Let me talk to him," Thomas insisted, appropriating the walkie-talkie. "Not children, Anthony. Cherubs."

"Cherubs?"

"Uh-huh."

"No survivors?"

"I don't think so. It's amazing they got this far north."

"Are you thinking what I'm thinking?" asked Van Horne.

"When cherubs come," said Thomas, "angels can't be far behind."

Pitted with rust, pocked with corrosion, the *Regina* was in no better shape than her crew. It was as if she'd been scooped up and sucked upon by God Himself—smashed against His cuspids, burned with His saliva—then spit back into the sea. Thomas started into the amidships deckhouse, following a sharp, fruity odor of such intensity it overpowered the cherubs' stench. His jugular veins throbbed. Blood pounded in his ears. The scent led him down a damp corridor, up a narrow companionway, and into a gloomy cabin.

On the far bulkhead hung Robert Campin's masterful *Annunciation*—either a copy or the original from the Manhattan Cloisters, the priest didn't know for sure. A lambent glow issued from the bunk. Thomas approached at the same respectful pace he'd employed three months earlier when greeting Pope Innocent XIV.

"Who's there?" asked the angel, propping himself up on his elbows. A black, fallen halo hung around his neck like a discarded fan belt from Van Horne Island.

"Thomas Ockham, Society of Jesus."

"I've heard of you." The bed sheet slipped to the floor, revealing the creature's wasted body. His flesh, though cracked and gritty, was exquisite in its own way, like sandpaper manufactured for some holy task—smoothing the Cross, buffing the Ark. A small harp bridged the gap between his knobby knees. His wings, naked as a bat's, rested atop mounds of shed feathers. "Call me Michael."

"It's an honor, Michael." Thomas pressed SEND. "Anthony?"

"Yeah?"

"We were right. An angel."

"The last angel," rasped Michael. His voice had a dry, brittle quality, as if his larynx had rusted along with his ship.

"Anything I can do for you?" asked Thomas, slipping the walkie-talkie into the pocket of his parka. "You thirsty?"

"Thirsty. Quite so. Please—on the bureau . . ."

Crossing the cabin, Thomas located a four-chambered glass bottle shaped like a human heart and filled with water.

"Am I too late?" The angel lifted the harp from atop his knees. "Did I miss His funeral?"

"You missed it, yes." Pressing the bottle to Michael's withered lips, Thomas realized the angel was blind. His eyes, milky and motionless, lay in his head like pearls wrought by some terminally ill oyster. "I'm sorry."

"But He's safe now?"

"Quite safe."

"Not too much decay?"

"Not too much."

"Still smiling?"

"Still smiling."

Michael laid his right hand on his harp and began picking out the famous zither theme from *The Third Man*. "Wh-where are we?"

"The Hebrides."

"That near Kvitoya?"

"Kvitoya's two thousand miles away," the priest admitted.

"Then I won't even get to visit the body."

"True." The angel's fever was so intense Thomas could feel the heat against his cheeks. "You built Him a beautiful tomb."

"We did, didn't we? It was my idea to inter Him with His masterpieces. Whale, orchid, sparrow, cobra. We had a tough time deciding what to include. Adabiel made a big pitch for human inventions . . . argued they were His by extension. Wheel, plow, VCR, harpsichord, hardball—we're all such Yankees fans—but then Zaphiel said, 'Okay, let's put in a .356 Magnum,' and that settled the matter."

A crepuscular cabin on a derelict freighter in the middle of the dreary North Sea: not a likely setting for revelation, yet that was what now struck Thomas Wickliff Ockham, S.J.—a revelation, a luminous truth blazing through his mortal soul.

"There's a fact I must know," he said. "Did God actually *request* the Kvitoya tomb? Did He come to you and say, 'Bury Me in the Arctic'?"

Michael coughed explosively, peppering the Campin *Annunciation* with droplets of blood. "We peered over the edge of heaven. We saw His body adrift off Gabon. We said, 'Something must be done.' "

"Let me get this straight. He never asked to be buried?"

"It seemed the decent thing to do," said the angel.

"But He never asked."

"No."

"So in sending His corpse to earth, He may've had something other than a funeral in mind?"

"Possibly."

Possibly. Probably. Certainly. "Do you want extreme unction?" asked Thomas. "I have no chrism, but there's a ton of consecrated firefighting foam on the *Maracaibo*."

Michael closed his sightless eyes. "That reminds me of an old joke. 'How do you make holy water?' Ever heard it, Father?"

"I don't know."

" 'You take some water and you boil the hell out of it.' Extreme unction? No. Thank you—but no. The sacraments don't matter anymore. Precious little matters anymore. I don't even care if the Yankees are still in first place. Are they?"

Thomas would never know whether Michael heard the good news, for the instant the priest offered his reply—"Yes, the Yankees are still in first place"—the archangel's eyes liquefied, his hands melted, and his torso disintegrated like the Tower of Babel crumbling beneath God's withering breath.

Thomas stared at the bunk, beholding Michael's ashy remains with a mixture of disbelief and awe. He drew out the walkie-talkie. "You there, Anthony?"

"What's going on?" demanded Van Horne.

"We lost him."

"I'm not surprised."

The priest ran his fingers through the soft gray ephemera on the mattress. "Captain, I think I've got the answer."

"You've discovered a TOE?"

"I know why God died. Not only that, I've decided what our next move should be."

"Why'd He die?"

"It's complicated. Listen—tonight's supper will be a private affair. I'm inviting only four people: you, Miriam, Di Luca, your girlfriend."

"Whatever your theory, I doubt that my girlfriend will accept it."

"That's exactly why I want her there. If I can persuade Cassie Fowler to disinter the corpse, I can persuade anybody."

"Disinter it?"

Thomas bundled the divine dust and holy feathers into the bedsheet, securing the corners with a convoluted knot.

"Answer me, Thomas. What do you mean, 'disinter it'?"

For reasons known only to himself, Sam Follingsbee bypassed the *Maracaibo*'s normal stores that evening and instead cooked up a copious Chinese buffet using the last of the meat they'd salvaged from the sinking *Valparaíso*. After Thomas said grace, he and his guests dug in. They ate slowly—reverently, in fact, even the habitually sacrilegious Cassie Fowler. Di Luca, too, seemed to approach his meal with piety, as if he somehow sensed its source.

Swallowing a mouthful of artificial mu gu gai pan, Thomas said, "I have a theory for you."

"He's solved the great riddle," Van Horne explained, devouring a mock wonton.

"I'll start with a question," said Thomas. "What's the most accurate metaphor for God?"

"Love," said Sister Miriam.

"Try again."

"Judge," said Di Luca.

"Besides that?"

"Creator," said Fowler.

"Close."

"Father," said Van Horne.

Thomas ate a morsel of bogus Szechuan beef. "Exactly. Father. And what would you say is every father's ultimate obligation?"

"To respect his children," said Van Horne.

"Provide them with unconditional love," said Miriam.

"A strong moral foundation," said Di Luca.

"Feed them, clothe them, house them," said Fowler.

"Forgive me, but I think you're all wrong," said Thomas. "A father's ultimate obligation is to stop being a father. You follow me? At some point, he must step aside and allow his sons and daughters to enter adulthood. And that's precisely what I think God did. He realized our continued belief in Him was constraining us, holding us back—infantilizing us, if you will."

"Oh, *that* old argument," sneered Di Luca. "I must say, I'm saddened to hear it from the author of *The Mechanics of Grace*."

"I think maybe Tom's on to something," said Miriam.

"You would," said Di Luca.

"A father's obliged to step aside," said Van Horne. "He's not obliged to drop dead."

"He is if He's you-know-Who," said Thomas. "Think about it. As long as God kept aloof, His decision to enter oblivion would remain a secret. But if He incarnated Himself, came to earth . . ."

"Excuse me," said Di Luca, "but at least one of us at this table believes just such an event happened about two thousand years ago."

"I believe it happened too," said Thomas. "But history marches on, Eminence. We can't live in the past."

Fowler sipped oolong tea. "What, exactly, are you saying, Father? Are you saying He killed Himself?"

"Yes."

"Cripes."

"Knowing full well His angels would die of empathy?" asked Van Horne.

"That's how much He loved the world," said Thomas. "He willed Himself out of existence, simultaneously giving us ponderous proof of the fact."

"So where's His suicide note?" asked Fowler.

"Maybe He never wrote one. Maybe it's inscribed on His body in some arcane fashion." Thomas loaded his fork with counterfeit calamari in black bean sauce. "I don't know about the rest of you, but I, for one, am quite moved by our Creator's selflessness."

"And *I*, for one, think you're way out on a limb," said Di Luca, eyes narrowing. "Could you tell us exactly how you arrived at this bizarre conclusion?"

"Jesuitical deduction," Thomas replied, "combined with a crucial fact I learned this afternoon from Michael."

"What fact?"

"God never asked to be buried. The archangels acted completely on their own. They looked down, saw His body, and with the last of their strength they built Him a tomb."

"Pretty meager data," said Di Luca, "for such a lofty hypothesis."

Van Horne tore into his ersatz Hunan chicken. "When you radioed me from the *Regina*, you said you knew what our next move should be."

"Our duty is clear—at least, I think it is," said Thomas. "After supper, we must bring the *Maracaibo* about and go back to Svalbard. We'll re-enter the tomb, hook ourselves up to the body again, and take it on a grand tour."

"On a *what*?" said Di Luca.

"Grand tour."

"The hell we will," said Fowler.

"Have you lost your mind?" said Di Luca.

"We'll visit every major Western port, corpse in tow," Thomas insisted, rising from the table. "If the *Maracaibo* can't handle the load, we'll press other tankers into service en route.

The news will travel ahead of us. We can count on CNN. Okay, sure, initially the public will react with denial, terror, grief, everything we observed on the *Val* when we told the sailors the score, and, yes, as the Idea of the Corpse takes hold there may be an epidemic of anomie such as occurred on Van Horne Island—though, of course, as the captain here explained to Tullio in the wardroom, that was primarily an effect of prolonged and intimate contact with the body—but in any case the categorical imperative will soon kick in, and after that euphoria will follow. Are you seeing this, people? Can you picture the excited mobs charging through the streets of Lisbon, Marseilles, Athens, Naples, and New York, thronging onto the docks, eager for a peek? The human race has been waiting for such an hour. They may not know it, but they've been waiting. Bands will play. Flags will fly. Vendors will hawk hot dogs, popcorn, T-shirts, pennants, bumper stickers, souvenir programs. 'We're free!' everyone will shout. 'Today we are grown men, today we are grown women—the universe is ours!' "

Thomas sat down and quietly loaded a flaky pancake with pseudo mu shu pork.

Fowler snorted.

Van Horne sighed.

"I must say, Professor," said Di Luca, "that is quite the most ridiculous proposal I have ever heard in my life."

Despite Thomas's profound lack of respect for Di Luca, the cardinal's rejection hurt, cutting into him like the negative review *The Christian Century* had given *The Mechanics of Grace*.

Have I reasoned incorrectly? he wondered.

"I want to know what the rest of you think. I promised myself I wouldn't pursue this plan unless a majority at this table tonight favored it."

"I'll tell you *my* opinion," said Fowler. "If humankind ever learns en masse that God Almighty can no longer fog a mirror, they won't feel like rushing out and climbing mountains—they'll feel like crawling into holes and dying."

"Well put, Dr. Fowler," said Di Luca.

"And I also think, as I've been saying all along—I *also* think that, once they return to daylight, they'll institute a theocracy so stifling and misogynistic it will make medieval Spain look like the Phil Donahue show."

Thomas bit through an egg roll, pointing the stump toward Sister Miriam. "That's two votes against my proposal and one vote—my own—for it."

The nun patted her lips with a white linen napkin. "Goodness, Tom, it was so blasted much trouble laying Him to rest. The idea of undoing our efforts—it's a bit overwhelming." She wrapped the napkin tightly around her hand, as if bandaging a wounded palm. "But the more I think about it, the more I realize we probably have a responsibility to share the Corpus Dei with the rest of humankind. It's what He wanted, right?"

"That's two for, two against," said Thomas. "It's up to you, Captain."

"If you vote yes," said Fowler, "I'll never speak to you again."

For an entire minute, Van Horne said nothing. He sat silently before his egg noodles, absently combing the pale yellow strands with his fork. Thomas fancied he could see the workings of the captain's brain, the throb and flash of his five billion neurons.

"I think . . ."

"Yes?"

". . . that I would like to sleep on it."

September 30.

Night. A starless sky. A 10-knot wind from the east.

So the angels lied to us. No, they didn't *lie*, exactly. They trod beyond the truth; they permitted their grief to obscure God's will. And if Raphael was overstating the case for an entombment, maybe he was overstating a few other notions as well—like my father being the man to absolve me.

When angels dissemble, Popeye, whom can you trust?

We're steaming round and round the Hebrides, and my mind's moving in circles too. I can see both sides, and it's making me insane. If I give the padre his grand tour, it won't be for personal gain. "Exhume Him," Cassie tells me, "and I'll walk out of your life forever."

And yet I wonder if Ockham and Sister Miriam aren't right. I wonder if we don't owe our species the truth.

I wonder if hearing the bad news might not be the best thing that's ever happened to *Homo sapiens sapiens*.

For the first four years they lived like peasants in the cramped cottage Cassie had been renting in Irvington, but after they struck it rich they decided to indulge themselves and move into the city. Despite their newfound wealth, Cassie held onto her job, doggedly explicating natural selection and other unsettling ideas for the God-fearing students of Tarrytown Community College while Anthony stayed home and took care of little Stevie. Best to play it safe, they decided. Their money might run out sooner than expected.

Being a parent in Manhattan was a sobering and faintly absurd undertaking. Police sirens sabotaged naps. Air pollution aggravated colds. To make sure Stevie got home safely from Montessori each afternoon, Anthony and Cassie had to hire a Korean martial-arts instructor as his escort. Still, they would have had it no other way. The spacious fourth-floor walk-up they'd acquired on the Upper East Side included full roof rights, and after Stevie was asleep they would snuggle together on their beach recliners, stare at the grimy sky, and imagine they were lying on the fo'c'sle deck of the late *Valparaíso*.

Their fortune traced to an unlikely source. Shortly after landing back in Manhattan, Anthony got the idea of showing his private papers to Father Ockham, who in turn delivered them to Joanne Margolis, the eccentric literary agent who handled the priest's cosmology books. Margolis forthwith pronounced Anthony's journal "the finest surrealistic sea adventure ever written," showed it to an editor at the Naval Institute Press, and secured a modest advance of three thousand dollars. No one ever imagined so strange a book becoming a *New York Times* best-seller, but within six months of publication *The Gospel According to Popeye* had miraculously beaten the odds.

At first Anthony and Cassie feared the bulk of the royalties would go toward lawyers' fees and court costs, but then it became clear that neither the United States Attorney General nor the Norwegian government had any interest in prosecuting what appeared to be less a criminal case than an instance of fantasy role-playing gone horribly awry. The families of the three dead actors were infuriated by this inertia (Carny Otis's widow journeyed all the way to Oslo in an effort to move the wheels of justice), and their rage persisted until the Vatican Secretary of State intervened. Having hired the impetuous Christopher Van Horne in the first place, Eugenio Cardinal Orselli naturally regarded it as his moral duty to recompense the bereaved. Each next of kin received a tax-free gift of three and a half million dollars. By the summer of '99, the whole messy affair of Midway Redux no longer haunted the Van Horne–Fowler household.

Anthony couldn't decide whether his decision to leave the corpse in place was courageous or a cop-out. At least once a week he would travel uptown and join Thomas Ockham for a picnic lunch of Brie sandwiches and white wine in Fort Tryon Park, after which they would stroll through the Cloisters, puzzling out their obligations to *Homo sapiens sapiens*. Once Anthony thought he saw a robed angel swoop through the Fuentidueña Chapel, but it was only a beautiful Columbia grad student in a long white dress, applying for a job as a docent.

The deal they'd cut with Di Luca and Orselli was a paragon

of symmetry. Anthony and Ockham would not reveal that *The Gospel According to Popeye* was factual, and Rome would not appropriate the corpse and burn it. While the notion of a grand tour continued to intrigue both the captain and the priest, they were coming to realize that such a spectacle might very well lead to something far sadder and bloodier than the brave new world Ockham had envisioned the day he'd explored the derelict *Regina Maris*. Then, too, there was the appalling presumption of it all. Nobody, Anthony felt, had the right to take the illusion of God away—not even God had that right, despite His evidently having attempted to do so.

The party Anthony and Cassie threw when Stevie turned six served a dual purpose. It celebrated the boy's birthday, and it brought together seven alumni of the *Valparaíso*'s last voyage. They came bearing gifts: stuffed whale, jigsaw puzzle, six-shooter and holster, electric train, first-baseman's mitt, toy tugboat, set of Fisher-Price homunculi. Sam Follingsbee baked the cake, Stevie's favorite, Swiss chocolate with cherry frosting.

As the moon rose, the confessions began, each sailor admitting to an intense private terror that his knowledge of what lay entombed above Svalbard might one day deprive him of his sanity. Marbles Rafferty disclosed that suicide figured in his fantasies with much greater frequency than before his trip to the Arctic. Crock O'Connor frankly discussed his impulse to call up *Larry King Live* and tell the world its prayers were falling on ruptured eardrums. And yet, so far, they'd all managed to become functional and even flourishing citizens of Anno Postdomini Seven.

Rafferty was now master of the *Exxon Bangor*. O'Connor, retired from the sea, currently spent his days and nights trying to invent a holographic tattoo. Follingsbee ran the Octopus's Garden in Bayonne, an atmospheric waterfront restaurant whose menu included not a single item of seafood. Lou Chickering was playing a chronically adulterous brain surgeon on *The Sands of Time* and had just been featured as Heartthrob of the Week in

Suds and Studs magazine. Lianne Bliss was working as the technical director of a radical feminist radio station broadcasting from Queens. Ockham and Sister Miriam had recently coauthored *Out of Many, One*, a comprehensive history of humankind's ever-changing images of God, from the radical monotheism of the Pharaoh Ikhnaton to the Cosmic Christ of Teilhard de Chardin. The introduction was by Neil Weisinger, presently a rabbi serving a thriving congregation of Reform Jews in Brooklyn.

After the party, while the grown-ups lingered downstairs, indulging in second helpings of cake and admiring the conches and birds' nests Cassie had collected on her honeymoon cruise to the Galápagos, father and son retired to the roof. The wind was crisp, the night miraculously clear. It was as if the island itself had set sail, flying beneath a cloudless sky.

"Who made them?" Stevie asked, pointing to the stars.

Anthony wanted to say "an old man at the North Pole," but he knew this would only confuse the boy. "God did."

"Who's God?"

"Nobody knows."

"When did He do it?"

"A long time ago."

"Is He still around?"

The captain inhaled a lungful of gritty Manhattan air. "Of course He's still around."

"Good."

Together they picked out their favorites: Sirius, Procyon, Betelgeuse, Rigel, Aldebaran, Orion's belt. Stevie Van Horne was a sailor's boy. He knew the Milky Way like the back of his hand. As the child's eyes drooped, Anthony chanted the several names of the mariner's best friend: "North Star, Lodestar, Polestar, Polaris," he sang, over and over—"North Star, Lodestar, Polestar, Polaris"—and by this method brought his son to the brink of sleep.

"Happy birthday, Stevie," Anthony told the drowsy child,

carrying him down the ladder. "I love you," he said, tucking the boy in bed.

"Daddy loves Stevie," squawked Pirate Jenny. "Froggy loves Tiffany. Daddy loves Stevie."

As it turned out, Tiffany hadn't wanted the bird. She didn't like animals, and she knew that Jenny would function less as a sweet memento of her late husband than as a remorseless reminder of his death. Anthony had spent over twenty hours teaching the macaw her new trick, but it'd been worth it. All the world's children, he felt, should fall asleep hearing some feathered and affectionate creature—a parrot, a mynah bird, an angel—whispering in their ears.

For a time he stood looking at Stevie, just looking. The boy had his mother's nose, his father's chin, his paternal grandmother's mouth. Moonlight poured into the room, bathing a plastic model of the starship *Enterprise* in a luminous haze. From the birdcage came the steady, clocklike tick of Pirate Jenny pecking at her mirror.

Occasionally—not this night, but occasionally—a dark mantle of pungent Texas crude would materialize on the parrot, rolling down her back and wings, flowing across the floor of the cage, and falling drip-drip-drip onto the carpet.

Whenever this happened, Anthony's response was always the same. He would press Raphael's feather against his chest and breathe deeply until the oil went away.

"Froggy loves Tiffany. Daddy loves Stevie."

Anthony loves Cassie, he thought.

The captain turned off the bedroom light, pulled the blue silk canopy over Jenny's cage, and stepped back into the dark hallway. Sea fever rose in his soul. The moon tugged at his blood. The Atlantic said, Come hither. North Star, Lodestar, Polestar . . .

How long would he be able to hold out? Until Cassie got her next sabbatical? Until Stevie was tall enough to take the helm and steer? No, the voyage must come sooner than that. Anthony could see it all now. In a year or so he'd get on the phone and make the arrangements. Cargo, crew, ship: not a supertanker, something more romantic—a bulk carrier, a freighter. A month later the whole family would rise at dawn and drive to Bayonne. They'd eat a fantastic breakfast at Follingsbee's restaurant on Canal Street. Scrambled eggs slathered with catsup, crisp strips of real bacon, wet crescents of honeydew melon, bagel halves mortared together with Philadelphia cream cheese. Bellies full, all senses at peak, Anthony and Stevie would kiss Cassie good-bye. They'd get on board. Light the boilers. Pick a port. Plot a course. And then, like those canny Dutch traders who inhabited their blood, they'd set out toward the sun, steady as she goes: the captain and his cabin boy, off with the morning tide.